ISABELLA

ISABELLA

An Orphan Jilted

Mary Crewe

Realized by
Louise Page

BBC BOOKS

Published by BBC Books,
an imprint of BBC Worldwide Publishing.
BBC Worldwide Limited, Woodlands,
80 Wood Lane, London W12 0TT

First published 1997
Realization © Louise Page 1997

ISBN 0 563 38317 8

Set in Bembo by Keystroke
Printed in Great Britain by Martins the Printers Limited,
Berwick upon Tweed
Bound in Great Britain by Hunter & Foulis Limited, Edinburgh
Cover printed by Belmont Press Limited, Northampton

❧ CONTENTS ❧

ꙮꙮ ONE ꙮꙮ

*In which Isabella Broderick arrives at
Ducoeur Castle, finds a home and almost
loses it through her wilfulness*

When Lady Sophia Ducoeur arrived home from France and
alighted from her carriage carrying in her arms not the expected
monkey or parrot in a cage but a child of about three years old,
it was only to be expected that there would be conjecture
among the servants at Ducoeur Castle.

'It's a bairn!'

'I can hear that.' The infant certainly had a fine pair of lungs.

'What's my lady want that for?'

''Tis another plaything.'

'It'll not stop crying if she jiggles it about like that!'

For Lady Sophia was swinging the child in her arms as if she
were a blacksmith at an anvil. In the moments it took for the
postilion to pull out the steps and the lady to descend from
the carriage, many suppositions were made about why she had
returned home with such a souvenir. There were some who
said she had adopted the child in order to fill the place in her
affections left empty by the death of her monkey some two
months before, a death at which she had wept more tears than
for her father who had died at about the same time. It had not
been expected that she should weep for her mother, that lady
having died very much disgraced.

Others imputed that Lady Sophia was perhaps not as strict in
her morals as she required her servants to be and remembered
the time, almost three and a half years ago, when the sociable
young lady had insisted on closeting herself in the country at the

home of a distant and elderly relation. It was quickly remembered that this relative suddenly became possessed of quite a sum
of money within a week of Lady Sophia's return to Ducoeur
Castle. Whatever was thought about the provenance of the child,
there was one fact on which all agreed: Sir Roderick Ducoeur, if
apprised of its existence, would not allow its presence in the
castle. However, Lady Sophia seemed not to have considered
such a possibility and, dismissing the servant who had gone forward to take the golden-haired child, walked up the outside
stairs and in through the great stone portal and down the corridor to her brother's chambers.

Sir Roderick Ducoeur had always been aware of his status
and the privilege that went with it. He had grown up handsome,
even in the eyes of his own sister. She always thought it a very
good trick to show her female acquaintances his miniature
without any explanation of who the young man was.

It was always the sight of universal admiration.

'The nose. I do declare it is the most Roman I ever saw.'

'What eyes; so bright!'

To which the fond sister would always reply. 'I assure you, the
portrait shows only half their dazzling brightness and passion.'

'Such a high brow! What an intelligent and clever gentleman
he must be.'

'Pray tell me – it is always so difficult in a miniature – what is
the young cavalier's height?'

Lady Sophia's reply that he was 'something above six foot'
only confirmed that the gentleman was, in every way a gallant
and that more could be expected from him than from any young
man in England.

Then there would be whispers: Did she know the young
man? How familiar they must be for him to give her his picture!
Oh, and on the reverse of it such a lock of black hair.

'If it would not be impertinent . . . '

'My most beloved brother, Sir Roderick Ducoeur.' The
enamoured sister would answer, often taking the liberty of kissing the picture before she closed its case.

Then how quickly she would hear confidences and professions of friendship! They were all eager for her to bring them home to Ducoeur Castle so they could all admire him in person, a thing Lady Sophia had no intention of allowing, not liking, on the rare occasions that she and her brother were together, to lose any of the affection she regarded as her due.

Those wishing for Sir Roderick to explode when presented with Lady Sophia's souvenir were disappointed. Her maid, Jane, who expected that she and her mistress would be thrown out of doors that very afternoon to sleep under hedges, and who, it must be added, thought she would make a very pretty picture by moonlight, slept that night in the truckle with her mouth thrown open. Indeed, had the late Mr Handel wished to write the music for the encounter of brother and sister he would have needed very few notes.

'Sir,' said Lady Sophia, standing before her brother. 'I will not put you to the trouble of enquiring after my journey, for there was nothing of interest in it to report except that I have brought this child back with me.'

'For what purpose?' asked Sir Roderick.

'I mean to raise her.'

'And if I have an objection to make about her being brought up under my roof?'

'There is none you can have. Her name is Isabella Broderick. She shall not trouble you.' And with this Lady Sophia retreated from the room.

After this meeting with his sister, Sir Roderick took the infant into his household without any more complaint. His only public pronouncement on the day of her arrival was that she should be put into mourning for his father.

How the child cried when she was taken out of her fustian and at the sight of the scissors that were needed to cut her out of her winter swaddling of woollen binder smeared with goose-grease. She screamed as if they were going to cut off her ears. Jane, who had been deputed for the task of undressing the infant, promised that she would use the scissors on the infant's tongue if she were not quiet. Thus was Isabella Broderick first made to submit to the will of her new guardians except in one particular. She would not, even for the sake of a bath, have a small gold locket, edged with pearls and rubies, removed from around her neck.

'No!' was her retort when the servant tried to remove it. 'Mine!'

'I'd like to know what right you have to such a thing,' said Jane, who did not like being put down from lady's maid to nurse.

'Mine!' said Isabella again.

'I shall not be afraid to beat you, for you are certainly no better than you should be,' replied the servant. 'And you may be my lady's favourite now, but it will not last. She is all passion one minute and all neglect the next. She wept for her monkey, but I know she poisoned it by giving it bitter herbs so she might amuse herself with its convulsions.'

Isabella, wide-eyed, struggled to understand her. The crafty servant made another attempt on the locket, but the child was too quick and placed her fingers around it with such force that Jane, for all her attempts, could not prise it off.

It was generally supposed that if the locket could be examined more carefully it would give a clue to the child's provenance by containing some image or a lock of hair which might be identified. When the jewel was at last opened – Jane having persuaded Isabella to compare her locket with one that had been Lady Sophia's pride and joy when a young girl and which contained a most flattering picture of her brother – there was general dissatisfaction at its being quite empty and containing as little information as if it had been newly crafted.

Lady Sophia had let it be known that the child's surname was Broderick, a compliment that was obviously intended to flatter her brother without being too familiar. There were wagers taken for Isabella being the bastard of Sir Roderick or even Lady Sophia. If this were the case, the servants, from the butler to the laundry drudge, agreed that it would have been better for the child to have been christened Janet Smith and left to dwell in obscurity.

When asked about her mother or father, Isabella would only shake her head and say 'Gone,' a remark that satisfied no one.

Other attempts were made to discover the child's origins. Jane was made to describe her lady's journey in such detail that a map might have been made of it. Her account was that near Warwick Lady Sophia had stepped out from the inn at which they were breaking their journey on the pretence of making a picnic with some acquaintances and had returned carrying the child and asking for her dinner. Which direction Lady Sophia had taken was not known, Jane being occupied with remaking a gown that her mistress had given her that very morning. Enquiries of the coachmen, even when made with pints of ale, could explain the puzzle in no greater detail. The lady of the house was not inclined to say anything that could illuminate her adoption of Isabella.

No one could believe the pet that Lady Sophia made of the child. She doted on her as she had previously doted, when first introduced to them, on her dogs, horses and monkey. To make the child love her, the young lady would get down upon her hands and knees to play find and fetch. It was in vain. Isabella, in her black silks, would not look for the dainty titbits hidden about the drawing-room. When Lady Sophia sat her on her knee and put hardbake into her mouth, Isabella would first bite her fingers and, if the sweetmeat was put into her own mouth, spit it out upon the floor. Yet still Lady Sophia continued to pet her. When Jane declared the child to be hard-hearted, Lady Sophia exclaimed: 'I was often so as a child.' A fact that Jane, who was used to her mistress's temper, could only suppose was true.

Then Lady Sophia would kiss Isabella and call her pretty names.

For the first three years of her life at Ducoeur Castle, Isabella was hardly aware of the existence of Sir Roderick, the gentleman being more often than not away from home, intent on enjoying his pleasures. One day, when she was about six years of age and engrossed in showing her doll Phoebe the pleasures of the Italian Garden, she encountered Sir Roderick, who had stepped out to avoid the troublesome necessity of an interview with Lady Sophia about a female servant whose condition made it impossible to employ her longer. The lady's condition being entirely due to Sir Roderick, he did not wish to receive the venom it would elicit from his sister.

'Good day, sir,' said Isabella, and, being very much frightened of the gentleman, she dropped Phoebe, whose wax face flew into a thousand fragments.

'You have killed her, sir!' cried Isabella, turning her bright eyes on Sir Roderick. 'You are a bad man. Poor Phoebe!'

'Isabella,' said Sir Roderick with great severity.

'I hate you!'

'Isabella, you will apologize.'

'No!' said the child, whose heart was full of hate for the death of her darling.

This was an arrogance that proud Sir Roderick could not endure.

'How dare you speak so to your elder and your better? How dare you speak so to me, to whom should be owed your duty?'

'I owe my duty only to my father, sir!' And with this the wilful orphan, gathering what remained of Phoebe into her arms, ran into the house to seek the protection of Lady Sophia.

Isabella was in the process of stammering out how Phoebe, a present from Lady Sophia, had come to lose all her features when Sir Roderick entered the room.

'Sir!' cried Lady Sophia, for Isabella's tears about the doll were the first ever expression of regard for anything that Lady Sophia had given the child, 'See what you have done to my darling's poppet.'

'What care I for that?'

At this, Isabella began to cry so piteously that the gentleman rounded on her. 'Leave us!' he commanded.

Isabella looked at her protectress, who indicated by her glance that this was what she wished the child to do.

The left-hand door of the chamber gave out upon the Long Gallery. When the weather was inclement it was often Isabella's habit to regard the family portraits that hung here. Her favourite face was that of Sir Penrose, Sir Roderick's father. Young though she was, Isabella could not but compare the portrait painted of him when he was a young man with that painted some thirty years later. The bearing and carriage were the same, but the face showed that some great suffering had taken place, though the eyes were still gentle, in marked contrast to those of Sir Roderick's, whose picture had taken its place on the wall beside it some six months after Isabella's arrival. Where the son's face was proud, the father's was sad. There was also a portrait of Arabella, Lady Ducoeur, a bold, dashing woman in the guise of Diana the Huntress. It was easy to remark on the resemblance of Sir Roderick and Lady Sophia to the Roman goddess with her dogs at her feet and slaughtered stag hanging from a tree behind her. To Isabella's young mind there was always something of a similarity between Sir Penrose's eyes and those of the stag.

While Isabella was occupied in the consideration of the paintings, she was the subject of a great argument between Lady Sophia and her brother. Sir Roderick described what had happened in the garden. Lady Sophia, already angry at the role she had had to play over the dismissing of the servant, retorted that he had frightened the child.

'That is nonsense, Sophia. From what I have seen of the child and her temper this morning, I realize I was wrong to have ever admitted her to this house.'

'She has been no trouble to you!'

'Had she not been, it would have been better.'

'What do you mean by that, sir?'

'I mean that she has been corrupted by your nature and temper. You have made her as wilful as I know you to be.'

'That is not true, sir,' cried Lady Sophia, hating the aspersions that her brother was making about her character.

'I insist that she is sent away at once.'

'Sir, I beg you.'

Isabella, whose tears had now dried, was in the happy perusal of a tapestry that pictured a lively mass of creatures, both mythical and real, being driven into the Ark. So absorbed was she in the procession of elephants and unicorns that she was quite unaware of the danger she had thrown herself into through her protection of Phoebe.

'Sir, the child is now of an age to remember and to talk. Think of how it might reflect on us, if it became known that we have sent her away, through your temper. Pray, sir, let her stay. If you wish my influence to be lessened upon her – though I cannot imagine why you should think such a precaution necessary – could that not be done through her education?'

'What good did your education do for you, or for my poor mother?'

'That is not the matter. I am talking of Isabella Broderick.'

'What purpose does the education of any woman serve?'

'Matrimony.'

'A subject of which neither of us knows anything.'

Lady Sophia took the taunt as it was intended. She bowed her head and waited for her brother to continue.

'I should not wish her to be a spinster at twenty.' This was something of a concession on the brother's part, for he had been generous enough some days before to present his sister with a gold bracelet on the occasion of her twenty-fifth birthday.

'You know I have not wished to leave you or our family home.'

'I have too often been made aware of it,' her brother replied testily.

Lady Sophia decided to make one last entreaty to her brother. 'Roderick, I beg you to call in the child and explain to her what her duty is and then to put as much of her education as you think necessary into the hands of such governesses and tutors as you choose to employ. If by this means her temper is corrected, might she then not stay?'

'She shall be entirely at my command?'

'She will, sir.'

Isabella was called back into the room.

'Isabella,' said Lady Sophia. 'Sir Roderick wishes to speak to you. You must attend to him with your greatest concentration, for, if you do not do as he wishes, you will be sent away.'

The child having submitted to be lectured to, Sir Roderick explained to her how her conduct must be governed in future.

The girl's head and her pretty curls drooped in front of him. Sir Roderick could not help noticing what a pretty infant she was, and thought that if her beauty continued she might grow into a very charming young lady.

'Do you understand me, Isabella?'

'I do, sir,' said the child, looking directly at him for the first time. There was, thought the gentleman, a touch of defiance in the bright, dark eyes. It was clear to him that his duty was to master Miss Isabella Broderick.

'Now that is done,' said Lady Sophia to the child, 'will you not shake hands with Sir Roderick?'

'Nay,' said her brother. 'I should prefer to have a kiss. Would that not make us better friends, Isabella?'

'I do not know, sir,' was the child's reply.

'You will like me better, by and by,' said Sir Roderick, consenting, for now, to forgo the kiss.

As a result of this interview a governess was appointed, a drawing teacher, a clergyman to supply enough Latin to enable Isabella to decipher the motto of any great families she came in contact with, and a music master, Sir Roderick taking great pains to find one who was old and ugly and whose gout made him an unlikely candidate for an elopement.

⚜ TWO ⚜

In which Lady Sophia is mortally threatened and Isabella leaves her home in the company of Sir Roderick

From this time on Sir Roderick involved himself more fully with Isabella, often insisting that she went alone to his rooms so that he could hear her lessons. This, however, was an occurrence that her tutors took the greatest pains to prevent happening, all fearing to be exposed by her stumbling over her multiplication tables or mistaking India for the West Indies.

Though lessened by the hours she spent in the schoolroom, Isabella's intercourse with Lady Sophia continued. Called to sit with the lady every night she often read to her very prettily, even out of novels she did not understand.

It was on one such evening that Isabella ventured on her origin. She had been reading *King Lear* and remarked on the fact that Cordelia, while pretending to deny her duty to her father, had made her love of him very plain.

'Madam,' said Isabella, 'may I presume, with a youth of only ten years, to ask you what you know of my own father?'

'You may not!' was the haughty reply.

'It is hinted, madam . . . '

'By whom?'

Here Isabella, for all her youth, paused, thinking that if the tales Jane and the other servants had told her as to her birth were made known to Lady Sophia, that the servants might be dismissed. A prospect that Jane, every day, assured her could be Isabella's own, a prospect she did not wish to inflict on any other person.

'I have been led,' said Isabella, 'by my own thoughts and the care that Sir Roderick has paid me and my own surname, to think that he might, in some way, be a relation of mine.'

'You are mistaken,' cried Lady Sophia.

'But he is so good to me. You are both so good to me,' continued the child on seeing the look in Lady Sophia's eyes.

'Why should we not be good to you? You are an orphan, and it is our duty.'

Young though she was, Isabella was aware that Lady Sophia did nothing out of duty, unless it suited her own purpose to be seen as the best of women. The child had sat beside her as Lady Sophia had made up charity bundles and poured her scorn upon the recipients, condemning them as lazy, feckless and in other ways undeserving of her charity.

'But could not that duty . . . ?'

'Silence! I have heard enough of your impudence,' shouted Lady Sophia. 'All talk on this matter is at an end!'

Isabella, through her reading of another play by Mr Shakespeare, was well acquainted with 'The lady doth protest too much, me thinks'.

And so Isabella took Lady Sophia's denials of Sir Roderick's being her parent as an affirmation that the gentleman was indeed her father and that she did indeed owe him the duty of being an obedient child.

That Isabella grew up to be a beauty could not be disputed. At fifteen she promised to develop all the features in the proportions that were most pleasing to the eye. Her brow was high and her lips were full. Her cheeks were exquisitely tinted, and the hair that curled around her brow would have been the envy of any young lady in the land. Her arms resembled those on the alabaster statues that Sir Roderick had long collected despite his sister's condemnation of their natural state. All these attributes, together with a quick wit and disposition to cheerfulness, had she any prospects, promised a choice of husband of a rank at least equal to Sir Roderick's.

Meanwhile the meagre charms possessed by Lady Sophia

dwindled. She became stout, and her teeth, which had never been good, demanded a constant chewing of caraway seeds.

'I had rather you chewed quid!' Sir Roderick would remark when unable to escape his sister's company of an evening. Lady Sophia would swallow as quickly as she was able, protesting that she was trying only to freshen her breath.

'For what purpose?' her brother would retort, though he was equally unscrupulous about his person, not changing his shirt or cravat as often as he should.

Whatever Lady Sophia's attentions to Isabella, they did nothing to diminish her devotions to her brother. Waistcoats and slippers were embroidered in profusion, he was waited up for at nights, and any chill resulted in the calling of a doctor.

'Pay your attentions to Isabella,' he would grumble as Lady Sophia's hot, moist hand attempted to soothe his brow. Yet he remained more and more at Ducoeur Castle, despite possessing an estate with much better hunting some three hours' ride off. One of the reasons given for Sir Roderick so much avoiding that place which had for some time been his chief residence was a disagreement between him and a young noble-woman who for many years had had certain expectations of him and who had finally found neither she nor her wealth could expect anything from Sir Roderick's affections. Fortunately, the lady was still young enough for her broken heart to be repaired. She pined for Sir Roderick for six months, spent another half-year forgetting him then married for love. It was supposed that the happiness of this union, which was openly flaunted, made Sir Roderick aware of what he had lost. Thus he continued often at Ducoeur Castle, taking the trouble to be very civil to his sister, for by that means he was put in the company of Isabella.

Though she did not have her own maid, when it was neces-sary for her to be attended on, Isabella was given the services of Abigail, a girl only a little older than herself but much more conversant with the ways of the world.

'My lord seems mighty attentive to you,' said the curious servant as she tidied Isabella's hair.

'He is indeed mighty good to me,' replied Isabella.

'He has been heard to remark that you are very pretty.'

At this Isabella blushed.

'Has he not said so to you?' continued Abigail.

'He has been kind enough to say that I looked in good health.'

'Do you not think him a fine and handsome gentleman?' said the maid, who knew more of Sir Roderick and his caprices than Lady Sophia would have liked.

'If he were a little more concerned about his person . . . '

'Fie, I do believe he is one of the best-turned-out young men in the county.'

'I do not call him young,' said Isabella. 'He is of an age . . . ' And here she stopped.

Her silence could not but inflame the maid's curiosity. 'What age, madam?' she asked.

'You are not to repeat this, Abigail.' The maid bobbed and assured Isabella she would not, at the same time considering how much attention she would gain in the servants' hall because of whatever Isabella was to say.

'I know it is not admitted,' said Isabella, 'but I sometimes suppose that Sir Roderick is my father.'

'How, madam?'

'Abigail, you know me and dress me. Would you say there was a likeness between myself and Sir Roderick?'

'Indeed not,' said the maid, who had her own reasons for considering Sir Roderick the most handsome and beneficent man in the kingdom.

'You are right,' said Isabella. 'Consider the portraits of Sir Penrose. Do you not think I have the same high brow?'

Abigail, who had not considered the possibility before now, could only admit that Isabella was correct.

'I have often,' said Isabella, 'stood before his portraits in the gallery and looked into my mirror, observing in it half his face and half mine. My conclusion to this has been that there is a likeness between us, both in the chin and the eyes, and I have read that such features can pass over a generation and declare themselves in the next.'

Abigail now took time to consider her mistress, and, having made her observation, could only agree with Isabella that there was indeed a likeness between the supposed orphan and Sir Penrose. From this moment on, Isabella was convinced that she was in some way related to Sir Roderick and Lady Sophia, a fact that was clearly evinced by the care Sir Roderick took of her on the occasion of Lady Sophia becoming grievously ill.

Lady Sophia had complained of headache for some time. A dozen times a day she had begged Isabella to 'Put down the blind!' only to have it put up again half an hour later. She complained that her crewel-work was all gone wrong because she had such a pain in her eyes. This was an old excuse to Isabella, who was accustomed to play the Penelope to her guardian, being used to taking out the stitches that were badly done and replacing them with her own quick needle. Then Lady Sophia began to complain of the oppression in the weather. Isabella decided that Lady Sophia was ill and that a doctor must be sent for, but being only seventeen years old and still by no means certain of her status in the castle she doubted if she had the authority to embark on the expense that any cure might require. But neither could she bear to see the lady suffer, and so she went in search of Sir Roderick.

Isabella was no longer afraid of Sir Roderick, though she found him both overbearing and careless towards others, especially his sister. She hoped that by interceding for a doctor to be called to Lady Sophia, Sir Roderick would agree to the necessary expense. Having determined on this course, Isabella ran down the great staircase, crossed the entrance hall and knocked with her fist upon the door of Sir Roderick's chambers.

The great thickness of the door could not be permeated by her hand. Sir Roderick went on with his perusal of certain libidinous works of Italian art until he became aware of the whining of his dog, Scar. Isabella, screwing her hand into a fist, knocked again and this time was heard. Sir Roderick folded the tissue over his etchings and called: 'Come.'

Isabella halted, her hand on the knob, took courage in the thought that by an interview with Sir Roderick she could do the best for Lady Sophia, and entered the room.

Sir Roderick regarded her. The speed of her journey from Lady Sophia's chambers to his had given Isabella a pinkness in the cheeks, which might have been called a flush had she not spent so many moments outside the door. Though she did not appear to pant, it was obvious from the rise and fall of her bosom that she had been through some great exertion. Scar opened his jowls and growled at her as he did at anyone who caused his master to rise quickly from his chair.

'Pray, sir . . . ' began the young lady, and then, remembering her manners, dropped a curtsy so deep that Sir Roderick could see over the back of her head and down the moonlight white of her nape. He crossed to her before she could rise and stood very close, drawn to her by the passion in her countenance.

'Pray, sir, good Sir Roderick.' Where she obtained the epithet 'good' for a man whose true nature she knew so little can only be conjectured. Isabella felt only that she must appeal to him out of the duty she owed Lady Sophia. 'My lady is ill.'

Sir Roderick, used to the humours and vapours of his sister and very often grateful to them as a means of confining his sister to her chambers, if not her bed, could only wonder at the palpitations they caused in Isabella's breast. He knew as well as any gallant that such distress must be comforted by any means at his disposal, and was not unaware that ladies thus comforted were bound to be grateful to their protector. 'Do you feel faint?' he asked. 'You must take my arm.' A shake of the head indicated that an arm was not necessary for Isabella.

'Perhaps some wine, then?' Again the head shook and all its pretty curls with it.

He indicated a sofa on which he had often made himself comfortable whenever he had taken vigorous indoor exercise.

'No, sir. I wish that a surgeon may be sent for.'

'A surgeon! My sister has been maladied before now and the

apothecary has not thought it worth his half-crown visit!'

'She complains of dying.'

'Then it's the toothache.'

Isabella was at a loss to explain how serious she thought the illness to be. In an entreaty she put out her hand and touched Sir Roderick's arm. 'Sir.'

'Isabella?'

She breathed in so deeply that for a second her creamy bosom was quite separated from her corset. Sir Roderick, being above a head taller, could not but notice the inhalation, and so entranced was he with her beauty that he was in a far more receptive frame of mind towards her when she spoke again.

'Sir Roderick, I have not known sickness except the boiling fevers of childhood, which, mercifully, I recovered from.'

The gentleman was surprised by this. Surely if such a creature had taken the measles or the croup and he had known, he would have asked after her every day, commanded grapes, sent out for such pomegranates as broidered Isabella's pannier. He looked up again and into her eyes and thought of figs. If she were confined to bed, figs, then, would have been the only fruit.

Calm and composed, the orphan continued:

'But from what I know, sir' – another curtsy – 'it is the pox!'

The blood drained from Sir Roderick's face. The pox was the disease he was most frightened of acquiring, though he thought of the biter-off-of-noses while Isabella referred to the smallpox.

'My sister?' he asked.

'Yes, sir,' she replied.

He tried to reflect on his sister's conduct and in what circumstances and from whom she might have caught the intimate contagion.

'How many times before now have I been told my sister is ill only to discover that her illness was merely an attempt to obtain sympathy from me?'

'Believe me, sir, the lady is very sick.'

'You shall tell me next she will die!'

'I believe she may.'

'Then let her get it over with,' retorted the callous brother.

'Sir, you are too cruel.'

'What do I care if my sister lives or dies?'

'She would care very much if you were so indisposed. She has all the symptoms. Her pupils are inflamed beyond anything that a tincture of eyebright and elderflowers can do for them.'

Sir Roderick wondered on this use of herbs. Any man knew that the only true remedies for such an infection were mercury and abstinence. Then it came to him that Isabella was entirely ignorant of the nature of his own fears. She prattled on about the smallpox, which anyone might take, whatever their virtue and station in life.

In her anxiety Isabella was anxious to gain more of Sir Roderick's attention. She reached out and touched him now on the hand. In a moment his attention was all hers. She continued without relinquishing her hold on his thumb. 'I fear it will spoil her features.'

Sir Roderick saw before him in his imagination the many beauties who had been smashed down from their pedestals in the fortnight of the disease's course. Women who now painted themselves so thick that in a year they used more mortar than would have held up a small house. Looking at Isabella's bright eyes and heaving bosom, he knew in a moment that she must be protected from the disease before it could spoil her beauty.

'Send for whomever Lady Sophia requires,' said Sir Roderick.

'Thank you, sir,' said Isabella, and in her gratitude she rained tears upon his hand. Sir Roderick turned his palm upwards and put his hand under her chin. 'But once the man has been sent for, you and I shall leave this house immediately.'

'But my lady?'

'She will recover if she must, but she cannot be so selfish as to inflict her sickness upon you, whom she has adopted as her own. Or upon me, who, in the event of calamity, will be your only protector. I will have the horses put into the curricle immediately.'

'You will drive me yourself, sir?'

'We will take no servant with us, for fear that they harbour the infection.'

'I must send for my clothes.'

'You must bring nothing. Our expedition must be entirely untainted. We will find a mantua-maker. And a milliner. You will be quite made over. Indeed, I have never thought my sister dressed you as you should be dressed. Always plain, and never showing you to your full and very pretty advantage. But then the moon does not like to be outshone by the sun.'

Isabella was becoming tired with her interview. Here was a man to whom she had never spoken above twenty words together, insisting that they must go away in a chariot without a servant. She wished now that she had some close relation, so that if it was truly necessary to take sanctuary from Lady Sophia's illness she might be able to do so with the propriety she felt necessary.

But Sir Roderick carried all before him. Isabella, brought up to be grateful (which always induces timidity), could do nothing but let him bear her away from Ducoeur Castle.

She looked back as they left the gravelled sweep in front of the house. Lady Sophia's apartments were on the first floor, all their blinds drawn down as if death had crept into them already. Then, for a moment, one lifted. Lady Sophia, blistered and red-eyed, looked down at them. Isabella, with a ghastly pity, lifted a hand to her.

The curricle containing her brother and Isabella Broderick, with Scar running behind them, and the small, white raised hand of Isabella put the sick lady into such a fever that, having seen them depart, she fell down beside the window in a dead faint.

☜ THREE ☞

*In which Isabella is taken to an inn by
Sir Roderick and there undergoes a strange
and alarming adventure*

As Sir Roderick and Isabella left Ducoeur Castle, Isabella sat silent, lulled into a reverie by the motion of the magnificent and finely matched horses.

'They are mighty fine stallions,' commented Isabella, venturing to say something to Sir Roderick.

'They are the envy of three counties.'

'I can much believe it, sir.'

'I have been offered five hundred guineas for them.'

'Indeed, sir.'

'They did not cost me a tenth of the price.'

'No, sir?' said Isabella, thinking it strange that anyone should make such a great gift to Sir Roderick, who, she was sure, would not in any way return the favour.

'I won them!' cried Sir Roderick, bringing his whip down on their backs so that they might step higher and show more of their prowess. Having lashed up the pair, Sir Roderick then proceeded to tell Isabella how he had come by them as a gambling debt. Isabella, who had never been interested in the intricacies of cards, had soon ceased to follow the triumph of knaves over kings but gathered, from the levity with which Sir Roderick told the tale, that it had not been an altogether honest game.

'What is honesty?' cried Sir Roderick. 'When a man is too drunk to tell a spade from a club? Especially when I was the one who had been keeping him in brandy and notes of credit for half the week.'

Isabella did not reply. She was not used to such confidences, especially from one she considered to be a gentleman, a man who, she had been instructed from the beginning by Lady Sophia, was the most open and most upright, and who only ever acted from the best of motives. It displeased her to think that a man whom she believed to be such a close relation to her as Sir Roderick could act in so duplicitous a manner.

''Twas a mighty good thing I beat Chaser and took my payment of him that very night.'

'How, sir?' ventured Isabella, hoping that now she was to hear something that reflected well on Sir Roderick.

'He could not ride home and so had to be accommodated where he was. Chaser mounted would jump anything, and so I prevented his neck being broken at the first turnpike he came to on the Richmond Road. Indeed, he thanked me for it when he realized what I had done. More than that, he put me in line with the best pairing of any horses in England.'

Isabella remained silent.

'Do you not wish to know how I came by the other?'

'If you wish to tell me, sir.'

Sir Roderick pulled on the reins. If the horses did not stop with the alacrity that should have been natural to the finest in England, they were not at that moment the object of his concern.

'Isabella, we must get along together. There is but one way of passing a journey quickly, which is to have as much conversation as possible. Indeed, to know one another.'

'But, sir,' she cried, alarmed at their stopping so far from the last habitation they had seen and fearing every moment to be attacked. 'What more do I need to know of you than I have heard every day from your sister? Which was all such good report!'

'Then I shall essay to know more of you!' said Sir Roderick, to Isabella's relief jolting his horses into motion once again.

'There is nothing that makes me interesting, sir. I do not even have the advantage of family or connections. Except those that you and your sister have been good enough to grant me,' said Isabella, hoping by this means to gain some information as to her parentage. None came.

Poor Isabella! Quick though she had been with her needle and her books, she had learnt nothing of the art of coquetting. She could not appear interested when she was not. Her laughter, sylvan though it was, could come only naturally. Her glances were direct, and she could not chatter for half an hour on something that had no merit. Thus, in order to keep up the required conversation, Sir Roderick had to dwell on himself. So familiar was he with this subject that three hours passed in self-flattery and descriptions of heroics so great that if Isabella had read them in a story-book she would have believed the man who had performed them to be a brother of Hercules rather than Sir Roderick Ducoeur. It was now necessary that the horses should be taken out of harness and some refreshment applied for at the next inn.

As they approached the place, Sir Roderick said: 'I must warn you, Isabella, that though this place looks very mean, the haunt of thieves and vagabonds, I am well known here.'

Looking at the building in front of them, Isabella was much surprised by Sir Roderick's assertion that he had friends within. 'How, sir, did you ever become acquainted with such a place?' she asked.

'It is not the first evening I have been caught out thus on the road.'

'But is the place not very dirty, sir? And in our hurry we omitted to carry our sheets with us.'

'That is no matter.'

'But we might be put into beds which are very damp and quite infested with vermin.'

'I promise you, Isabella,' said Sir Roderick, now looking at her with great kindness. 'If you think the bed is dirty, I will have a boy put into it to take the fleas off on him. Nay, I shall have him roll the sheets as many times as you think prudent to make the bed safe.'

'I had rather sit up all night!' cried Isabella. 'When you insisted that we left Ducoeur Castle, I imagined we were to go to friends.'

'That was indeed my intention.'

'Do they lie far off? Would it be possible by merely walking the horses to arrive there without them becoming too tired?'

'Only a fool walks his horses. Besides, my dear, look back over your shoulder and you will see why it is necessary for us to seek shelter at once.'

Isabella did so and saw behind them black, leering clouds approaching with all the speed of a cutpurse. It was clear that a great storm might be upon them at any moment. Having no change of clothes with her, Isabella recognized the wisdom of taking immediate shelter however ominous the abode.

The first drops of rain descended on them as they entered the yard. Sir Roderick called for servants, which produced two miserable specimens, one of a man and the other of his help-mate. The woman grabbed up to help Isabella down. Sir Roderick, seeing her reluctance to give the creature her hand, was instantly available. He felt Isabella shiver as she stepped into the dirty yard which was fast becoming mud, and, throwing his coat around her, drew her into the shelter of a porch and instantly called for brandy. To Isabella's entreaties that she would prefer chocolate, he begged her to remember the length of the journey they had come and prevailed upon the landlady to insist that Isabella should take some spirits to keep her strength up and step at once into the house.

'Madam,' said Isabella, 'I will take some brandy, if there is a place that is out of the public eye and if you' – addressing Sir Roderick – 'will then suffer me to sit alone a little while.'

'Surely he will,' answered the landlady. 'I have a little parlour that will suit your purpose in every description, and not reached through the house either. Let me take her there, sir, and when she is recovered you may come to her.'

Sir Roderick's appreciation of this was shown by a guinea, which the landlady trusted well enough not to bite but to put straight into her bosom. She begged Isabella to follow her: 'To a dry place, and quite private.'

Though Isabella would dearly have loved to protest, the approaching storm made any objection impossible, and she permitted herself to be taken into the house, where the landlady – which, despite her appearance, she obviously was – threw open the door upon a small, surprisingly snug chamber. A fire was lighted in the hearth, which, with well-trimmed candles, gave the room an atmosphere of such comfort that Isabella could only rejoice in after her apprehensions of filthiness. Sitting down on a smart chair, its leather covering as well studded with brass nails as any at Ducoeur Castle, she reflected upon the folly of drawing conclusions from first appearances.

At this point the landlady came in, carrying a glass and the brandy Sir Roderick had insisted upon. Isabella noticed that since she had left her the woman had covered and smoothed her hair and replaced the bit of sacking she had worn as an apron with a bib of the purest white. Five minutes was all it had taken for this transformation from slattern to honest country woman. So delighted was she with this change of circumstances that Isabella wished she had some small money about her that she might reward the woman in some way. Then she remembered that she was now entirely dependent on Sir Roderick for all the necessities of her life.

'My lady, your brother . . . '

'My brother?' Isabella looked around the room in alarm.

Though they were alone, the landlady decided it was best to be discreet. She came very close to Isabella and whispered: 'The gentleman thinks it is best that you should be considered brother and sister. I know it is not the truth.' And she added piously: 'I know we should not lie, but sometimes we must help the Lord in protecting us from arrogant questions. Especially' – and here she dropped a curtsy to Isabella so low that she might have been saluting a countess – 'where a young lady as fair as you is concerned.'

'Your brother' – she grew loud again now – 'begs that when

you are ready he should dine with you.' Again the voice fell. 'He would eat alone, in the other room, but it is not a proper place for him. Greedy eyes.'

Here the landlady rolled her eyes with such a degree of ferocity that she looked more dangerous than Isabella's first sight of her. She started.

The landlady having made her hit ran home with: 'I would not like you to put him to the inconvenience of being robbed. Not when, from what he has told me, your brother undertakes the journey merely for your protection. But I press you, and the gentleman gave me half a crown against doing that!'

She had gained the very monetary reward that Isabella had wished to give her, and so the young lady agreed to dine with her new-found 'brother'. Secretly she thought it would have been far better, and certainly more believable to the landlady, if Sir Roderick had called himself her father, for was not such propriety more fitting than a brother and sister travelling alone?

A cloth was spread upon the table and two covers brought in when there was suddenly a great commotion and a knocking on the door. Isabella's heart was in her mouth. She could think only that such a ruction was the prelude to the mischief that she had feared and at which the landlady had openly hinted. She wished that she had called Sir Roderick and his pistol to join her immediately she had sat down in the chamber. Now, the illumination that had been so welcome to her could only alarm her, with its lack of shadows and dark corners, its inability to provide any sort of hiding-place. There was but one hope: to take up the knives which some providence had placed on the table. Hiding one in her waist and taking the other in her hand, Isabella placed the heavy chair against the door and waited.

There was running and confusion, as if the whole house was laying itself under siege. Then silence, then footsteps and the landlady's voice begging admittance. She has dressed like a friend and then betrayed me, thought Isabella! I am lost, and Sir Roderick has not defended me!

The handle of the door turned. The portal opened and

struck against the chair. Isabella recognized that in her hurry she had not placed the chair close enough, and that she had left a space into which a pistol might be admitted, a sighting taken and a shot made.

'My lady,' came the rough voice of the innkeeper's wife.

'What? She has made a barricade to keep out her brother?'

It was the voice of a woman, neither high nor sharp, neither fawning nor carping. In short it was a voice with all the attributes Lear had given Cordelia's, of being soft and low in women and, being so, was most distinctive. It continued: 'Pray, my dear, do me the duty of one of my sex: grant me admittance so that I may divest myself of my wet dress. Indeed, that is not the last of it. My petticoats and shift are as if they have been put on me straight from the tub.' Here the lady gave a small sneeze, indicative of the fact that she was close to catching a cold.

Isabella was all confusion. What attacker could this be? She had heard of women who rode the highways in search of pocket-watches and jewels. But would such a woman complain of the elements, would she not rather have boasted of her discomfort, would she have talked of it at all or possessed such a gentle voice?

There came another sneeze. Isabella, mindful of the cold she had been protected from by her arrival at the inn, ran to the door and pulled away the chair.

In a moment the lady – for so she obviously was from her looks and dress, though it was black and declared the death of some relation – stood in the space it had occupied. She resembled nothing so much as a statue in an old-fashioned water-garden. She dripped, she ran, and yet her beauty was entirely undiminished. The lady's adversity had taken nothing from her manners. Advancing on Isabella, she made her curtsy.

Isabella could not but look graciously on her. She was charmed that she should meet such a beauty by chance.

The beauty looked at her. 'Madam,' she said, 'I am thrown into your company by misfortune. Please, for my sake, set down your knife. You have no cause to use it against me.'

Isabella was entirely astonished to notice that she bore a weapon in her hand. Instantly she dropped it. The implement clattered to the floor, at the feet not of an avenger but of an angel.

The angel, who was as practical as any principality, angel or archangel who ever acted in the interests of humanity, picked up the knife, polished its dirt on the wet stuff of her cloak and set it again on the table, smiling at Isabella as she did so. She then proceeded to pull the chair away from the door, placing it in the darkest corner of the room.

The landlady, beholding all this as it behoves the keeper of any establishment to do, had said nothing until this moment. Now she came forward, addressing Isabella and stroking her new-found white apron, and said: 'I am sure your brother will esteem you all the more for your graciousness to this lady here.'

'You have a brother,' stated the lady; 'I have none. I had a cousin once . . . ' The lady would not go on, and it appeared to Isabella that there had been some great grief between them. Then the lady continued: 'Alas, where his friends were concerned he was never strong. And as soon as my influence was removed from him, his good nature was sorely exploited by a gentleman I can never forgive, and who encouraged him in every vice and removed from him every scruple. In short, my cousin was cultivated into becoming a drunk and a gambler.'

Here the lady's affection quite overcame her, and she burst into tears. The hostess of the inn, who feared nothing as she feared emotion, instantly forsook the pair, and Isabella was left to offer what help she could.

She begged the lady to sit down. Within a second of being seated the lady was up again, walking the length of the room and saying: 'I must be rid of these wet things. For the death of my much-loved husband has turned me almost into a pauper, and I am now on my way to see my cousin, in the hope of obtaining some small settlement, which I am not confident he will give me, even for our former affection. And if he is to turn me out and I have caught . . . ' She paused to contemplate her future.

Isabella regretted instantly that she had left Ducoeur Castle without a trunk or even a bundle. Being unable to provide the lady with a change of clothes, Isabella had to content herself by leading her to the fire, where, in a stream of apology and steam from her clothes, the lady poured out her thanks for the kind way in which she had been received.

'Madam,' said Isabella, 'you have no need to reproach yourself to me. I only wish I could give you greater comfort.'

Here the lady forgot all dignity and sobbed wetter than the night from which she had come 'Oh, madam,' she wept, 'now my husband is dead, I never thought to receive comfort again, certainly not from one so young and who I hope, will never suffer as I have done.'

Isabella could not but fall at her feet and, taking up her hands, beg her to be less agitated. For a moment the lady looked at her. Her face was calm but full of wonder.

'I pray, if it is not too much of a liberty, will you tell me your name?'

'So please you, I am Isabella Broderick.'

'Then I am mistaken. I thought I saw in you some slight resemblance, but your humility makes it impossible for you to be a relation of the person of whom I think.'

At this point the lady shivered so violently that Isabella feared for her wits. She rang the bell and, when a surly youth demanded to know what was required, she sent him straight away for his mistress, from whom, at length, a change of rough clothes was obtained.

The lady, now dry and warm, took more notice of her surroundings. She acquainted Isabella with the fact that her name was Lady Henry Amory, but she begged that Isabella might call her Louisa. She had been married, with all bliss, for five years when her husband had been suddenly taken from her by the canker. A misfortune in the will and the fact of her childlessness meant that she had no claim over her husband's estate. So now she was thrown out.

At this point the landlady came in to put some bread on the

table. Isabella noticed that the poor unfortunate's eyes were all upon it. From such a demeanour it was obvious that she had not eaten for some time.

'You shall dine with us!' Isabella cried with her usual generosity of heart, forgetting that any such invitation should be Sir Roderick's prerogative.

'Madam,' was the reply, 'you have already been too kind to me.' However, Lady Amory could not keep her eyes from the bread.

It was clear to Isabella that if her new friend did not take some nourishment soon, then her strength might break down entirely, which, together with her recent wetting, would put her into severe danger.

'Madam,' she said, indicating the chair with which she had blocked the door, 'sit down in this chair, for it is the most comfortable in the room.'

'Then it is your place,' replied the lady.

'I have no need to be kept out of the draught and it would give me pleasure to know that you are comfortable.'

Lady Amory did as she was requested and sank down on the chair, saying: 'I am truly very tired and very hungry.'

'You shall be hungry no longer,' said Isabella, who took one of the pewter plates from the table and, putting a piece of bread on it, carried it to Lady Amory.

She picked up the bread and said to Isabella: 'I have eaten nothing these three days. I have always heard that hunger must be gradually relieved, that a surfeit given to a starving person does them more harm than little fragments given at short intervals.' She broke the bread into small pieces such as might be given to sparrows and finches.

As she did so, Isabella took the opportunity of looking at her more carefully. The deep shadow that was thrown on to Lady Amory's face by the chair made it difficult to estimate her exact age, but Isabella guessed she must be about six and twenty. Apart from a heaviness in her eyes, her face was, as yet, unmarked by the grief from which she suffered.

One by one, Lady Amory took up the crumbs from the table and savoured each one as if it were the finest dish at some banquet. Overhead, the storm raged, and Isabella could not help contrasting its fury with the calmness with which her guest took her repast.

There were still some five or six pieces of bread on the table when the eyes of Isabella's new-found friend began to droop. Before many minutes she had fallen into a deep stupor, sinking down in the chair until she was almost entirely invisible. Suddenly, for a few instants she roused herself and said to Isabella: 'I do not know who and what you are. But your kindness will always have my gratitude, and if I can ever assist you . . . ' But the effort of conversation became too much, and she gave in to the sleep that overwhelmed her.

This utterance put Isabella in mind of Lady Sophia. She wondered how that lady did, if the dread hand of death had yet seized her. She might be dying now, deserted but for her maid, Jane. Isabella trembled as she realized, with full intelligence, that though she had just assisted one lady she had deserted another, and one to whom, for the sake of Sir Roderick, she owed alliance.

Taking the plate so that it should not fall from Lady Amory's lap and wake her, Isabella vowed that she would ask Sir Roderick to return her to Ducoeur Castle as soon as the storm abated, so that, if there was anything she might do for Lady Sophia, she could perform it.

At that moment Sir Roderick entered the room. So great was his drunken swagger as he threw open the door that it extinguished the candles on the table. Isabella prepared to send for them to be lighted again.

Sir Roderick stopped her. 'You have been exerted too much today. I can dine as well by firelight as anything else. Indeed, in places such as this, where the victuals are not always of the highest quality, I sometimes find it preferable. If we sit close, we will see one another well enough.'

And so saying he went to the table and drew nearer together

the two wooden chairs that were placed there – so close that Isabella feared her knee would touch that of Sir Roderick.

The food was brought in. It smelt passably well, and Isabella put off her fear that they might be poisoned. She followed Sir Roderick to the table and took her place beside him. He helped her to the dishes with great delicacy, but before Isabella could pick up her knife he sprang from his chair, crying: 'Madam, I must move further off. Sitting so close makes me too hot.'

'Then, sir,' said Isabella, 'sit further from the fire.'

For a second Sir Roderick said nothing, then he resumed his seat, saying: 'I will grow used to it.'

'But, sir, I see you are flushed,' said Isabella, noticing the sweat that had broken out on his brow and the high colour in his cheeks. 'Perhaps you have caught a chill on the journey.'

'I never take a chill – or perhaps I might have.' He took up Isabella's hand and held it to his forehead. 'Tell me. Am I hot?'

'A little, sir,' she replied, trying to draw her palm away.

'No,' he whispered to her urgently. 'Hold it there. It is so cool. See. I begin to become calm already.'

Isabella began to grow alarmed. To see a gentleman who was usually so aloof now so agitated concerned her. There began to grow in her the notion that he had perhaps caught his sister's sickness and that their flight from Ducoeur Castle would prove entirely hopeless. She thought that it would be best if he were put into bed; she ventured to broach the subject with him.

'To bed?' he exclaimed.

'I think you would find great relief there, sir.'

'Indeed, indeed!' cried Sir Roderick with such vehemence that his voice penetrated the sleep of Lady Amory, who until this point had remained unnoticed in her chair. As people who are agitated in their sleep are wont to do, the lady could not help uttering some words. Isabella could make nothing of what she said, but to Sir Roderick they seemed as audible as a church bell striking midnight.

'Curse me not!' cried Sir Roderick, the brightness of his countenance evaporating at once.

Lady Amory spoke again. This time Isabella could comprehend her, though she said only one word and that was 'Always!' At which, Sir Roderick Ducoeur did the strangest thing he had done in his life. He fell in a dead faint on the floor as if he were some young lady who had just discovered that her man of fortune was truly a younger son whose only expectation was of a small country living.

❦ FOUR ❧

In which Sir Roderick survives and Isabella returns to the home from which she has lately fled

Inns on lonely roads are often thought to be haunted, and though it had long been the boast of the house at which Isabella and Sir Roderick had stopped, that a young girl had been murdered there by a blow to the head with a chamber-pot, no proof of such a spectre had ever been received. Thus, the land-lady and her husband were delighted when Sir Roderick fell on the floor and rolled his eyes. There was no difficulty in putting him into the best room the place afforded. Sir Roderick had seen a ghost and they were grateful – particularly as they had not been put to the trouble of being witnesses themselves.

The commotion in removing him from the parlour could not but rouse Lady Amory. She awoke trembling and complaining of having had the strangest dream she had ever had in her life. Isabella hoped she would be told what was the import of this dream, but the lady shook her head and, being surprised to find the place so much darker than it had been when she fell asleep, begged only that more light should be brought into the chamber.

When it was again possible to see every corner of the room, she began to pace it anxiously, knocking on the panelling, in the hope, Isabella presumed, of finding a secret room. She kicked a small rug from in front of the fire – was she in search of some cellar? – and finally stooped to peer under the table. Her searches revealed nothing, and with a deep sigh she resumed her chair.

Isabella, now firmly convinced that she had been in the presence of two visitations and witness to neither of them, was agog to know if the lady's story bore any resemblance to Sir Roderick's. To this end she revealed nothing of what had happened while she and the gentleman had been at table.

Lady Amory remained silent such a great while that when she spoke it was quite startling to Isabella. 'Listen!' she said, laying her finger on her lips. Intent on hearing cries and chains, Isabella listened as acutely as any servant at a door. She heard nothing. For there was nothing to hear. The storm had abated.

'Will you do me a favour, my dear?' Lady Amory asked.

'Anything that is in my power, madam.'

'It is a small thing.'

'I should still be very happy to do it.'

'Will you open the casement for me so that I may see how the weather now stands?'

'Certainly,' said Isabella, rising and going to open the window.

'Why do you tremble?' asked Lady Amory when Isabella's hand was on the latch.

'I do not tremble, madam.'

'Indeed you do,' replied Lady Amory.

'I . . .'

'What can you be frightened of in the night?'

'I just wondered, madam, what it was that agitated you while you were sleeping.'

'I was not agitated,' said the lady in her soft voice.

'Forgive me, but you were. I thought you had had some strange dream or thought that perhaps some apparition . . .'

'I dreamed certainly, and it was not a dream I should like to repeat either in my sleep or to you. So, my dear child, you may open the casement without expecting to find some macabre face looking in on you.'

The lady having made this assurance, Isabella, very disappointed that she was not to know of Louisa Amory's dream, now öpened the latch, to discover that there was indeed no terrible visage staring in on her and that the storm had completely passed over and that the wet countryside was now illuminated by the light of a full moon.

Isabella could not help but feel a little disappointed. She had been told by her governesses and tutors that the purpose of her education was to make her rational. Now she feared they had performed the task too well.

The moonlight made Lady Amory restless. She went to the window herself to see what effect it had on the countryside. 'It is as bright as day,' she declared. 'I must go on.'

'Madam!' cried Isabella. 'I beg you not to venture out on such a night!'

'I must!' answered the lady.

'Consider the state of the roads and the danger you might be in from attack!'

'It would be impossible for me to be in any danger greater than that in which I felt myself to be in my dream.' Here the lady gave a little laugh which Isabella was sure was an attempt to build up her spirits. She continued calmly: 'It is quite imperative that I finish my journey and undertake the interview that I must have with my cousin. Now that the night is kind enough to let me continue on my way, I will do so with no further ado but to bid you goodbye.' With this she walked to the door, dropped another curtsy to Isabella and departed.

The young lady, now left alone to reflect on all that had happened to her that day, could reach only one conclusion: which was that, in some way, both Sir Roderick's vision and the lady's dream had been presentiments that Lady Sophia was now in a better place. She was confirmed in these thoughts by Scar, who, having been left in the other room when his master came in to dine, now gave a great howl. Isabella had heard of grief in animals, but this cry chilled her blood and reminded her that she must try to let fall a tear or two.

She had got very comfortably into crying when the landlady entered to remove the dishes, which were virtually untouched. Having for many years often been visited by young gentlemen and their 'sisters', and young gentlewomen and their 'brothers', she naturally drew the conclusion that Isabella wept for her sibling who lay upstairs.

She was all courtesy, even down to taking a handkerchief from her sleeve and presenting it to Isabella, who took it up and wiped her eyes without looking at it and observing the many purposes for which it had previously been used.

'Madam,' said this supporter of young lovers, 'I pray you go up to your lord. He is waiting for you.'

'Is he recovered, then?'

'No, madam, but he insists that he will have no one in his room except you.'

'Do you think my presence there will be a comfort to him?'

'How could it not be so?' replied the landlady. 'Especially being as young and pretty as you are.'

'But I am so inexperienced in such matters.'

'You have only to see to the gentleman's comforts,' said the landlady, wondering why Isabella was so reluctant to go upstairs.

'I owe him no more than that,' said Isabella, 'for he has, in his own fashion, been good to me.'

'I dare say. And now, I beg you, madam, do not make any further delay.'

At this Isabella asked the landlady to light her up the stairs and was led, at length, into a small, fetid closet. She went immediately to the windows and threw them open to disperse the odour. When she turned, her eyes met those of Sir Roderick, who reached out his hands towards her. 'Isabella!'

'What is it, sir?' she cried, going to the bed and taking Sir Roderick's hand.

His grip was very firm for a man who had seen a ghost but half an hour before, and all the brightness was back in his eyes.

'Say you will not leave me.'

'No, sir, not if there is anything I can do for you.'

'Do for me!' said Sir Roderick, sitting up in the bed and regarding Isabella. 'Do you know that you are very pretty?'

'This is not of the moment, sir.'

'Do you not like to be complimented on your looks?'

'I am not used to it, sir.'

'That is because my sister is jealous of you.'

'Oh, sir!' cried Isabella, letting go of Sir Roderick's hand. 'I fear the worst has happened to your sister. I am sure your fit was a premonition of her death!'

In her bedroom at Ducoeur Castle, Lady Sophia, though not dead, was very near it. Jane, who had been her faithful attendant since Isabella had left the house that morning, was so convinced that Lady Sophia would expire that she had taken the opportunity of removing a few valuable trinkets that Lady Sophia had promised her in order to prevent them falling into other hands during the chaos of death. It was a comfort to her to know that when Lady Sophia died and she was dismissed the house – for you cannot have a lady's maid without a lady – that she would be hedged round by a flurry of snuff-boxes, candlesticks, miniatures, bracelets, pieces of excellent lace and a very remarkable scent-bottle. Lady Sophia was unable to make any comment on the foresight of her servant because the surgeon had ordered that his patient's eyes should be completely bandaged to prevent any light reaching them.

The first part of the night had been spent watching and waiting. Then as midnight approached, Lady Sophia had begun to shudder, and that sweating which augurs the breaking of a fever took hold of her. When the moment of crisis was over, Lady Sophia lay back upon her pillows and whispered to Jane: 'I shall live.'

'I never had the least doubt of it,' said Jane, still hopeful of the disease developing a complication.

At the mention of his sister, Sir Roderick gave a ghastly groan. 'Why must you talk of her?'

'Because, sir,' said Isabella, thinking of the piteous moans that had come from the lady that morning, 'I do not think we should have left her, all alone in the company of servants.'

Sir Roderick laughed.

'Why do you laugh, sir?'

'I have always thought my sister very happy in the company' – and here he snarled – 'of certain servants.'

'Sir, I came here to comfort you and not to listen to abuse of Lady Sophia.'

'Then come closer.'

Isabella moved nearer to the bed and sat down on a small stool, some little distance from Sir Roderick.

'I cannot see you.'

'I shall move the candle, sir.' This Isabella did.

'You are still not close enough.'

Sir Roderick's statement frightened Isabella very much. Lady Sophia's illness had begun in her eyes and now she feared, from all that Sir Roderick said about not being able to see, that he was, despite leaving Ducoeur Castle, already afflicted.

At this precise instant Sir Roderick gave a great groan and threw himself back on his pillows. Isabella at once went to him and put her hand on his brow. The pulse in his temple raced. She withdrew her hand and went to the door.

'Where are you going?' asked Sir Roderick.

'I am going to call for a surgeon.'

'I do not need one.'

'Sir, I believe you do, and as I insisted that I should send for one for Lady Sophia, I now insist on doing the same for you.'

Isabella left the room, and Sir Roderick consoled himself by springing from the bed and taking a large draught of brandy.

At first the landlady showed great reluctance to have such a person in her house, insisting that Isabella was mistaken in thinking Sir Roderick ill. Nothing that the landlady could say would dissuade Isabella from her course. Thinking that by her arguments the landlady wasted time, Isabella reproached the woman and demanded if she would have Sir Roderick's death on her conscience. Finally, the landlady, thinking of her house's reputation if it got abroad that the presence of one ghost had brought about another, gave way under Isabella's insistence.

The surgeon having been sent for, Isabella returned to Sir Roderick's room. He lay silent, with his eyes closed. Lady Sophia had talked continuously in her pain, a constant litany of her ills and inconveniences. Her brother said nothing, and as Isabella walked up and down his chamber, moving as silently as a shadow, she believed that he knew nothing of her presence in the room.

She did not realize that Sir Roderick observed her, watching as she approached the window, where the moonlight glowed on the soft lustre of her gown. Isabella was so lost in her own thoughts that she was suddenly surprised by Sir Roderick whispering her name. 'Isabella!'

'What is it, sir?'

'There is something I must tell you.'

Isabella's heart trembled. It could only be that he was about to impart to her some great secret. She placed her ear close to his lips, thinking at last to hear his admission of being her father. There came a little sigh, and then, with sudden violence, he took hold of her person, drawing her to him with great ferocity.

'You need not be afraid of anyone listening at the door,' cried Isabella, trembling at the prospect of what was about to be revealed to her. Sir Roderick brought his lips so close that they brushed her ear.

'Look at me,' he demanded, taking her head between his hands and drawing her nose close to his own.

At this moment the surgeon, who, in his urgency to see his patient and thereby obtain his fee, had not even paused to knock upon the door, entered the room. At the suddenness of the interruption, Sir Roderick loosened his hold on Isabella and fell back on his pillow. His cheeks, so pale before, were now flushed, and his breathing came heavily, almost in pants; it seemed to Isabella that he was very discomforted.

She approached the physician. 'I beg you, sir, whatever you can do to comfort him, do it.'

'I will,' said the surgeon, much surprised at being called to such a place so late at night and by such a young and beautiful lady.

Knowing that, very often, the performance of medicine is as of much comfort as any good advice, he immediately began to perform his art. He brought out his cupping glasses, placed his jar of leeches on the table, opened a small box containing vials filled with all hues of medicine, shook a bag in which all manner of surgical instruments rattled very satisfyingly together, and set to his task.

In vain did Sir Roderick moan at every touch of the physician. He was ill and must be cured. Boiling water for poultices was called for, a cut was made for bleeding him, and powerful emetics forced between his jaws. The physician finished by giving the patient such a draught of laudanum that he was almost instantly asleep. The surgeon, confident now of Sir Roderick's recovery, made his adieus and left.

Isabella, who felt she had done all she could to relieve Sir Roderick, left the pot-boy watching at his bedside and went to her own rest. She did not pass a good night, dreaming much and sleeping little.

Yet it was beyond nine o'clock the next morning when she performed what toilette she could and went to enquire after Sir Roderick. To her surprise, she found him already in the parlour, deep in conversation with a gentleman who was dressed so soberly that he could only be a lawyer or a parson.

She entered the room just in time to hear Sir Roderick mutter the words: 'A full confession?'

And the gentleman, in an accent that she believed to be Scottish, replied: 'I thought it was better that I should come in person.' When Sir Roderick looked up and saw Isabella, he said: 'We will return to the matter again, sir, when we are at the liberty of having a more private interview.'

Isabella might have been a stranger to Sir Roderick, so curt was he with her, merely nodding when he noticed her entering the parlour. Even Scar disdained to recognize her, growling as she approached the table, which had been spread with a small repast. Only when Sir Roderick hit the dog with the tip of his boot did Scar back off and Isabella was allowed to sit at the table.

Once seated, she waited for the chocolate to be passed to her. It was not, until Sir Roderick, glancing at her, remembered his manners.

He poured a cup for Isabélla, which she drank quickly to stave off her hunger, having eaten little the evening before. As she set her cup down upon the table, Sir Roderick begged her, with great formality, to step out of the room so his discussion with the sober gentleman could continue in privacy.

Isabella did as she was requested, sure that Sir Roderick would explain himself in due course. But she was instantly confronted by the landlady, who had lost all her dignity of the previous evening and become, once again, a slattern. This apparition laid her finger on her lips, indicating that she wished to communicate with Isabella without the lady giving any shrill reply.

Isabella's thoughts went to Lady Sophia. Here was the news she had not been vouchsafed the previous evening. 'Tell me,' she said in a low voice.

The landlady spoke. 'You are to return at once to Ducoeur Castle.'

Isabella's look of astonishment at this information was answered by the landlady thrusting a folded piece of paper into her hand. There was no seal upon it, and it had obviously been hastily quartered. Isabella opened her communiqué, a swiftly written note in a hand she did not recognize but which she could only presume, from the contents of the letter, to be that of Sir Roderick. The letter ran thus:

I have met, by mischance, this morning, a gentleman on his way to do business with me. He presses me to attend to the matter (which is nothing I would trouble you with) immediately. We must both, you and I, therefore quit this place and go our separate ways. I have arranged for your return to Ducoeur Castle.

Here Isabella wondered that a man who was so anxious for her to leave her home in the first place was now so desirous that she should return.

There will be no problem with your journey. You will travel by coach and in daylight. Leave without delay. If my sister lives, I beg you will not distress her by my going away with the gentleman. Indeed, knowing my sister's temper, I think it better that you should mention nothing of what passed last night. I shall return to you, think well of me and do not forget me, for know I will always have your interests at heart.

The note perplexed Isabella. It compelled her to return to the place from which Sir Roderick had insisted she fled less than twenty-four hours before. She could not understand it and would have gone back into the room in search of some explanation from him had the landlady's demeanour showed that she was anxious that Isabella should be gone as soon as possible.

A coach stood ready at the door. It was a sad contrast to Sir Roderick's equipage. If his horses had been the best matched and the envy of three counties, these were exactly the opposite: a huge bay and a piebald that would have shamed a dalmatian. The furnishings were dirty, and a pane of glass was missing from one of the windows. But it was her conveyance and, as instructed by Sir Roderick, she must go.

Nothing on the journey seemed familiar. They went through woods of oak, not firs that Isabella thought she had travelled through with Sir Roderick. Yesterday she had traversed dry roads; today they seemed all mud. The houses and cottages had no happy families outside them. Everything seemed bleak. The horses stumbled and the coachmen used language that caused Isabella to shudder. It seemed to her that at any moment she would be precipitated into the nearest ditch. Several times Isabella stopped the coachmen in order to enquire after their destination.

'Ducoeur Castle,' one replied, touching his hand to his faded cockade. Yet Isabella was in no way reassured that he spoke the truth.

Then, slowly, the countryside began to look familiar. She recognized the spire of a church, the sign of an inn, the face of a farmer driving his cows to market. When she understood that all was in order, Isabella's thoughts began to turn on what awaited her at her journey's end.

As they reached Ashton, the nearest village to the Ducoeur estate, she expected every moment to hear the mournful tolling of the church bell, ringing out the death of Lady Sophia, even putting down the window to hear it more clearly. Then it came: the first dreadful chime, then another, and another, and yet one more, the fourth, and the bell fell silent. It was four o'clock in the afternoon, and Isabella had been seven hours on a journey that the previous day had taken three. There must still, then, be some hope for Lady Sophia.

Not wishing to disturb the lady with any unexpected noise, Isabella requested that she should be set down at the park gates. The coachmen did so with the flurry of bows and salutes which usually made a very favourable impression. They were to be disappointed; Isabella had no time to notice them. Her chief aim was to reach the house. She fairly flew along the gravel, so great was her anxiety to know what awaited her in the castle.

It had often occurred to Isabella that the word 'castle' was somewhat inappropriate for the seat of the Ducoeurs. A castle had been built on the site; antiquarians had attributed it to the reign of Richard I. This impregnable fortress had had all the attributes it should: a moat, a portcullis, a gatehouse, turrets and battlements. It had had a noble family who, feeling secure behind their walls, had adopted the sport of feuding with their neighbours. Alas, it was a sport for which they showed as little aptitude as ladies do for cricket. Gradually they were forced to leave off this hobby in favour of advantageous matrimony – unions that provoked feuding of another kind, very few husbands and wives ever being able to live in harmony within the walls of the castle. Their most successful alliance had been with the daughter of a duke, which made it necessary for them to support the king against Parliament.

It took twenty days of siege and bombardment for the castle to fall and the family to flee. Having won its prize, Parliament then decreed that that the building should be made uninhabitable. For over fifty years it had remained a very pretty ruin, then Sir Roderick's grandfather had bought it and built a house out of it, somewhat in the style of Chiswick. And since a man's friends must know where he can be found, he called it Ducoeur Castle.

It was this edifice that Isabella now approached.

❧ FIVE ❧

In which a certain Mr Jackson, with the aid of Lady Sophia and her friends, compromises Isabella

The servants, their master being absent and their mistress regardless of what they did, had decided to spend the day in sport. The butler had broached a barrel of ale, and the cooks had been busy with the dry provisions. In this manner the day had passed very satisfactorily.

As Isabella walked into the hall, a game of nine pins was in progress, on which the wagering, as befits a holiday, was high. It was the footman's turn to strike. Such was his eye that all the pins went down. He expected cheers; none came. He turned and saw the reason for the silence. Isabella, whose going away with Sir Roderick had been one of the chief conversations of the day, stood in the doorway, returned as suddenly as she had gone. For a moment there was general astonishment; then it was remembered that if she had come back, Sir Roderick must have also returned. There was an instant bustle. The footman, pausing only to pick up his winnings and his wig, struggled into his livery. Food vanished from the tables as if the biblical plague of locusts had descended on the hall. Laundry-maids sank back into the laundry. Kitchen-maids ran to fetch their caps and aprons, and the cook started shouting for the fire to be made up while rapidly calculating how long the venison had been hanging. It seemed to Isabella as if bedlam had broken out in the hall.

It was a matter of some minutes before one of the maids remembered her duty and went to take Isabella's cloak. The maid was Abigail, who was always curious about any adventure concerning Sir Roderick, and who had perceived that the undoing and removal of Isabella's cloak would provide an opportunity for conversation on the subject.

She unfastened the ties at Isabella's throat, saying: 'And how is Sir Roderick?'

'Very well,' replied Isabella.

'We did not expect you to return so soon,' said Abigail, looking around the hall, now almost empty of its previous flotsam.

'Nor I, but Sir Roderick insisted on it.'

'And the master will always have his way,' the maid said saucily.

'Let us not talk of Sir Roderick. How is Lady Sophia?'

'She will live,' answered Abigail. 'But where is the master?'

'That subject can wait. I must go to Lady Sophia, for I know now that I should not have deserted her yesterday.' And saying this, Isabella brushed away the maid and went at once to Lady Sophia's bedchamber, leaving the maid to conjecture what she would about the night Isabella had spent in Sir Roderick's company.

Jane, who had spent much of the day computing how much she had lost by her employer's survival, was much startled to see Isabella, being certain that once Sir Roderick had removed her from Ducoeur Castle he would deprive her of her virtue and in no way permit her to return. Having seen that Lady Sophia slept, Isabella indicated that Jane should step out of the room so that they might talk without disturbing her.

Jane got up from her place at the bedside, taking care to push a bracelet, which she was sure Lady Sophia had forgotten, up her arm and into her sleeve. In the dressing closet, questions tumbled from Isabella's lips. How was Lady Sophia? Would she recover? How long was that recovery likely to be? Would she be marked? How bad had her eyes taken it? Was she awake or sleeping? Could she relieve Jane of her post?

Jane was happy enough at this offer of assistance but begged Isabella to give her a moment to put the chamber straight before she entered it. Isabella assented. When she took her place in the room, the bracelet was back in its casket and the other trinkets back on their shelves.

Isabella approached the bed, with its high plume and yellow hangings. Lady Sophia lay there, her face almost as yellow as the curtains, her eyes bandaged, snoring, as was her wont. It was instantly clear to Isabella that her face had been ravaged by the disease; the oozing, broken blisters indicated as much. She was so much a picture of misery that Isabella could not forbear making an involuntary sigh.

The noise caught Lady Sophia's ears. 'Jane?'

'No, it is I, Isabella.'

'Isabella?'

'Yes, madam.'

'You are gone away with Sir Roderick,' said Lady Sophia fearfully.

'I have gone and I have returned.'

'You dare to return here?'

'I have done so at Sir Roderick's insistence,' replied Isabella.

'He dared to insist that you should return to this house.'

'He arranged all the means.'

Lady Sophia gave a great cry. Supposing her to be in pain, Isabella demanded to know if there were drops or any other comfort she could administer.

'The only pain I have is from my brother's behaviour!'

'My lady, what has he done wrong except by going away?'

'I saw you!' cried Lady Sophia angrily. 'My eyes were not bandaged then.'

'Madam,' said Isabella, not liking to see the agitation that their conversation was provoking in Lady Sophia, 'calm yourself.'

'How dare you say that to me?' cried Lady Sophia, trying to turn her bandaged face in the direction of Isabella's voice. 'And you have come back, expecting, nay hoping to find me dead.'

'No, madam,' said Isabella, venturing to take Lady Sophia's hand as she had taken Sir Roderick's the previous evening.

'Do not touch me!' cried Lady Sophia. Then, more to herself than to Isabella, she said: 'After all I have done for you!'

'And I am grateful.' Isabella was at a loss to know what she could say to bring some comfort to Lady Sophia. She offered to fetch her a cup of water, but the lady insisted that it would choke her. She would take nothing from Isabella's hand.

It remained so for the length of her illness. For six weeks Lady Sophia did not cross the threshold of her room. It was left to Isabella to keep order in the household as much as she could. The servants, always aware of her status as an orphan, were never anxious to take orders from her. Now, with her exile from Lady Sophia, they were still more disinclined. If Isabella were out of favour, what could be gained by impressing her?

She could keep the servants in check only by persuading them that Sir Roderick's return was every day expected. But as the weeks passed, this threat held less and less authority. In her anxiety for the master to regain hold over the household, she looked for him every time a carriage was heard and waited to hear from him by every mail. Anyone who did not know her situation would have said that she exhibited every trait of a young lady in love, with his name constantly on her lips, the snatching up of letters, and the expressed belief that he would return at any moment.

Isabella had been right in supposing that the Scottish gentleman she had found at breakfast with Sir Roderick had been a lawyer. The business he had come on was very urgent and necessitated Sir Roderick's going away with him at once, being concerned with certain difficulties that had suddenly arisen through some estates that had come to him from his mother. The properties in question being in the West Indies, Sir Roderick had gone first to London and then to Southampton, where he took the first available ship, hoping that speed would resolve the problems quickly. There being some delicacy in the matter, he declined to commit any details of it to paper, and so the fact of his being abroad and remaining there for some time was not universally known.

How often, during her banishment from Lady Sophia's company, did Isabella reflect on the strange night she had spent at the inn. She wished that she had begged Lady Amory for her address, for she wished to know how the lady had fared in her interview with her cousin. She hoped for the lady's sake that he had treated her with kindness, for she did not see how anyone who had made the acquaintance of the lady could regard her in any other way.

At length, Lady Sophia was well enough to descend to the downstairs rooms. A fire was put into the grate, and the servants were ordered to keep below-stairs. Isabella was uncertain as to where she should be in this scheme of things and decided to remain in her room, passing the time, as she often did, with a novel. It was clear to all that Lady Sophia did not wish to be seen and that her disfiguration must be very great.

Isabella was intent upon her reading when she was called to the salon. She put down her book, Mrs Sheridan's *Memoirs of Miss Sidney Bidulph*, and followed Jane.

Lady Sophia sat in state, a stool under her feet, and for the first time Isabella saw the true enormity of the damage that the smallpox had done to her face. It was not just the pitting. The sore throat which accompanied the disease had prevented Lady Sophia from eating for many days together, and such had been the wasting of her flesh that the skin now drooped in long dewlaps. The inflammation of the eyes had damaged them to such an extent that the lady could see only by making slits of them. She had attempted to paint, but so inexpertly it might have seemed as if she had done it for a joke. In truth, she was a fright. She looked now at Isabella, waiting to mark her reaction. Isabella made none.

'Do I turn you to stone?' asked the gorgon.

Lady Sophia's smile was the worst thing of all, but Isabella would not let it disconcert her. She approached Lady Sophia's chair. 'I am only glad to see you out of your room.'

'I do not believe you,' was Lady Sophia's cold reply, and it seemed to Isabella that this interview was to be conducted in a similar manner to the one she had had at her bedside. 'What do you think my brother will make of me?'

Isabella did not know how to answer for Sir Roderick, but she did not need to, for the lady continued: 'It is the face *he* should wear, not I.'

Isabella was aware that Sir Roderick had not been quite the gentleman over his sister's health. His lack of correspondence with Ducoeur Castle she felt indicative of his indifference to Lady Sophia.

'Madam,' she said, hoping to put herself in sympathy with Lady Sophia, 'I can understand how painful it must be for a sister who so loves her brother to be neglected by him as you have been.'

'Where is he?'

'I do not know.'

'I will turn you out of this house if you do not tell me the truth.'

'It *is* the truth, madam.'

'Do you not have a clandestine correspondence with him?'

'I do not. I have received but one letter from him in my life, and that was to tell me to return here.'

Lady Sophia continued to berate her brother in a manner that was the exact opposite of her manner towards him before her illness. This Isabella attributed to Lady Sophia's usual self-pity and endeavoured to talk her out of it. She soon discovered that the more she defended Sir Roderick, the more his sister abused him; so Isabella, at the first opportunity, turned the conversation towards more pleasant topics.

She told how the curate's wife had just given birth to her tenth child, who had surprised no one by being a tenth daughter; how the gardener who had strived for many years to produce a pineapple had again failed; and how one of the local magistrates had ventured his entire fortune on a speculation for making velvet from bulrushes and how the unsuccessful project had bankrupted him. In short, she told Lady Sophia so many stories of misery that the lady, at long last, was almost persuaded to think herself fortunate. And when she dismissed Isabella there was even a degree of amity restored between them.

It was some days after Lady Sophia's first adventure into the salon that, at last, a letter arrived from Sir Roderick. It bore greetings, of a sort, to Lady Sophia, made no mention of Isabella and announced that the business Sir Roderick was involved in could not be concluded until he had paid a visit to the West Indies, so hurried had been his departure that he had not been able to write until they reached the Canaries to take on fresh water.

Isabella expected this information to cause Lady Sophia to pour more scorn on her brother; instead, it seemed to cheer her. She turned to Isabella, observing her very closely, and saying: 'I do not reckon on him being home for above six months.'

'Do you think his business can really be concluded so quickly?' asked Isabella.

'I thought you would wish him home at once.'

'No, madam, for I have observed that though you are unhappy when Sir Roderick is not here, his behaviour towards you when you are together gives you still greater grief.'

'Do you indeed believe that?'

'I do, and I would protect you from it if I could, for I do not like to see you so oppressed by one . . . ' Isabella paused, wondering if she should dare to broach to Lady Sophia, what she believed was her own relationship to Sir Roderick.

'Pray continue,' said Lady Sophia.

'Perhaps you think me foolish, madam . . . '

'The matter, the matter!'

'I have sometimes supposed my relationship with Sir Roderick to be . . . that I am not an orphan.'

'Why should you, after everything I have ever told you concerning your parentage, think such a thing?'

'His care over my education, his taking me away when he supposed me to be in danger.'

'You think he is some relation?'

'Yes, madam, I believe he is my father, for I would not, I swear to you as I have sworn before, gone away with him and left you so ill if I had not believed that to be my duty.'

Lady Sophia laughed, as Isabella had never seen her laugh before, crying at least a dozen times 'Your father!' as though it were the best joke in the world.

'I see now,' said Isabella, 'that I have been mistaken. I should not have presumed . . .'

'You would not have gone away with him had you believed your relationship to be otherwise?'

'It would not have been right, unless perhaps he were my brother,' said Isabella, remembering the appellation Sir Roderick had given himself at the inn.

'He is nothing to you,' cried Lady Sophia, 'and you have no right to think otherwise.'

'Is nothing known of my origins, then, not even the name of the mother whom I suppose to have given me this jewel?' asked Isabella timorously.

'Nothing.'

Isabella dared say no more. She feared that her presumption in connecting herself with Sir Roderick would turn Lady Sophia completely against her, but the effect was otherwise: she was once again petted and pampered as she had been as a small child, and Lady Sophia even talked of taking her into society with her.

'I did not know you were fond of company, madam.'

'I have always rejected it for my brother's sake, but now I mean to take it up again for yours as soon as I am well enough.'

It might have been expected from Lady Sophia's so much altered appearance that the lady should feel awkward going among people. But Lady Sophia, as soon as she was well enough to go outdoors, seemed to delight in showing off her countenance. She would take tea with acquaintances she had formerly snubbed, and any excitement at the assembly rooms would find her there.

Lady Sophia going around, Isabella went around also. Never had she had so much entertainment. She was the subject of much conjecture. It was generally decided that, because of her looks, her parentage must be good and that she could not be a foundling, however much she insisted on the fact. Her arrival at Ducoeur Castle was remembered by the parents of the younger dancers, and those who had declared that Isabella Broderick would be a nine-day wonder now insisted that they had always declared that she would do well.

It was inevitable that through these entertainments Isabella should be introduced to the young gentlemen of the neighbour-hood. And it must be said that Lady Sophia, wrapped in her own interests as she was, did not perform the function of chaperon as strictly as might have been expected. It was noticed that despite the lack of check, Isabella conducted herself with the utmost propriety: she would stand up to dance with any gentleman who asked her, never pretending she was fagged when a partner was not to her liking. She favoured younger sons as much as their elder brothers (something Lady Sophia had never done in her youth). Before long she was a universal favourite among all.

Isabella was engaged one morning in moving some lace between Lady Sophia's gowns, the lady being unable to choose between the Brussels on her green frock and the Arles on her blue, when the footman entered to announce that a Mr Jackson had called on a very urgent matter. Lady Sophia, hastily unpinning the trim that Isabella had placed around her cuffs, said she would go to him immediately.

Isabella was surprised by this, knowing Mr Jackson to be one of the roughest farmers to whom Sir Roderick rented a subsistence. 'Madam,' she said, 'it is not right that you should see such a person alone.'

'Why not?' asked Lady Sophia, almost tearing her lace in an effort to be gone.

'If he has a grievance he should make it to Sir Roderick's agent and not to you.'

'I shall be more effective than any agent,' shouted Lady Sophia in a frenzy. 'Unpin me!'

Isabella took out the fastening and watched as Lady Sophia primped and preened herself for a meeting with one of the most disreputable farmers on the estate.

Mr Jackson had been shown into a small antechamber close to Lady Sophia's rooms. He was a rough man, who stood with his hat in his hands, turning it through his fingers the entire time.

'How dare you come here!' were Lady Sophia's first words on entering the room.

The farmer looked at her with disdain.

'Answer me!' she cried.

'There is the matter of some money.'

'Money! Always money!'

'You must pay me or I will starve.'

'What care I for that?' asked Lady Sophia haughtily.

'I think you care very much,' replied the farmer, approaching her boldly.

'How dare you!'

'I dare,' he said, 'for you are old and ugly now and have no sway over me.'

'You are unkind,' said Lady Sophia, biting her lip so she did not cry.

The matter was this: a bill had been run up by Lady Sophia when she was a young girl. The business had come to the attention of her father, who remonstrated with his daughter. She had promised him that she would not again give in to the same temptation. Then a young lady in the neighbourhood obtained a scent bottle from London decorated with a very pretty love scene. Lady Sophia must have one like it – indeed, one better – but her pin-money being spent, she again dipped into her funds for relieving the poor.

The scent bottle was procured and flaunted, which inevitably brought it to the attention of Sir Penrose. The young lady was called to interview with him. He asked her about the provenance of the phial. At first Lady Sophia pretended it was a present, but, when she would not say from whom, Sir Penrose pressed her further. The sly girl then tried to pretend that she had had it for many months and her father had not noticed it. At last she was forced to admit the source of the money. Sir

Penrose, normally a mild man, was doubly angry, first because his daughter had broken her word to him, and secondly because she had shown herself to be a liar. His action was swift and firm. Lady Sophia would have no money of her own for six months. He would discharge her duties to charity but would contribute not a penny for her clothing or amusements.

Lady Sophia thought this very hard-hearted. She had no mother to apply to, Arabella having made an unfortunate assignment with a music master and absconded to the Continent, so lacking this recourse for pin-money, Lady Sophia took her grievance to Sir Roderick. He, in his own way, was also short of funds and said he could let her have nothing. She decided she would borrow and discovered that Caleb Jackson, who at that time prospered, was always happy to lend in return for certain favours. An agreement was formed between them that satisfied them both. Lady Sophia was very confident that as soon as she was in funds again, she could discharge her debt. But then there was a patch-box she must have, some shoe-buckles, and every new novel. Instead of repaying her loan, she borrowed again and so the debt grew.

The matter might have been settled when Lady Sophia came into her own money, but it was more convenient to forget it and Caleb Jackson, preferring to have Lady Sophia as a friend than an enemy, did not press her to return what she owed. And she in her turn felt that she held such great sway over Mr Jackson that he would never press her for repayment. But now, due to the demise of his farm and his penchant for strong liquor, he required his money with interest. So he had approached Lady Sophia.

'I do not know what you are talking of,' said Lady Sophia when Mr Jackson again told her that he must have his money.

'Perhaps this will refresh your memory,' he replied, searching around in his pockets and eventually finding an ancient piece of paper. 'I have here an agreement made between us and signed in your own hand.'

'Give it to me!' cried Lady Sophia, attempting to snatch it from him.

'What, and have you throw it into the fire. No, madam, if you will not repay me, your brother will have this piece of paper and an account of all our proceedings.'

'You would not dare!'

'I would, madam.'

'But I cannot find the money you require at such short notice.'

'Sell something.'

At this moment a letter was brought in for Lady Sophia, a letter she knew instantly to be from her brother. She at once broke the seal, hoping that the letter would contain details of Sir Roderick's being detained in the West Indies. But the import of the letter was very different, informing Lady Sophia that Sir Roderick was in Madeira and hoped to be at Ducoeur Castle in little more than a month. The letter concluded by Sir Roderick's sending his warmest regards to Isabella Broderick, who he trusted should have a dress in the latest fashion for his home-coming.

Having finished the letter, Lady Sophia turned to Mr Jackson. 'Sir,' she said, 'I think that there may be a way in which I can repay you.'

'What is that?'

'You will marry my ward, Isabella Broderick.'

'Miss Broderick?' said Mr Jackson, who thought the young girl a goddess.

'She is not rich, but she has a dowry that will provide you with an income that will support you both very comfortably.'

The matter was agreed and shaken upon, and Lady Sophia returned to Isabella.

'Isabella,' she said on entering the room, 'how should you like to be married?'

'Married?'

'Surely you must have sometimes considered the matter?'

'Indeed, madam, I have sometimes wondered what it would be like to have my own establishment.'

'You do not like it here?'

'Madam, you and Sir Roderick have been good to me . . . '

'It would please me to see you married.'

'Then, madam, I hope I shall find a husband who will win your approbation.'

'You have done.'

Isabella was quite amazed.

'I received just now an offer for your hand.'

'Not from Mr Jackson!' cried Isabella, her voice wavering and full of disgust.

'Yes, and I have accepted it.'

Isabella fainted.

Sal volatile was brought: it did not revive her. Cold water was applied to her head: she sat up. Feathers were burnt under her nose: she fainted again and was carried to bed.

When she awoke, Lady Sophia was at her bedside.

'Madam, tell me that I have dreamed it and that Mr Jackson has not asked for my hand.'

'He has asked for it and desires to be married with all possible haste.'

Isabella could only shake her head at this. She knew Caleb Jackson to be a rough man who had occasionally remembered to touch his hat to Isabella as she went into church. His cattle were bags of bones, and his house was of the humblest sort. Isabella could not imagine how he presumed to make an offer for her hand. Surely this was some jest as a result of too much drink and provocation?

'But I know nothing of him.'

'Your marriage will give you time enough to do that,' was Lady Sophia's firm reply.

'I beg you, madam, let us be better acquainted before I say yes or no.'

'The matter is done. You are to be married as soon as it can be arranged.'

Was she, then, not even going to shake hands with the bride-groom before they met in church?

'Please, madam, leave me a little time so that I may discover

Mr Jackson's interests.'

Isabella could not for the life of her think what the man's interests could possibly be or how they could correspond with hers. She did not believe the man could even read. And she was being pushed into the alliance without being the least way consulted on the matter. This was the event that must shape a woman's life, and she did not even know the age of the gentleman, though it seemed from his appearance and grey hair that he must be past fifty and she but eighteen. She sought to make another entreaty to Lady Sophia. 'Sir Roderick . . . '

'What of him?'

'Should he not be consulted as to whether or not he has any objection?'

'What objection could he have to seeing you set up in a home of your own?'

Isabella's mind was all commotion. Since she could not appeal to Sir Roderick, she began to think if she had any other friend who might prevent this match. She conjured up before her the vision of the sweet lady she had met in the inn. But what hope could Lady Amory be to her, even if she knew her place of abode? Isabella, penniless, could not throw herself on another woman in the same situation. There was no one among the servants who would take her part over Lady Sophia. Lady Sophia stood firm. Caleb Jackson had proposed, and Caleb Jackson had been accepted.

It was decreed that Isabella should take tea with the proposed bridegroom. Lady Sophia, on the pretext that it would not do for the household to know what was afoot, arranged for the interview to take place at the house of two impoverished sisters.

The Misses Timms were the daughters of a local clergyman, who had hunted so hard and expensively that his untimely though hardly unexpected death on the hunting-field inevitably had left his family with very little provision. Their father's way of life had led them to be the most proper ladies. Every nicety was observed, and propriety could have taken lessons from them. They never did anything unless they observed it to be right both morally and socially – indeed, the two were for them indistinguishable. It may be supposed that their life lacked amusement, but being so upright they had great pleasure in observing those around them and commenting on their foibles. It had been their father who had christened Lady Sophia, who had fortunately been born on a Thursday during the close season, and the sisters had remained grateful to her for the honour her baptism had done their father. For Lady Sophia's sake they had been attentive to Isabella, asking after her progress and reminding her of the duty she owed her guardian.

The tea-party was to be held on Wednesday. Isabella spent the night in advance of it in an agony. She had still not devised a plan that would bring Lady Sophia's preposterous suggestion to an end. She wished now she had made a favourite among the young gentlemen in the assembly rooms that she might send a message offering to go with him to Gretna and was ready to leave that very night. Even John Clewless, who could talk only of pistols, would have been more preferable to her than Caleb Jackson. At length she decided that she would submit to the interview at the Misses Timms' abode. She would use her strength of character to make the man see that a marriage between them was quite impossible. She was not fitted to be a farmer's wife, had never separated milk and cream or made cheese. She would convince him that she would make him but a poor wife who was more trouble than she was worth, who could not make a loaf of bread or a barrel of ale.

The couple were to meet at four o'clock, by which time Isabella had very prettily worked out her speech on her lack of domestic ability. All she required now was a moment alone with the grey-haired farmer so that she could make it. She was helped in this by Lady Sophia's declining at the last moment to accompany her. This had always been Lady Sophia's intention, though she had wavered to the last moment as to whether to use a headache or the toothache as her excuse. Then it occurred to her that Isabella might insist on staying by her side, so she pretended instead that she had twisted her ankle and needed nothing but to rest on the sofa. Isabella set out alone.

She had made no attempt to impress the farmer. The gown she wore was of the drabbest shade and quite out of the fashion. It was a dress that Isabella thought did not become her in any way. She had not pinched her cheeks to give her colour and steadfastly reminded herself that she must not bite her lips, wanting them to appear as pale and sickly looking as they could.

The path she took was the lowest and muddiest, one she normally avoided. Today it gave her great satisfaction to see her stockings splashed. She had put on no ornaments and even considered taking off the trinket from around her neck until she realized that, today of all days, she was most in need of her amulet. Unfortunately for Isabella, none of these precautions could stamp out her beauty. Her looks must impress Mr Jackson whether she liked it or not.

The Misses Timms opened the door to her themselves. 'We are so honoured!' said Miss Ann, the elder.

'So very honoured!' simpered Miss Betty and, then, remembering her instructions, added: 'But where is Lady Sophia? We so expected to see her.'

'So expected!' echoed her sister.

Miss Betty again took up the cause. 'Poor Lady Sophia. She has always been such a martyr to the toothache.'

'Indeed, madam, but it is not that which troubles her,' replied Isabella in her frank way.

'Her poor head! How I feel for her!' As she said this, Miss Ann drew her hand across her forehead and made the very image of pain. 'I am so afflicted by them myself, am I not, my dear Betty?'

'We must remember, Ann, that Lady Sophia's constitution has always been most delicate.'

'Indeed, they did not think she was likely to last . . . '

'Our father, you know, had the honour to baptize her,' put in Miss Betty.

Isabella felt she must correct them as to Lady Sophia's indisposition. 'Her Ladyship has twisted her ankle.'

The two sisters looked at each other. It was obvious that this was not the information they expected to hear. Isabella began to suspect a ruse on the part of Lady Sophia, but before she could further question Miss Ann and Miss Betty there was such a hard knock at the door that it was a wonder that the knocker did not fly through the wood and into the hall.

'Quick, my dear!' cried Miss Betty. 'Go up and make yourself comfortable. Ann will come with you to make sure all the proprieties are observed. I will let Mr Jackson in. Such a good neighbour!' she uttered brightly as the door gave another shudder.

Isabella was shown up into the parlour. The grate, which had not held a fire the whole of the winter, now burnt brightly. The furniture had been arranged for a tête-à-tête and a small table put ready to receive the tea things. Its deliberateness made Isabella shudder, and she entered the room with as much fear as she would have done the Fleet. Miss Ann begged that she would sit down. Isabella did so, taking care to keep her back to the light. Instantly Miss Ann was at her side, urging her that she could not be comfortable on such a hard chair and that gentlemen never liked to sit on a chair with cushions. Isabella kept her place, determined to secure the advantage in the interview.

Miss Ann, failing to achieve her point in this, decided to extemporize on the farmer's virtues. This honest lady made a paragon out of him, reminding herself all the while that it was her Christian duty to think well of her neighbours. If Isabella had known nothing of him, Miss Ann's description would have made him seem the finest farmer in the neighbourhood, an advocate of everything good and progressive, when in truth he had never had a good word to say for the improvements of Viscount Townshend or Robert Bakewell.

There was a lumbering on the stairs, very comparable to thunder, something said softly and then almost a roar of a voice. 'Why?'

'It is manners to take a hat off indoors,' said Miss Betty.

The hat had evidently been removed, for holding it

awkwardly in his hand Farmer Jackson entered the room. He was a large man who would have sold pigs very profitably if they had reached his gigantic proportions. Miss Betty, who had followed him in, urged him to sit down. He crossed the room, causing the floorboards to creak at each step, and took the seat that had been intended for Isabella, crushing the cushions as thin as pie-crust. Isabella stared at the astonishing mountain who was intended to be her husband.

He had not one redeeming feature. It was obvious that he possessed neither brush nor comb, nor, Isabella suspected from the state of his coat sleeve, a handkerchief. He wore no waist-coat, it was impossible to guess at the colour of his hose, and shirt and breeches were not united. In short, he would have presented a better appearance if he had come in his smock. Isabella wondered how it could occur to Lady Sophia that she and this man could ever sit down together. His very presence in the room oppressed her.

The farmer in his turn regarded Isabella. He had done well out of his bargain and wanted to secure his prize straight away. For his part he would have done without the whole business of taking tea and its necessity for him putting on his best clothing.

The Misses Timms ventured on some small talk by way of making an introduction, but the farmer had no interest in the fact that a near neighbour had grown a pelargonium with the most interesting scarlet flowers and that they were to have a cutting. Isabella, who usually showed quite an interest in horticultural matters, declined to evince any curiosity, and the conversation soon faltered.

It seemed like an age until the maid brought in the tea things, and another age while the tea was made and prepared. Mr Jackson had said nothing, for he had nothing to say. The matter was arranged, and he saw no necessity to make any more to-do about it. When Miss Betty offered him the sugar, he took it out of the bowl and placed it straight in his mouth. Miss Ann shuddered, but in a second she reminded herself that Isabella was an orphan about whose provenance very little was known and that marriage to Mr Jackson might be regarded as being to her advantage.

The tea helped to revive Isabella's spirits a little. She began to look for an opportunity to make her speech. She thought that if she praised the domestic practice of the Misses Timms, she might mock her own inadequacies in this art. But before she could do so there was a great commotion from downstairs. Miss Betty, begging her visitors and her sister not to get up, put down her cup and fled down to deal with it.

Mr Jackson was slowly heard to say that he hoped it was not a fire. Isabella silently agreed with him. She did not want him to have to put himself to the trouble of rescuing her.

The tumult downstairs ceased, and Isabella assumed that calm had been restored when Miss Ann suddenly declared: 'I do not like the silence. My dear brother, who died at sea, always insisted that there was a calm before the storm.'

Isabella saw her chance to escape from the room. 'Pray, madam, let me go down and put your mind at rest!' But Miss Ann, who had practised her exit several times that morning, was already on the stairs. Isabella and her paramour were left alone. In a second, possessing an agility that she did not expect from so much flesh, the farmer had left his chair with its flat cushions and advanced upon her. Isabella shrank back, holding out her arm in front of her to keep him at a distance.

'Sir!' she cried. 'Think of me, respect me.'

But the brute thought only that if he kissed her now the matter would be settled as well as if they had already gone to church together.

'Pray, sir, what if Miss Ann or Miss Betty should enter?'

Mr Jackson did not seem to have heard her and continued his advance. Isabella ran to the casement, thinking that she might throw it up and call for help. But the Misses Timms had had it fastened against draughts in the interests of their household economies. The other windows in the room were even more firmly sealed – bricked up to avoid the window tax. The only avenue of escape was the door, and that she was prevented from reaching by the body of Mr Jackson. Then Isabella thought that by falling to the floor she might crawl between him and the furniture, but before she had dropped to her knees he had seized her around the waist. Isabella screamed, and then her lips were sealed.

At that moment Miss Ann and Miss Betty re-entered the room, having dealt with the confusion they had quite expected, the maid having been charged with returning the fish kettle, dog pan and jelly mould to their shelves. They witnessed Mr Jackson's attack on Isabella and saw that she had been compromised. Her only salvation now lay in uniting herself with Mr Jackson as soon as the banns could be proclaimed.

❧ SIX ❧

In which Isabella is jilted

In vain did Isabella protest that the kiss had been none of her doing and that she detested the man who had inflicted it. Lady Sophia was adamant that the marriage must take place, for the propriety of the Misses Timms had required that the attack should be broadcast throughout the town. It was impossible that Mr Jackson could have made overtures to Isabella, brought up at Ducoeur Castle as she had been. No farmer in his position would have the audacity to presume on the affections of one so far above his station. Isabella, therefore, must have invited his attentions.

If her fate was to be sealed, Isabella begged it might be with the utmost quietness, but even this was forbade her. Lady Sophia, who hobbled on her twisted ankle when she remembered it, declared the wrong could be put right only by the marriage taking place in as public a manner as possible. To this end, the daughters of several lowly families in the district were sought out to be bridesmaids, the families very flattered by Lady Sophia's attention and the bridesmaids comforting themselves that if they must dance with Mr Jackson after the wedding at least they would be doing so in new dresses and petticoats. It was also known that Tabby Roberts had been given a silver bangle for attending at her aunt's wedding and the aunt had grown up above a blacksmith's shop, not in the elegance of Ducoeur Castle.

There was soon hardly anyone for twenty miles around who did not know that Caleb Jackson was to marry Isabella

Broderick. The dressmaker had told the haberdasher, he had told the packman, and the packman had carried the word to every door where he sold pins. But the one man who might have prevented the match knew nothing of it.

Sir Roderick, who had made good time from Madeira, had then been delayed in London by the delights of Ranelagh Gardens and Vauxhall and found himself less eager to see Isabella than he had been after seven weeks at sea, a journey on which he had not had good company. But three days before the intended wedding, he fell in to a dispute about some money. The other party insisted he should call Sir Roderick out, and Sir Roderick, despite having a pair of pistols for such occasions, decided a more prudent course to a duel would be to return to Ducoeur Castle. The speed of his departure from London meant that he dispensed with messengers so that no one at Ducoeur Castle expected his arrival.

A journey at speed is always thirsty work, and as they passed through Ashton he ordered his coachman to stop at the Green Man. It was obvious from the noise coming out of the house that some celebration was in progress. Sir Roderick hesitated a second and then decided that his thirst was such that he would step in. He arrived at the moment a toast was being drunk. Sir Roderick recognized the swaying hulk who lifted his tankard as his tenant, Caleb Jackson, a messy fellow and a tenant his overseer had several times to threaten with eviction before his rent had been forthcoming.

The farmer raised his mug above his head, and on this occasion it was a good thing that he was wearing his hat indoors, for his balance was so unsteady that quite half the ale poured down upon his head.

'Gentlemen,' he cried, though to Sir Roderick's glance there was no one except himself in the room who deserved that title. 'Gentlemen, I give you Isabella Broderick.'

'Isabella Broderick!' was the reply from a dozen men, who though they had always avoided Mr Jackson before had suddenly become his friends on the promise of free drink.

Mr Jackson spun around on his heels, surveying the room as he again got to the bottom of his vessel. He recognized Sir Roderick. Before he could put his cup down on the counter, Sir Roderick had demanded of the company: 'By what right do you drink to that young lady's name?'

Silence fell in the room.

'I asked a question, sir.'

The landlord, weighing up the situation and deciding that there was more to be gained from Sir Roderick's patronage than Mr Jackson's coin, said: 'She is to be married tomorrow, sir.'

This was the first he had heard of the matter. 'She is to be married tomorrow? To whom?'

Here the farmer beat on his chest in the manner of a true fee, fi, fo, fum giant and cried: 'I am the man.'

'You are in jest, sir.'

''Tis true,' one of the crowd was heard to utter.

'I got her of Lady Sophia Ducoeur,' said the farmer.

The look on Sir Roderick's face was terrible. Members of the company who had been contemplating another draught suddenly remembered it was the middle of the day and they had work to do and drained from the inn as quickly as they had drunk their beer. The landlord, remembering that he had promised his wife that he would put some hooks in the ceiling, went in search of his tools, and Sir Roderick and the farmer were left alone.

Inevitably, Sir Roderick triumphed in the subsequent interview. When Mr Jackson left the inn he was 'damned' if he would marry Isabella Broderick. It had all been a scheme of Lady Sophia, in which Caleb would not have played any part had he known how displeasing it would be to Sir Roderick, who had offered to be generous to him to the tune of two hundred pounds if he would leave the county forthwith.

By the time Sir Roderick rode through the gates of Ducoeur Castle, Mr Jackson had made arrangements with the butcher over the sale of his livestock, ordered a cart to carry away his few possessions and made an inside reservation on the next stagecoach, declaring that he had been undone by Isabella and her tricks and would not remain in the area to be ensnared again. The whole town knew that Isabella was an orphan jilted before any information on the matter reached the ears of the lady herself.

While Mr Jackson had been carousing at the Green Man, the bride had been in her room with the dressmaker. Isabella had had so little appetite over the past week, despite Lady Sophia's attempts to persuade her with dainties, that it was necessary that the dress should be taken in at all the points it touched Isabella's form. Isabella stood like Hermione's statue in *The Winter's Tale* while the dressmaker pinned and tucked and kept up a stream of prattle about Isabella's future happiness.

As soon as Sir Roderick entered the castle he demanded an interview with Isabella. When she came to him, he could not believe the alteration that had been made to her countenance by unhappiness. He asked her if it were true that she was to be married the next day.

'I am, sir, but it is greatly against my wishes.'

'Why, then, did you consent?' asked Sir Roderick.

'He compromised me.'

'In what way?'

'He kissed me,' cried Isabella, shuddering at the thought that there were more such kisses to come on the morrow. 'I pray, sir, if there is anything in your power to save me from going to church with him, do it. I beg you, sir, save me. Find me employment in some humble occupation. I had rather sew shirts at threepence a day than be married to such a man.'

Her eyes implored him; for all her crying, their beauty had not been dimmed. Sir Roderick felt the exquisite pleasure of releasing such a supplicant from her torment.

'I must tell you, Isabella . . . '

Here Isabella placed her hands over her ears, thinking that Sir Roderick was going to insist on supporting his sister's wishes. He drew them away. 'I must tell you, you are not to be married.'

'Not?'

'Mr Jackson is going away from the district today.'

Isabella stared at him. 'Going away?'

'You have been jilted.'

Think of all the young women who have had such a pronouncement made to them! Who have swooned and protested
that it could not be true! That they were loved by their swains
and could not be unloved! Ladies who have pined away and died
when they realized they would never see their chevaliers again.
Isabella suffered none of these afflictions. She grasped Sir
Roderick's hands, kissed them and swore she would be in his
debt for life. In truth, he was her saviour. The colour came back
into her cheeks, and she stood half a head taller.

As soon as she was dismissed by Sir Roderick, Isabella ran to
her chamber. She snatched the dress from the dressmaker, tore it
from top to bottom and then across, and, when it was in small
patchwork-sized pieces, gathered them all up and, laughing,
threw them into the fire and told the dressmaker that her
services were no longer required.

Lady Sophia heard of her brother's return with scarcely
concealed anger. She had not seen Sir Roderick since she had
watched him and Isabella leave Ducoeur Castle when fleeing
her and the smallpox. Her plan had been that, by the time he
returned from the West Indies, Isabella should have been put in a
position where she would no longer attract his attention. Lady
Sophia's jealous nature with regard to her brother had corrupted
her whole life.

She had longed for him to notice her. She had flattered and
forgiven him to the point where she felt he must return her affection for him. Her regard for him had been more than filial attachment. Now she did not even have the little beauty she had once
possessed to charm him.

The news that his first interview on his return had been with
Isabella enraged the lady. Here was proof indeed of the way Sir
Roderick regarded the girl. In but another twenty-four hours
she would have been out of his reach for ever. She was requested
to attend on him.

The encounter between brother and sister was all anger on either side. Sir Roderick instantly told her that he had dismissed Mr Jackson.

'It is all prepared,' cried Lady Sophia, not knowing that Isabella's dress was issuing from the chimney in puffs of smoke.

'I have cancelled it.'

'But the banns . . .'

'Had I been here I would have objected.'

This was a strange statement for a man who never went into a church if he could possibly avoid it.

'Her reputation . . .'

Sir Roderick seized the chance to wound his sister. 'Whatever her reputation, it is better than yours was at her age!'

The knife cut deep, and Lady Sophia could answer only in the same tenor. 'And what of your character?' she asked.

'I never pretended to have our father's reputation, but you have had all our mother's.'

There was nothing Lady Sophia detested more than to be compared in any way to her mother. That lady's reputation had been for looseness in all her morals and a liking for strong liquor. Her children had suffered because of her: three in infancy because she had not enquired properly as to the suitability of their wet-nurses, who had rolled on one, neglected another and given the third such a dose of laudanum that it had slept itself into the grave. This was a loss scarcely noticed by Arabella, Lady Ducoeur, who had always preferred her hounds to her children. The two that had survived infancy, Sir Roderick and Lady Sophia, had, despite Sir Penrose's attempts to remedy the situation, run almost wild, a neglect that shaped their characters for life. These two were the brother and sister who now fought like cat and dog.

It was Abigail, the maid who had been so curious as to Isabella's flight, who decided it was necessary that the argument between the two scions of Arabella should be carried to Isabella. She had prepared herself for this task by listening at the door with half a dozen other servants. Now she went in search of

Isabella to tell her that Lady Sophia was insisting that she must be married to Mr Jackson and Sir Roderick was insisting that no nuptials would take place.

Isabella, whose usual caution had deserted her on hearing that she had been jilted, could not resist making a confidante of Abigail and telling her the whole story. The maid (who, truth to tell, would have been glad to be married to anybody and so put into the way of running her own household and being at the call of one husband instead of assorted butlers, cooks and footmen) could not believe that Isabella would not have Mr Jackson sought after and sued for breach of contract.

'All I care,' said Isabella, 'is that he is gone. And as far away as possible, for I hope never to meet him on any walk or ride.'

'I am sure you have your own reasons for wishing so,' the dauntless maid replied.

'I do!' cried Isabella. 'It is my greatest desire to be married for love and to a man I respect, and whom I can trust to protect my interests.'

Now Abigail had it all. This was as frank a declaration of love for Sir Roderick by Isabella that she could expect. She congratulated herself mightily for being the first to hear it and began to contemplate what pernicious advantage she might acquire from such a frank confession.

The interview between Sir Roderick and his sister ended when he insisted that he would have Mr Jackson blackguarded in every parish in the county for first presuming on and then jilting Isabella. Lady Sophia, who had been a great jilt when she had her youth and looks (and she did not like to be compared to her mother) could find nothing further to say on the matter, and so brother and sister parted. Sir Roderick determined that he should never again be in company with Lady Sophia, and the lady determined that he should never again be in company with Isabella without her presence.

Sir Roderick insisted that messages should be sent immediately to disappoint all the bridesmaids. This was a message that contained as much mirth as grief. They would not have to stand up with Mr Jackson, but, equally, without a bride there could be no bride gifts. Tabby Roberts triumphed with her silver bangle. It was half tin, but why should she not enjoy it?

The parents of the girls who had been chosen to go to church on the morrow, and whose hopes were now so cruelly dashed, rejoiced that they had been noticed and that the providing of new clothes for their daughters for the Whit Monday celebrations had all been at Lady Sophia's expense.

The night of her jilting was the first time that Isabella sat down at table with both Sir Roderick and Lady Sophia. All her appetite had returned, and she took food from each dish as it was handed around. The goose, the mutton, the pie, the fish, she enjoyed with all relish. She could taste the onion which had stuffed the goose, the caper sauce for the mutton; she could make out that the ingredients of the pie were good; and though she had never liked eel, the way in which it was served, with a butter sauce and the bones taken out, so inflamed her appetite that she took some more when the dish was again handed round.

All the conversation was between Isabella and Sir Roderick, the shyness she had always had of him being completely evaporated by his bringing her the news that she was not to marry Mr Jackson. Lady Sophia glowered and, despite Isabella's attempts to draw her into conversation, would say no more than yea or nay.

The next day, which should have been her wedding-day, Isabella saw nothing of Sir Roderick. He was completely engaged in putting his affairs in order and avoiding his sister. And the day seemed very long until he joined them that night at dinner. The meal was a repetition of the previous night, and again Lady Sophia sat in watchful silence. In an attempt to amuse her, Isabella, who had divulged nothing about what happened the night she and Sir Roderick spent in the inn, decided to turn to the subject of apparitions. She asked Sir Roderick if he had witnessed any of the infamous witches that were supposed to inhabit certain parts of the West Indies.

'I did not,' he replied, 'though they are believed in universally.'

'Is it true, sir, that they are called up with the blood of a white chicken?'

'So I have heard.'

'How I should like to see one!' cried Isabella, clapping her hands together at the thought.

'I have a morbid terror of such things,' replied Sir Roderick.

Though she said nothing, her brother's admission surprised Lady Sophia, who had never known him to be frightened of anything in his life.

Isabella, who as a child had been taught to overcome her fear of horses by being put back on every time she tumbled off, now suggested to Sir Roderick that the best way to conquer his aversion was to submit himself to it.

'It is a good notion, Isabella, but one which for the instance I would prefer to decline.'

From this the conversation moved to more general subjects and was soon forgotten.

As Sir Roderick sorted his affairs, he had greater liberty to spend in Isabella's company. Lady Sophia kept up a constant watch so that they should not be left alone together. But the more Sir Roderick was deprived of intimate conversation with Isabella, the more he craved it. It was noticed that he and his sister would vie to turn over the music when Isabella was at the spinet and that he had taken to leaving the door to his apartment open so he could observe whoever was passing.

One night, as Abigail was putting Isabella to bed, she happened to mention to her that the players were in the neighbourhood and expected at Ashton the next night. Isabella had never been to the play and expressed a wish to go, a wish that became stronger when she found that Mrs Jordan was in the company. Lady Sophia, when she heard the news the following morning, declared that she would go with them. Abigail, always desirous of being of service to Isabella, mentioned all this to Sir Roderick and was immediately dispatched to command a box at the theatre.

It being the night of a full moon, there was no difficulty in travelling the six miles to Ashton. At the theatre a lively crowd had assembled. The throng was so great that Isabella feared she might be separated from Sir Roderick and Lady Sophia. But Sir Roderick took hold of her arm and they were soon seated in their places.

Isabella, who had not been seen in public since her jilting, was the subject of universal interest. As she sat down all heads turned towards her and wondered that such a creature could have been betrayed by a man like Mr Jackson. Isabella, completely taken up with the novelty of being in a theatre, was unaware of the excitement caused by her arrival. She admired the gilded masks of comedy and tragedy, the velvet curtain that concealed the stage. In short, she longed for the play to begin.

Sir Roderick watched as Isabella's lively glance mastered every detail. She was silhouetted against the light, and he could see the excited pulse that beat in her throat.

The play began. Isabella was quite transported. She fled from the cruel duke who had usurped his brother's place into the enchanted forest of Arden. She took on the mantle of Ganymede and let Orlando woo her in that guise. She suffered at all the revelations and thought the epilogue the most delightful speech she had ever heard.

Sir Roderick saw not more than twenty minutes of the performance. His Rosalind was Isabella Broderick. His sister was completely aware of this infatuation and decided she would acquaint Isabella with his character.

Accordingly, after they had come home from the play and Sir Roderick had bidden them both good night, kissing Lady Sophia's hand so he, in turn, could kiss Isabella's, she called for a glass of cordial which she herself carried up to Isabella's room.

Isabella, who was determined not to lose a single detail of the evening, had decided she would, as from that night, take up the keeping of a journal. Consequently, she had dismissed Abigail, saying she would undress herself, and now sat at her writing-table noting down every particular of the evening.

It was thus Lady Sophia surprised her, with pen in her hand, scribbling away for all she was worth. Lady Sophia had in her youth been one of the most ardent of chroniclers. It was a habit she had got into at the hands of her governess, who had promised her that in her old age she would find it a great comfort to remember how many hearts she had broken. She assumed now that Isabella was writing her heart out about Sir Roderick. To establish so, she came close to the table, but, before her weak eyes could make out any of the words, Isabella sprang up and closed the notebook she had chosen to receive her most intimate thoughts.

She took the cordial from Lady Sophia and, thinking the lady must have something particularly serious to say to her, the hour being after one o'clock in the morning, sat down to listen. Lady Sophia poured forth a catalogue of complaints on her brother. Isabella heard her in silence, wondering why Lady Sophia, who had always championed Sir Roderick over all other men, had suddenly taken so violently against him.

'What has he done to you,' she cried, 'that you should suddenly hate him so much?'

Lady Sophia looked at Isabella and saw in her everything that had so enchanted her brother. She turned away from her, catching sight of her own face in the mirror, a face that she constantly had to remind herself was her own, so ghastly it appeared every time she saw it. Now she said bitterly: 'He has ruined others, and he means to ruin you.'

'Why should he have any intentions of that sort?' was the innocent's reply.

'I know him!' cried his sister.

'Madam, if he meant to ruin me, did he not have every opportunity the day we went away together during your illness?'

'You have always declined to tell me what happened.'

'Because I so deeply regret that I left you when I might have been of some assistance.'

Lady Sophia laughed spitefully, as if to doubt the truth of what Isabella said.

'Madam, it is true!'

'Then why did you go?'

'He persuaded me out of my objections.'

Lady Sophia laughed again.

'Madam, he asked me to say nothing of this!' said Isabella.

'Now we are to have it!' cried Lady Sophia.

'While we were at the inn, your brother was taken with a strange fit which required him to be put into his bed.'

Lady Sophia gave a little scream.

'Don't alarm yourself, madam, I did everything I could for him, and when we parted the next day he seemed to me entirely recovered.'

'Why did you part?'

'He met with a gentleman who was coming to him on business.'

'What business?'

'I do not know. Sir Roderick did not do me the honour of making an introduction.'

'He did not want the gentleman to know who you were!'

'No, madam, I think they were too much occupied with the business in hand.'

'What *was* that business?' Lady Sophia asked Isabella.

'I do not know, except that it required him to leave at once for the West Indies. And I heard nothing more from him until his return.'

'That unfortunate day!' cried Lady Sophia.

Isabella, thinking that this alluded to the breaking of her engagement, could say only: 'Madam, I do not consider myself unfortunate in being jilted. It was, as you know, a marriage I never desired. My only intention of going through with it was out of my duty to you.'

'Will you always do your duty to me?'

'I will.'

'Never marry my brother!'

It had never occurred to Isabella that she should have any such ambition.

'Madam, I feel towards Sir Roderick as I would to an uncle

or a cousin and could never feel the affection of a wife towards him.'

With many assurances on Isabella's part that she admired Sir Roderick but would never love him, the interview ended. Lady Sophia went to her room and woke Jane to undress her. Isabella took up her pen again and noted down what had passed between her and Lady Sophia, in as much detail as is recorded above.

For the next few days the diary became an obsession with Isabella. She took it up after breakfast to record in the minutest detail that Lady Sophia had complained that the butter was not fresh and that Sir Roderick had drunk five and a half cups of coffee. She carried it into the garden and noted down all the blossoms that were out. In the hen-house she recorded the exact number of eggs laid every day. In short, wherever Isabella went, the book accompanied her, a fact that did not go unnoticed by Sir Roderick. He tried to joke Isabella into letting him see it by pretending that she scribbled so much she must be writing a novel, but she would not show it to him.

Sir Roderick longed to know what was in Isabella's book. He was, of course, as anyone in love, anxious to see how often his own name was mentioned and if the lady thought of him as often as he thought of her. He was beginning to dream away whole mornings and nights in the thought of Isabella and felt that her journal must be the cure.

Sir Roderick, as has been indicated, was a man who liked to get what he wanted. He gave Abigail the charge of bringing the notebook to him. The maid watched and waited, but no opportunity of obtaining the book ever presented itself, Isabella even sleeping with it under her pillow. Then, one Sunday, there being some confusion about the time she and Lady Sophia left for church, Isabella was so hurried that she forgot to turn the key in the drawer where the diary was deposited, on this occasion being obliged to carry her prayer book with her rather than her diary. As soon as Isabella had left the house Abigail was upon it, and within five minutes Sir Roderick was engrossed in the conversation Isabella and Lady Sophia had had the night they returned from the theatre. He read that Isabella would not marry him; but he knew she must, and by whatever means he could bring about their marriage. Turning through the other pages, he began to feel that Isabella was not quite as indifferent to him as she had told Lady Sophia. For what young woman would record the exact colour of a gentleman's cravat without being in love?

By the time Isabella returned from church, the precious book was back in its place with no indication that it had ever been removed. And Isabella recorded her thoughts on the morning's sermon quite oblivious of the fact that her notebook had been read by Sir Roderick.

That evening at supper Sir Roderick suddenly announced that he was expecting a friend to arrive at the castle on the morrow, a young man by the name of Edgecliffe. Isabella, who had never met any intimate friend of Sir Roderick's, could not wait to make his acquaintance.

Mr Edgecliffe arrived at the due time. He was some years younger than Sir Roderick, being just over thirty while Sir Roderick was just over forty. Isabella asked him if he had been in the neighbourhood before.

'Never,' replied the gentleman, 'though I live but two hours off.' He begged Isabella to tell him what charms the neighbourhood had to offer, and she gave him as comprehensive a list as she could, all of which Edgecliffe nodded at and said he would like to see. Then he asked: 'Miss Broderick, can you tell me how far it is to Carrick-on-Soar?'

'I could not tell you, sir, having never been there myself.'

Mr Edgecliffe asked Sir Roderick if he could give him any better information and was told that the little place lay some ten miles away.

'And are the roads good?' asked Mr Edgecliffe.

Sir Roderick assured him that they were.

'I have a great desire to visit the church there.'

'Is it very fine?' asked Isabella, thinking how pleasant a June adventure would be with the young man and that a journey of ten miles, there and back, might easily be accomplished between breakfast and sunset.

'It is something more than fine. It is remarkable.'

'In what way?'

'It is declared to be the most haunted place for a hundred miles. What say you, Ducoeur, that we ride over and experience the phenomenon ourselves?'

'If you wish to look for ghosts, Edgecliffe, you must go alone. Or in the company of Isabella,' said Sir Roderick.

The young man turned to her, his face all eagerness. 'What say you to that proposal, Miss Broderick?'

Isabella was certain she would like it very much, but that she did not think it was possible that they should go alone.

'Mr Edgecliffe is my friend, Isabella. Do you not trust him?'

'Sir, I feel I should be quite safe and am sure there would be no impropriety from Mr Edgecliffe, but I do not like to think how such an adventure might appear to other people. I think it better, therefore, that the offer should be rejected.'

'Have you no other friends who could accompany us?' asked Mr Edgecliffe, who was obviously most eager to undertake the adventure.

Isabella replied that she did not. Mr Edgecliffe turned back to Sir Roderick. 'Sir, I beg you,' he said, 'overcome your scruples enough to come with us. You need not enter the churchyard if you are afraid of what we might find there.'

Sir Roderick looked at his friend and then at Isabella and said: 'Very well. I would not disappoint you or the young lady.' He raised his glass to Isabella, a gesture that was at once copied by Mr Edgecliffe.

Hah, thought Lady Sophia, you are afraid that Mr Edgecliffe will carry her off! And desirous of this eventuality she decided she would do everything possible in her power to throw Isabella and Mr Edgecliffe together as often as possible during the young man's stay.

Mr William Edgecliffe had been introduced to Sir Roderick at a cock-fight, where Sir Roderick had taken a great liking to the bird owned by Mr Edgecliffe. When the rooster had been successful in fighting off all opposition, Sir Roderick offered to buy him from his master. Mr Edgecliffe had demurred. He had been offered a large sum if he would put the bird into the ring the following week. Sir Roderick immediately suggested that they should go shares on the bird, and the deal was struck. Unfortunately, three days before the champion, of which Sir Roderick now owned half, could show his mettle, a fox got into his coop and devoured him. This was of little advantage to the fox, as he was hunted down the following day, but it left Mr Edgecliffe greatly in Sir Roderick's debt.

At first the young man feared that the elder one would turn the full face of the law on him for negligence, but Sir Roderick had other plans. He enlisted Mr Edgecliffe as an ally whenever he should need one. It was in this capacity that he had been instructed to present himself at Ducoeur Castle.

The expedition was arranged to take place on the Thursday, that being the darkest night of the week. As the day approached, Isabella was in a frenzy of excitement. She was to travel in Sir Roderick's curricle with Mr Edgecliffe, while Sir Roderick rode in front to show them the way, and Isabella passed many happy hours anticipating the tête-à-tête she should have on the way to Carrick-on-Soar.

So eager was she to be on her way that she was in the hall a full half-hour before the party was to leave. She had done herself up very prettily, and Lady Sophia had been kind enough to give her some attar of roses to sprinkle on her neck. The party set out full of mirth, and their destination was soon in sight.

It was a small hamlet, now almost deserted, the great house which had supported it having been burnt down some years ago. They ate their picnic on a small hill overlooking the church and its burial ground. Sir Roderick was most insistent that Isabella ate well, urging her that it was important to keep up her strength.

When they had done their meal, she begged the gentlemen to walk down to the graveyard with her so she might read the names on the tombs and therefore know what apparitions to expect. Sir Roderick insisted that Mr Edgecliffe stay and smoke a cigar with him, so Isabella went down alone.

The place was not well tended, the sexton being in his eightieth year and worried that some accident might befall him when there was no one nearby to give him assistance. The grass grew long, with a profusion of wild flowers. In some places it was so high that it was impossible to see the gravestone. Isabella felt the sad neglect of the place and thought it very proper that it should be haunted. Then, suddenly, going to the back of the church, she came upon a plot that had obviously been tended very recently. The grass had been cut back and the stone but recently erected. She hurried forwards to read the words on the headstone. The inscription was simple:

Henry Amory, erected by his grieving widow

The date of his death was given as the previous year.

Was this, then, the grave of Louisa's husband? Isabella could only think so, and if that were the case the lady must live very close, for there were fresh flowers laid at the foot of the head-stone. Isabella shuddered. She dreaded to think of the corruption of the body that lay beneath her feet. What if Henry Amory was the spectre she saw, and what if he asked her to take a message to her friend Louisa? Isabella turned and ran. At the gate she met Mr Edgecliffe and Sir Roderick.

'Miss Broderick,' cried Mr Edgecliffe, 'you must congratulate me. While we have been smoking I have convinced Sir Roderick not to sit outside this piece of consecrated ground but to join us at our watch.'

'And I should not like to put you to the trouble of appearing braver than I!' added Sir Roderick, bowing low to Isabella.

The ordeal must be gone through, then, and Isabella must watch and wait for come what may.

The shadows began to lengthen and the darkness began to fall. Mr Edgecliffe, who had provided the company with two lanterns, now took out his flint and lit them, hanging one from the branch of an old yew tree near the gate and placing the other by the door of the church. Bats began to fly from the roof of the church.

Isabella waited. She began to grow quite cold and Sir Roderick to become quite impatient. Several times he took out his watch as if by looking at it he could call up an appearance. Mr Edgecliffe urged him not to agitate himself, saying all was in hand and that Sir Roderick would not be disappointed. Eleven o'clock struck and suddenly there came the sound of an approach.

Isabella trembled. The apparition was there, a ghostly white and coming towards them as if it knew its way. She shuddered and could not look. She felt its presence only as it went past her and entered the church.

'Quick!' cried Sir Roderick. 'We have not a moment to lose!'

He grasped Isabella by the hand and, not loosening his grip for one second, almost dragged her after him into the church, taking the lantern from the door as he did so. Mr Edgecliffe followed. They entered the shrine. The ghostly figure stood before the altar. Sir Roderick addressed it: 'You are quite ready?'

The spectre nodded.

'The ring, Edgecliffe,' demanded Sir Roderick. As the young man fumbled in his pocket to bring out a thin gold band, it suddenly came to Isabella that the spectre was a priest and that he was to join her to Mr Edgecliffe.

'I am to marry Mr Edgecliffe?' she gasped.

'You are to marry, Isabella, the man who loves and adores you. Everything is ready. You may forget the promise you made to my sister,' said Sir Roderick. 'In five minutes we will be man and wife!'

'No!' she cried.

'I pray, hurry, sir,' called the vicar, beckoning that Isabella and Sir Roderick should approach him.

'I will marry for love, sir, and I will marry legally. I have been duped once by your sister, and now I find I have been duped by you. I, an orphan, who believed that you were my protector, now find you are my enemy.'

'Enough!' cried Sir Roderick, who wanted the whole business over and done with so he might get on with the real excitement of marriage. Isabella stood firm.

'Take her other side, Edgecliffe!' said Sir Roderick, pulling Isabella so hard that her arm almost came out at the shoulder. Between them, Mr Edgecliffe and Sir Roderick drew her in the direction of the priest.

Isabella saw how she had been tricked and betrayed. She had been led here on a false pretence. Sir Roderick had used Mr Edgecliffe to help advance his plans and now meant to wed her in secret in front of a priest who might, she saw, be some other friend of Sir Roderick in fancy dress.

She struggled to break free from her captors. Sir Roderick tightened his hold on her arm. She began to scream. Alarmed that the noise might discover them, he put his hand over her mouth. Isabella bit it and tasted Sir Roderick's blood. In his pain he let go of her and, Mr Edgecliffe's grasp not being so firm, she wrenched herself free.

Mr Edgecliffe, who had obviously not learnt from the death of his cockerel, had omitted to close the door to the church. Isabella fled.

Within a second she was through the porch and running along the path. She went out of the gate, gathering up her skirts to run faster. The blood beat in her ears and she was quite unaware that a coach was proceeding down the lane at a tremendous rate.

The driver tried to pull up the horses, but they were going too fast to be checked. The first horse hit her a glancing blow on the side which caused her to tumble backwards and out of the way of the wheels.

The coach stopped and a young man jumped out and ran towards her. He found her lying senseless with blood at the corner of her mouth.

SEVEN

In which, our heroine exchanges the name Broderick for Napier

When Sir Roderick and Mr Edgecliffe ran from the church in pursuit of Isabella, presuming that she would have run downhill and not up, the first thing they noticed was a coach stopped in the middle of the roadway. It was obviously in difficulty from the commotion by which it was surrounded. Sir Roderick cautioned his companion to move more deliberately, and together they approached the scene of the accident.

A flare had been lit, and by its light they could see that the body lying in the road was that of Isabella. Beside her knelt a young man, most proper in every particular. He patted Isabella's hands in an attempt to revive her and, when this would not do, plucked the feathers from his own hat and set fire to them under her nose. Still she did not revive. Sir Roderick approached the scene.

The cleric, meanwhile, was very grateful for this diversion, for it allowed him to slip away unnoticed, which was always his chief wish on such occasions as clandestine marriages. Accordingly, he untied his donkey which he had tethered to a tree, and kicked the poor animal until it consented to carry him uphill and away from Carrick-on-Soar.

The gallant gentleman who attempted to bring some sort of animation to Isabella looked up in surprise at Sir Roderick's approach. He did not know whence he had come but called to him eagerly: 'Sir, I beg you will assist me. There has been a terrible accident. I had urged my driver to make as much speed as we could, not expecting to find anyone, except those of ill repute, on the road at this time of night.'

Sir Roderick bristled, believing that the young gentleman's remark was meant as an insult to him. He at once decided that, however noble the young man, he was his sworn enemy.

At this point, Mr Edgecliffe, always happy to defend Sir Roderick, stepped forward, intending to protest that his friend was one of the best men in the county, and, indeed – if Sir Roderick had not given him a sharp dig in the ribs – the country.

'But,' said the object of Sir Roderick's hatred, 'there was this young lady, to whom I, in my hurry, have done a great injury. I pray you, assist me to get her into my coach so that I may bring her to a place where I may get her some aid.'

Sir Roderick looked down at Isabella, whose face was very alabaster in the torchlight. Then he turned his glance on the young man who knelt at her side and made a small bow. 'Sir,' he said, 'it is obvious from your description of your progress that you are engaged in a matter of some urgency. Let me assist the lady while you continue on your way.'

'I will not hear of it!' cried the young man, who was determined to play the good Samaritan for the sake of Isabella's beauty. 'The fault is mine, and I must remedy it. I see from her countenance that her birth must be good and that some terrible mistake has led her to be on this road at this hour of the night. She requires help and' – casting another anxious glance on Isabella – 'if she lives I shall give it to her.' The young gentleman stood up, as the coachman covered Isabella with a travelling-blanket, and for the first time was able to regard Sir Roderick and his companion properly.

From their clothes and their bearing he at once saw that their station in life must be very similar to the young lady's. The sight of two fine gentlemen so late at night, and the proximity of a deserted church, together with a certain train of thought he had been perusing on his journey, at once suggested to him that he had happened on the plot of a clandestine marriage.

'Sir,' he said to Sir Roderick, 'may I presume from your

desire to help the young lady that you and your companion are acquainted with her?'

A glance from Sir Roderick informed Mr Edgecliffe that he should say nothing, a glance that did not go unperceived by Isabella's intended rescuer.

'No, sir,' said Sir Roderick, 'I have never before seen her in my life. But for such a creature to be alone - why, it is no more than my Christian duty to assist her, and' – glancing at the young gentleman – 'to assist you by allowing you to continue on your journey.'

At this moment Isabella gave a little sigh. This was almost too much for the man who in his hurry had caused her injury, and he cried: 'She will die, and I will have killed the most beautiful creature in the world!'

Sir Roderick seized his opportunity. 'Sir, you are too distressed to deal with this calamity. I beg you let me relieve the lady!' And he bent down, indicating to Mr Edgecliffe that between them they should pick Isabella up.

The young gentleman stopped him, laying his hand on Sir Roderick's arm. 'But where will you take her, and by what means?'

'My companion shall ride for a carriage,' said Sir Roderick, gesturing to Mr Edgecliffe that he should at once set out on such a course.

'Do not trouble yourself, sir,' said the young man. 'I have a carriage here, and she shall be put into it without further delay.'

'I cannot allow it, sir,' cried Sir Roderick.

'Then tell me at once: are you certain that you have never seen her before?'

'Never, never, never!' shouted Mr Edgecliffe, wishing to leave the gentleman in no doubt of Sir Roderick's story.

So loud was his protestation that nothing was heard of the approach of a horse until the beast and rider were upon them, and the fellow announced his arrival by brandishing a pistol and shouting out: 'Whoever draws his weapon against me, I shall shoot first!'

They had been fallen upon by one of those devils of the night, who ride so masked and caped that their identity may never be known. At the first glance at the fellow, Sir Roderick and Mr Edgecliffe turned and fled, Sir Roderick shouting at his friend to throw down any money he had in his pockets. But the brigand, who had at once ascertained that the young man wore finer lace and better buckles and was therefore the greater prize, did not pursue them.

'Sir,' he cried in a gruff voice, 'you would be wise to follow the example of your friends and give every one of your valuables into my possession.'

'Here!' cried the young gentleman, thinking the only thing that had any value to him at that moment was the life of Isabella. He threw his purse at the hooves of the brigand's horse. 'Take it. Only do not touch the lady!'

'The lady?' came the husky response. The gentleman stepped back and revealed Isabella, her jewel shining on her neck. The highwayman drew his horse closer and looked down at her. He made a low bow from his saddle, saying: 'I would not hurt her, if there was anything in my power to prevent it.' Then, turning, he rode off and was swallowed up in the night, leaving the gentleman's purse where it lay.

Within a minute of the highwayman's departure, the young gentleman had had Isabella put into the coach, jumped in beside her and, ordering the coachman to make as much speed as he could without doing any injury to the young lady or any person on the road, drove away from Carrick-on-Soar.

Sir Roderick and Mr Edgecliffe made their own rapid retreat to Ducoeur Castle, stopping only to discuss what they should say to Lady Sophia to explain the disappearance of Isabella. It was decided that they should use the highwayman as their excuse, saying that he had stolen Isabella away at gunpoint and that they had been powerless to prevent her abduction. The ferocity and desperation of their attacker was given still greater credence by Sir Roderick instructing Mr Edgecliffe to go to the trouble of removing all the silver buttons from his waistcoat, a sacrifice Mr

Edgecliffe made with the greatest possible alacrity.

Meanwhile Isabella travelled, quite senseless, through the night without any idea of where she was being taken or by whom. At every place they stopped to change horses, the gentleman, who could not resolve to himself whether he was her destroyer or her rescuer, enquired if anyone recognized her description. But between Carrick-on-Soar and the entrance to his own park, he found no one who could resolve the mystery.

It was just after dawn that they drove in at the gates of a large estate, but Isabella did not see the grounds which had been newly created by Mr Repton, nor the great house which had been built in the reign of Queen Elizabeth and which could have accommodated several Ducoeur Castles.

The owner of the house, on alighting from the carriage, instantly called for a room to be made ready with all possible speed. The maids, not yet up, were woken from their sleep, then ran hither and thither furnishing the best lodging that was available. They made little noise, but the constant movement in the house caused the young lady of the house to waken. Putting on her wrap, she went to enquire about the commotion. She was met by her brother, who carried Isabella in his arms.

'See what I have done,' he said in an anxious tone. 'I have injured a creature who, I am sure, has never hurt anyone.'

'Montagu,' cried his sister, 'how could it be possible for you to wound any creature in the world?'

'My coachman was, at my insistence, driving too fast.'

'But what reason had you to be in such a hurry?'

'I wanted only to be of assistance to you,' said Lord Angelsea, looking at his sister's drawn countenance and dull eyes.

'That matter is over,' said his sister, turning aside. 'I bitterly regret the harm it has done to me and to my friends, and now to a stranger. But she will have all my care. Now bring her at once to the chamber that has been prepared for her.'

The young man did so, laid Isabella on the coverlet and withdrew while his sister and the housekeeper undressed Isabella and put her into bed. When this was done, the young lady went at once to her brother, who waited in an adjoining room.

'Will she recover?' were his first words to his sister.

'It is believed so.'

'Thank God!' he replied.

'I wished now to hear that you are well and that your heart is not broken.'

'My complexion is not good,' said his sister, 'nor my spirits high, but as for my heart . . . ' She paused and her brother dreaded to think that she was planning some appeal about the behaviour of a young man who had drawn her into a very unsuitable attachment. An alliance that had ended not at the altar but with the complete breakdown of Lady Caroline's health when she had discovered that her lover was descended from an ancestry which had in it more than its fair share of lunatics, and that the madness that was inclined to skip a generation had been present in his grandfather.

'As for my heart, I was giddy more than in love and, being so, thought his madness giddiness. But,' she added, 'I will not forget him, even if you order me, for it is he that deserves your pity more than I ever did, for, alas, there is nothing we can do for him, unlike the beautiful creature that you have brought here this morning.'

All day Isabella hovered between life and death. The medical men who came offered little hope, some saying she would drift from her coma into death, others predicting she would get her life back but not her senses. Whenever they were not required elsewhere, Lady Caroline and her brother sat at her bedside, anxious for the smallest gesture that would indicate her return to consciousness.

'If only we knew her name!' was the young man's constant lament. 'We could find out her relations, and they might be able to penetrate her consciousness.'

'Perhaps,' said Lady Caroline, reaching towards Isabella's neck, 'this jewel might give us some indication as to who she is.'

But before she could turn it over, Isabella, sensing the movement, put up her hand and grasped her locket as if to save it from all interference.

'She is sensible!' cried the young man, starting to his feet.

Isabella opened her eyes and saw before her such an angel that she thought she was in heaven and that the features of the young man were the most perfect example of masculine beauty.

There was no one in the world who did not think Montagu, Lord Angelsea, handsome: even his enemies, of whom there were few, and none so ill-disposed towards him as Sir Roderick, granted him that privilege. He was tall, so much so that when he visited the humble dwellings of the cottagers on his estate he needed to duck so that he did not dash out his brains on their doorways. His features were even, his jaw was strong, and he cursed himself for having a smile on his lips even when he wanted to be most stern.

'What is your name?' he asked, whispering so she should not be frightened.

For a moment Isabella could not speak. She was sure that in heaven her name would be known, and now she cast her eyes about her to discover in what sort of place she lay.

Seeing her agitation but not understanding it, Lord Angelsea endeavoured to put her mind at rest by saying: 'Whatever your secret, it shall be safe with my sister and myself. Only I beg you, tell us your name.'

'Isabella!' she whispered and fell back upon the pillows.

Instantly, servants were sent out to make discreet enquiries in the district of Carrick-on-Soar about whether a young lady of that name was missing. But no information of any sort was forthcoming, except the fact that one old woman had thought she had seen a light at the church. It was this beldam's habit to see so many lights and hear so many voices that her few neighbours were adamant that she should not be believed. Thus, one piece of intelligence that might have helped establish Isabella's identity was lost.

It was hoped, when Isabella recovered her health, that she might recall something of the events of the night on which she had met with her unhappy accident, but it was soon clear that the blow to her head, though it had not deprived her of her memory of certain facts and figures, had deserted her on all information pertaining to her identity except that her name was Isabella and she was an orphan. No matter how often Lord Angelsea described what had happened at Carrick-on-Soar, not a single detail of the event remained in her mind. In vain did he make the most accurate drawings of Sir Roderick and Mr Edgecliffe; to Isabella they remained strangers.

'Perhaps it is for the best,' said Lady Caroline. 'If she were involved in some elopement, and that by a trick, is it not better that she should remember nothing?'

Her brother did not agree with her. 'It is my fear,' he said, 'that if whichever of the gentlemen duped her while she had her wits about her, he may do the same again and much more easily in her present state.'

'But how should he find her, unless, when she is recovered, you mean that she should go away from Angelsea Court?' replied Lady Caroline, who was certain that her brother Montagu had no intention that Isabella should leave them.

Some four weeks after her arrival at Angelsea Court, Isabella was well enough to take a short turn around the gardens at the front of the house, leaning on Lady Caroline's arm. The pair strolled along the formal walk, and Lady Caroline begged Isabella to take some notice of a very fine pelargonium of an unusual shade. For a moment Isabella considered the plant and, turning to Lady Caroline, said to her: 'I think it may have been that I was about to be married.'

Lady Caroline stopped her perambulation and turned her eyes on Isabella. 'To be married?' she said.

Isabella nodded.

'Can you name the gentleman?'

Isabella could not.

'Did some obstacle occur?' enquired Lady Caroline.

'I was jilted.'

'My poor Isabella!'

'I think perhaps I had some objection to the matter,' said

Isabella, though at a loss to recall what that objection had been and remembering not the slightest detail of Mr Jackson or his courtship.

No sooner had Isabella finished her exercise and gone to take some rest than Lady Caroline went straight to her brother and told him the information she had gleaned. Between them, they soon had it all. Isabella had been on the point of getting married when suddenly the gentleman had changed his mind or had some ghastly revelation made about him. Either way, the poor bride had been completely shunned and so had fled and run into the path of the carriage.

At Ducoeur Castle, Lady Sophia greeted Sir Roderick's news of Isabella's abduction with scarcely concealed delight. It seemed to her that this incident with the highwayman must for ever put Isabella out of her brother's reach. She trusted that never again would Isabella Broderick's name be mentioned between her and her brother. Mr Edgecliffe, sworn to secrecy about what had happened in Carrick-on-Soar, was dismissed to await another chance of rendering service to Sir Roderick.

As the days shortened, Isabella recovered her strength and was made one of the family at Angelsea Court. No entertainment was held without her, and she was constantly consulted by both brother and sister about plans for a new livery or the redecoration of a boudoir. Isabella had never lived in such felicity. Lady Caroline and Lord Angelsea were a brother and sister who understood each other perfectly, except in the matter of Lady Caroline's unfortunate affair of the heart. As the autumn approached, it began to appear to Isabella that it would soon be necessary for her to go away. 'But my dear Isabella, where can you go?' cried Lady Caroline when the idea was first mentioned to her.

'Anywhere I can earn a living.'

And, indeed, she had spent much time considering how such a thing might be achieved. She had some aptitude with her needle which might earn remuneration from some dressmaker. Her education was good, and there might be some family in need of a governess. She read aloud very pleasantly, which might fit some person who had lost the ability of sight. In short, she felt certain that with the right introduction she might, in a small way, find some means of supporting herself.

Lady Caroline, seeing that Isabella was in earnest, sought to humour her, constantly promising that she would enquire after certain situations and then delaying so much that the vacancy was filled and another one must be looked for. By this means, Isabella, who had found no employment in October, had found nothing by December, at which time Lady Caroline and her brother begged her to stay with them so that she might assist with the children of their elder sister, who was expected for the Christmas festivities and who, journeying from Ireland, planned to stay above three weeks.

Isabella consented. Here at last was a way of repaying some of the kindness she had received. So when Penelope, Countess of Mullingar, arrived at Angelsea Court with her six children, Isabella was on the steps to greet the party.

The countess had grown up with the same happy disposition as her younger brother and sister. Then she had married – against the advice of her family and friends (who had been too kind-hearted towards her to absolutely forbid the match) – the Earl of Mullingar. At first they had been happy, and everyone thought that Penelope had known her own heart. But then, after the birth of six children, four boys and two girls, the earl had become bored with domestic pleasures and decided he could no longer be happy on his Irish estate. He announced to his lady that he planned to spend some time in London.

Lady Penelope, always anxious to be with him, instantly began to make plans about the shutting up of the house, the journey and what sort of establishment they should have in London. She was greatly pleased by the prospect of being little more than three days' drive from her brother and sister. Then the earl announced that he planned to go alone but would send for her and the children.

Penelope, who had always obeyed her husband in all things, waited for his summons. But none came. She then heard a rumour that he had struck up a friendship with a certain Miss Tanner. At first Penelope dismissed this as gossip, but as her husband's letters home grew less frequent she began to consider it more. She had felt the necessity of consulting her brother on the matter. He had ridden to London and found that not only was the rumour true but that Miss Tanner was in 'an interesting condition' and that she quite openly boasted about the expected child being the son of an earl.'

Anxious not to break this news to his sister by letter, Lord Angelsea had ridden straight from London to Pembroke and taken the first boat from there to Dublin, from whence he travelled on to Mullingar. Lady Penelope knew from the fact of her brother's arrival that all her worst fears had been realized. Her husband, with whom she had lived in great amity for eight years, no longer wanted to have anything to do with her.

With stone in her heart, she had refused to listen while her brother put to her the necessity of a proper legal separation, insisting that she would not cut herself off from her husband in such a manner. So Lady Penelope found herself in the situation of one who was less a wife and more a widow and with nothing signed by a lawyer to establish her real status in regard to the earl, her husband.

The estrangement between her and the earl and the fact that she was the injured party had hardened her heart, and she had spent many hours reflecting that, though he had elevated her rank, her husband had trampled the rest of her life into the dust. She became more and more aware of her status and all the deference that was attached to it. In a word, though brought up to respect the interests of others, she had become a snob, and, in her anger, she had inflicted the same pretensions on her children.

She had been fully informed of Isabella's arrival at Angelsea Court and had supposed that, as soon as she was recovered, she would be returned to her friends. Lady Penelope was therefore surprised to find her still in residence and waiting to receive her children.

Isabella was introduced as Miss Napier, this being the name she had chosen in place of the one she had forgotten. When she made her curtsy to Lady Penelope, the lady immediately expressed her surprise at Isabella remaining at Angelsea Court for so long.

'It is at my request, Penelope,' said Lord Angelsea 'and at Caroline's. All we entreated was that Isabella, I mean Miss Napier, should remain with us until after the festivities, and she agreed on one condition: that you would allow her to help with the care of the children and their education while she is here.'

The children, on hearing this and used to being on holiday when at Angelsea Court, at once took a dislike to Isabella – something their mother had done likewise when she heard her brother call her Isabella instead of Miss Napier.

Before she had even entered the house, Lady Penelope started to lament that she had not brought her children's instructors from Ireland: the boys had been educated by a very pious and deferential clergyman, who had – and Lady Penelope always assessed it as rather more than it was – some connection to the Archbishop of York. (He was, in fact, a second cousin on his mother's side, and apart from the time of his ordination had never been in any correspondence with the great man.)

The girls were under the care of a Miss Foxe, who it was known had once given up the best proposal of marriage that she was likely to receive in order to instruct Lady Miranda and Lady Julia Mullingar into such a position that they might receive an offer from one or other of the royal dukes. She had extracted from the young ladies a promise that when this inevitable event occurred she would receive a room in a palace and a new dress for every celebration of the king's birthday.

The children, having made up their minds to dislike Isabella, were disposed to ignore her whenever they could. The spinet was banged rather than played, and Australia declared to be part of Africa. Their mother, who now had nowhere to place her affections except in her children, saw only that Isabella could not manage them.

'Montagu,' she complained to her brother when the party was out walking and George was complaining that Isabella was insisting that it was possible to tell an oak from an ash without its being necessary to have the leaves to look at. 'Her company is so tedious I do believe her family sent her away on purpose.'

'I do not find it tedious.'

'But she knows no one and has done nothing.'

'She does not gossip, that is true,' said Lord Angelsea. 'And now I shall hurry along and catch her up before the children torment her further.'

From this moment on, Lady Penelope's conviction that the pair were in love could not be shaken. She set her children to spy on the pair, insisting to them that she wished very much that they should be observant. Consequently, she was soon possessed of a great deal of information on what Uncle Montagu had said to Miss Napier. By this means it became clear to Lady Penelope that if something were not done to separate the pair an offer would be made, an offer she did not believe that any young woman in Isabella's circumstances would reject.

She found herself presented with two courses of action: either she could find an excuse for sending Lord Angelsea out of the way, perhaps with a message to her husband about the boys' education, or she must get rid of the young lady herself. As any intercourse with her husband was painful to her, she decided on the latter, considering that Isabella could be dismissed most easily from Angelsea Court. It was provident, therefore, that she should receive a letter from a friend who had decided to spend the winter in the northern spa of Hawbury saying that she did not want to leave a place where she found the waters so helpful to her rheumatics. The lady wrote to tell Lady Penelope that she had had to discharge her companion for lewdness. Indeed, she wrote to Lady Penelope, that after hearing a strange noise from the disgraced lady's chamber, she had put herself to the trouble of looking under the door (it says a great deal for the efficacy of the waters in that Derbyshire town that she was able to do so) and had seen a pair of naked feet, that from their size could only be those of a man. And that there being none of this sex in the house apart from her footman, the rest was self-evident. The lady begged to know from Lady Penelope if she could suggest some suitable replacement, as it was dull being at a spa out of season. Lady Penelope decided that her friend should look no further than Isabella.

Accordingly, she went at once to the schoolroom and, dismissing the children, said to Isabella: 'My dear Miss Napier, have you ever considered taking the waters for your health?'

'Madam, thanks to the kindness of your brother and sister, my health is perfectly restored.'

'But should you not like to go?'

'Very much. But it is not in my power to afford it.'

'I may be able to assist you in that,' said Lady Penelope. 'No, I should not say that. You might be able to assist *me*.'

'In what way, madam?' asked Isabella.

'I have a friend, who currently resides at Hawbury and who has been compelled to send away her companion. Now she writes to me, saying that she is in very low spirits and does not know how she will endure the winter without some gentle-woman to be her companion.'

'The poor lady. Though I gather that much development has taken place there recently, I believe there is not much entertain-ment in Hawbury during the winter months.'

'Indeed not,' replied Lady Penelope. 'But in the season there are entertainments aplenty, and my friend, being almost resident in the place, is bound to be among the first invited. And if you would agree to go to her now, would see that you received the same invitations, and at no expense to yourself or my brother.'

When Isabella saw by this means that she might become independent, she vowed that she would take up the role of companion to the lady.

'You will not go, you must not go!' cried Lord Angelsea

when Isabella made her plan known to him.

'I have already written to the lady.'

'Write again. Tell her your friends will not permit it.'

'My plans are all in motion.'

'Why did you not consult me first?' he cried.

'Because . . .' But Isabella could say no more to Lord Angelsea and ran from the room in tears.

❦ EIGHT ❧

In which Isabella's jug is broken by a clergyman

Ten days after the New Year began, Isabella bade a tearful goodbye to Lady Caroline, shook hands with Lord Angelsea and curtsied to the countess and her naughty children and departed on her journey to Derbyshire.

Though her passage was often across some of the bleakest and most inhospitable country she had ever seen, the voyage passed without incident and Isabella was able to concentrate on wonders of nature of which she had only read.

She arrived in Hawbury at ten o'clock in the evening to find that everyone in the house except one of the maids had gone to bed and that she must wait until the morning to meet the lady to whom she had come to be companion. Isabella burnt her candle just long enough to say her prayers, in which she made sure to ask that special care should be taken of Lord Angelsea.

The young lord for whom she prayed did not commend Isabella to God but played with a lock of her hair which he had stolen from her when she had been bent over her needlework, the deed being done before Isabella could complain.

Miss Napier and Mrs Cox sat down to breakfast at nine o'clock the next morning. Mrs Cox seemed a lively woman and not at all the invalid that Isabella had anticipated. She could only suppose this was due to the waters that had kept Mrs Cox at the spa when many others had deserted it for more lively places.

Mrs Cox was all concern for Isabella after her journey. Her first words to her were: 'My dear Miss Napier, you must be quite fagged, and I assure you there would have been no trouble in sending you up a small repast.'

'No, indeed, madam,' replied Isabella, 'it has always been my custom, when in health, to rise early. I find that lying in bed too long produces in me a lassitude that sometimes cannot be shaken off until after dinner.'

'I suspect,' cried Mrs Cox with delight, 'that is because, like all young ladies, fatigue is lifted when the gentlemen come in for their tea!'

Isabella did not quite like the tone in which this was said and endeavoured to point out that in her own case such ennui was lifted not by company but by exercise. Mrs Cox gave a shudder. To her, all motion that required her to stand on her feet, other than dancing, was quite abhorrent. 'I believe,' she said, 'that I should be happy to be in bed all the day.'

Isabella felt that she had behaved most insensitively to Mrs Cox and remembered that Lady Penelope had told her that she must not be surprised if Mrs Cox, due to the ailment that affected her joints, spent a great deal of time in her room or on her bed.

Having enquired after Isabella's health, Mrs Cox turned her attentions to Lady Penelope. 'How is my dear countess?' was her next question.

'Very well.'

'And her spirits?'

'Again very well.'

Mrs Cox gave Isabella a look of remonstrance. 'How can she be in spirits, after what the wicked earl has done? It might be excusable with a lady, but to choose a *woman*, who by all accounts is very little better than an actress!'

'My dear Mrs Cox, I know very little of the countess and her history,' assured Isabella.

There was a pause for a moment. Mrs Cox took up the pot and poured the coffee, stopping for a moment to look into Isabella's cup to make sure it was entirely clean. Then she settled back into her chair and prepared to acquaint Isabella with all she knew of the relationship between the Earl of Mullingar and Miss Tanner. She did not pause for a moment to think of Isabella's youth or to consider the fact that a conversation of ten minutes' intimacy should be engaged into enquiring after the likes and dislikes of the new associate. She did not ask if Isabella had found her room satisfactory or make any apology for not sitting up to wait for her the previous evening. Mrs Cox had a wide circle of friends, all of whom liked to write to her, sending long snippets of gossip. She would always reply the same day as the letter arrived with some equally interesting details. Many of her correspondents begged that she would put their letters into the fire directly she had read them, and they all implored her to the utmost secrecy. Mrs Cox could not abide secrecy, except in the matter of where she kept such epistles. Thus, she was one of the chief conduits of information between the four corners of the kingdom.

She started her discourse on the Earl of Mullingar and Miss Tanner with a comment on Lady Penelope, saying: 'Lady Penelope, as you know, is one of my very dearest friends. We were at school together, and, as you know, such friendships endure for ever.'

Isabella, who had no recollection of whether she had learnt her facts from a school or a governess, replied that she believed it must be so.

'She married for love, and that, I always say, was the root of the problem.'

'How can that be?' asked Isabella.

'Because she did not believe that she might ever cease to interest him.'

'But if the earl loved her . . . ?'

Mrs Cox, who did not like to be distracted in the middle of a discourse, looked at Isabella and said in a firm tone: 'You will come to understand, Miss Napier, that a man cannot love a woman of seven and twenty as much as he loved her at eighteen. After six children, it is not possible. They have become too familiar. Their intercourse is all at the same level. It is necessary that the lady finds ways to make herself more interesting, some-thing I fear that Lady Penelope never considered.'

Isabella thought it very unfair that the effort of being interesting must be all on the wife's side, especially when she was occupied by so many other cares. She also thought it something better not to be discussed but her role of companion to Mrs Cox prevented her from expressing this concern.

The lady rattled on. 'He therefore sought to interest himself outside his family. And where better for a man to find the inter-course he craves than in London?' She paused for breath, and Isabella could not help herself breaking out with the words: 'Could he not have asked his wife and children to accompany him?'

Mrs Cox gave her a look which could only be described as one of contempt.

'I hope, Miss Napier, that I shall not have to cancel my invitation to you before we have been in each other's company half an hour.'

Isabella cast down her eyes and begged pardon.

'Why?' asked Mrs Cox (a question she did not expect to be answered), 'should a man who finds his wife dull in the country find her more interesting in town? There he will always find half a dozen women who have more time to be interested in him than his wife does.'

Isabella took a sip of her coffee, and Mrs Cox, glad that she had instituted silence in her, now came to the thrust of her story.

'I have not heard precisely how he and Miss Tanner were introduced. But they were, and very soon came to an accom-modation together.'

Isabella did not wish to hear the lady any longer, but she sat at her table and ate her bread, and was apparently expected to pay for it by listening.

'I dare say it was not quite proper,' said Mrs Cox with a little laugh. 'But given it is the custom of most married men, we must look on it as almost being a law. The long and short of it is, that she has had one son by him and intends to bear him as many more as my dear Penelope has. Though' – and here Mrs Cox became very secretive – 'it is my belief that they will part before she has accomplished it. Indeed, I expect every day to hear that they have separated. Well, if that be so, it is my wish that they should both find a new amour.'

Isabella was so shocked by this statement that her cup rattled as she put it down.

Mrs Cox seized instantly on her discomfort. 'You must not be so nice, Miss Napier. This is the way of the world, as I am sure we both know.' She gave a little wink at Isabella.

When it was not returned, she cried: 'If you have come here with Mr Wesley's sermons in your luggage, you must make a choice of disposing of them or returning to Angelsea Court.'

Isabella would have liked nothing better at that moment. She turned her eyes to the window, hoping to avoid the gaze of Mrs Cox, and noticed that during their interview it had begun to snow very thickly and that the hills beyond the town were now quite white; all the usual morning activity in the street had ceased because of the weather. At the same moment Mrs Cox, too, became aware of the deterioration in the weather. 'What are we to do?' she cried. 'How will James come home?'

'Who is James?' asked Isabella, believing the household to consist entirely of women.

'My footman, who is quite devoted to me, and to whom, I, always anxious to repay that devotion, granted a holiday.' Mrs Cox pushed back her chair and went to the window. 'I do believe it will stop very shortly,' she said, although every indication was to the contrary.

The snow did not stop. For several days Isabella and Mrs Cox were confined to the house and forced to spend their time in each other's company as agreeably as they could. Mrs Cox thought that the snow was providential and that their being enclosed at close quarters gave her an admirable opportunity to turn Isabella's mind to enjoying the things that gave Mrs Cox pleasure.

She began by insisting that they must play cards and was

most perplexed when Isabella seemed not to know the rules of the simplest games and never to have even heard of a trump. It would have been easy for Mrs Cox to exploit this ignorance and to insist that they played for threepences; that she did neither must be admitted to her credit. On Isabella's side it must be said that she was anxious to please Mrs Cox and quick to learn, and along with cards and other amusements they managed to pass the time in a tolerable fashion.

James returned as soon as the weather grew milder. Mrs Cox, whose infirmity, Isabella had noticed, was not at all affected by the ice and snow, complained that the thaw had produced a dampness that caused the most severe pain in her joints, and that there was nothing for it, she must retire to her room. Isabella asked if she might find a glass of water from the town well of any help and, the lady declaring it might, offered to go for the water herself, for she had been in Hawbury above a week, and, having become acquainted with everyone Mrs Cox considered to be anybody, through that lady's gossip she now had a very natural desire to see the place for herself.

Accordingly, Isabella ventured out on her pattens bearing a heavy jug. Mrs Cox had given her instructions as to how to find the well, even going so far as to make a map of the place. The map was of little purpose because instead of the information Isabella needed as to the names of the streets it was entirely marked with such information as 'Mr Perks' inn', 'a house where I won three pounds at macao', 'a noisy place where it is said lunatics are kept', 'ballroom, where no one likes to dance because of the unevenness of the boards', 'the house where the Scottish queen stayed when she, being as ill as I, came to take the waters'. In consequence, she had left it on her dressing-table, and she had not gone far before she needed to ask for directions, stopping for the purpose at a bookseller's, where it must be supposed Mrs Cox did not buy books, for there was no mention of it on the map. Isabella had to wait before she could be attended to and spent the time looking around the shop. It was part-bookseller and part-library, and there were tables at one end where those anxious to peruse various journals and magazines might sit and read in comfort. One table was marked as being exclusively for ladies. She decided that the library was a place to which she might come, thus providing her with an opportunity of being out of Mrs Cox's company, rendering that company, when she must be in it, more easily bearable.

Thus, when it was her turn to be attended to, her first question was as to the cost of a subscription and the hours at which the books and periodicals might be consulted. It was only when she had obtained these particulars that she recalled the main purpose of her journey and was told that she had gone right instead of left some small way back.

Isabella retraced her steps. She knew she was approaching the well when she noticed a line of people waiting to take their turn. Isabella joined the throng until it might be her turn for her jug to be filled. She could see infirmities of every kind. Some of the crowd had completely crooked limbs; others had to be constantly restrained by their attendants because of the spasms in their bodies. The rolling eyes of some and the vacant stares of others proclaimed that they had come to be cured of some disorder of the brain. As ever, when she was in any sort of a crowd, Isabella could not resist pausing on some of the gentler faces and wishing that the owners of them might recognize her and suddenly exclaim that they were some friend or relation.

It was her turn. She stepped up for her jug to be filled and also took a glass of water for the sake of her own health. Lord Angelsea had made her promise that this was something she would do every day, and Lady Caroline had said that she must write to Angelsea Court the moment any recollection came to her about the past. Accordingly, Isabella drank the water as a toast to her dear friends Caroline and Montagu and set off to return to Mrs Cox's. The walk was all uphill, and soon the jug became very heavy. The only thing to do was to set it down and take a rest, which, coming to a low wall, Isabella did. The hand which had held the pitcher was now very cold, and she drew it into her muff to chafe some life into its fingertips.

At this moment there was a hullabaloo as a brindle cat came around the corner in an attempt to escape a dog which ran close on its heels. The cat, seeing the wall and thinking there must be some place to hide behind it, leapt past Isabella and disappeared into some bushes. The dog, as dogs are wont to do, followed, and the next second cat, dog and jug were all on the other side.

There now came around the corner a man whom Isabella could only presume to be the owner of the pug. Indeed, he somewhat resembled the dog himself, being small of stature and obviously fond of eating. His garb proclaimed him a clergyman, something above fifty. He paused, panted and mopped his brow. The cat by this time had quite escaped the dog and was spitting at it from the safe height of a large oak. The dog, defeated now, returned to the clergyman, who fastened a string around its neck and, instead of kicking or beating it, proclaimed that he would forgive it if doing so lay in his power.

The dog having been forgiven as if it were the greatest sinner ever to return to the fold, the clergyman turned to Isabella and asked if she was hurt.

'Only a little frightened, sir.'

'But you had some package, I think, which has fallen off the wall,' said the clergyman, peering anxiously over and hoping that there was some means by which he could retrieve any such parcel. All that came to his notice were some shards of pottery.

'I see Captain has broken your pitcher!' he cried, as full of remorse as if he had been the one who had sent it flying.

Isabella felt positively sorry for the old man. 'I assure you, sir, it is of no consequence.'

'Of course it is. You would not be carrying it up the hill if it were of no consequence.'

Isabella explained that she had been to the well.

'You have carried it so far? If only I had been on hand to assist you. I will go home at once and return Captain to his mistress,' he said, confiding that the animal's mistress was his good wife, who did not like to go abroad when the weather was so inclement. 'Then I shall procure a jug as similar in shape and size to the one that has been broken, fill it and bring it to you, if you will be so kind as to give me your address.'

Isabella begged that he would not put himself to such trouble, but he was not to be put off, saying he would walk twenty miles carrying such a weight, if by that means he might be of service to Isabella.

Finally, the lady was persuaded. And the clergyman asking again for her address, she told him that she was lodged just off the road towards Staffordshire with Mrs Cox. The gentleman repeated the lady's name. It was obviously of some surprise to him.

'Well,' said the clergyman, 'I have promised to set things right and that is my duty. That, therefore, is what I must do.'

He gave a small bow to Isabella, set his wig straight upon his head and his hat upon his wig and departed, pulling the dog after him.

Isabella walked home musing on his final speech. She had discovered during her days of confinement with Mrs Cox that the lady had no liking for religion or any of the trappings that went with it, and she presumed this must have led her into some argument with the clergyman.

When she arrived home, Isabella discovered that the weather had not deterred several of Mrs Cox's friends from calling on her and that Mrs Cox, on hearing of their arrival, had decided to leave her room. It was insisted that Isabella should come and sit with them. She did so, drawing her chair into a line with her neighbours.

'No, no!' cried one of the company. 'You are making a circle. And Mrs Cox' – and he simpered in the direction of his hostess as he said so – 'has quite thrown off sitting in a circle for conversation.'

He whispered to Isabella: 'We like to be in the fashion here, you know.'

Isabella said she supposed Hawbury liked to keep up with the fashions as much as anywhere else and moved her chair back to its fashionable place from which, she discovered, it was possible to listen to the conversation without the necessity of taking part.

The talk was very trivial, and she was very glad not to be part of it. Much of it was gossip of the most malicious kind, and though she had never met them she felt sorry for those whose reputations were being shredded like paper. Try as she would to listen, her mind constantly returned to Angelsea Court and the talk she had joined in there about the latest advances of the day.

Suddenly, Mrs Cox clapped her hands and cried to Isabella: 'My dear, such a remarkable story and appertaining to a name-sake of yours.'

'Do tell us, Mrs Cox,' said a long young man who talked through the side of his mouth to avoid showing his teeth.

'Who did you have it from?' cried one of the ladies, disappointed that Mrs Cox had heard something she had not.

'It came to me in the course of my correspondence. I do not know the young gentleman to whom it happened, but I have it on the best authority that the facts I have are true.'

'Do you not long to hear the tale, Miss Napier?' asked an elderly gentleman who sat beside her.

'If Mrs Cox wishes to tell it,' replied Isabella, knowing the lady would whether she herself wished it or not.

'The young gentleman who recounted the story to my friend had got up a party to go ghost-hunting.'

'Where?' asked the long young man.

'That I cannot tell you,' replied Mrs Cox. 'The party consisted of three, the gentleman, a friend of his, who would not undertake the expedition without a wager, and a young lady, who was very pretty and who said she was quite without fear at the thought of a ghost. They entered a church. It was on the stroke of eleven, but before he and the other gentleman had seen or heard anything, the young lady ran from the church insisting that she would stay there no longer.'

'What had she seen?' asked one of the ladies of the party with a shudder.

'It is not known, but when the gentleman and his friend ran

out after her, they found her lying in the road, still breathing but almost dead. They ran to her but before they could give her assistance, they were struck down by the most ferocious highwayman, a felon who cared for nothing but gain. The young man fought him to the ground, completely fearless of the robber's pistol, so intent was he on rescuing the young lady. But it was to no avail. His companion who might have helped him had instantly fled on the arrival of the highwayman, and unarmed and alone it was impossible that the young man should not be overpowered, though he fought like a dog, breaking the attacker's jaw and tearing out half his hair. But the highwayman fired on him, a shot that glanced off the young man's pocket-watch, so that instead of being killed he was merely grazed. He struggled once more to his feet, determined as he was to give his life to save that of the young lady. But his enemy was too quick and in a moment had snatched up the young lady on to his horse, which was twenty hands high. All the poor gentleman could do was watch as her fair hair shimmered in the moonlight and shudder at the thought that there was nothing to come to her but disgrace.'

Mrs Cox's story being finished, the eyes of the company all strayed towards the window. They were all very surprised and delighted to discover that it was still daylight. This being the case, they now flung questions at Mrs Cox: had any more been heard of the young lady, what had her family thought?

Isabella heard nothing of these questions, her mind completely preoccupied in pitying the young lady. She had been rescued by no Lord Angelsea; she had found no favour with his sister. Isabella wished that she might find the young lady wherever she was and befriend her and comfort her. She was interrupted in these thoughts by a knock upon the door. Expecting the old clergyman with his jug of water, which she doubted at this moment Mrs Cox required, she got up and went downstairs.

But instead of a jug a letter was put into her hands, addressed in a script that was all too familiar. Isabella intended to go to her room at once to read it in private, but, passing the salon door, which she had left ajar on her descent, she was called to rejoin the company. She slipped the letter into her bosom, but the rustling paper was heard by Mrs Cox, who called out as Isabella entered the room. 'I believe Miss Napier has received a letter.'

Belatedly, Isabella remembered how very interested Mrs Cox was in all correspondence. The young lady blushed very deep; she had known on seeing the letter that it was from Lord Angelsea and must bring her news that she longed to hear. Isabella's colouring was noticed by all the company, who now grew agog to know who had sent the letter and what it contained. One of the gentlemen present even went so far as to offer Isabella a paper-knife for the purpose of opening it. Isabella refused. The company chattered to one conclusion: the letter must be from a lover, and they would have his name. Mrs Cox took the lead in this teasing.

'I do declare it is a billet-doux!' she cried. 'Ah, Miss Napier, I understand now why you were so anxious to step out into the town.' She turned to the company 'I would have sent a servant, the weather being so dirty, but Miss Napier would go!'

Isabella saw that an answer was required and said simply: 'I only wished to be of assistance, madam.'

One of the gentlemen broke in with: 'Fie, to give assistance to somebody else without doing any good to oneself? Where is the reason in that?'

From the nods that were given by the rest of the company, it appeared to Isabella that all in the room except herself were in complete agreement with this statement.

'Come, Missy,' said Mrs Cox. 'I have seen you looking out of the window some half-hour at a time.'

'I was only admiring the view.'

'Hah!' cried a very thin, pale lady in a costume of so many feathers and choices of colour that she resembled nothing so much as a piece of patchwork of the most organized design. 'A young man, strolling up and down the street, always makes a very admirable picture to my mind.'

'And young gentlemen, as we know, never take cold. They are always too active,' cried the most elderly of the gentlemen present, in a tone which gave Isabella to understand that he regretted the passing of his own youth.

'And it is a small matter,' added the patchwork lady, 'to slide the sash up a finger's width and slip out a letter to inform someone below as to one's name and situation.'

The taunt inspiring rather than intimidating her, Isabella became brave. She cast her steady gaze on Mrs Cox and her friends, who from this conduct, expecting some explanation from her, gave her liberty to speak. 'I have always had a great regard for nature and was constantly drawn to look out of the window by the fine aspect of the snow and the hills.'

This remark was greeted by the company with such laughter that it might have been the best joke in the world.

'I assure you,' she continued trying to be heard, 'I have no friends in this town,' forgetting at this moment the kindly clergyman who had come to her aid but an hour before.

'Fie, fie, Miss Napier!' cried Mrs Cox. 'Am I not your friend?'

Isabella was put at a disadvantage by this. She could not count the lady as anyone with whom she would have chosen an acquaintanceship; equally, it was quite impossible to admit this to Mrs Cox.

Fortunately, she was spared the effort of replying by the patchwork lady, who, the daughter of a shoemaker and thus always keen to improve herself through her acquaintances, fawningly cried: 'Who could not be friends with you, Mrs Cox?'

This remark soon prompted so many similar statements that, without Isabella uttering one word, Mrs Cox felt that she was universally beloved. Once this tide of admiration had died down, Isabella's letter again become the focus of the room. But she was resolute. Indeed, during the tributes to Mrs Cox she had planned that she would throw the missive into the fire rather than be forced to present it to the company.

At this juncture the footman entered the room and announced that a clergyman by the name of Mr Bunce was at the door. This produced more universal laughter among the crowd, Mrs Cox becoming almost hysterical in her response. When she had recovered herself, she turned to her friends and pronounced: 'This is a very good joke. Who can have been put up to it?'

Several names were offered and Mrs Cox put them to the footman, who rejected them all and repeated: 'It is Mr Bunce. He is asking for Miss Napier.'

'I suppose he must see her,' said Mrs Cox, 'or he will haunt the doorstep, like a dog that has lost its master.'

She turned to Isabella and warned her: 'He likes to think it his duty to call on every arrival, in an attempt to turn us all from our pleasures. It is regarded best not to invite him in but to tell him his duty lies in saving the humbler souls of the parish.'

'Very true!' cried the oldest gentleman. 'We want no French-type mobs here.'

'Wicked, very wicked,' shuddered the patchwork lady, whose disgust at the mob was influenced by the fact that some of her relations remained in a station of life such as to be excellent candidates for the carrying through the streets of burning brands and effigies of the local magistrate.

Isabella was about to leave the room when Mrs Cox uttered another exhortation. 'He will try your views on the abolition of slavery, to which our response is' – and the company all chimed together – 'what is tea without sugar and what is company without tea!'

Isabella vowed that if Mr Bunce gave her such a piece of paper she would take it from him and do him the honour of reading it. Isabella, for the second time that morning, ran down to the front door. It was obvious from the stamping he was making with his feet that the clergyman had been kept waiting some time. Isabella wished she could invite him in, not only to thank him for providing a new jug of water and taking the trouble to carry it to her but also so that he could warm himself before setting out in the cold again.

'Thank you,' she said, taking the jug from him. 'Mrs Cox will be most grateful.'

Mr Bunce looked as if he did not believe this statement. He was about to turn away when Isabella, feeling sorry for the kind old man, and looking behind her to see that she was not observed, stepped into the street, closing the door a little.

'Sir,' she said, 'it was clear to me when we parted earlier that you had some difficulty in coming here.'

The old man's glance told her it was so.

'And, indeed – believe me, sir, it pains me to say this – the announcement of your arrival was greeted with much mirth by the company above.'

'I am used to being the object of ridicule to Mrs Cox and her circle,' the gentleman replied.

'But I am glad to see you,' Isabella added, hoping by this to ameliorate her last speech a little.

'And I believe you to be sincere. In which case,' he added, putting his hand into his greatcoat pocket, 'I beg you to accept this. It is from my wife. I told her what mischief was made by her naughty dog this morning, and she would like the honour of apologizing to you herself if you are ever at liberty to call on her.' And he handed her a written invitation from Mrs Bunce.

'I should be happy to,' said Isabella, 'if at any point I should be at liberty to do so. But I must inform you that my first duty is to Mrs Cox.' Isabella could almost have said the clergyman had tears in his eyes. She shivered, having come down without a wrap of any kind.

'Go in,' he said, 'or you will take a chill. And Mrs Bunce would never forgive me.' He saluted Isabella and took his leave. She returned upstairs and noticed that the footman who had followed her out of the room had shut the door.

It took but a moment to run to her room and secrete her two letters. She looked around for a piece of paper she might substitute for her first letter, should she once again be asked to present it in the salon. Her eyes fell upon the map Mrs Cox had made her and which she had discarded. Isabella snatched it up, tucked it into her bosom where Lord Angelsea's epistle had lately lain, and returned to the others.

She was very provident to have done so, for after a few remarks to the detriment of Mr Bunce, Mrs Cox again returned to the subject of Isabella's letter.

'Very well, madam,' said Isabella, 'you shall have it of me,' and drawing out the map she handed it to Mrs Cox with the words: 'In my hurry to return to you, I dropped this from my muff, a mishap which happily was witnessed by someone who was good enough to take the trouble of returning it.' It was a lie with which Isabella felt entirely justified in duping Mrs Cox.

The map was seized upon and instantly became the new subject of conversation. Disputation as to the name of the innkeeper and the denomination of the chapel being Congregational or Presbyterian entertained the party until it broke up under the necessity of returning home in time for dinner. Isabella was at last free to return to her own room and her two letters.

She had determined that she would change as quickly as she could so that she might spend as much time as possible reading her correspondence before being called to the table. Once she was attired, she opened first Mrs Bunce's letter, which was most civil and assured her that she would be welcome to call even if her visit were outside the hours convention set down for such appointments. The second, from Lord Angelsea, Isabella opened with trembling hands and a beating heart.

My dear Isabella (she read)
For such, as you know, Caroline and I always presume to call you, Miss Napier being but an invention. We have been very dejected since your going. We talk about our happy days together twenty times a day, and hope your time with Mrs Cox goes quicker than ours here at Angelsea Court. Caroline begs me to remind you of your promise to take a glass of water every day in the hope of restoring your memory.

How glad was Isabella that she had done what he desired that very morning. She returned to her letter.

If we had our wish we would have you home immediately.

At the notion of Angelsea Court being called her home, Isabella's heart was filled with joy. How she longed it could be so! It was some minutes before she put this fantasy away from her and returned to the letter.

But you have given your word to stay with Mrs Cox until Easter, and I know that no entreaty will make you break that promise.

Isabella's heart grew heavy, and she wished that Lady Penelope had not been so persuasive in the matter of Mrs Cox's needing a new companion. But then she remembered that it had been the result of her insistence that she should make her own way in the world, a course that Lord Angelsea and his sister had tried to persuade her from.

Caroline and I have therefore decided that we will carry ourselves to you in the hope that Mrs Cox may agree to share you a little or make up a foursome with us. Penelope and the children have quitted us and returned to Ireland without the earl making any attempt to contact them. She still insists that she will not have a legal separation made between them, saying she will not give the children over to the care of such a father.

Caroline interrupts me again, this time to ask me to insist on your writing by return, as I know you will, and saying on what date our visit will be convenient to you and Mrs Cox. I hope that it may be soon.

I remain, Isabella, your devoted servant, Montagu

Isabella read and reread the letter which had been signed with his name. Indeed, she lapsed into such a reverie of her time at Angelsea Court that the servant knocked on her door three times before Isabella realized it was time to dine. She went to the table with such a bright eye and so much colour in her cheeks that Mrs Cox, drinking the water that the much despised Mr Bunce had brought her, became suspicious of her conduct and kept a stream of questions about young men and lovers until Isabella pleaded to go to bed on the grounds of a headache.

Sophia Ducoeur's delight in being relieved of Isabella by so neat a contrivance as a highwayman soon gave way. The lack of an appropriate companion drove her more and more often to Sir Roderick's chambers on any number of small pretexts, until Sir Roderick, unable to bear her sight a single moment longer, had removed himself to friends. Consequently, at that time of year when it is most pleasant to surround oneself with family and friends she was left alone at Ducoeur Castle, and mocked by the boughs of green holly and ivy which denote the arrival of Christmas.

Sir Roderick spent the holiday hunting across half a dozen counties and making love to three times as many pretty women, none of whom, to his mind, could hold a candle to Isabella. One of his favourite speculations was to imagine what had happened to her at the hands of the highwayman, and he envied the wretch his prize. He imagined that Isabella had been debased and that he might come across her in some dark street plying the only trade open to such women.

He was, therefore, greatly shocked to hear from a young lady, who had been sure, from the size of her fortune, that she had had every hope of winning Lord Angelsea's affections, that his lordship had taken a young lady into his house, claiming he had rescued her from a highwayman.

'The lady's name?' asked Sir Roderick.

'Isabella, but she has quite lost her memory and cannot remember any other.'

Sir Roderick had never been a man who believed in coincidences, but this was too great for him to ignore. He pressed the lady for more information.

'Pray, madam, do you have any description of the lady?'

'I never saw her in my life,' replied the lady, tossing her head, 'and I never trust reports of beauty from Angelsea Court, for I have met Lady Caroline and think her very plain. But then in that family all the looks were given to the brother.'

'What of the relations of this Isabella?'

'She is supposed to be an orphan, but I suspect that her family have spent all their fortune on her clothes and mean to have their return by her marrying Lord Angelsea.'

'Is that possible?' asked Sir Roderick, hating Lord Angelsea at that moment more that he had hated him when he had met him on the road.

'If he is such a fool, I wish him joy of it. They will end up in a worse pickle than the earl and the countess.' The lady drew close to Sir Roderick and said in a voice meant for his ear alone: 'Believe me, sir, you are twice the gentleman, and you would have the sense not to throw yourself away upon a pauper.' She threw back her head and gave a little laugh, showing off her diamonds to good effect. The lady could have sixty thousand a year for all Sir Roderick cared. His only thought was Isabella, and he cursed himself for a coward at the hands of the highwayman, telling himself he had retreated only because Mr Edgecliffe had done so. He was distracted the rest of the evening and came to his host the next morning to say that it was most essential he leave. No inducements that the host could make of hunting the best coverts or calling up the best champagne could persuade him to stay.

His first instinct was to ride straight to Angelsea Court and declare himself to be Isabella's friend and protector, but then he remembered that he had insisted to Lord Angelsea that he did not know her and decided that there was no possibility of taking any such form of action. It was necessary for him to be circumspect. Thus a Mr Whistler, an ambassador of a very similar type to Mr Edgecliffe, another man whom Sir Roderick had put in his debt, presented himself at Angelsea Court in the guise of a near-relation of Isabella's.

Mr Whistler, who had had no acquaintance with the orphan

and had been told only of her beauty and her height, and who did not anticipate with any relish a confrontation with Lord Angelsea, considered himself a fortunate man to be confronted instead by the young lady as soon as he entered the park. Here she was, quite alone, without even a dog and out of earshot of any assistance, running forward to greet him and ask if she could help him in any way.

Mr Whistler decided in an instant that Sir Roderick would prefer the creature herself to any information about her. In a second he was off his horse, his hand was over her mouth and the lady was his captive.

How she struggled! She kicked, she spat, she scratched, she bit – but all in vain. With Lady Caroline mounted before him, Mr Whistler rode out of the park gates before the gatekeeper had finished telling his assistant that he had ridden in. The fear and tumult that Lady Caroline felt can only be imagined. The weather being quite fine that morning, she had ventured to walk to the village to ask after some of the old people and to dispatch a letter to her beloved Isabella. Now she was captive and being taken she knew not where; she knew only that the gentleman who had abducted her declared that he was doing so for Sir Roderick Ducoeur, of whom she had never heard.

It was often Lady Caroline's habit to take the walk to the village, a custom her sister Lady Penelope detested on the grounds that anyone might walk but only Lord Angelsea and Lady Caroline had the right to the Angelsea coat of arms on their carriage. It was therefore some time before any alarm was raised as to her disappearance.

When the news of it was carried to Lord Angelsea, he at once suspected that his sister had been abducted in a fit of madness by her former lover. He remembered how she had come to him that morning insisting that she must call at the home of their old nurse, who had been laid very low by a fever. He had tried to persuade her not to go in case some infection still remained there, but Lady Caroline had been adamant that she would go.

He went at once to the old woman and demanded to know if she had seen his sister.

'Certainly,' said the nurse, 'and looking in better spirits than I have seen her in since the sad business . . . '

'Let us not talk of that!' said Lord Angelsea.

'And she said she had put on her newest gown to cheer me. So pretty!' sighed the old woman.

Lord Angelsea would have preferred to have heard that his sister had been dressed in rags than in the mode. 'Where did she intend to go when she left you?'

'Back to tell you that I was almost quite recovered.'

'Were those her very words?' asked Lord Angelsea, hardly able to believe that his sister would lie to the good woman.

'I always like to remember the things you and she say to me, Montagu,' was the nurse's reply, 'but I know by your coming here that she cannot have come home.'

'She has not.'

'Then it is a sorry business.'

'My dear Jemima,' said Lord Angelsea, taking her hands in his, 'I know you will say nothing of this, but it is my fear that Caroline has deceived us all.'

❧ NINE ❧

In which a murder is committed

Lady Caroline and her captor had not gone far when Lady Caroline realized that struggle was in vain. The more she fought, the harder he held her. Had they travelled on the highway she might have stood some chance of rescue, but Mr Whistler, not wanting to be seen, travelled cross-country. She decided that she might gain more from cooperation than obstruction.

'What have I done, sir, that I should be treated in this manner and dragged away from family and friends?' asked the lady.

'You are to be returned to your true friend,' replied her captor.

'What friend is that?' asked Lady Caroline, fearing that this was another consequence of the liaison she now condemned herself for ever having entered.

'Sir Roderick Ducoeur.'

'But I know no one of that name.'

'Madam, I have been informed by Sir Roderick about the infirmity of your mind,' said Mr Whistler, who had been warned that Isabella might refuse to recognize Sir Roderick's name.

'There is no infirmity. There has never been any. It is you and your . . . master – or whatever power he holds over you – who are mad. I have done you no wrong that I know of, and if I have I shall recompense you for it,' said she, thinking that perhaps she was being taken in the hope of obtaining some ransom from her brother. 'Return me to Angelsea Court and I shall beg from Lord Angelsea whatever sum you require. I will plead for you before him so that you will not be punished. Only pray, sir, take me home!' So saying, Lady Caroline, who had been resolute until she thought of all the things she was now parted from, broke down in tears.

Mr Whistler, who could cry a great deal at a tragedy himself, nearly gave way before such a show of feminine emotion, but he steeled himself by giving a mighty blow to the flanks of his horse.

At the surge of the steed and the fact that at every stride it carried her further from Angelsea Court, Lady Caroline's tears became sobs.

'I beg you, Miss Broderick!' entreated Mr Whistler, who was beginning to wish that he had stuck to the original intention of an interview with Lord Angelsea, and in that way had been introduced to Isabella.

In a flash it occurred to Lady Caroline that here was a case of mistaken identity.

'Sir,' she said, 'pray tell me who this Miss Broderick is so that I may convince you that I am not she.'

'You can be no one else,' answered Mr Whistler.

'But indeed I am!'

'You cannot trick me,' said Mr Whistler. 'You are she in every particular.'

'There may perhaps be some similarity between me and this person.'

'She is beautiful, you are beautiful. She is above average height, and so are you. The eyes have a brightness to them, and the brow is high.'

'There are many such women in the country,' said Lady Caroline, her eyes flashing.

'And she has a temper,' added Mr Whistler, 'which is not usual in a lady of quality. I venture to say that *you* are the Miss Broderick you pretend not to be. But Sir Roderick will know you well enough.'

Sir Roderick, anxious that his reunion with Isabella should be in the most secret of circumstances, had arranged to take on a small farmhouse in a flat and out-of-the-way place in the county of Lincoln. Here he had installed a man and his wife who were to perform all the offices necessary and keep their mouths shut. It was to this place of rendezvous that Mr Whistler and Lady Caroline were headed.

Sir Roderick had sat up half the night, musing on different plans for removing Isabella once her presence and movements at Angelsea Court had been ascertained by the always useful Mr Whistler. He was delighted when the serving-woman came in to say that her husband had heard a horse, though far off, and barely had this news been digested than the very husband himself appeared with the information that two riders on one horse were approaching, and that he was sure, from the little moonlight there was, that one of the party was a lady.

Sir Roderick was thrilled. There was only one possible interpretation. Isabella here – and come of her own accord! He had only time to dismiss the servants until the morrow and make some small adjustment in his dress when the door opened and there came into the room . . . not Isabella Broderick but Lady Caroline Angelsea.

Sir Roderick could only stare. He looked to Mr Whistler for some explanation. Mr Whistler, expecting fulsome thanks from Sir Roderick, stepped forward and said: 'Sir Roderick, I have the honour of presenting to you Miss Isabella Broderick.'

'You have mistaken me for Isabella?' cried Lady Caroline.

'She is the exact description,' said Mr Whistler.

'She is not!' shouted Sir Roderick.

'Then, sir, I beg you, since there has been a mistake, return me at once to my family.'

But Sir Roderick did not hear her, all his attentions focused on Mr Whistler, whose arrival with a young woman had caused his hopes to rise that she was Isabella, and who now, by a hideous mistake, had dashed them to the ground.

'What have you done?' shouted Sir Roderick.

'Only what you asked of me.'

'I wanted Isabella,' cried Sir Roderick.

Mr Whistler tried to stammer something but, before the words could form, Sir Roderick, in a fury, advanced on him, snatched up the fire iron, which had been left in the grate when the servants departed, and before Lady Caroline could stop him he brought it down with a crack on Mr Whistler's skull. No man, not even one as strong as Mr Whistler, could have withstood such a blow. He crumpled and fell stone-dead at the feet of Sir Roderick.

Lady Caroline, who some might suppose would have been grateful to be rescued in this manner, looked on in horror. As Sir Roderick stooped to turn over the body, hoping against hope that there would be some breath in it, she picked up a candle, and, drawing close to Sir Roderick, she registered every detail of his face and person as acutely as if she were painting his portrait, and knew instantly it was the face that her brother Montagu had drawn when trying to force some recollection from Isabella.

Suddenly, Sir Roderick became aware that he was being observed and that there had been a witness to the murder. He sprang upright. Lady Caroline shrank back, but he advanced on her, his eyes blazing. In vain, the lady looked for some escape. There was none forthcoming. His hands reached out to grasp her around the neck. She felt the wainscoting behind her. Suddenly, all went dark.

Sir Roderick stood amazed. It was as if the lady had disappeared through the wall! He threw himself upon it, trying to find the secret lever that Lady Caroline must have touched, but to no avail.

For several seconds Lady Caroline did not know what had happened to her. One moment she had been in an oak-lined room; now, she believed, from feeling along the wall, she was in some damp passageway.

It occurred to the lady that she had been given the same means of escape that had been given to priests who had performed the rites of mass when to be a member of the Church of Rome was a capital offence. Everything pointed to it: the remoteness of the house, the panelling, and now she felt the shape of a crucifix set into a small alcove in the wall. Frightened though she was, Lady Caroline was certain that the passageway must, at some point, provide an exit.

By the device of putting one hand after another, she came eventually to a place where the cold wetness of the wall gave way to the warmth of wood. Her hands fumbled for a latch. There was none but, by keeping her reason and exploring every inch of the door, she discovered a small knob, which, though rusted, turned when she applied her full strength to it. Lady Caroline stumbled out into the bitter air of the January night.

She dared not seek any form of shelter so close to Sir Roderick. All her readings of Arctic journeys had taught her that in the cold to lie down means death, and so she walked, dragging herself up every time she stumbled.

Sir Roderick, meanwhile, had woken his servants and, swearing them to terrible secrecy, led them to the place where the body of Mr Whistler lay. On seeing the corpse, the woman screamed and said she would have nothing to do with murder. The man asked Sir Roderick to grant them a few words in private and, having convinced his wife of the danger of going against their employer's wishes, a plan was devised for bestowing Mr Whistler's remains in a shallow grave. When dawn broke, there was nothing to remind the world that any such being had ever been in existence.

The day that did not dawn for Mr Whistler found Lady Caroline on the point of exhaustion. For all her will, she began to feel that she could go no further. Then, as light began to fill the sky, she noticed the silver sheen of a river, and built into its bank the sort of house which is used for the protection of boats. With her last remaining strength, she dragged herself towards it and, since the door had not been locked, went in. There she found a pile of sacks, on which she sank down and fell asleep.

On the night of all this adventure, Isabella had suffered from the most terrible dreams concerning her dearest Montagu and Lady Caroline. She had wakened herself by calling out to them to save them. Then she had tossed and turned until sleep again claimed her and the dream would be repeated. The last time she dreamed it, which was as morning was almost breaking, a name suddenly came to her, that of Sir Roderick. She knew it at once: at least one piece of her memory had been restored, and if she still did not know her former friends, she did know the name of her enemy. She arose at once and wrote it down, intending to never forget it again.

Lady Caroline did not expire in the boat-house. She had been sleeping there above an hour, an hour in which, despite the sacks, she had gradually grown, because of the cold, more and more insensible, when the local squire, intent on a day's duck-shooting, and knowing that the birds were very dense in a certain area of reeds, came to collect his punt for the purpose.

He was surprised to find, on opening the door and as the weak winter sunlight flooded in, a young lady obviously, from her clothes and looks, of good breeding. Instantly, he put down his gun and took her in his arms, all thought of sport quite forgotten.

In this manner, and with Lady Caroline still asleep, he carried her to his abode, where she was received by his mother with every attention that could restore her to warmth.

The fire was made up, a hot brick put under her feet and a warm blanket around her shoulders. At length, Lady Caroline's teeth stopped chattering and she was able to look around her and ascertain her situation. She was in a small, snug parlour, fitted up in a mode which, though a little old-fashioned, was as clean and trim as if it were new. In front of her, wearing an anxious look, sat a neat woman in black, and behind her stood a slightly overweight young man with exactly the same look of concern. The similarity of the looks between the two could only proclaim them to be mother and son.

Lady Caroline felt great relief at being in the company of such a pair. She opened her mouth to ask their names, but though her mind formed the words, no sound came; she had been struck quite dumb by her experience.

Seeing her distress at not being able to make any form of communication, the young man introduced his mother as Mrs

Percival and himself as Richard Percival.

Lady Caroline, anxious by some means to explain to the mother and son who she was, made certain gestures which Mr Percival instantly understood to be a request for writing materials. These were brought instantly and, taking up the pen, Lady Caroline wrote: 'My name is Lady Caroline Angelsea, sister to Montagu, Lord Angelsea.'

As soon as she had read these words, Mrs Percival rose to her feet, saying: 'You must think us very humble!'

Lady Caroline could only motion her to sit down and wrote upon the paper: 'It is I who should stand, being in your debt.'

'I beg you, madam, think of your feet.'

Lady Caroline looked down and saw that her shoes were quite worn through with walking. She knew she must give these good people some explanation as to her presence. Her hands now began to fly across the paper, writing the words 'I will tell'. Here she scratched out the word 'tell' and wrote 'write you my story, but first let someone go to my brother and tell him I am safe. Have you some reliable servant?'

'I will go myself,' cried Mr Percival. Lady Caroline scribbled again, imploring him to wait quarter of an hour so she could write a note to her brother.

'We will leave you alone,' said Mrs Percival. 'I must see that my son is provided with some nourishment for the journey.' While the kind mother and son were out of the room, Lady Caroline wrote the following note to her brother:

My dear Montagu,
I have been in great danger, but now, thanks to chance and to Mr Percival, who bears this letter, I have been brought to a place of safety. I have been the witness of such horrors that my voice has gone from me. I am only thankful that I am capable of taking up a pen and writing to you. Do not be too much alarmed: no wrong has been done to my person, only to my spirit and my desire to think the best of everyone. I will not let it harm me, as I have seen by the example of our

sister Penelope how much more bitterness harms those that nurture it, than those whom it is intended to wound. The kind people with whom I find myself will keep me as long as it is necessary, but I would not wish to put them to more inconvenience than I have already done, or to bring the danger on them that my presence here may provoke. I therefore beg you, if you cannot come yourself, to send Mr Fairley, for I know I can rely on him, and he will come for my sake. If it is Mr Fairley or yourself, I must urge you the utmost caution on one point. Should you at any time come upon a gentleman by the name of Sir Roderick, do not trust him. He abducted me in mistake for Isabella, and, from the short time I was in his company, I believe him to be the man you met on the road on that fateful night.

Caroline had got this far in her letter when Mr Percival and his mother entered the room. Anxious for Mr Percival to leave as soon as possible, she added a few more lines and quickly made her conclusion.

The letter being signed and sealed, she gave it to Mr Percival with a look that expressed her most sincere thanks. The gentleman put it into the right pocket of his greatcoat, the left one being filled with bread and cheese so that he need not break his journey should he be hungry. Kissing his mother and she returning that kiss, and with a bow to Lady Caroline, Richard Percival set out with all speed for Angelsea Court.

Lord Angelsea had not slept that night. He had gone constantly to his sister's rooms as if there he could find something of her presence. He picked up her Prayer Book and read the service of matrimony and wondered if she might be saying those very words in the same instant he read them. When his mind did not dwell on his sister, he thought of Isabella and of the comfort she might have been to him. He felt sure that, if Isabella had remained among them, Caroline would have opened her heart to her and received the most prudent advice.

'My dear,' said Mrs Cox when Isabella sat down to breakfast after her dreadful night, 'you look a proper fright!'

The young lady explained that she had not slept well.

'So much is obvious from your countenance,' said Mrs Cox, and then, with, for her, a remarkable energy, added: 'The day is good. You should go about in the air.'

'But, madam,' said Isabella, 'will you not have need of me?'

'Not if you are so sick looking. You appear worse than sickly, you look unhappy, and that I could never abide.'

This, thought Isabella, was one of the truest statements Mrs Cox had ever uttered. She sometimes thought that Mrs Cox was ill only to give her the excuse of spending her time at watering-places and enjoying the entertainments they provided both in and out of season. In the past two years alone she had been at Cheltenham, Scarborough, Malvern, Bath and Matlock. In addition, she talked of leaving Hawbury and going on to Tunbridge and then to the Continent.

Though Isabella had gone every day to drink the waters since the first occasion on which she had toasted her dear Montagu and Lady Caroline, Mrs Cox had always gone with her. This morning, when Isabella was almost bundled out of doors so that she would not appear unhappy, was the first morning she had been at liberty to properly explore the town.

She determined that she would first go to the library and pay her subscription there, perhaps pausing to consult some of the periodicals. Accordingly, she went to the bookshop and for a small fee was permitted to sit down at the table reserved for ladies. Here she made every attempt to concentrate on an article pertaining to the latest discoveries by Sir Joseph Banks. Yet try as she might, Isabella could make no sense of it. The words jumbled before her eyes, and the whole sheet of print reduced itself to the words 'Sir Roderick'. She endeavoured to reconcile this scrap of information with what else she knew of her life before her meeting with Lord Angelsea's horses. She knew that any child's first duty is towards its father, and that his should be the first name to be heard from its lips. Was it possible, then, that this Sir Roderick was her parent?

Yet she was still as certain as she had been when she first protested the fact to Lord Angelsea that she was an orphan.

Isabella had spent some time in this train of thought when she became aware, from a small cough, that an attempt was being made to attract her attention. Isabella looked up and observed Mr Bunce. She had not seen the clergyman since the day of the broken jug and, closing the journal she had been attempting to read, got up and gave him her hand.

Mr Bunce regarded her very intently and said: 'Miss Napier, I fear you are not well.'

'I confess, sir,' Isabella replied, 'that I did not sleep well.'

'It does not surprise me,' said Mr Bunce sadly.

'Mrs Cox has sent me out to walk.'

'That was her way with her former companion,' said Mr Bunce. 'Do you know for what reason she was sent away.'

'I do,' said Isabella, 'and I am greatly surprised that Mrs Cox declined to dismiss the footman.'

Mr Bunce did not reply to this. Instead, he said: 'My dear Miss Napier, since by your own admission you are at liberty, may I request you to honour my wife's invitation?'

Isabella answered that she would like nothing better, and so they walked together to Mr Bunce's house. Without any ceremony, Mr Bunce took her at once into the room in which his wife sat, surprising the good lady, who was engrossed in reading a pamphlet which she immediately put down on seeing that she had company. Isabella wondered how she would ever find it again, for there were papers and bulletins on every surface in the room, and so many on the floor that they threatened to flow out of the room and down the stairs. On top of one of these piles sat the pug, his only chance of procuring a place before the fire.

If Mr Bunce resembled the pug, Mrs Bunce resembled it even more. Standing side by side, the couple resembled nothing more than two pepper castors, though their natures in no way resembled the fiery nature of that spice. If Mr Bunce still wore a wig, Mrs Bunce kept him company by still wearing Watteau pleats at the back of her gown.

They sat down together and the tea was brought in, the tray placed on top of a pile of papers as thick at least as the five volumes of Miss Burney's *Cecilia* piled one on top of the other. Mrs Bunce having poured the tea and Mr Bunce having handed it around, Isabella looked about her, expecting the sugar.

'Ah, my dear,' said Mrs Bunce. 'You will think this most particular of us – indeed, I know we are laughed at by many people for it – but we have quite given up the use of sugar . . . '

Mr Bunce finished his wife's sentence: 'We will have nothing here that is produced by slavery.'

'Indeed, not!' said his wife, taking up the thread of conversation again. 'There is no point in saying anything, if one does not act upon it.'

'But if you must take your tea sweet, Martha shall bring you honey,' said Mr Bunce.

Isabella said she would take her tea with nothing but a little cream. She had just placed her spoon in the saucer when Mrs Bunce exclaimed: 'My dear Mr Bunce, why do you stare so at Miss Napier?'

It was obvious from the clergyman's reaction that his wife's interruption had startled him. 'I am sorry, my dear,' he said in a flustered tone. 'It is only that I seem to have some recollection of a locket that was very similar to the one that Miss Napier is now wearing.' And he begged Isabella that he might have a closer look at it.

She unfastened the jewel and handed it to Mr Bunce. He turned it over in his hand several times, then shook his head, saying: 'There must be many such lockets in the world.'

'Pray, Mr Bunce,' said his wife. 'You have never been interested in ornament or adornment, so why should a locket have caught your attention?'

'It was the occasion of a wedding . . . ' He stopped. 'Miss Napier is not interested.'

'No!' cried Isabella. 'I am very interested and would hear every detail. If it is a story you feel you can tell,' she added, thinking of the imprudent tales of weddings and the lack of them she had heard from Mrs Cox.

'It was the occasion of a wedding,' explained the clergyman, 'the happiest wedding I have ever attended, excepting my own.' He cast a fond glance at his wife.

'If only all couples could be as happy as we!' said Mrs Bunce, returning his look.

'I remember the jewel because the bride wore something very similar around her neck.'

'Can you remember the name of the lady and gentleman, sir?' asked Isabella, thinking that if the bridegroom had been called Sir Roderick . . .

Mrs Bunce put out her hand to Isabella. 'My dear, I am afraid you will be disappointed. Mr Bunce has such a hard time with names. I have been variously Amelia, Augusta and Alicia before he has settled on my proper name of Amy.'

'I fear what Mrs Bunce says is true,' said Mr Bunce, at length giving up the effort of remembering. 'I have quite forgotten the name of the happy couple, though I can still remember their happiness.'

Isabella was disappointed. She had always felt that her locket held some clue to her true identity, and even the discovery of the owner of a similar locket might have led to the name of the jeweller who was responsible for their design.

The Bunces and Isabella sat the whole morning in conversation, and Isabella was much more in spirits when she returned to Mrs Cox's house. She had half run home, expecting to be chided for staying out so long. But Mrs Cox, who seemed oddly fatigued with her morning activity, asked her only if she had enjoyed her walk.

At Angelsea Court, Lord Angelsea, intending to send out fresh enquiries about his sister, drew her face with the purpose of having an engraving made and bills posted saying that her friends were anxious to have any information of her. He tore up half a sketchbook until he made a likeness that satisfied him.

Then, deciding that he did not want to play the tyrant and hunt down his sister like a common felon, he decided to destroy that sheet of paper.

In the moment before he severed Lady Caroline's mouth from her eyes, he noticed some pencil marks on the other side of the leaf. He turned it over and saw a sketch that he had made of Isabella when she was unaware of being observed. He remembered now the happiness of the evening. Caroline had been at the harp playing a selection of country airs, Isabella had been embroidering the slippers he now wore, and he had been sitting at the table supposedly occupied in consulting a gazetteer but more engaged in looking at the two young ladies. He had pulled his sketchbook towards him and, in the pretence of listening to his sister, had drawn a likeness of Isabella.

The young lord now turned the paper before him, looking sometimes on the likeness of Isabella and sometimes on that of his sister. They were both very different in beauty, but each had her own will. Isabella had determined on going to Mrs Cox, whom Montagu had met once and thought to be an odious woman, and Caroline . . . he preferred not to think of what had been her choice.

If Lord Angelsea had been such a fop as the late-departed, and not lamented, Mr Whistler, he would have put his head on his arms and wept. He did not; instead he sought to divert himself by the balancing of some accounts.

Lord Angelsea was still engaged in this pursuit when Mr Percival, his horse near dead under him, rode into the courtyard, demanding that the letter he carried be taken at once to the master of the house.

The trepidation that Lord Angelsea felt when he saw that the letter was in his sister's hand can be imagined. As soon as he had read it, he called at once for Mr Percival to be brought to him.

Before Mr Percival had made his bow, Lord Angelsea asked him: 'Are you the Mr Percival mentioned in this letter?'

'I am, sir.'

'And is this letter true?'

'I do not know,' replied the young man in some confusion. 'I have not had the liberty of reading it.'

'But did my sister write it of her own accord?'

'Yes, sir,' and she instructed me to bring it to you without delay, which for her sake I have done.'

'I believe you, sir,' cried Lord Angelsea, noting the respect with which Mr Percival spoke of Lady Caroline. 'I will go at once to fetch her. You shall stay here as my guest for as long as you wish.'

'Thank you, sir, but I cannot accept.'

'But you must be exhausted from your journey.'

'I am tired, certainly, sir, but I know from what your sister wrote down for my mother and myself that there is some danger in our neighbourhood. She could not tell us how far she had walked after her escape, but I cannot imagine it to have been more than ten miles, given the nature of the terrain. If there is so much danger at so small a distance from my mother, I must return to her as soon as I can borrow a horse.'

'You shall have any horse. You shall have my own horse!' cried Lord Angelsea, offering Mr Percival a favour he had never yet granted to anyone else.

'I should not trouble you about your own horse,' said Mr Percival, thinking that any horse that was Lord Angelsea's favourite must be very valuable and that in his anxiety to be home he might lame the beast.

'Stay!' cried Lord Angelsea. 'Why do we talk of horses? My carriage will be here in ten minutes. We shall travel together. You shall tell me every detail of how you found my sister and her condition.'

So Montagu and Mr Percival set out together.

Lady Caroline spent the day engaged in writing down an exact record of the adventure that had befallen her. When she had covered every sheet that was in Mr Percival's desk, Mrs Percival had brought her receipt book, and so after a recipe for fricassee of pigeons came the information of Mr Whistler's death. Mrs

Percival watched her as she wrote, reading with disgust each sheet as it was finished and thinking perhaps that, once all the horrors were recorded, Lady Caroline's voice might return to her and enable her to dwell on the happier circumstances of her life. Yet when Lady Caroline retired for the night, Mrs Percival's chamber having been put at her disposal, it was only with a glance and gesture that she could thank the good lady for all her hospitality and kindness. She did not know that the lady's generosity went so far as Mrs Percival's sitting up all night outside the door, guarding Lady Caroline with Richard Percival's cocked pistol.

It was a wise precaution, for, as her son had guessed, Sir Roderick lay little more than an hour's ride away. Being a man of some intelligence, even if some of that intelligence had been squandered by the nature of his life, it did not take long for Sir Roderick to guess at the name of the woman Mr Whistler had mistaken for Isabella. It was necessary now to find Lady Caroline with all speed and to find some way of silencing her.

Still in delirium from the previous evening and with his mind fuddled by drink, he could think of only one way in law that this could be done, and that was marriage. If he could find some means of making Lady Caroline his wife, her evidence would not be admissible in any court in the land. But how to achieve such a union? Then the necessity of putting another log on the fire and the memory of how hard it had been to break the ground to bury Mr Whistler, reminded him of how keen the previous night had been. He congratulated himself on being rid of an encumbrance by the simple expedient of the weather, imagining Lady Caroline lying as stiff as a board in some ditch, as silent as the grave. And having disposed of one lady, his thoughts turned to another. He would find Isabella, and he would have her! He owed it to Mr Whistler's death.

Isabella knew nothing of this, of course. After she had returned from the Bunces, Isabella and Mrs Cox had gone to the baths, where Mrs Cox decided she would be totally immersed and

urged that Isabella do the same. The young lady declined, preferring to take a glass of the water and to make her silent toast to
her dear Montagu and Lady Caroline.

When she reached the tap, there was a scene of great excitement,
and enquiring its cause of a young lady, Isabella was told that a
masked ball had been announced to celebrate the anniversary of
St Valentine. It was to be the largest assembly of the winter, and
since the new assembly rooms were not yet completed and the
dancing must be in a room of a only moderate size, invitations
would be at a premium.

'But,' said the young lady, recognizing Isabella as Mrs Cox's
companion, 'Mrs Cox is sure to be invited.'

'Do you think so?' replied Isabella.

'For certain. It is to celebrate love' – and she stressed the
word 'love' – 'and if Mrs Cox goes, surely you must go too.'

'That must depend on Mrs Cox,' answered Isabella.

'Do you not want to go?' asked the young lady with the
greatest surprise, for she craved nothing more than to know her
own invitation to the ball was secure.

Isabella considered the matter. Was the prospect of sitting at
home with a novel in any way comparable to the prospect of a
masked ball?

The young lady rattled on: 'If Mrs Cox is invited and you
decline to go, I should be very happy to supply your place.
Should her infirmity mean that she cannot stand up to dance, I
should be very happy to sit with her and see that she is supplied
with all she requires.'

Isabella thanked her and said: 'I should not like to disappoint
you, but I think that if Mrs Cox is invited and asks me to go
with her, I must accept. Can I trouble you to tell me what the
theme of the costumes is to be?'

'Vice and virtue,' replied the young lady, who, seeing some of
her companions, went to join them. Isabella began to consider
what sort of costume she might choose, and then checked herself
for being premature.

She need not have troubled for, on their arrival home, James the footman told them that an invitation had arrived not five minutes after they had left the house.

'Well, Miss Napier,' said Mrs Cox, 'I know it is not possible to go against nature. I suggest therefore that I assume the guise of one of the vices and you adopt that of virtue.'

The evening was spent in discussion as to which morality Isabella should represent and which sin should be adopted by Mrs Cox, Mrs Cox taking great delight in discussing wickedness without any reflection on the quality of virtues. At length, they decided that she would go as Sensuality and that Isabella should go as Prudence.

'We must be certain to advertise what we have decided on,' said Mrs Cox. 'There is nothing in the world so tedious as a masked ball when one's friends do not find one out!'

Long before the hour at which her brother's arrival could be expected, Lady Caroline, still silent, was looking out for Lord Angelsea's arrival. She stood at the window, her hand on the glass, surveying the small village street that ran in front of the house. She was so intent on looking out for her brother and his carriage that she did not notice a lone man on horseback. He seemed just part of the traffic of the highway.

However, Sir Roderick saw her. So great was his shock that he almost tumbled off his mount. Here was another creature presumed dead returned to haunt him. He looked back but was not mistaken. Lady Caroline Angelsea still lived and breathed.

With whom was she accommodated, and for what purpose? He would have his answer at the nearest inn, where he knew all information on the neighbourhood would be forthcoming for the cost of a few pints of beer.

The inn at which he stopped was a small place and wary of strangers. Nevertheless he ascertained that the house in question belonged to a gentleman called Mr Percival. This knowledge having been ascertained, Sir Roderick determined that he would destroy the lady by any means in his power rather than undertake the necessity of a marriage as a way of obtaining her silence. He took a positive pleasure in imagining his hands around her neck, her imploring eyes, just enough temporary release of pressure for her to tell him the whereabouts of Isabella, and then the death of Lady Caroline Angelsea would dispose of any threat to him.

He was all for going at once to Mr Percival's house and destroying the lady when he noticed that the agitation this thought had provoked in him had attracted the attention of several other customers, who seemed to be taking the greatest interest in him. It became clear to Sir Roderick that these men might be proved very creditable witnesses to his being in the district, and it was therefore necessary for him to construct an alibi for himself before he could safely murder Lady Caroline.

He settled his bill and set off to visit Sophia, who he knew from past experience would keep any secret of his entrusted to her. And so he set off for Ducoeur Castle.

Lord Angelsea was all for driving directly to the snug Queen Anne house that Mr Percival had described as his and his mother's abode, but the said Mr Percival, with a prudence he had possessed since childhood, insisted that they should put in at the local hostelry to make a fresh toilette. Lord Angelsea understood the wisdom of appearing before his sister in the most normal state that his agitation could assume, and accordingly he agreed that he should step down from his coach with Mr Percival.

Mr Percival, being somewhat more used than Lord Angelsea to making his toilette in a country inn, was washed and refreshed before Lord Angelsea had re-tied his stock and had stepped down into the body of the inn, hoping for a kidney or two, some sausage, perhaps a piece of bacon and a couple of new-laid eggs.

He was half-way through his meal when he was approached by the innkeeper, an amiable fellow who, through his profession and good nature, knew the secrets of half the neighbourhood. He begged that he might have a word with Mr Percival and was instantly invited to sit down with him. This done, the landlord broached the fact that certain enquiries had been made in the same room not some two hours before, by a stranger whom he believed to be of a certain rank.

Mr Percival begged the landlord to let him know the exact nature of the information which had been requested. The gentleman was just about to embark on his story when Lord Angelsea joined them. Not liking to sit down, even in his own house, with such fine company, the landlord got up and said that he would leave the gentlemen alone, but Mr Percival insisted that he should stay and tell Lord Angelsea about the stranger.

The tale told, and with the greatest accuracy, no exaggeration being made as to the height of the stranger or the fact that his only question had been to know the name of the owner of a certain house towards the edge of the town. When the landlord had left them, Mr Percival and Lord Angelsea addressed themselves as to what motives a stranger should have for asking such a question and to try to deduce his name and his intentions.

Mr Percival came to the conclusion first. 'I fear,' he cried, 'that in some way he has found out the presence of your sister at my house.'

'I must agree with you,' replied Lord Angelsea.

'Then,' said Mr Percival, pushing his plate away from him and declining to finish his meal, 'you must come to the house and take her away at once, before the fellow can lay any further plans for her abduction. And I vow by all that is good, that should the blackguard try to take any further advantage of her, he shall have me to answer to!'

'It is not only my sister you must think of, sir, I fear you have placed yourself and your mother in some danger.'

'I should not wish anything I have done to bring harm to my mother!' cried the impetuous young man.

'Your sentiments as a son do you credit,' said Lord Angelsea 'But I fear that the damage is already done. The stranger knows your name and your abode.'

Mr Percival nodded his head in acknowledgement of this fact.

'Therefore,' continued Lord Angelsea, 'when I take my sister away, I shall insist on your mother joining us for her own protection.'

'Sir, you are too good.'

'Mr Percival, I shall be very strict upon this matter. And as I fear that your mother will not agree to accompany us, and leave you at home, I invite you now to also be one of the party.'

Mr Percival could only reply that this should be governed by his mother's opinion, though in truth he had already in his heart vowed that he would accompany Lady Caroline to the ends of the earth, in the hope of performing any small task that might give her comfort.

Lady Caroline's joy at the arrival of her brother quite overwhelmed her. She ran to him and threw her arms around his neck. She then burst into tears but could give no word of greeting and, though supplied with paper and pencil, her agitation at her meeting with Lord Angelsea prevented her from forming letters in any shape that might be easily read.

While brother and sister were being thus united, Mr Percival took the opportunity of passing Lord Angelsea's fears about their safety to his mother.

The lady, who had the advantage of him in having read every word of Lady Caroline's account of her abduction, had already made up her mind that flight was necessary but feared throwing herself or Mr Percival on any of their relations, in case through their own peril they should bring danger to others. She agreed readily that she would put herself under the protection of Lord Angelsea and accompany Lady Caroline wherever her brother thought it sensible to bestow her, and she begged her son, her only child to have survived infancy, to think of the duty he owed her and to go with them.

Within the space of an hour, Mr Percival had put his papers into a strongbox, paid off the few servants that attended on them, at the same time presenting them with testimonials to which Lord Angelsea put his name and seal. The servants, though thus recommended to positions far higher than they had had in the Percival household, were very sorry to be dismissed in such a hasty fashion. In order to rectify this situation, Mr Percival had to explain a little of the danger that threatened him and their mistress. When this was done and their own interests considered, they agreed that flight was the only answer. They begged, however, that they might be given some address in order to inform their old employers as to how they prospered.

It was arranged that all such letters should be lodged at the inn from whence the warning had originated and that all such letters should be sent for at such time as it was safe to do so.

The Percivals had little plate, but what they had was put into its bags and carried out to Lord Angelsea's coach, that gentleman being determined that the home of his sister's rescuer should be as safe from burglary as he could make it. The shutters were put up and their bars placed across them. Having handed his sister into the coach, Lord Angelsea lent his assistance to Mrs Percival with the words: 'Madam, it shall all be put right, and, if it is in my power, I shall make up for your inconvenience twenty times over.'

And so Sarah Percival quitted the house to which she had come as a bride with no certainty of ever returning.

🌿 TEN 🌿

In which Sir Roderick Ducoeur enters Isabella's bedroom

Lord Angelsea's first thought had been to take Lady Caroline to stay with her sister, Penelope, Countess of Mullingar, in Ireland. But it being less than a month since his eldest sister had returned home together with the necessity of having to explain how Lady Caroline come to lose her voice caused him to reconsider this strategy. He also felt that Penelope might not receive Mr Percival and his mother as he, Montagu, would wish. His first instinct to Mr Percival had been gratitude for what he had done for Lady Caroline, but on closer acquaintance he had come to regard the young squire as a man of intelligence and Mrs Percival as a woman of quiet sense and practicality. He also thought there might be some advantage to Lady Caroline for having on hand so fervent a protector as Mr Percival and so motherly a woman as Mrs Percival.

Next, his fervent desire to see Isabella led him to suggest that they should all go to Hawbury.

'No, sir, I cannot allow it!' cried Mr Percival.

Lord Angelsea was at a loss as to what in his suggestion could provoke such an outburst from Mr Percival.

'My lord, consider how your sister was abducted in the place of the young lady who you have known as Isabella Napier and whose name we have now discovered to be Broderick and ask yourself if you do not think that Sir Roderick will make another attempt to abduct that young lady.'

'For Isabella's sake I would do anything to prevent it,' said

Lord Angelsea, so afraid for Isabella that he did not attempt to disguise his feelings for her.

'Do you not think that by our bringing Lady Caroline and her friend together in the same place, that Sir Roderick finding out one lady might discover the other?'

Lord Angelsea at once saw the wisdom in this argument, and since he would do nothing that could introduce Isabella to any danger he saw that any plan to visit Hawbury must be abandoned.

The possibility of some seaside resort was then discussed, but they decided that, its being so out of season for visiting such places, their arrival would almost certainly be noticed. Since this was the thing that Lord Angelsea and Mr Percival were determined to avoid at all costs, they decided finally that their safest means of obscurity lay with some small country family, who might very properly expect to see their relations at this time of the year.

Lord Angelsea, being possessed of such a set of relations in the form of second cousins, immediately ordered the coachman to take the road in the direction of Borsetshire. The journey was slow, Lord Angelsea having made it a rule with himself, after his collision with Isabella and his subsequent encounter with the highwayman, never to travel fast at night unless the moon should be at its brightest. It was therefore the end of the week before they began to approach the final stage of their journey.

When they came to about ten miles off, Lord Angelsea stopped the carriage at a blacksmith's. He demanded to know where the best horse in the neighbourhood could be obtained. The blacksmith boasted that he himself was the man fortunate enough to own the animal requested, and Lord Angelsea, having looked over the salient points of the beast and ascertained that this was true, rode on in before them to announce the imminent arrival of Lady Caroline and the Percivals at the house of his cousins.

Everything was made ready to receive the party, and by the time they arrived it was as if their visit had been decided upon six months earlier. The kindness and tact with which the visitors were greeted was everything that Lord Angelsea could have wished for. And that night, for the first time since Lady Caroline had been snatched, he slept deeply enough to wake refreshed.

Meanwhile, Isabella looked every day for a letter from Angelsea Court. None came, Lord Angelsea being most anxious not to alarm her in any way. She felt this separation from Lady Caroline and her brother very keenly, something she was often chided for by Mrs Cox, who on one occasion, finding the butter rancid, said that she put it down completely to Isabella's appearance and not to the fact that the butter had been kept too long. Isabella, trying the butter herself, could find nothing wrong with it, but Mrs Cox insisted it was so bad that it made her ill.

A similar fault had been ascribed to the coffee the day before, and the bread the day before that. Indeed, it seemed to Isabella that taking any form of breakfast so little agreed with Mrs Cox that she ventured to suggest that the lady should leave off taking that repast altogether.

The suggestion made Mrs Cox quite cross. 'I am not to blame if the food makes me ill,' she said, promptly leaving the room.

It became Mrs Cox's daily habit to insist that Isabella must take the air for the sake of her spirits. Should Isabella offer any excuse of the weather being inclement, the lady would insist that there was some essential errand to be run, pins to be obtained, tonics to be bought and, whenever she could not think of anything else, the water on which the town's fame had been established to be fetched so that Mrs Cox might take a glass.

On the occasions when it was not very wet underfoot, Isabella delighted in having a chance for an excursion, which not infrequently ended at the library or in the Bunces' crowded parlour. When her steps did not lie in either of these directions, Isabella was at liberty to explore the town, discovering on her expeditions numerous little byways and soon becoming so familiar with the town that she thought she might walk through it blindfolded without any difficulty.

It was on one of these rambles that she was observed by the ever-obsequious Mr Edgecliffe, who had come to the baths in the wake of an heiress, who, though pretending to spurn his attentions had, nevertheless, let her movements be known in most precise detail.

On the first occasion he saw Isabella, Mr Edgecliffe doubted the evidence of his own eyes, but when he saw her on a second occasion and then a third, he became convinced that the young lady who issued from Mrs Cox's house each morning was Isabella Broderick.

No intercourse had occurred between Mr Edgecliffe and Sir Roderick since the former had been compelled to cut off his buttons and present himself to Lady Sophia Ducoeur in the guise of one who had been grossly attacked upon the road. However, calculating that being known as the friend of Sir Roderick would go some way in improving his standing with the parents of the heiress, Mr Edgecliffe now decided that it was his duty to at once inform Sir Roderick that Isabella was living in Hawbury with every appearance of being well connected.

After discovering the name Percival at the inn, Sir Roderick had returned to Ducoeur Castle with every intention of being able to declare, should any questions be asked, that he had spent the whole of the previous week in residence. He doubted there would be any difficulty in keeping up this pretence, for he felt certain that he would be supported in it by Lady Sophia. To be sure of this, he made great play of being her fond brother, even going so far as to purchase some ruby ear-rings. That they were paste was no matter. To Lady Sophia's weak eyes they sparkled as if they had been found in the deepest mine. And to the lady their real worth lay in the fact that when she expressed a wish to kiss her brother in thanks, he assented to her placing her lips on his cheek. The memory of this moment was relished by Lady Sophia a hundred times a day thereafter, a delight that was in no way comparable to the pleasure that Sir Roderick felt on receiving the news that Isabella Broderick had been discovered. Sir Roderick had never desired to go into the North of England and had often declared Bath to be the only spa worth visiting, but now he was on fire for Hawbury and would not be deterred from going there by the fact that it was out of season.

Mr Edgecliffe had been making his own enquiries about Isabella, thinking by such means to put himself even more in Sir Roderick's favour. He had discovered that she was invited to the ball on St Valentine's Day, and, thanks to Mrs Cox's desire to be known, the costumes that the two ladies intended to adopt.

Isabella had begged Mrs Cox that she might be allowed to make their disguises. The lady would hear nothing of it and insisted on calling a dressmaker, with whom she had her fittings in the strictest confidence, maintaining that she wished to surprise Isabella with the finished garment.

Isabella's own dress as Prudence was based upon the image of Britannia, the prudent guardian of a great nation. The design was taken from the back of a penny, and thus the garment was somewhat loose, which, when the face was obscured by a mask, would make the figure of its wearer impossible to guess.

All this information was conveyed to Sir Roderick, Mr Edgecliffe having gone to some trouble to procure an invitation for him. Sir Roderick was determined to arrive at the town and present himself at the ball in his own disguise. Thus he might have the pleasure of making love to Isabella without her being able to guess who he was. He vowed that he would woo her and reveal his true identity to her only when she said that she loved him. He decided to present himself to her as a Virtue, and to this end ordered a costume to be made up which proclaimed Constancy, this being symbolized by a combination of elements of classical costume with artefacts connoting the passage of time.

The night of the ball arrived. Mrs Cox and Isabella retired to their rooms to dress. Isabella had just finished arranging her hair when she was summoned to Mrs Cox's room, where she was surprised to find that the lady had made only half her toilette.

'Is something the matter, madam?' asked Isabella, who, it being nearly half-past six, expected the chairs to be at the door at any moment.

'That wretched woman!' cried Mrs Cox, stepping up to the mirror and regarding herself.

'Pray, what is the matter?'

'The matter? The matter is, that having stuck pins in me for seven days together, my dress is too tight!'

Mrs Cox was made so angry by this fact that Isabella did not like to suggest that the cause of the dress not fitting might have been the craving for cake that the lady had recently developed, something that Mrs Cox said was caused by her not being able to take breakfast.

'Madam, if the dress is too tight, I will run and get my work-box so it may be altered,' said Isabella.

'There is no time for alterations!' cried Mrs Cox. 'Your dress hangs very much looser than mine. There is nothing for it. We must swap clothes. You must see it is the only solution!' And Mrs Cox almost grabbed at Isabella, saying: 'We shall be late. It must be done at once!'

Isabella had no inclination to adopt the disguise favoured by Mrs Cox. It was immodest almost to the point of vulgarity, the skirt cut very short and the stomacher very low. Most of the arms were exposed even above the elbow, and it had no petticoat.

'Make haste!' cried Mrs Cox.

Isabella, seeing she was insistent, began undressing herself, supposing Mrs Cox would instruct her maid to do the same. But the mistress, with a touch of modesty that was not hinted at by her costume, insisted that she would not stand in her shift in front of Isabella, and that her maid would bring the outfit to Isabella's room as soon as Mrs Cox was divested of it.

Isabella flew to her room, thinking about what alteration she could affect in the costume it was now ordained that she should wear. She had, very fortuitously, unpicked some net from a dress that afternoon, and, in the time between removing her own costume and being brought Mrs Cox's, she had managed to devise a way of attaching it to her new dress in such a way that would extend the length of the skirt. This alteration, together with a fichu at the neck, would make the costume appear a little less like a chemise.

She had threaded her needle before Mrs Cox's dress was brought into the room, and, being the most competent of seamstresses, it was the work of a few moments to make the alterations. By the time she joined Mrs Cox in the hall to await their chairs, she felt that if her costume was not dignified it was, as far as she could make it, decent.

Mrs Cox was amazed to see what a transformation she had made in such a short time and began to wish that she had agreed to Isabella fetching her workbox when it had first been suggested.

The chairs arrived and they joined the throng progressing towards the assembly rooms. Some of the gentlemen had declined any mode of transport excepting that of their own two feet, so Isabella overtook not only Patience but also the Devil before she was set down at the place where all invitations were to be handed in, this being a precaution to keep out imposters, something that was greatly approved of by those who had gone to the desperate lengths to obtain their tickets. Her admittance being given in, she was then almost carried along by the multitude and into the rooms. Mrs Cox, now dressed as Britannia, was prudently only just in time to join her.

Sir Roderick, who had arrived in the town that afternoon, had come to the assembly rooms very early and procured a vantage point from which all those admitted might be observed. The best position from which this might be done was at the head of the stairs, and it was here that he now placed himself with Mr Edgecliffe and some of his companions. All the men appeared to be engaged in earnest conversation, but in truth each one was looking for his own inamorato, all having been furnished with every detail of the chosen young lady's apparel.

In the same way, Mrs Cox had furnished her friends with the information that she would appear as Sensuality and her companion as Prudence in the dress off the back of a penny.

The tide swept forwards before Sir Roderick and his friends. Mr Edgecliffe felt quite at a loss. His heiress had made a particular point of telling him that she would appear as Chastity, and now it seemed as if this was the virtue that had been decided upon by half the ladies in the company. Finally, he thought he saw her and left his companions, swearing that he would stand up to the first dance with her or know himself to be a fool.

Still the crowd came and still Sir Roderick searched, sure that even if he did not know every detail of Isabella's costume, the fact that it was worn by that lady would instantly cause him to recognize her. At last he was rewarded by seeing a woman who was dressed in the exact outfit Mr Edgecliffe had described to him as that chosen by Isabella. Though the gown was loose, he noticed that Isabella had thickened a little around the middle since he had last seen her. Had he not known her character, he might even have described her as being in an interesting condition.

Anxious to follow her, Sir Roderick quickly broke off his conversation in order to follow the lady to the great room that stood at the heart of the proceedings. The figure stopped and looked around, obviously expecting some gentleman to come up and invite her to dance, but no man appeared. Sir Roderick, thinking that in the circumstances his interest might be very well received, went up and offered his own hand.

The lady seemed surprised and backed away from him, saying that she did not mean to dance and was only looking out for her friends. After a couple of minutes, still no friends having been forthcoming, Sir Roderick repeated his offer to give her his hand. Again he was declined, the lady insisting that she had no intention of dancing. Sir Roderick then offered to show her to a chair, thinking that a little intimate conversation might serve his purpose as well as any set of quadrilles. To this suggestion, Prudence did assent, and Sir Roderick, who had already ascertained the most discreet corner in the room, led her to it and was surprised by the lady's immediate demand for a glass of punch. This he did at once, congratulating himself on the fact that, if Isabella, whom he had formerly known to take only the smallest amount of liquor, had developed a taste for it, he was now provided with a ready means for overcoming her senses.

While Mrs Cox was giving orders to Sir Roderick, Isabella had been invited by a gentleman dressed as Avarice to take her place on the floor. She was surprised at being approached so quickly and gave her ready consent. During the dance, she became aware that her movements were being closely scrutinized by a small group of ladies who stood at the edge of the floor. From this notice, Isabella feared that all her attempts to make her disguise a little more modest had failed and that she was being condemned for her want of taste.

The dance came to an end and Isabella was led back to her place, where the gentleman pressed her hand and whispered, 'It was not supposed you would dance.'

Isabella thought this a very strange remark. What was a ball for but dancing? The gentleman indicated that he wished to go in search of other friends, making a small bow and parting by saying: 'We have never been introduced, but I have always admired a woman of your spirit, above all others.'

Isabella expected to be left alone and provided with an opportunity to inspect the throng. Scarcely had she had time to turn around before the ladies who had been observing her surrounded her, swallowing her up in their company. Isabella was addressed by the tallest lady, who had taken advantage of her height by disguising herself as a Brobdingnagian.

'My dear!' the giantess cried. 'Are you not afraid of causing some accident to yourself?'

'Indeed not, madam. I am fond of exercise. It has been my habit to walk regularly.'

Here the circle gave a merry laugh, and one of the ladies, tapping Isabella's shoulder playfully with her fan, said: 'You cannot puzzle us.'

'We know your preference as to exercise,' continued another. 'And with whom!' put in a third.

'You have mistaken me for someone else,' said Isabella, trying to make a motion to move away. The giantess detained her by placing a hand on her arm. 'We are all aware of how much a certain condition may be disguised by tight binding,' she said.

This was too much for Isabella, who almost wished to fling off her mask and reveal her true identity. She sought to bring the unpleasant interview to an end by saying: 'I do not know whose condition you refer to, but I assure you it is not my own.'

'Mrs Cox!' remarked the lady with the fan, and Isabella saw in an instant what had happened. Mrs Cox, who had so arduously broadcast what her appearance at the ball was to be, had confounded her friends by changing dresses with Isabella at the last moment. The ladies that surrounded her believed Isabella to be Mrs Cox and Mrs Cox to be with child.

Isabella understood now why the seamstress had been consulted behind closed doors, why the dress had suddenly appeared so tight and why, when an exchange of clothes was insisted on, Mrs Cox had made hers in the privacy of her own room. Mrs Cox was with child, and there was no Mr Cox in existence.

'I am Miss Napier!' she cried in a voice so loud that she might have been the giantess, the general noise in the room making it only audible to the ladies round her.

'Do you mean to try to trick us still?' asked the lady who had struck Isabella on the shoulder. Isabella sought furiously for some means of convincing the crowd of harpies around her that she was indeed who she said she was.

Suddenly, it came to her. 'I presume you are acquainted with Miss Napier?' she asked. The ladies nodded, and one of them opened her mouth to make some comment on Isabella's character, but before this could be done Isabella put her hand to her neck to draw their attention to her locket.

'Is this not the poor jewel she always wears?' said Isabella, turning so that it could be seen by all. The giantess assured her that it was.

'Then,' said Isabella, 'since you say you know Miss Napier, have you ever seen her without this locket?'

'No!' answered the lady with the fan, who was beginning to believe that Isabella was indeed the woman she purported to be.

'Do you think that if I were Mrs Cox, that Miss Napier would lend it to me? Or that I, supposing I were Mrs Cox, and having the quantity of jewels that that lady possesses, would choose to wear such a thing?'

The vehemence of Isabella's protest aroused in the ladies a suspicion that they might indeed have been mistaken, and very quickly the circle around Isabella shrank away on the pretext of something else in the room having caught their attention. Isabella, left alone, cast her eyes around for Mrs Cox. The information she had received from the ladies inclined her to turn her attention away from the dancers and in the direction of those who were seated.

Finally, after several minutes of inspection, she discovered Mrs Cox, in her loose dress, engaged in conversation with a gentleman whose costume proclaimed him to be Constancy. It occurred to her that Prudence and Constancy should appear a very fine union, were it not for what she now knew of Mrs Cox's condition. The time was not right for an interview with her mistress. Isabella turned back to the room, catching, as she did so, the elbow of a lady who stood beside her.

The lady was heavily disguised in the habit of a nun. Isabella would otherwise have recognized her as the young lady she had met at the pump, and who had first informed her about this evening's ball. Isabella apologized for the awkwardness of her movements. The young lady, who was in a very good humour, having achieved her heart's wish of obtaining an invitation to the ball at the very last minute, accepted the apology very gracefully, saying: 'It is not possible, in such a large crowd, to avoid running up against people.'

'You are kind to say so.'

The conversation having begun, the lady endeavoured to continue it a little longer.

'Can you tell me?' she asked Isabella. 'Do you think it true that there is to be waltzing?'

This was the first Isabella had heard of such a thing, and she answered that she did not know.

'I do hope there will be,' cried the young lady. 'They say the man and the woman must stand up very close for a waltz.'

'I have heard that to be so,' agreed Isabella.

'And the lady must place her hand on the gentleman's shoulder, and his behind her back. And I do declare, that under their disguise there are half a dozen young men I should like to dance with in that fashion!' The sheer thought of such dancing was almost as pleasurable to the young lady as the dance itself.

At this moment Isabella was approached by a gentleman who, though he wore the apparel of Complicity, was actually Mr Edgecliffe. He bowed low and offered Isabella his hand, which, anxious to get away from the chatter of the young lady, she was eager to accept.

Mr Edgecliffe did not have many accomplishments except in the eyes of the heiress, but one of them was dancing. Isabella found her enthusiasm for the reel matching his, and she so thoroughly enjoyed herself that when the dance was finished she felt quite dizzy and begged that they might stand a while.

Mr Edgecliffe offered to fetch her something to cool her. Isabella declined, saying she would go and stand beside one of the windows that had been opened. For though it was February, the assembly and the sheer number of wax candles which illuminated the room had made the atmosphere very stuffy. Mr Edgecliffe, having established that his heiress was occupied with a couple whom he knew to be her parents, accompanied her.

After the usual remarks made in such circumstances, Isabella found herself surprised by the person disguised as Complicity suddenly saying: 'Madam, there is a fact with which I must acquaint you. Miss Napier is not the person she appears to be.'

Isabella was amazed. She was not aware that she was familiar enough with any young man for him to penetrate her disguise. 'Can I ask how you have found her out?'

'I have met her before. Her name then was not Napier but Broderick.'

A weaker woman than Isabella might have given way at the pronouncement of a name so similar to the one that had come to her the night of her horrible dream and which, being written down, she had read over twenty times a day in order to provoke her memory. Isabella herself, scarcely believing what she heard and uncertain as to whether she had caught it aright due to the commotion in the room, took the opportunity of asking Mr Edgecliffe to repeat the name.

He did so. Isabella gasped, holding her hand to her throat. As she did so she disturbed her fichu, and the locket that had convinced the giantess of her true identity now proclaimed itself to Mr Edgecliffe.

'Is it possible,' he exclaimed, 'that you are Isabella Broderick?'

'My name is Isabella, certainly.'

'But was it not put out that you were to wear the guise of Britannia to symbolise Prudence?'

'Indeed, but at the last moment I was put to the necessity of changing garments with the lady to whom I am companion.'

'And I thought all the time I was talking with Mrs Cox.'

'You are not the first to make that mistake,' said Isabella, thinking of what she had heard earlier.

'Then let me correct that mistake by re-acquainting you with the friends from whom you were so roughly parted. See there, that gentleman in the shape of Constancy?'

Isabella was surprised that she was being invited to regard the gentleman who was in a very close tête-à-tête with Mrs Cox.

'He is your most constant admirer.'

For a moment Isabella entertained the hope that the person she was being invited to observe was Lord Angelsea. But he and his sister were not expected for another month, and Isabella knew his character well enough to know that he would not use the occasion of a masked ball to renew their friendship. Neither could she imagine him choosing to single out Mrs Cox, especially considering what she had now discovered about that lady's character. The gentleman now lifted Mrs Cox's hand to his lips, kissed it and held it while some joke passed between them, a motion that was not observed by Mr Edgecliffe, who continued to press Sir Roderick's cause to Isabella.

'He was parted from you by a most unhappy accident, the very day you were to marry, and has been searching for you since.'

'Pray, sir, what was that accident?'

'Do you remember nothing of that day?' asked Mr Edgecliffe, surprised it did not play the part in Isabella's memory that it played in his.

'I do not,' replied Isabella. 'I know only that there is something pertaining thereto, which I believe has caused me great unhappiness.'

'Do you not remember being carried away by a highwayman?' said Mr Edgecliffe, who had told the story so many times that it had achieved the status of a truth.

Isabella wondered at this fact. Lord Angelsea had told her of their strange encounter with the brigand, and how, on seeing her, he had ridden off, refusing even to take Lord Angelsea's purse. Then she remembered the story she had heard at Mrs Cox's house, and it came to her that the two events were one, and that the lady who featured in each story was none other than herself.

'Sir,' she asked, 'were you present at the encounter when, if I am to believe you, I was carried away?'

Mr Edgecliffe assured her that he was, even going so far as to mention receiving a scratch on the arm in her defence.

'And the other gentleman also?'

Again Mr Edgecliffe confirmed that this was the case, and that Sir Roderick had fought with the strength of Hercules. Isabella now asked the name of her champion.

'Madam, his name is Sir Roderick Ducoeur.'

If her face had not been covered, Mr Edgecliffe would have

seen all the blood drain from it as Isabella learnt the true identity of Constancy.

'I beg you, sir,' she said to Mr Edgecliffe, 'give me a few moments to reflect upon what you have told me. I should like the opportunity to make my own mind clear on the matter.'

Mr Edgecliffe assured her that this would be done.

'When I have had a moment to think,' she continued, 'I should like the opportunity of talking to Sir Roderick. I should not like my presence here to come as a shock to him, and I ask you, Mr Edgecliffe, to please prepare him. I shall wait here.'

'Sir Roderick will be happy indeed to know that you desire to speak to him,' said Mr Edgecliffe, and with a bow he left to do what Isabella had requested of him.

Isabella did not need time to think. The lie she had been told about the highwayman, the stranger who had tried to wrestle her care from Lord Angelsea, while denying he knew her, what she had that moment heard from Mr Edgecliffe, and the fact that the whole incident had taken place at midnight, outside a church, all indicated that the marriage Mr Edgecliffe had mentioned was clandestine. And Isabella, though she did not remember the details of the night, knew it was not in her nature to perform such an act. Her purpose in requesting some time alone was to find some means of escape.

She looked towards the doorway by which she had entered less than an hour before. It was now completely filled up by spectators, who watched the crowd in an attempt to discover the identity of the dancers.

Isabella turned to the door at the other end of the room, but it had been filled up in the same manner and among the mass was the figure of Sir Roderick. Isabella's attention now turned to the window, struck by the sudden tapping upon it of the branch of a tree which grew outside. The music starting and the eyes of the whole assembly fixed on the novelty before them, and the sash being already half open, it was the work of a moment for Isabella to throw it up completely and climb out.

Using the tree, and in her flight completely oblivious to the perilous footholds it afforded her, Isabella descended to the ground, tearing her scant costume almost to pieces as she did so. Almost at the same moment, Mr Edgecliffe succeeded in reaching Sir Roderick and imparting the news that by virtue of her locket the real Isabella had been discovered and wished to see him. Sir Roderick instantly demanded to know where she was; Mr Edgecliffe indicating the window, it was discovered that Isabella had vanished.

The sash pushed up to its topmost point indicated how the escape had been made. Without even an 'excuse me', Sir Roderick thrust his way through the crowd in the doorway and ran down the stairs by which the servants supplied the rooms. The door to the street at the bottom of these stairs stood open, so that the man who had been sent to the pump could regain access without the necessity of putting down his buckets. Sir Roderick arrived on the pavement just in time to see the sheen of Isabella's dress disappearing around a corner. He threw off his mask and followed her.

Isabella ran. It did not take her long to discern that she was being followed. She dared not slow her pace by turning around to discover her pursuer, but she remembered Mr Edgecliffe's words and guessed that it must be Sir Roderick, a suspicion confirmed by Sir Roderick's calling out to her: 'Isabella, why do you run from me? I, who have never intended you any harm.'

The lights of the assembly rooms were soon behind her. A few more steps must bring her to the utter darkness where she must make her way with caution to avoid falling. They came now to the hill, where Isabella gained some slight advantage by being accustomed to walking up it every day. But as soon as the ground began to level out again, Sir Roderick easily made up the distance. Isabella felt that at any moment she would feel his breath on her neck. Sir Roderick calculated that ten more paces would bring her within his grasp.

The door of one of the houses suddenly opened. A man appeared with a lantern to see what was causing the commotion. Seeing Isabella's state of dress and the way in which she was pursued by a gentleman who had obviously been at the assembly rooms, he concluded that some harlot had robbed the man of his watch or pocket-book. In no way wishing to involve himself in the matter, he closed the door as quickly as he had opened it, but not before its beams of light had shown Isabella Sir Roderick's face, the face from her terrible dream, but it also provided her with a means of escape by illuminating the entrance to a small alley.

The darkness again surrounding them, she flew to where she had seen the ingress and hid herself, putting her hand over her mouth so that Sir Roderick should not hear her breathing.

Sir Roderick, who had not noticed this sudden diversion of Isabella's, ran on for some distance before he discovered that he had been eluded by his prey. How far he had stopped from her hiding-place, Isabella did not know. But she guessed that as she could hear his curses it was not very far. She dared not go back the way she had come for fear of attracting his attention by her movement. She must continue down the way she had taken, which, from her familiarity with the town, she believed to link with the turnpike road.

She went on, through the puddles, steeling herself not to scream when a rat ran over her feet. At every moment she expected that the alley would lead out on to a street. Suddenly, however, she found herself faced with a brick wall. The way was completely blocked! Isabella could do nothing without going back the way she had come. She had gone almost three-quarters of the way when, reaching out to feel her way, she felt a hand touch her own. She shivered in alarm.

'Who are you?' asked the voice of a small child.

'My name is Isabella, and, hush, we must be quiet.'

'Why must we be quiet?' asked the child, who from the tone of voice Isabella guessed to be a girl.

'Because I am being followed.'

'Who is following you?'

'A gentleman.'

'For what reason?' asked the child.

'He wishes me harm,' replied Isabella.

'Why?'

'I cannot explain that now. I must find my friends.'

'What friends?'

Isabella tried to think what friends she had in Hawbury and remembered the kindness she had been shown by Mr and Mrs Bunce. She felt sure that they would help her. 'They go by the name of Bunce.'

'Is Mrs Bunce your friend?'

'I hope so.'

'Is she the lady with the pug?'

Isabella answered in the affirmative and for some seconds the little girl ran out of questions. Then she asked: 'Are you going there now?'

'I would, but I am not certain of the way. Is there any path from here that does not go by way of the road I turned in from?'

'Why do you not wish to go by the road?'

'I fear the gentleman may be waiting for me.'

'How long have you been here?'

'It feels as if it has been a very long time, but I think in truth it has been only a few minutes.'

'Will you give me a penny,' asked the child 'if I take you to Mr Bunce's house?'

'Most certainly,' said Isabella. This arrangement being concluded, the girl took Isabella by the hand and urged her to follow. The child gave her name as Hester, asking in the same sentence if Isabella thought it a pretty name, and led her back towards the end of the alley. Just before the wall, the child turned suddenly to the right and, urging Isabella to lower her head, took a short passageway that gave into another alley. From this they gained a street that Isabella recognized as the one in which Mr and Mrs Bunce had their abode.

It was Mr Bunce's habit always to leave a light outside his front door, so that anyone in search of a parson might easily find his house without his neighbours being disturbed. Isabella trembled at the thought of stepping out into the light and being observed, so she opened her purse and showed the child a sixpence, promising that she should have the whole amount if she would step up and knock on the door.

The door was opened by Mr Bunce, who was in the process of putting his coat on with one hand while holding his Prayer Book in the other. Immediately he asked the child where he was wanted, and if for a birth or death, knowing no other reason for being called to his front door at this time of the night. Hester explained that she had come at the request of Miss Isabella, who hoped that Mr and Mrs Bunce would admit her. Mr Bunce threw the door wide open in a gesture of greeting and begged Hester to tell Isabella to step in, which, the child after being rewarded with her sixpence, did.

If Mr Bunce was shocked at Isabella's dirty, ragged, almost naked appearance, he did not show it. He called for Mrs Bunce, who apparelled Isabella from her own wardrobe. Then he listened to Isabella's account of what had happened that evening without the slightest interruption.

When Isabella had done, Mr Bunce turned to his wife, who answered his look by saying: 'Isabella now knows the true nature of Mrs Cox. There is no need to dwell on it longer.'

'I had hoped,' said the clergyman to Isabella, 'that you would have been reunited with the friends we so often talk about before Mrs Cox's condition should be known and your reputation tainted by your acquaintance with her.'

Isabella explained how she had understood from the Countess of Mullingar that Mrs Cox's morals were of the highest order. At this Mr Bunce shook his head sadly, saying he believed the lady to be the mother of several young children, each of whom was being raised in a different spa.

'How I pity them!' cried Isabella. 'I have always declared myself to be an orphan, but sometimes I cannot help thinking that my birth was not legitimate.'

'I cannot believe that to be so,' said Mr Bunce.

'Nor I,' said his wife.

'Though there is certainly some mystery to the conditions of your birth,' continued Mr Bunce.

'Which I am sure will be resolved,' finished Mrs Bunce.

The conversation then turned to what she could do to escape the attentions of Sir Roderick, a matter which, because of the lateness of the hour, Mr Bunce said would be better resolved in the morning.

Sir Roderick, meanwhile, had returned to the assembly hall, where the Master of Ceremonies made some fuss as to his being readmitted without the necessary ticket, the matter made good only when Mr Edgecliffe was called to vouch for him.

'You are a great fool,' said Sir Roderick as they went up the stairs together.

'Sir, how was I to know that a young lady should escape through an open window by way of a tree?'

'Why did you not bring her to me yourself?'

'You were engaged.'

'Damn me for it!' said Sir Roderick, cursing himself for kissing Mrs Cox's hand when he had presumed it to be Isabella's, 'and damn you for being as great a fool as Mr Whistler.'

'Mr Whistler?' said Mr Edgecliffe. 'I do not believe I have made his acquaintance.'

Sir Roderick would not be drawn any further on the matter, saying: 'Now, sir, you have left me with the unpleasant duty of acquainting Mrs Cox with the fact that Isabella Broderick has run away.'

Mrs Cox was surprised when Sir Roderick attempted to talk to her again. She had been on the point of enjoying his flirtation when a disparaging remark about Lord Angelsea by Sir Roderick had caused her to realize that she was being wooed in mistake for Miss Napier. Mrs Cox, who had always been of a jealous nature, had instantly dismissed his attentions. No sooner had Sir Roderick moved away from her to be greeted by Mr Edgecliffe than she regretted this action, thinking that it would have been far sweeter to have encouraged Sir Roderick's attentions to herself and thereby deprived Isabella of her lover. Now the opportunity presented itself again, she was determined to take it.

She invited Sir Roderick to sit down beside her and asked if he had found Miss Napier.

'Madam,' replied Sir Roderick, 'there is no such person as Miss Napier.'

'How can that be?'

'Miss Napier is an imposter. Her real name is Isabella Broderick.'

'You surprise me, sir.'

'And there is another fact of which I must inform you.'

'What is that?'

'Do you see the lady in the room?'

Mrs Cox looked around and was forced to admit that she could not see Isabella anywhere. 'No, sir.'

'Let me tell you, madam, she has run away.'

'That is not possible.'

'Madam, I observed her escape.'

'Perhaps she has returned home with a headache.'

'Without informing you, her friend?'

Mrs Cox was forced to admit that this was unusual, but she still maintained that this might have been the case.

'Then, madam, I pray you send to your house to find out if she is there.'

Mrs Cox, thinking that by this ruse she might gain an extra half-hour of Sir Roderick's company, readily agreed. Sir Roderick was instantly on his feet, insisting that he would go himself as they had brought no servants to the ball. Mrs Cox was forced to give him her address, adding that any linkboy would know it.

Sir Roderick, on the door of Mrs Cox's house being opened to him, explained his purpose and was told by James that Miss Napier had not returned. 'Then,' said Sir Roderick, 'it must be supposed that she has run away.' And he begged the footman that he might be let in to Isabella's room to ascertain if this were indeed true. For a moment the footman hesitated, but Sir

Roderick pressed his point home, saying: 'There may be some piece of note, or it may be possible to discover from which of her possessions are missing what direction she intended to take.' Having thus convinced the footman, Sir Roderick was brought candles and shown to Isabella's room.

The very fact of being in a place that Isabella had inhabited filled Sir Roderick with the most delicious sensations. Her workbox, still lying open on the table with her thimble beside it, aroused his intense interest. He picked up the thimble and toyed with it between his hands, kissing it for the sake of the finger that had inhabited it. He then turned to her wardrobe, taking each dress in turn from its peg and examining it quite minutely. He caressed the chemises, imagining that they had touched Isabella's skin, and fell into raptures at her shoes, taking each in turn and stroking its kid and placing his hand inside where Isabella's warm foot had been.

Then he sat down at her dressing-table, picking up in turn each of her brushes and combs and all the dainty items necessary to a lady's toilette.

Sir Roderick then went to her bed and lay down upon it, imagining that Isabella lay beside him and returned his kisses and embraces. He was drawn from this reverie by James enquiring at the door if he needed any assistance. Sir Roderick said he did not and, leaping from the bed, started to pull out drawers from the tallboy so that he might be supposed to be in search of something.

He quickly found a packet of letters, which Isabella had made tidy by tying them up with a ribbon. Unfastening their binding, Sir Roderick soon discovered that they were all from Lord Angelsea or his sister. These he perused in the hope of discovering where Lady Caroline and her brother had hidden themselves. To his dismay they all dated from before Lady Caroline's abduction, and in his anger he had no more use for them than to throw them into the fire.

There was no need now for Sir Roderick to linger, but he could not bear to leave Isabella's room without some intimate, physical memento. He searched for something to take away with him and saw her fur muff. Crossing the room, he seized it from the small table where it had been left by Isabella. To conceal it about his person, he tried to fold it and discovered that there was something in its pocket. Sir Roderick drew it out. It was the invitation from Mrs Bunce.

⫷ ELEVEN ⫸

In which several proposals are made

The following morning, at their conference about Isabella's future, Mr and Mrs Bunce said that they feared for her safety if she remained in the town a moment longer than was necessary. They urged Isabella to return to Angelsea Court and the protection of Lord Angelsea.

'I fear that is impossible,' replied Isabella.

'Surely, my dear, they would not wish you to be in danger?' said Mrs Bunce.

Isabella, who had not before confessed that she had not heard from Lord Angelsea and his sister for some time, and feared that they had lost interest in her, replied: 'Madam, I have had no correspondence from them for nearly three weeks.'

'So long! Did you not tell me when we first met that it was their custom to write each week?'

'That was the agreement when I left Angelsea Court. But though I have kept to my side of the bargain, I have received no reply.'

'That is certainly peculiar,' said Mr Bunce.

'Most!' added his wife.

'So you see, I am in some difficulty as to where to go.'

'I have been thinking half the night,' said Mr Bunce, 'about the name Broderick. I am sure it is one I have come across, but whose it was I cannot at this moment recall.'

'Mr Bunce, I have told you before, you should keep a note of these things.'

'I know, Mrs Bunce, but as I have pointed out to you, my

dear, if I spent my time taking note of everybody I met, I should only meet half the number.'

Isabella supposed this to be true, but she could not but be disappointed at the vagueness of Mr Bunce's memory for recalling names.

After further discussion on the subject, Mr Bunce suggested that the three of them should travel to Angelsea Court and that Mrs Bunce and Isabella should put up at an hotel, while Mr Bunce had an interview with Lord Angelsea as to whether he and his sister wished to sever their connection with Isabella.

'Mr Bunce, I cannot agree to it!' cried Isabella.

'Why not?'

'They have not written . . . I cannot presume on them.'

'But, my dear, from all you have told me of Lord Angelsea, he has protected you once, and I am sure he will protect you again,' said Mrs Bunce.

'Montagu . . . ' Isabella stopped, her cheeks crimson.

'So that is how it is, Mr Bunce,' said his wife, giving him a knowing look.

Isabella felt quite uncomfortable at having betrayed so much of her emotion.

'Any lord who rescues a young lady deserves to be loved by her,' said Mr Bunce, for he had seen his daughter blush just as prettily when she was in love.

'Perhaps he has not written because he is ill.'

'Ill?' cried Isabella.

'Would you go to him if he were?' asked Mr Bunce.

'Indeed I would,' was her reply.

'Then why not go to him now, when he might help you?'

Isabella gave way, and they decided that they should set out for Angelsea Court as soon as they could. Mr Bunce hurried off to see his curate about the care of his little flock while he was away. Isabella and Mrs Bunce occupied themselves by making some adjustments to an old dress of Mrs Bunce's, the sending for Isabella's clothes having been categorically rejected.

By noon everything was ready, and the party set out on

horseback. Isabella having expressed the opinion that Sir Roderick would have spies posted at all the coaching-inns in the district, they decided, despite the weather, to travel cross-country to the first place from which they felt they could take a coach in safety. It had been agreed that Isabella would travel as the daughter of Mr and Mrs Bunce. At first Mr Bunce had reservations about telling such a lie, but Mrs Bunce pointed out that they did indeed have a daughter, one by the name of Charlotte, who had changed her name from Bunce to Gerrard by marrying an American gentleman and who had gone to live with him in his own country, and that if they kept their remarks general, no falsehoods would occur.

As dawn was breaking that morning, Sir Roderick Ducoeur, having drunk even more than was customary with him, had been carried back to the rooms that Mr Edgecliffe had taken for him and had been put into bed by the servants. As a consequence, he did not wake until late that afternoon and it was almost dark again. Mr and Mrs Bunce and Isabella could have taken the coach from Hawbury in perfect safety. The reason for his waking was the delivery of a note from Mrs Cox which begged him to call on her so that the two of them might meet undisguised. Having nothing better to do, and hoping that Mrs Cox might have heard some news of Isabella, Sir Roderick arrived at Mrs Cox's house within the hour. The lady herself came down to greet him.

'Madam, I am come in reply to your note,' said Sir Roderick.

'Sir,' said the lady, all aflutter, 'I did not expect you to come so soon and therefore have invited no company to sit with us.'

'I have no objection to our sitting alone if you have not?' said Sir Roderick.

'Indeed, no,' replied Mrs Cox, who had been determined on this course since she sat down to write her note.

'I am sure, sir, that since you are a friend of Isabella's, there can be no impropriety however we meet,' and, so saying, she took him upstairs.

Once they were seated, Sir Roderick found Mrs Cox a much

more handsome woman than he had supposed her to be the previous night when he had detested her for disguising herself in the costume Isabella should have worn. She, in her turn, was most impressed with the gentleman's looks. They fell into a very natural conversation and for whole quarter-hours together the subject of Isabella was quite forgotten. Mrs Cox congratulated herself on making a conquest of the gentleman, Sir Roderick congratulated himself of making a conquest of the lady. On parting, it was agreed by both of them that another interview would be necessary the following day. Sir Roderick returned to his rooms completely satisfied but without having made any enquiry regarding the Bunces.

To remedy this, Sir Roderick next day called very early on Mrs Cox. Though he explained to the servant that he enquired only after an address, the servant returned to say that Mrs Cox was not yet dressed but had something particular to say, and that she begged Sir Roderick to wait while she put on her clothes. Alternatively, she might talk to him from behind a screen.

'I would not wish to put the lady to the trouble of dressing,' said Sir Roderick, who was, in consequence, invited to step into the lady's bedroom. His interview with Mrs Cox was soon concluded satisfactorily, the lady begging him to come to her again the moment he had any news concerning Isabella. Reminded of his true love, though still desirous of keeping up his intercourse with Mrs Cox, Sir Roderick set off to make enquiry at Mr Bunce's house.

He knocked on the door several times, but no one responded, and Sir Roderick concluded that the place was deserted. He noticed that a piece of paper had been attached to the door, which at first glance he had assumed to be a bill for an auction or some such thing. On closer examination, he perceived it to be the name and the address of the curate who was to supply Mr Bunce's place. At this point a young girl, not above seven years of age, stepped up to him and asked: 'Why have you come here?'

'To pay a visit to Mr Bunce,' replied Sir Roderick, carefully observing the fresh-faced young girl.

'Are you a friend of his?' asked the girl.

'I should like to be.'

'Why would you like to be?'

Sir Roderick thought the child enchanting and, wishing to be on more familiar terms with her, asked her name.

She replied that it was Hester.

'It is a pretty name, and you are a pretty girl.' He was reminded of how he had first taken notice of Isabella when she was about the same age.

'Why does everybody wish to see Mr Bunce?'

'Everybody?'

'Do you know the name of the young lady who came here?' Hester asked.

Sir Roderick replied that he did not.

'If I tell it you, will you give me a penny?'

'I shall certainly give you a penny, and if it is the right name I shall give you more.'

'What is the right name?'

'You must tell me.'

'Isabella,' the child pronounced.

Sure on this point, Sir Roderick now asked the child if she could conduct him to the curate's house. When she said she could, he took her hand in his saying that he should not like to lose her.

'I want my penny,' said Hester when they arrived in the street where the curate lived.

'You shall have sixpence,' said Sir Roderick, 'if you will give me a kiss as well.' The kiss was permitted, and Sir Roderick could not desist from winding some strands of her hair around his fingers, for the girl reminded him so much of Isabella at a very young age.

'That is enough, sir,' said Hester, waiting to see if any more money was forthcoming. When it was not, she ran off in search of another means of procuring a living.

Sir Roderick approached the curate's door.

On being asked the whereabouts of Mr Bunce, the clergyman's deputy was only too keen to boast of how he had lent his superior a gazetteer of the county in which Angelsea Court was located.

Sir Roderick at once assumed that this was the destination of Isabella and the Bunces and determined to follow them with all possible speed, mindful not just of Isabella but also of the fact that she would lead him to Lady Caroline.

In consequence, he did not attend Mrs Cox that night. As a result the lady, who had dressed in her finest for him, turned instantly from love to a violent dislike, determining that she should have her revenge on Sir Roderick. She then called in James and bade him spend the evening in entertaining her.

When Isabella and her companions arrived in the vicinity of Angelsea Court, Mr Bunce installed the ladies in a small hotel and, despite being begged to take something to eat by both his wife and Isabella, set off straight away for Angelsea Court.

Isabella had described the house to him in some detail, but even her description had not prepared him for the magnificence of the place. The house had been built some two hundred years previously and was designed in such a way that, when the rooms were illuminated, the whole residence glowed as if it were a lantern. The light of the setting sun now played on the panes of the windows, making them appear like rubies. Mr Bunce, determined on his interview with Lord Angelsea and running over the nature of its contents in his head, did not notice.

His hopes were cruelly dashed when he discovered that Lord Angelsea was not at home and had not been for some days. Mr Bunce enquired of the servant when he could be expected, but was told that no one knew. He then asked if there was any possibility of directing a letter to Lord Angelsea, the answer again in the negative. The poor clergyman, his heart full of pity for Isabella, set off across the park with the step of a man twenty years his senior.

Isabella was waiting in a state of great trepidation. Mrs Bunce attempted to keep her entertained with a string of anecdotes about her own daughter, but Isabella scarcely heard them. The return of Mr Bunce, some hour before he was expected, confirmed her worst fears. Lord Angelsea and Lady Caroline had forgotten her.

Mrs Bunce, who had always been of the opinion that it was want of eating that killed pining lovers and not broken hearts, now insisted that the three of them should sit down to dinner and discuss what should happen next. Isabella declared that she had no appetite.

'It is our duty to eat,' said Mr Bunce, the meal having been brought in. 'If we do not eat, how does the agricultural labourer earn his bread?' And by this means Isabella was persuaded to take a little chicken.

Throughout the repast, various proposals were made concerning Isabella's future. Mrs Bunce wondered if an old school friend who had married a Scottish gentleman would consent to have her in the role of companion. Mr Bunce suggested that she went as governess to the family of a lady who was one of his keenest supporters in the abolition of slavery. Isabella herself thought that she should advertise, her movements by this means being completely anonymous. Despite all the suggestions that were made, not one could be universally agreed on, and they had fallen all into a silence when Mrs Bunce suddenly cried out: 'I have it!'

'What is that, my dear?' asked the fond husband who wished with all his heart that a plan should present itself with which all three of them could concur.

'We will go to America and live with Charlotte and Mr Gerrard.'

The enormity of this announcement was so great that Mr Bunce and Isabella could only regard each other. When finally he regained his tongue, Mr Bunce said: 'My dear, I have loved you these thirty years and have never yet heard you venture such an insane opinion.'

'It is not madness!' his wife replied. 'Charlotte begs us to come to her by every letter, and I should dearly love to see her little boys.' And at this, Mrs Bunce, who had tried always to think of others before herself, blushed, as she had done on first being introduced to Mr Bunce.

Isabella ventured a word. 'I think Mrs Bunce's plan of my going out of the country is a very good one. I have always heard that America is a place where anyone wishing to work is sure to find a reward. If Mrs Gerrard would have me and make some introductions for me, I would be very happy to go.'

'Alone?' asked Mrs Bunce.

'I have no fear of going alone,' answered Isabella.

'My dear Mr Bunce, you cannot permit it!'

'For Miss Napier's part' – for it was quite impossible for a man who had as much trouble with names as Mr Bunce did to remember she was now Miss Broderick – 'I can see the advantage, but as to the question of going with her . . . ' he said doubtfully.

'Then, sir, let us make a visit, taking Miss Broderick with us and returning alone,' said Mrs Bunce.

'My dear, think of the expense!' said her husband.

'Has not Mr Gerrard often said that he would bear the cost?'

'For us, Mrs Bunce, but what of Isabella?'

'If he will advance me the money, I shall repay him with interest as soon as I can find some employment,' said Isabella. 'And as I have said before, I feel quite confident of going alone.'

Mrs Bunce would not entertain this suggestion. At last it was agreed that they would all go, Mr Bunce having considered that there was as much, if not more, need of clergymen in America as there was in England. Accordingly, they planned to go the next day to Liverpool and take the first ship on which a berth could be provided.

Isabella slept fitfully that night. To be so near a place where she had been so happy, to be within a half-hour's walk of the dear room that had been given to her as her own, to remember the happy times she had spent with Lady Caroline and her beloved Montagu, all agitated her not a little.

It was but seven when she woke in the morning and went to

the window of her room to see a cold frost lying on everything before her. She knew that Mr and Mrs Bunce, being somewhat older than herself and tired with travelling, had asked that they should not be woken before eight o'clock, and she considered, therefore, that if she hurried into her clothes, as the cold demanded, she might walk to a place from which she might observe Angelsea Court and by such observation take her leave of it for ever.

Having decided on this measure, she dressed herself in the outfit that she and Mrs Bunce had so hastily cobbled together the morning of their departure, and, opening her door very quietly so as not to disturb the Bunces, who slept in the next chamber, she went along the passageway, descended the stairs and emerged into the cold fresh air. The ground was frozen beneath her feet, and she was able to keep up a good pace. Not many minutes passed before she could see the full magnificence of the house.

Isabella did not know how long she had been in contemplation of it when she heard a horse behind her. She turned, quite expecting it to be Sir Roderick, but looked instead into the eyes of none other than Lord Angelsea.

The gentleman kicked his horse on to the grass to prevent its slipping on the roadway, and the moment it had stopped he threw its reins over its head and dismounted.

Isabella trembled, expecting at any moment to be sent away.
'Isabella?' said Lord Angelsea, a tone of wonder in his voice.

'It is I.' Before Isabella could utter another word, Lord Angelsea had run towards her and embraced her most fondly, saying again: 'Isabella.' Then, without letting go of her hands, he fell to his knee on the frosty grass and begged her to be his wife, kissing her hands all the while.

'Do not kneel to me, sir,' cried Isabella.

'Why should I not kneel to the most beautiful woman in the country?'

'You flatter me.'

'You will flatter me more by accepting me,' said Lord Angelsea.

'Sir,' replied Isabella, 'for myself I would gladly marry you, if I were certain of what my past has been. But since I have been in Hawbury I have found out some particulars about myself which might in some way be able to lead me to my relations, who in return might have some information that would make it impossible for me to be your wife.'

'What sort of complication could there be?' asked Lord Angelsea, springing to his feet.

Isabella shook her head.

'Why should you presume there to be some objection?'

Again her pretty side curls jigged in the early sunlight.

'Isabella, I beg you.' Lord Angelsea seized hold of her hand, but she took it from him saying: 'I have discovered my true name. It is Isabella Broderick.'

'Yes, I know it,' was his reply.

'By what means, sir?' asked Isabella, not a little surprised.

'I will not answer you,' he chided, 'until you call me Montagu and, believe me, Isabella, for I care nothing if you are Napier or Broderick or plain Miss Smith, I will marry you!'

Tears came into the young lady's eyes, making them even more lustrous than usual. 'Oh, sir,' and she could say no more because her heart was too full. But it was certain from her demeanour that she would willingly give her hand to Lord Angelsea, a kiss all the affirmation that was required.

When they drew apart Isabella looked before her at all that would become hers upon her marriage: the great house, the park, Lord Angelsea . . . She was almost overwhelmed.

Lord Angelsea knew what she was thinking. 'You will be mistress of all this, Isabella. I only wish I had more to give you.'

'It is already too much.'

'No, indeed, it is too little. I would give you the world were it in my power. You have sealed your bond with a kiss, and I never knew a lady that was more certain to keep her promise. Oh, how happy Caroline will be for us!'

'How does your sister?'

Lord Angelsea saw now that he must dwell on the sad matter

of his sister and how she was mistaken for the lovely creature that stood before him, and the grievous consequences. But he did not want to alarm Isabella.

'How did you come here?' he asked.

'With some very good people.'

'May I ask their name?'

'It is Bunce. Mr Bunce is a clergyman. They . . . I beg you, sir, do not be distressed by this . . . they believe me to be in a certain danger.'

'Do you believe it also?'

'Yes.'

Lord Angelsea wished he had his pistol with him that very moment so that he might use it in defence of the lady. 'Tell me what it is, and I shall prevent it.'

'It comes from a gentleman that I know as' – Isabella's voice quavered – 'Sir Roderick.'

'Oh, my dear Isabella, I must tell you now that you are indeed in danger, and that it is very great. My sister Caroline was stolen from almost this very spot in mistake for you. Do not fear, she is safe, but she has lost the power of speech. She was taken in the roughest manner, to a secluded place and there introduced to a man whose name she has written down as Sir Roderick Ducoeur and where she was introduced as Isabella Broderick.'

'I have brought this danger to her!' cried Isabella.

'There is more, Isabella. It is very shocking.'

'I will hear it.'

'When Sir Roderick – he should not be addressed by the title of a gentleman – discovered that the lady who had been brought him was not you, he struck the fellow who had done the deed such a blow that he killed him stone-dead. My sister was the witness to the murder, and I am sure he would have closed her mouth by the same method had she not, by some divine grace, discovered some mechanic in the wainscoting by which she was propelled into a secret passageway. By this means she escaped, her body and mind intact but her tongue unable to make any accusation against the murderer.'

Isabella shivered.

'I have said too much!'

'No, sir, it is the cold.'

'Then before I proceed any further in the matter, you must be warmed. Where are your friends?'

'At the hotel.'

'Then we will go there immediately.'

They arrived at the hotel exactly as Mr and Mrs Bunce were leaving their room in search of Isabella. The introductions were soon made. They were both extremely shocked to hear what had befallen Lady Caroline and asked after her health with great solicitude. Yet both Mr Bunce and his wife realized from Lord Angelsea's story that Isabella was in even greater danger than they had at first supposed her to be.

Mr Bunce explained to Lord Angelsea his wife's intention of going to America. Lord Angelsea, though seeing the sense of the plan, put the strongest objections in its way, saying that Isabella's presence in the country was necessary to bring Sir Roderick to justice.

'Then, sir, what do you recommend?' asked the clergyman.

Lord Angelsea now explained the role of Mr Percival and his mother in the rescue of his sister and their going into hiding with her, and suggested that Mr and Mrs Bunce joined the party.

'I understand your reason, sir,' said Mr Bunce. 'But it means that if this wicked man – I use the word wicked with great sorrow but there is no other – if this wicked man finds one lady, he finds the other.'

As the conversation continued, it became apparent to Isabella that the threat to her person from Sir Roderick had reached out its hand and touched all those who were closest to her. How great was her responsibility for placing all these good people in danger!

She decided that, for the sake of the love and respect she bore them, it would be best that she should separate from them and go to live the rest of her life as a stranger to them. Compelled by this thought, and taking one long glance at Lord Angelsea, she slipped out of the room on the excuse of fetching a shawl that Mrs Bunce had been kind enough to give her.

Arriving in her room, she sent for pen and paper, meaning by way of a letter to explain to her friends that her departure had been her own decision and she had not been forced to it by Sir Roderick. She wrote first to the Bunces, thanking them for all they had done for her and asking them to remember her in their prayers. Then she addressed her lover:

> My dearest Montagu (for that you are) You suppose me to be the woman in the world most trusted to keep the vow I have made to you. I would keep it if I did not recognize the harm that might come to you through that vow. I shall always be a danger to you unless I am a stranger. It is my plan, therefore, to go away from this place and never see you further.

Here a falling tear made a blot on the paper.

> I would not wish for us to part without shaking hands and saying goodbye, but it must be so. Farewell.
> Isabella

She folded the note and kissed it and could not resist kissing it again. Then, leaving the hotel, she took the opposite direction to the one that she had taken an hour earlier.

So deep in conversation were the Bunces and Lord Angelsea that not for some time did they realize that the fetching of a shawl, which should have taken five minutes, had taken half an hour. Lord Angelsea ran to Isabella's chamber as though he were the wind. The room was empty. But there, in a spot where they might command the most attention, lay Isabella's letters. Lord Angelsea snatched up the one addressed to him and read the terrible truth. He then carried it and the letter addressed to Mr and Mrs Bunce downstairs, Mrs Bunce, that always practical woman, bursting into tears when she read what theirs contained.

Lord Angelsea determined at once to go after Isabella. But no one could say in which direction she had gone and the thickness of the woods which lay directly at the boundary of the little town would give any fugitive the cover he – or she – desired.

The path through the woods was the one that Isabella had taken, thinking that if she was followed she could hide herself in a thicket or in the branch of a tree. She had proceeded at a great pace for some way when she perceived a clearing in which a charcoal-burner and his family were at work. They were much surprised at the appearance of Isabella, not being used to seeing strangers. The woman of the group came forward and, recognizing that Isabella was of a station much above her own, asked if she could be of any assistance.

Isabella begged the woman for a cup of water which, it being brought, she drank in one gulp. Her thirst having been satisfied, she asked the woman if she could tell her of anywhere she might find employment. The woman looked at her with some surprise, making a sly comparison between her own hands, which were permanently black and gnarled from the fire, and Isabella's.

'It is of the utmost necessity that I find some means of providing for myself, for I have no one in the world to whom I can appeal for assistance.'

At this she was informed that there was a small town by the name of Weyton some ten miles off, where perhaps some employment might be obtained. Isabella asked if she could reach it before nightfall and was told that it would be dark before she could even hope to see the town and that the path she must take was very indistinct. But the woman added that she was going there herself the following morning, market day, and if Isabella would condescend to spend the night in their hovel, she could travel with her.

Isabella, who thought it preferable to stay in the humblest abode among company rather than on her own in the woods, assented. She passed the rest of the day playing at cat's-cradle with the children, and, after dining on a humble dish of vegetables and barley, she settled down to sleep.

The exercise she had taken that day and the lack of sleep she had had the previous evening meant that she soon fell into a heavy slumber, and when the woman woke her just before dawn she could have sworn that she had only just closed her eyes.

The woman walked so fast, despite carrying a heavy bundle on her back, that Isabella was hard put to keep up with her. It was just past nine o'clock when they arrived in the busy little town. Isabella, rewarding the charcoal-burner's wife with her last three pennies, parted from her and went in search of some form of employment that would provide her with food and accommodation.

Having taken careful note of all the industries in the town, Isabella decided that she would apply first at the milliner's, but no one was wanted there, and she heard the same story everywhere she applied. By two in the afternoon she was beginning to grow very anxious and had to keep bucking her spirits with the thought that the course she had taken was the right one. Soon she began to grow very hungry and could not help staring in at the window of a pastry cook's, as if by that means alone she could assuage her appetite.

When at last she withdrew her eyes from a tray of ginger-bread, she became aware that someone was standing behind her. She looked into the glass and saw his reflection. She recognized the man – it was Sir Roderick. Before she could make any sort of escape, he reached out and seized her by her elbow.

Isabella let out a small scream, which attracted the attention of a passer-by. His offer of assistance was spurned by Sir Roderick, who turned on him with the words: 'Sir, my sister has been grossly disobedient, leaving home against the express wish of her father. It is my intention to return her to him.' The gentleman touched his hat and passed on, with a final glance at Isabella. She opened her mouth to cry out after him, but Sir Roderick squeezed her arm so tightly that all she could think of was the pain.

Still holding her in this fashion, he began to lead Isabella along the street. His grasp was such that it was impossible to escape. Isabella feared that she had fallen into the very hands she had hoped to avoid.

'Where are you taking me, sir?' she demanded to know.

Sir Roderick laughed and looked at Isabella, saying: 'Your little friend is not half as pretty as you.'

Isabella tried not to make any reaction at the mention of Lady Caroline, but her feeling for her friend made this impossible. Sir Roderick, noticing the anxious look that had appeared in her eye, demanded to know where Lady Caroline was.

'I do not know.'

'I cannot believe you,' said Sir Roderick. 'I already know you have had an interview with her brother.'

'How?'

'On discovering you had left Hawbury, it was an easy task to find out your destination.'

'We told no one.'

'It was an error, then, to borrow a gazetteer.'

Isabella remembered how Mr Bunce had read to them on the journey about landmarks they had passed, though preoccupied as she had been in her own thoughts she had hardly heard him. To be found out by such a simple means! She feared it would never be possible to escape Sir Roderick and that whatever she did he would make her his victim.

'Sir, anything you do to me, you do from the evil of your own soul and not for love. I despise you, sir, and I will despise you to my grave, if I am brought to that grave by my own hand. I should be happy to be buried at the crossroads with a stake through my body for the sake of haunting you.'

Sir Roderick remembered what had happened that night at the inn when he had first tried to seduce Isabella. It put him in such a terror that he let go of her arm. Instantly, Isabella thought to throw herself into the crowd that thronged the market-place, considering that in this instance her greatest safety lay in being part of a large multitude.

It was some moments before Sir Roderick recovered his senses. When he looked around to see where Isabella was, she had entirely vanished. He spent the rest of the day enquiring for her, with the promise of a substantial reward for any information, but could find out nothing. He did not, this time, even have a curate he could approach.

When they realized that there was no hope of discovering which direction Isabella had taken, the Bunces and Lord Angelsea had once again discussed what should be done. Lord Angelsea decided that the best way forward lay in the apprehending and bringing to trial of Sir Roderick, and in consequence of this he decided that he would travel into Derbyshire and enquire there for any information. Mr Bunce begged to return with him, but Lord Angelsea decided that the clergyman and his wife should be kept out of the way of a man so unpredictable as Sir Roderick.

The Bunces finally agreed that they would travel north with Lord Angelsea and continue on to Scotland to stay with Mrs Bunce's school friend. Lord Angelsea promised that he would keep in regular correspondence with them. If Mrs Bunce was still more inclined to America than to Scotland, she did not say so but sat down obediently at her husband's request that she write to let her friend know that they were to be expected.

Not wishing his presence at the spa to be generally known, Lord Angelsea decided that he would put up in the next hospitable place and ride over whenever it was necessary.

When finally he reached the town, he went first to visit Mrs Cox. He had not been with her for more than ten minutes before he had evinced a strong dislike of her manner and her morals. He marvelled that his sister's disappointment in her marriage could have led her to renew a friendship with a woman whose standing in society called her own behaviour into question even more than those of the Miss Tanner whom she so despised. If he had little respect for Mrs Cox's manners, the information she gave him about Sir Roderick made Lord Angelsea detest him all the more. He did, however, gain one useful piece of information from the interview, and that was that

Mr Edgecliffe was still in the town.

When Lord Angelsea quitted Mrs Cox's, the lady holding out her hand to be kissed, which he did with great reluctance, his lips not even touching it, he begged that he might be allowed to send for Isabella's things.

'I am sorry to disappoint you, Lord Angelsea,' said Mrs Cox, 'but it has been necessary to dispose of them already.'

'Indeed?'

'Yes, I am afraid I was put to not some little expense by taking Miss Napier . . . Broderick to live with me. And I thought that by the selling of her things to recoup a little of my losses.'

At that moment a tradesman was heard in the hall below demanding to see Mrs Cox about the payment of some bill. It was obvious to Lord Angelsea that the lady was living beyond her means and that Isabella's possessions had been sacrificed for this reason.

Lord Angelsea then went in search of Mr Edgecliffe and found him at an hotel, engaged in conversation with a group of young men. Mr Edgecliffe was at the centre of the crowd and, having taken rather too much strong drink, was entertaining them with stories, in all of which he himself was the hero. Lord Angelsea approached the edge of the group and listened. Mr Edgecliffe was embarking on the story of how he had been involved in a fight with the most menacing of highwaymen. He was just about to describe how Isabella had been carried away when there was an interruption from Lord Angelsea. 'Sir, I beg to correct you.'

Mr Edgecliffe looked around to see who had spoken.

'Go on with your story,' cried one of the audience.

Again Lord Angelsea interrupted, this time stepping forward to make his point more precisely. 'This gentleman, whom I believe to be Mr Edgecliffe,' – Mr Edgecliffe gave a nod to indicate that this was so – 'is a liar. He put up no resistance. His only instinct, and the instinct of the gentleman who accompanied him and whose name I know to be Sir Roderick Ducoeur, was to run off, leaving me to protect the lady. Do you deny it, sir?' he asked, looking Mr Edgecliffe full in the face. 'Perhaps I should remind you of the place. It is called Carrick-on-Soar.'

'Sir, you have the advantage of me in knowing my name. May I be permitted to know yours?'

'I am Lord Angelsea. And I would request you, sir, to step somewhere quiet so that we may have this argument out in private.'

Mr Edgecliffe did not wish the degree of his falsehood to be generally discovered in case it should come to the ears of his heiress, on whom, when he had first told it, the story had created a great impression. He agreed, therefore, to step into a small antechamber off the room for the purpose of talking to Lord Angelsea.

When they were alone, Lord Angelsea demanded to know the precise details of what had happened directly preceding Isabella's running into the road on the night that Mr Edgecliffe had been describing in such great detail only seconds before. Mr Edgecliffe tried to evade the subject, pretending he had forgotten the evening in question. His attempts at such evasions began to annoy Lord Angelsea, who knew they were only attempts to gain time, while Mr Edgecliffe tried to invent some plausible explanation.

'The truth, if you please, sir!' demanded Lord Angelsea.

'Sir . . .'

'The truth.'

The matter came out in such dribs and drabs that to anyone without such a personal interest in it as Lord Angelsea, the tale would almost have seemed dull.

'And you meant to go along with Sir Roderick in the matter of this clandestine marriage?'

'I had no choice.' And to prove this was the case he told Lord Angelsea the story of the cock and the fox.

Lord Angelsea heard him out, despising anyone, who by such a foolish act as not closing the door to a hen-run, could throw himself into the hands of Sir Roderick. For though he certainly thought Mr Edgecliffe a silly young man, he did not consider him to be dangerous in the manner of Sir Roderick.

In return for Mr Edgecliffe's confidences, Lord Angelsea told him about the abduction of his sister. Remembering his heiress and thinking that he could not live if he was ever deprived of her, Mr Edgecliffe paled.

'I must tell you, sir, worse was to follow.'

'What was that?' asked Mr Edgecliffe in a low tone, expecting to hear of the dishonouring of the lady.

Lord Angelsea told him of the murder of Mr Whistler. At the mention of the name, and remembering the comparison that had been made on the night of the ball (between himself and Mr Whistler), Mr Edgecliffe now, despite the wine he had taken, suddenly very sober, sank so much at the knees that Lord Angelsea placed a chair behind him and begged he should sit down.

'I wish, sir, I had never been acquainted with Sir Roderick.'

From his demeanour and the paleness of his skin, Lord Angelsea was convinced that Mr Edgecliffe spoke the truth.

'Can I rely on you, sir?'

'If Sir Roderick could, how much more should a man of your nature and disposition.'

'Will you help me to find him and bring him to justice?'

Mr Edgecliffe considered for a moment. 'Sir,' he said, 'I have already revealed myself to you as not being a brave man. But I will do all that is in my power to assist you.' And springing up from the chair, he added: 'Here, I give you my hand and take yours for inspiration.'

It was decided that Mr Edgecliffe should remain in Hawbury in case he received any communication from Sir Roderick, while Lord Angelsea should return to his sister and Mr and Mrs Percival. Mr Edgecliffe made a very fine and solemn promise that should he have any piece of information, however small, about Sir Roderick, he would send it post-haste to Lord Angelsea, who was to ride south to discover if any progress had been made in Lady Caroline's recovery of her voice.

Lord Angelsea's first act on arriving at the house where his sister and the Percivals were lodged was to send for Mr Percival, who, he was firmly convinced, in contrast to Mr Edgecliffe was a very sensible young man, and who, Lord Angelsea suspected, regarded Lady Caroline's interests as his own. He acquainted Mr Percival with everything that had happened since he had left the company to return to Angelsea Court to find out if any enquiry had been made there by Sir Roderick or one of his minions.

Mr Percival insisted that since the matter pertained to them all, his mother and Lady Caroline should hear every detail, its being his firm opinion that the more minds that were concentrated on a matter, the more likely it was that the right solution should be found. Lord Angelsea asked him to prepare Mrs Percival for the interview, and, while this was being done, he took the opportunity of a few minutes alone with his sister to tell her how he had proposed to Isabella and how she had accepted him before her flight.

At the news of the engagement, Lady Caroline's looks were all happiness; at the news of Isabella's flight all sadness; and so eloquent were these emotions in her face that she had no need of the little book of paper and pencil she had fastened to her waist so that they might always be to hand. When her brother had finished his story, he stood in silence. Lady Caroline knew he was thinking of Isabella. She went up to him and wrote the words: 'You will find her.'

'I do not dare to think so,' replied her brother.

Again the pencil moved across the paper: 'I am sure of it.'

Mr and Mrs Percival entered the room at this moment and there was no opportunity of continuing the conversation either by way of words or on paper.

When they were all sat down together, Lord Angelsea told Mr and Mrs Percival and his sister everything that had passed since they had last met. Lady Caroline and Mrs Percival were both greatly grieved to hear about the true nature of Mrs Cox. Lady Caroline regretted now that she had not found a position for Isabella when she first requested one, but she was too wise a woman to dwell on the past and now endeavoured with her brother and her friends to find a way of making all their futures safe.

'Sir, I pity you and Lady Caroline for the loss of Miss Broderick, and I am only sorry that my mother and I have never had the opportunity of making her acquaintance. But it appears to me that the person we must find is Sir Roderick Ducoeur. Once he is stopped, everything else will come right,' said Mr Percival with his usual sharp intelligence.

Lord Angelsea consulted Mrs Percival as to her opinion on the matter. 'I am in agreement with Richard,' the good lady replied. 'And I think you should attend to the matter with all speed before he can do any other danger in the world.'

'In that case,' said Lord Angelsea, 'as soon as I and my horse have had an opportunity to rest, I shall set out to find the blaggard.'

'I beg you, sir, let me accompany you,' cried Mr Percival with a glance at Lady Caroline.

'No, sir, I think it would serve our purpose best if we were to divide. You will go to London, to find out the word that is on him there, and I shall endeavour to gain admission at Ducoeur Castle, for though I do not think it conceivable that I should find Sir Roderick within its walls, I may be able to gain a little information.'

Accordingly, the following morning Lord Angelsea and Mr Percival rode out in quest of Sir Roderick in much the same fashion as the knights of King Arthur had done long before. Mrs Percival and Lady Caroline watched them until they were out of sight and then, when the gentlemen could no longer see them, both took out their handkerchiefs and wept to think of the difficulties Lord Angelsea and Mr Percival now must face.

❦ TWELVE ❦

In which Isabella is doubted and Lord Angelsea makes the acquaintance of Louisa, Lady Amory

It now being the beginning of March and Sir Roderick having spent but one week at Ducoeur Castle since the New Year, a week when he had been so pleasant to her that he had gone as far as to allow her to kiss his cheek, Lady Sophia began to desire his return. As was usually his habit, she had no correspondence from him, Sir Roderick preferring to conduct all his business matters through his steward and never, apart from the paste rubies, having any personal matters that he wished to share with Lady Sophia.

The severity of the weather and the fact that Lady Sophia did not like to go out in the cold since she had had the smallpox had meant that she had spent the whole winter with very little companionship except that of her fawning maid Jane and the occasional visits of the Misses Timms, who were glad to find themselves being asked to sit down to tea as if, as they themselves said, the fiasco of Mr Jackson had been quite forgotten.

In consequence, Lady Sophia had been very lonely and had begun to reflect with more and more kindness on Isabella. She would often spend hours together thinking of what had befallen her at the hands of the highwayman. Sometimes she would enter these speculations in such depth that the morning would slip into the afternoon without her notice.

Sometimes, in her reverie, the villain was kind to Isabella, and she grew to love him with every show of love that she could give. At other times he was her despoiler and quite impervious to her cries and entreaties. It is hard to say which of these scenes was the most favoured by Lady Sophia. She had even tried setting them down, thinking perhaps to make out of them a booklet with some such title as *A Small Treatise on Highwaymen: Written for the Edification of Ladies who Venture Out Alone.* However, with her customary lack of application, the book had never progressed beyond her own imaginings.

Sir Roderick not being at home, and she expecting no company, it came as a great surprise when Jane came into the room with the announcement that at the door was a young gentleman by the name of Lord Angelsea, who was enquiring for her brother. Lady Sophia, hoping that from this gentleman she would gain some intelligence of her brother's movements, and quite expecting him to be Mr Edgecliffe or another of that ilk, asked that he should be conducted to the gallery, and she told Jane she would go to him as soon as she had the necessary half-hour with her pots of paints and powder.

While he waited, Lord Angelsea took the opportunity of surveying the portraits that, had he but known it, had so fascinated Isabella when she was a child. He recognized them not to be the finest portraits in the world, but in each, at least, the artist had certainly contrived to make some suggestion as to the character of the sitter.

The first Sir Penrose, who had been responsible for the rebuilding of the house and the placing of the gallery in which he would hang his portrait and those of his ancestors, was a fine gentleman with a high brow. From the devices surrounding him, it was evident that he had many interests, and Lord Angelsea felt that he must have had the greatest difficulty in remaining still long enough for his likeness to be caught. His son, another Sir Penrose, had his brow, but it was furrowed by cares, and a faint pallor of sickness hung about his cheeks. That he had died young, before his heir had attained the age of sixteen, was indicated by the fact that there were two portraits of the third Sir Penrose, father of Sir Roderick and Lady Sophia, one painted on his youthful accession to the Ducoeur estates and the other when he was approaching middle age. The first was by a local painter, whose execution of the face was good but who had not mastered the art of illustrating the hands. The second was by Mr Gainsborough, who was accomplished in all particulars: in it the gentleman was grown older and, if not wiser, certainly sadder.

Lord Angelsea moved on to the portrait which, though she was illustrated as Diana, the Huntress, he recognized at once to be that of the mother of Sir Roderick. He did not like it. The picture was all composition and no form and so he moved on, coming finally to the likeness of Sir Roderick.

It had been painted, when Sir Roderick was on the Grand Tour, by Signor Batoni. It was very similar to his own as painted by the same person, even down to the urn, yet it showed, however quickly it had been executed, the cold nature of the sitter. He recognized now the man who had tried to persuade him to give up his responsibility to Isabella when his horses had mown her down. Lord Angelsea shuddered to think what would have befallen Isabella if he had not insisted on taking responsibility for her and her return to health.

He then reflected that this was the face of the same villain who had caused Mr Whistler to abduct Lady Caroline in place of Isabella and who had, when the wrong lady had been brought to him, murdered Mr Whistler in cold blood. Lord Angelsea would have liked to have torn the picture from its frame and destroyed the hateful image.

At that moment Lady Sophia entered the gallery. When she had made her curtsy and invited Lord Angelsea to sit down, she requested to know the purpose of his visit to Ducoeur Castle.

'Madam,' said Lord Angelsea, 'I must declare myself at once. I am the friend of Miss Isabella Broderick, who I have been told by a certain Mr Edgecliffe was once your charge.'

'Does Isabella live?' cried Lady Sophia.

'I sincerely hope so with all my heart, but she has chosen to live apart from those who have been honoured to call themselves her friends.'

'For what reason?'

'The danger that is like to come to them from your bother.'

'Roderick!' cried Lady Sophia, recognizing that the young man before her could be no friend of her dearest brother.

'Madam, I must tell you now that your brother is a murderer and an abductor.'

'I will not hear my brother so abused,' said Lady Sophia, defending him without considering whether or not Lord Angelsea spoke the truth. 'I will hear no more,' she said, rising to her feet and meaning to end the interview.

'Madam, I must ask you to be detained a little longer,' said Lord Angelsea, reaching into his pocket. 'I have here a copy of a written statement from my sister, a statement that has been lodged with one of the highest justices of the land and which contains all the details of her abduction by one Mr Whistler, who carried her off in mistake for Miss Broderick. When Sir Roderick discovered the blunder, his fury knew no bounds and he struck Mr Whistler a blow on the head which killed him outright.'

'No!' cried Lady Sophia, who could not bear to hear these aspersions on her brother's name, even if in her heart she knew the accusations likely to be true.

'Madam,' said Lord Angelsea, 'if you will not trust my word, trust my sister's! I beg you to read these papers and then tell me that your brother is innocent.'

'I am sorry, sir, but my eyesight does not allow close reading.'

'Then, madam, I beg you to let me call someone to read it to you. Or if you prefer to keep the matter a close secret, I shall read it to you and no one in this house shall know what it contains except me and you.'

'I do not wish to hear it.'

'If you will not, I will publish it up and down the length of the country. Well, madam, will you hear me?'

With great reluctance, Lady Sophia agreed that she would and, after having requested Jane to see that no one was admitted (a sure invitation for Jane to listen at the door), she once again sat down.

'Madam,' said Lord Angelsea, 'if there is any point in this communication on which you are not certain, I beg you to interrupt me, for I should not like our interview to end with any doubt on your part.' And in his firm, clear voice, he commenced to read to Lady Sophia his sister's account of her abduction. As he read, he tried to observe the effect that Lady Caroline's statement was having upon its listener. In vain! The paint and powder on Lady Sophia's face were so thick that no evidence of pallor or embarrassment could be detected.

The lady sat, quite impassive, throughout the whole interview. She made no interruptions and no movements. At every point that Lord Angelsea expected a query, none came. For the whole time that Lord Angelsea read, Lady Sophia was as silent as Lady Caroline had become.

The statement concluded with the words: 'This is, in every particular, the true statement of Lady Caroline Angelsea as set down by her own hands and by her own desire, no part of it being influenced in any way by any other person. To this I set my name, Lady Caroline Angelsea.' As soon as he finished reading, Lord Angelsea looked for some response from Lady Sophia.

The lady had heard the gist of the piece but not many of the particulars. She had been too busy trying to reconcile what she felt about Sir Roderick and his passion for Isabella, with her own feelings towards him as her dearly loved brother, the brother to whom in her youth she had promised to give her life.

'Madam,' said Lord Angelsea, who was becoming anxious to know what Lady Sophia thought, 'I must press you to tell me whether you believe my sister's account of all that befell her on that dreadful day.'

Lady Sophia's deliberations about Isabella and Sir Roderick had come down, with the full weight of the blood of the Ducoeurs, on her brother's side. She had decided that she would, by all the means at her disposal, save him from the gallows, which, if Lord Angelsea's story were true, would be the means of parting Sir Roderick from life.

'Sir,' she said at last to Lord Angelsea, 'only a brother can truly know a sister. Do you believe that Lady Caroline's account is as correct as she declares it to be?'

'I do.'

'Then, sir, I must believe it too.'

No reply could have been more favourable to Lord Angelsea, and he congratulated himself on so easily winning Mr Edgecliffe and Lady Sophia to his cause.

'Madam, will you then assist me by helping me to find him?'

'I shall,' replied the lady, lying as effortlessly as that art becomes with practice. 'Only tell me what you require me to do, and I shall do it.'

'I wish to know as soon as you have any information as to the gentleman's whereabouts. I wish you to tell him that I will meet him at any time and in any place to settle this matter as private individuals. Do you understand me?'

Lady Sophia said that she did and, hoping to gain the advantage over him by knowing where Lord Angelsea could be found, asked where she should address her information. Lord Angelsea was too careful to fall into this trap. 'Madam, I shall not trouble you with sending your servant to me. I shall send one to you at regular intervals. A man who, without any bribery or promises on my part, I can trust to say nothing of the matter to anyone excepting you and myself.'

The matter being so settled, Lady Sophia was left to satisfy herself with the thought that any such servant might easily be followed.

This part of the interview being concluded, Lord Angelsea now tried to gain some information on the origins of Isabella.

'I can tell you nothing of her early life, sir. My first knowledge of her was from an acquaintance who asked me if I knew of any kind person that might be prepared to stand sponsor to a pretty girl, less than three years old and all alone in the world. I said that I would consider the matter and begged that I might see the child in order to be certain that it was really in existence and that the money I was to pay for her up-keep would truly go to feed and clothe her. The child being brought in, lisping very

prettily that her name was Lissy, which I was given to understand was her baby way of saying her name, and consenting to be
petted a little by me, I decided that, whatever my brother's
opposition, I would take her into my own house and raise her as
a mother would her daughter. This I did, and was for many years
rewarded if not for her love then by her loyalty to me until she
came under the influence of my brother, an influence which,
you will gather from our previous conversation, has had the
most fatal consequences for her and all who know her. That, sir,
is the story, as I know it, of Isabella Broderick.'

When she had finished, Lord Angelsea begged the liberty to
ask one more question.

'Madam, did you ever believe that, though she now detests
him with all her heart, Isabella ever had any true affection for Sir
Roderick?'

'I did. I do,' said Lady Sophia, remembering how she had
seen them drive off from Ducoeur Castle when she felt herself
like to die and hoping by this reply to sow the seeds of doubt
in Lord Angelsea's heart, doubts that might reflect on Isabella's
constancy.

With this, the interview concluded. Lord Angelsea gave a
small bow and, repeating his promise that his servants would call
upon Lady Sophia regularly, quitted the room.

As soon as he had gone, Lady Sophia called for Jane and told
her that it was necessary for Sir Roderick's whereabouts to be
found out at once or great danger would befall the whole
household. She was not specific as to the nature of this danger,
but Jane was sufficiently alarmed that it might threaten her
wages to make immediate enquiries among the other servants.

She did this with such efficiency that the whole afternoon
Lady Sophia was taking down names and sending letters, telling
her brother that she had had a meeting with a certain L– M– A–
and that she believed she had certain information for Sir
Roderick that might be to his advantage.

The last servant who was called before her was Abigail. Since
procuring Isabella's diary for Sir Roderick, Abigail frequently

had performed other services for her master, services that during their execution had led her to be privy to much private information, among which was the fact that, whenever Sir Roderick had very private meetings, he was in the habit of frequenting the house of a certain Mr Couchman, the owner of the said property being almost always abroad for the sake of his health, and whose household was informed that the place should be at the disposal of Sir Roderick whenever that gentleman's purposes required secrecy.

The house not being more than five miles off, Abigail, knowing exactly in which direction it lay and in what time it might be reached on foot, begged to be allowed to carry the note there herself. This offer was declined by Lady Sophia, who decided that, if it were true that Sir Roderick was so near, she would lose no time in going to see him herself.

For the giving of such information, Abigail expected some reward from her mistress, but Lady Sophia, knowing exactly for what purpose the quick-tongued maid had gone to Mr Couchman's house with Sir Roderick, rewarded her by saying she was to pack her box at once.

'For what reason am I dismissed, madam?' asked Abigail.

'I have not found you satisfactory.'

'I do not believe Sir Roderick would have me dismissed.'

'I shall tell him,' shouted Lady Sophia, 'that you have hinted at a certain lewdness on his part, which goes against all that he is, and who should know such a fact better than his own sister!' she finished, advancing on Abigail to box her ears.

Abigail ran from the room, intending that once she had seen to her things she would appeal to Sir Roderick about the way his sister had dismissed her.

Lady Sophia called for the carriage and set off straight away for Mr Couchman's house. Sir Roderick, who thought his arrangement with Mr Couchman completely unknown to his sister, was greatly displeased at hearing her name announced, and Scar felt the toe of his boot (the dog being frequently employed as a kind of whipping-boy for Lady Sophia). He was instructing his man to tell her that he was not at home when the lady entered.

'Sir,' she said, 'I have come here on a matter of the most utmost urgency and secrecy. We must speak together at once.'

The man was dismissed.

'What is the matter, Sophia?' asked her brother.

'Am I not to have a kiss first?'

The kiss being given with great reluctance on Sir Roderick's part, Lady Sophia announced: 'I have been called on today by a certain Lord Angelsea.'

Sir Roderick paled.

'I see he is known to you?'

'A little,' said Sir Roderick, almost stammering at the information.

'And what of a certain Mr Whistler?'

'I have never heard of him.'

'That is a lie!' said his sister, advancing on him.

'Sophia . . . ' said Sir Roderick, who was used to have his sister believe him in all things.

'You must listen to me, Roderick, for I believe I am your only means of escape,' said Lady Sophia, enjoying the power she now had over her brother. 'The gentleman showed me the copy of a written testament from his sister, Lady Caroline Angelsea, in which she alleges the most monstrous crimes against you.'

'It is not true!' cried out Sir Roderick, covering his face with his hands.

'Sir, if you will not be a coward, I will not be one,' said his sister, not liking to see her proud idol so brought down as to cover his face. 'I will help you, if you will answer me with one word: is the lady's testament true or false?'

'True,' cried Sir Roderick, meeting his sister's eyes.

'Then, sir, I have done the right thing.'

'What have you done?' asked her brother.

'I have fallen in with Lord Angelsea.'

'What?' Sir Roderick thought himself completely betrayed.

'I have done so for your sake. By joining in with his plans, I may more easily confuse them. I have convinced him that I have turned against you. But, as you know' – she ran her hand a little up and down her brother's arm – 'that I would never do. I shall send him whatever message you may instruct, so that you may have your revenge on him.'

'Sophia,' whispered Sir Roderick.

'All I require is that you will furnish me with enough information to draw him into a trap from which he may be dispatched, for I believe your greatest danger in this matter lies at his hands.'

In unusual harmony, brother and sister agreed that the device should be a suggestion as to the whereabouts of Isabella, so that Lord Angelsea, expecting to find her and not anticipating any danger, should fall into Sir Roderick's trap unarmed.

Sir Roderick suggested, cruelly, that it should be made known to Lord Angelsea that Isabella, unable to support herself by any other means, had sunk as low as she could do and was now a member of the oldest profession, an idea that delighted him, and that it should further be given out to Lord Angelsea's servant that she had entered one of the houses that carried on such a trade.

Lady Sophia fell in with this plan. 'I must have an address, sir,' she said.

'I shall give you one,' said Sir Roderick. 'Inform her lover,' he said with a sneer, 'that she is at Mrs Spendlove's and that the lady's business is at Muchcum House, Cunthorp.'

'Muchcum House, Cunthorp,' repeated Lady Sophia, not showing her anger at Sir Roderick's being able so easily to furnish the address.

'If you will carry out this part of the deception, I shall carry out everything else,' said Sir Roderick, and this being agreed Lady Sophia returned home to Ducoeur Castle, much delighted at having been of so much use to her dear brother.

When Lord Angelsea's servant called on her some five days later, everything was in place. Sir Roderick had consulted the mistress of the house in which Isabella was supposed to be lodged and had arranged that he should be concealed in a certain chamber, to which there was entry by a small back staircase, so that when Lord Angelsea, demanding to see Isabella, was shown up to it, Sir Roderick could be waiting for his arrival.

When the servant returned from Ducoeur Castle with the story of Isabella's fallen state and present whereabouts, which Lady Sophia claimed was the general gossip, adding a postscript informing him that even a certain Mr Jackson had preferred to jilt Isabella than to marry a woman whose heart he really knew belonged to Sir Roderick. By this means Lady Sophia hinted that Isabella's fall had been brought about by Lord Angelsea carrying her away from Sir Roderick on the night of the accident.

This was the only part of Lady Sophia's tale Lord Angelsea did not believe to be true. He felt that any affection Isabella had had for Sir Roderick had been quite obliterated by his attempt at a clandestine marriage and his further behaviour. He truly believed that when Isabella had accepted him, her heart and embraces had been his. How he regretted that his own fear of her being drowned on the projected voyage to America and his desire to bring Sir Roderick to justice had led to the degradation of one of the purest souls that he had ever met. His qualms about the place in which he believed Isabella to be lodged were so great that he did not attempt to communicate any detail of what he had discovered to his sister or to Mrs Percival. Isabella being in such a place seemed to indicate, in the most glaring manner, that she had given up any idea that she could ever be his wife. Yet, despite this, his previous affection for her determined him to rescue her and place her in some secluded spot in the country, where, like Mr Shakespeare's Mariana in the moated grange, she might pass the rest of her days safe from the prying eyes of the world. He thought it very likely that if he did such a thing, kind Mr and Mrs Bunce would return from Scotland to join Isabella, so that she should not be deprived entirely of society.

This plan having been arrived at, he then turned to the

consideration of where he should take Isabella as soon as he had liberated her. It was necessary that she should be placed with someone who would treat the matter with the strictest confidence, and after casting about in his mind for some time, Lord Angelsea at length decided to hide her at the home of his old nurse, Jemima, to whom he had confessed Lady Caroline's disappearance, until some more permanent arrangement for her lodging could be made. The nurse was consulted, and, after she had wept some tears at the thought of the fate believed to have befallen Isabella, she consented to take her under her roof for as long as Lord Angelsea deemed it necessary.

There was no time for any consultation with Mr Edgecliffe or Mr Percival about his designs. Thus, when Lord Angelsea set out for the town in which he had been informed Isabella was plying her trade at Mrs Spendlove's, his destination was known to no one but himself. He had chosen, for the sake of protecting Isabella from all unnecessary gossip, to take no servant with him.

Lord Angelsea arrived in the town and went straight away in search of Muchcum House. After several enquiries he found out the street in which it was situated. From its external appearance it looked no different from the other buildings in the street, and he began to wonder if the gossip that had alerted Lady Sophia to the whereabouts of Isabella had become confused. Not liking to make an enquiry at the house itself in case it was the abode of a decent family, Lord Angelsea decided to make some observation of the house, hoping, by the comings and goings of those entering and leaving the place, to ascertain its real nature. He was not aware that the gentlemen who regularly visited the house did so by means of a small back door, hoping by this means to avoid too much public notice.

At last an elderly gentleman approached the house. It seemed to Lord Angelsea that he looked around him for fear of being seen. Mounting the steps to the house, the gentleman paused and took the opportunity to look to both right and left. He then approached the door and knocked. The door being opened, the gentleman was admitted without any more ado. The elderly gentleman was soon followed by a man who was so corpulent that it was only with the greatest of difficulty that he stepped out of his coach and up to the house, pausing to regain his breath between each of the steps up to the door. He knocked, and the door was again opened, the gentleman stepping in with great deliberation. The door had barely been closed again when two young ladies stepped out into the street, both being dressed as brightly as if they had been dancers in the circus. Their appearance confirmed to Lord Angelsea that the information he had received from Lady Sophia was correct, and he decided with a heavy heart that he must now approach the place himself.

He knocked, the door was opened by a girl whom he guessed to be aged about twelve, and, on asking to meet Mrs Spendlove, he gained admittance to the house. It was immediately clear to him that the house was much busier than it appeared from the outside. There was a constant going and coming in the hall. While Lord Angelsea endeavoured to look about him, his pistol was subtly removed by the girl who had opened the door and who, when he ventured to remonstrate with her, said: 'I am sure, sir, that you are properly armed without it.' At this point she was shooed away like some bird by a matronly woman who announced herself to him as Mrs Spendlove.

'Madam,' he said, 'I have come to consult you on a matter I would prefer to remain private.'

Mrs Spendlove glanced around the room. 'No one here will give a fig for our conversation,' she said.

From the way in which the men and women in the hall were disporting themselves, Lord Angelsea guessed this to be true.

'I have come to enquire about a young lady by the name of Isabella Broderick.'

'Ah, Isabella,' sighed Mrs Spendlove, who, like his sister, had been well coached in her part by Lord Roderick. 'She is such a popular girl.'

'Indeed?'

'She is always very willing to accommodate anything that is required of her.'

Lord Angelsea, to whom this was a very painful conversation, bowed his head.

'And uncommon pretty.'

'Yes, madam.'

'It wouldn't surprise me if she did not manage to set herself up very nicely. The new trade in the town has provided a lot of openings for girls who are prepared to be discreet, like Isabella.'

The thought of Isabella as the kept mistress of some magnate who had made his money from screws was hardly less abhorrent to Lord Angelsea than her casual use by anyone who happened to call at the house.

He asked if he might see her. Mrs Spendlove gave him a wink and, knowing Sir Roderick would take a little time to get into his place behind the curtains of the room that had been decided upon for the purpose of his meeting with Lord Angelsea, told him that Isabella was at present engaged. If he would care to wait half an hour, she would be at liberty to receive him. There was little else Lord Angelsea could do but wait. He would have preferred to spend the half-hour in the street, but feared that if he left he would not be re-admitted and so was forced to remain in the house.

He could not believe that Isabella, who had always had a natural gentility, could have sunk to the level of the other women in this place in such a short space of time. He could not imagine her hanging around the neck of the gross young man and twisting his hair in her hands, or petting up the old gentleman who was all aquiver with excitement.

When he had sat for what seemed to him an age, Mrs Spendlove returned and begged that he should come upstairs. Their progress up the stairs was slow, owing to the corpulent gentleman who, completely fuddled with drink, had fallen and was now undergoing the ministrations of two young ladies, each of whom vowed that she could revive him, and each of whom was keeping up her spirits by application to a bottle of brandy which had previously been the property of the gentleman they now attended. The top of the stairs having been achieved, it was obvious that they had now come to the part of the house where matters were better managed than was the case below.

Mrs Spendlove led him up another short flight of stairs to a room where the door stood a little ajar. She knocked on the door and called, 'Isabella, my pet, there is a young gentleman here who wishes to have some intercourse with you. Shall he come in?'

Lord Angelsea did not hear the reply but gathered, from Mrs Spendlove's pushing the door open and indicating that he should step in, that it was in the affirmative. He entered the room, taking care to close the door behind him so that his conversation with Isabella should not be overheard.

His consternation on discovering that the chamber was empty was even worse than it had been when he was seated downstairs. To think that Isabella might have fled while her protector sat beneath her was almost too much to be borne. Then, suddenly, there was a movement behind the curtains.

'Isabella!' cried Lord Angelsea, crossing the room in an instant. But the curtains parted to reveal not Isabella Broderick but Sir Roderick Ducoeur.

'What have you done to her?' cried Lord Angelsea in an agony.

'That is my affair,' the villain answered, drawing out his sword, for he thought by such a weapon he could dispatch Lord Montagu more quietly than with a pistol. 'It is my intention that you will never know.' He advanced upon Lord Angelsea. 'Before you die, sir, I wish to know two things. Where is Isabella Broderick and where is your sister, Lady Caroline?'

With what relief Lord Angelsea heard that Isabella was not in the house. 'Sir,' he said, 'I know no more than you the where-abouts of Miss Broderick, and that of my sister I shall never tell you.'

Sir Roderick came nearer.

'You cannot threaten me, sir,' said Lord Angelsea. 'I would go silent to the grave rather than give you the chance of harming one hair upon the head of either lady.'

'And what of Mr and Mrs Percival?'

'I should do the same for them.'

'How I despise honour!' growled Sir Roderick. 'It always makes a man insipid.'

'Honour and virtue are the only two things that speak for a gentleman!' replied Lord Angelsea with a calmness that Sir Roderick, whose heart was racing, found unendurable.

'Tell me, where is your sister?'

'Sir, I have answered you on that point. I have said I shall be silent on the matter, as silent as you have made her by depriving her of her speech. You may kill me before I shall say anything. But first, sir, hear me on this point. You are a coward to advance on a man who is not armed!'

Lord Angelsea spoke again with that level calmness that makes a man a great general in the field. 'I am a Christian, and so I will forgive you. Do what you will, or put up your weapon.'

The agitation felt by Sir Roderick was only increased by Lord Angelsea's remaining so composed.

'Will you not dispatch me?' asked Lord Angelsea, looking Sir Roderick full in the face.

Sir Roderick grew livid. So extreme was his anger that a small vein stood out on his forehead, pulsating with every beat of his heart.

'Very well, sir!' said Lord Angelsea. 'I must take the necessity of turning my back on you. Perhaps, then, coward that you are, you will make your move.'

So saying, he turned away from Sir Roderick, stooping in the same moment to pick up the poker that lay in front of the fire. Before Sir Roderick could make his first thrust, Lord Angelsea had turned and, seizing the advantage of surprise, struck the sword as it was about to descend on him. Recovering himself, Sir Roderick aimed his next blow. Lord Angelsea stepped aside, but the blade cut through the lace on the cuff of the young man. The silver filigree on the edge impeded the blow just enough to prevent the cutting of an artery, but nevertheless Lord Angelsea received a deep and livid cut on the hand. Ignoring the wound, he again swung back the poker, meeting Sir Roderick's sword with a mighty clash.

The two men fought now blow for blow and with such a ferocity that it was impossible to say who had the advantage. Then Lord Angelsea stumbled and, being unable to regain his balance, toppled towards the floor, losing his grasp upon the poker. He put his hand out to reach for the curtains that surrounded the bed. These, being caught with his full force, gave way, falling as they did so on the head of Sir Roderick, who had leant forward to deliver a mortal blow. For a second Sir Roderick's whole vision was obscured, and he could not tell whether to strike to left or right. In this instant Lord Angelsea regained his feet, catching the curtain as he did so and binding Sir Roderick even more tightly.

Lord Angelsea considered. He saw that his only hope of escape lay in flight, and the time he had gained by the necessity of Sir Roderick's having to extricate himself from the curtains was to his advantage. The young lord was instantly at the door and out of it, and down the small flight of stairs before Sir Roderick was at liberty.

The large gentleman and his companions who had caused the previous blockage on the stairs had been removed by the expedient of the three revellers falling all the way down them, and so it was an easy matter for Lord Angelsea to regain the hall. Sir Roderick was now at the top of the stairs and would have gained on him had not, at that moment, the corpulent gentleman decided that he would like to continue his pleasures in one of the upstairs rooms and started to re-ascend the stairs with his companions, his great bulk so completely filling them that it was impossible for any other progress to be made.

Lord Angelsea made his escape into the street and would have waited to meet Sir Roderick again had he not become aware of the necessity of binding up his hand before any more blood could be lost. Having not expected to spend the night in the town, Lord Angelsea had made no arrangements regarding a place to stay. He was therefore in some difficulty in deciding in which direction to go.

At this moment he was overtaken by a carriage which, having passed on a little way, halted, and, the window being put down, a lady with the most fluting voice that Lord Angelsea had ever heard enquired if he was hurt and whether she, or those about her, could give him any assistance.

Lord Angelsea replied that he would be very grateful if the lady could inform him of some inn or other place in which he might pass the night. The lady said she would do so and begged that Lord Angelsea would step into the carriage.

Seated in the carriage, Lord Angelsea regarded his good Samaritan, who was obviously a widow of some fine degree, her carriage being very new and her clothes at the height of fashion. The lady in her turn regarded him so closely that it seemed to Lord Angelsea that she seemed to be trying to recall having seen him somewhere before.

'Madam,' he said, 'may I venture to discover the name of a lady who has been so good to a stranger?'

'Certainly. It is Louisa, Lady Henry Amory.' And the lady smiled at him, a smile that had a certain sadness to it, not being entirely able to illuminate a countenance that had once been very brilliant.

They travelled on a little further together without exchanging any more words until they arrived at a small inn that the lady recommended as the best in the town. Lord Angelsea thanked her, saying that she had done him a great service through her kindness. The lady in her turn replied that she was glad to have been of assistance and urged Lord Angelsea to have some stitches put into his hand so that as little harm as possible might come to him through his injury. Then, inclining her head in a gesture of adieu, she told the coachman to drive on, while the lady herself looked backwards, still regarding Lord Angelsea.

☙ THIRTEEN ❧

In which Louisa, Lady Amory, tells her part in the adventures of Isabella

The cut that Lord Angelsea had received during his fight with Sir Roderick festered, and for some days, despite the excellent ministrations of the surgeon, he lay very low with a poisoning of the blood. When at last he felt able to walk about and have a little conversation, he discovered to his surprise that Louisa, Lady Amory, had sent a servant every day to enquire after his health. On hearing of his recovery, she now begged that he would give her an audience.

Lord Angelsea, wanting very much to thank the lady for what she had done for him on the day of his injury, begged that she would call on him whenever was convenient to her. Accordingly, the lady arrived the next day. She was dressed very fine, but again Lord Angelsea noticed that her countenance had, at some time, been marked by a great sadness.

'Sir,' said the lady as soon as she had made her curtsy, 'I hope you are quite recovered?'

'Madam, thanks to your bringing me here and the excellent attention I have received, I am convinced my hand will mend.'

'I am glad of it, sir. For such injuries are often not without complication.'

'Madam, I have discovered that since I have been here you have been kind enough to ask after my health every day.'

'That is true. It was of great importance to me to know when I could hope to have some conversation with you,' said the lady in her mellifluous voice.

Seeing Lord Angelsea looked surprised at this, Louisa continued: 'We are already acquainted, you and I.'

'Madam, I cannot believe this to be true.'

'It is certainly true,' replied the lady. 'But I believe that I have a better remembrance of you than you of me.'

'Since I do not believe that I have ever seen you before, what you say must be correct. But I must press you to remind me of the circumstance in which we met.'

The lady laughed her silvery laugh. 'Do you not have any idea?'

'Perhaps it was at some ball?' Again the lady laughed. 'Or at the play?' Louisa shook her head.

'Then, madam, I am in error for forgetting you, and I pray that you will remind me of the circumstance.'

Here the lady changed her voice to such a degree that it came out in a deep growl. 'You begged me to spare the life of Isabella Broderick.'

Lord Angelsea grew amazed. Before him, with her small hands in her lap, sat the highwayman he had encountered on the night his horses had run down Isabella. Louisa could see from Lord Angelsea's face that his mind had apprehended the truth.

She said now in her own tones: 'We shall come to that in a minute, sir. At this moment what I desire to hear most is anything you might know of that lady. Did she recover? Is she well?'

It was obvious from the urgency with which Louisa asked after Isabella that her concern for her was entirely genuine and must be answered before he could have any satisfaction as to why the lady had been forced to take up the profession of highway robber.

'Madam, to tell the story briefly, after your departure and the returning to me of my purse . . . '

Louisa gave a brief smile and, interrupting, said: 'You are the only person for whom I ever performed such a deed, and I did it because of your devotion to the lady. I owe much to Isabella Broderick, who fed me when I was starving. But continue your story. I long to know how she is and what has become of her.'

Lord Angelsea saw that he must acquaint the lady with the whole story of Isabella as he knew it. Since the lady was so anxious about the health of Isabella, he started by telling of how he carried her to Angelsea Court and of how, though she recovered her body, her mind had not recovered in the same degree.

'The poor child!' cried Louisa.

Lord Angelsea lowered his head. 'The blame for her injury must rest with me. It was I, anxious to return home to see my sister who had just returned from the Continent after a most unfortunate affair of the heart, who had ordered my coachman not to spare any speed.'

'That does not explain why Isabella was on the road so late at night.'

'That was the fault of a great rogue, the rogue' – and here Lord Angelsea held up his hand – 'who did me this injury, and would have killed me, the man who . . . ' Lord Angelsea shuddered to think of all that he knew pertaining to Sir Roderick.

'Sir, I believe that I know the name of the gentleman.' Lord Angelsea looked at her. 'It is Sir Roderick Ducoeur, is it not?'

'It is,' said Lord Angelsea, amazed. 'What do you know of him and his dealings?'

'Too much,' Louisa replied, growing pale.

'Forgive me, madam, for this enquiry, but it must be made: what is the reason you have to fear Sir Roderick?'

Here Lady Louisa took a ring from her finger and handed it to Lord Angelsea.

The ring contained a lock of hair and was obviously some mourning token. 'The hair is that of my cousin,' explained Louisa. 'We were the children of twin brothers and brought up almost as if we were brother and sister. Sometimes as children we fancied we might be married and that I might still retain the name of Chaser, and as a girl I truly believed that Edward – for that was my cousin's name – would make an admirable husband.' She paused, and some tears fell on her cheeks. 'I should tell you now, that it is not for Edward that I wear these weeds, but for another so far above him – but I run away with myself. At the age of seventeen, my cousin, like most young men of his station, set off for Italy with the intention of mastering something of classical languages and an appreciation of art and nature. He travelled with his tutor, whom I, my father and my uncle greatly admired for his education and his manners. At Venice the tutor grew ill and within two days was dead of some continental fever, leaving my cousin without a protector. While waiting to hear from my uncle if he should return home or if another tutor were to be sent to accompany him for the rest of the tour, it was inevitable that Edward, being a young man, and used always to being surrounded by company, should look around for friends. It was thus he ran into Sir Roderick, who had all the advantage of him by being some years older. In short, they formed an acquaintanceship in which Sir Roderick was the chief influence.

'On first hearing of the friendship between his son and Sir Roderick, my uncle was most pleased, having known something of Sir Roderick's father, Sir Penrose, and always liking him, though that gentleman had by this time died. Then my uncle, while trying to raise a subscription for the widows of those killed in the mines, had occasion to run into another gentleman who had been acquainted with Sir Penrose and his family. My uncle told him how happy he was that my cousin had formed a friendship with Sir Roderick, the son of their mutual friend. The said gentleman, on hearing this, instantly urged my uncle to prevent Edward from seeing Sir Roderick by calling him home at once, saying by way of explanation that Sir Roderick was a cheat, a liar and prone to every natural and unnatural vice.

'My cousin was ordered home. On his arrival it was obvious from my cousin's demeanour that this was only because his father demanded his return: for his own sake he swore that he would have stayed at Venice until Sir Roderick had quitted the place.

'From this time I noticed a change in my cousin which I deeply regretted. I had always loved to walk with him when the weather had permitted it, but now I did not like his manner and preferred to stay at home even when the days were most clement. He was more often out of sorts than he was in them. It was not just I who recognized this change in him. Both my father and my uncle were aware of it and decided that it was the result of his spending too much time in idleness. It was therefore decided that my cousin should become more involved in their business, being the heir to both of them unless my father should marry again, a thing he said he never would do for my dear mother's sake.

'At first this proposal was greeted with apathy until it became known that the business would require some time to be spent in London. At this my cousin developed an absolute passion for the business, declaring it was all he had ever wished to do with his life. It was decided, my now being of an age to go into society, that I should travel with them. We were soon transferred to Richmond, my uncle preferring not to approach too closely to the smoke of the city. This decision was not to the liking of my cousin, who bemoaned the necessity of travel. It was not long before he resolved this problem by purchasing, at great cost, a pair of horses that were so perfectly matched that they made him the envy of the town. It was an expense that greatly disturbed my uncle, who, even though he was over twice his son's age, thought nothing of going about on horseback, even in the coldest months of the winter. However, there was nothing for it but that my cousin must have a carriage, and the matter was finally agreed on after the most dreadful argument between father and son. Neither I, nor my father, ever discovered what was said, my uncle refusing to divulge it even to his twin.

'It was not long before the carriage began to return home later and later, and it was soon apparent that, Sir Roderick being returned from Venice, my cousin had again become one of his circle. My father immediately urged that we should retreat again into the country, but the business in which he and my uncle were engaged was so far advanced that this could not be done without losing everything. Since my uncle could not quit the place, my cousin would not.

'One evening, and much against his new character, Edward begged that we go with him to Vauxhall, to the pleasure gardens, a thing which, after much entreaty, we arranged to do. It was at that place, my father and uncle being engaged in conversation with some friends, that Edward insisted on introducing me to Sir Roderick.'

Louisa stopped to see that her story was being attended to. Lord Angelsea being all attention, she continued.

'Knowing what I had heard of his behaviour in Venice, and the change he had effected in my cousin, I was not disposed to like him and wanted to move on as soon as the introduction had been made, but my cousin insisted that I should take some refreshment with them, something I did with so little grace that it tasted like poison. I then begged that my cousin would return me to my father and uncle, which at first he refused, saying that their conversation would bore him and me. I insisted, and at last he removed me from the company of the odious Sir Roderick, though he himself returned to him as soon as he had reunited me with my father.

'The next day I was surprised to find my cousin trying to deliver a note to me from Sir Roderick which he begged I should read. I would not. He pestered me in this manner for some days. I told him that if he endeavoured such a thing again, I would receive the letter and deliver it into my father's hands without going to the trouble of opening it. At this, my cousin fell on his knees, telling me that he was greatly in debt to Sir Roderick, and that if I would enter into a correspondence with the gentleman, he might by that means buy a little time. Whatever my feelings for my cousin at this moment, my former ones had not completely deserted me. I agreed' – Louisa gave a heavy sigh – 'that I should write one letter to Sir Roderick, but only one. My cousin begged that he should dictate if for me, but I would not consent to this, thinking that he would want me to make a long note, where I wished to make one that was as short as possible. The letter was indeed brief and contained nothing that could give Sir Roderick any encouragement, commenting only on the crowd at Vauxhall and the inconvenience of a wheel coming off our coach on the way home. Having written to him in so short a manner I believed myself to be out of danger from his attentions.

'Then my cousin came to me again and begged me to send a favour to Sir Roderick, in the form of some item that I carried on my person. I refused emphatically. Edward insisted that if I did not, Sir Roderick would call in all his debts. I urged him at once to go and make a clean breast of it to his father. This he insisted he would not do. That night, in what I believe to have been a fit of drunkenness, he gambled away the first of his horses to Sir Roderick and, one of a pair not being as valuable as two, finished the business by selling the other very cheaply to Sir Roderick, who, I believe, has them to this day. There followed another dreadful argument with my uncle, who, as soon as my cousin quitted the house, came to my father and me with tears in his eyes. We begged him to tell us what the matter was, but, before he could say anything, he fell down dead in front of us, of a stroke, the apoplexy having been brought on by the behaviour of his son.

'If you have any close brother or sister, you may imagine the pain that the suddenness of his death caused his twin, my father, grief that was greatly compounded by the fact that it occurred at such a precarious time. The whole business that had brought us to London collapsed, bringing my father and me close to ruin. It was immediately necessary for us to close up the house and return home in order to prevent ourselves getting into more debt than we were already in.

'We did not see my cousin again before we left town. Nor did we want to. He was not even present when his own father was laid in the earth. The day on which this happened was very wet, and my father caught a cold from which he never recovered.

'We lived very quietly in the country for six months, when the son of a neighbouring family offered me his hand in marriage. In former times it would have been an offer to which I would have been inclined, but now, with my father in poor health and no means of providing me with a dowry, I sadly declined.

'I was at this time, despite my youth and with my father's advice when he was well enough to give it, almost entirely responsible for the running of the estate, and though it could not be said that things were going well for us, we were making a little progress in all that we owed and had satisfied all those who would have sued us. It came as a surprise, therefore, to receive a visit from a bailiff. I would not have wished my father to have known of the man's presence in the house, but, since we were at dinner when he came, it was not possible for any interview to take place alone. When my father – for it was he who addressed the bailiff, not wanting to blame me for any mistake that I might have made in the accounts – asked on whose account the writ was signed, he was informed that it was by Sir Roderick.'

'Was Sir Roderick, then, involved in the business?' interjected Lord Angelsea, who had so far kept silent during Louisa's long speech.

'You run ahead of me, sir, and I must tell you now that the business is not what you suppose it to be. When my father asked what the debt was for, a note was put into his hands which caused him to tremble as if he had stepped out into the greatest hurricane. Without a word, he gave the paper to me. I was astonished to see that it was from myself. I have it here, sir. I would beg you to read it.'

The note that Lady Amory handed Lord Angelsea was a promissory one for a wager in which she promised Sir Roderick Ducoeur that if he should beat Mr Edward Chaser, on such a night, at such a game, she would be forfeit to Sir Roderick, as and when he chose, or recompense him with ten thousand pounds.

'A weaker man than my father,' said Lady Amory, re-folding the note, 'might have given way at the sight of such a letter. Instead he gave it, without a word, into my hands. I was shocked at first to see a style of writing so similar to mine that anyone not minutely acquainted with my hand might have mistaken it. However, I was fortunate in that, whenever we had been separated, it had been the habit between my father and myself to keep up a very detailed correspondence. It was he who turned to the bailiff and said: "The writing certainly pretends to be that of my daughter, but the strokes are too long. It is a forgery got up against her person, and I will swear to it."

'But from that moment on, the grief that his estate was to be inherited by his nephew, who had sunk so low and who by his behaviour had killed his father, my father's twin brother, compounded by the cold caught at his funeral, now hastened my own father's death, and I must be left with, as my closest relative, a man who would use me in any way he could to pay his debts. My father, seeking his own means of protecting me, and knowing that our neighbour Sir Henry Amory had already made an offer for me which I had refused, he now went to that neighbour, and having found as he thought a means of providing me with a small dowry, begged that he should ask me again. This Sir Henry did, offering me his heart as well as his home, in such a tender manner that I could not refuse him a second time.

'So we went to church to be married, my father by this time being too ill to accompany us, and when we returned home as man and wife he was dead. Though I was happy with my husband from the first, we now entered upon a time of the most dreadful trouble. My cousin insisted that he had come into the estate before the moment when we – my husband and I – were legally bound. The doctor who had been with him, and the priest who performed the marriage, both gave out their clocks as being at different times, and at last it was established in law that my father had died ten minutes before I had become Lady Amory, and that the provisions he had made for me had become null and void. Both my husband and I begged my cousin that he would honour the agreement that had been made concerning my future, my husband nevertheless assuring me at all junctures that, whether good or bad the outcome, his heart would still be entirely mine. It will not surprise you, sir, to know that my cousin tore the agreement my father had made in pieces.

'My husband, however, was as good as his word and never

mentioned the matter to me during the five happy years of our marriage. Our union was ended by my husband's being struck down by a canker, which progressed so rapidly that nothing could be done to save him. On my husband's death, and the fact that we had had no issue, a grief to us both, and his family not liking to be attached to me (for by this time the true and dissolute nature of my cousin was universally known), once I was made a widow, I was completely rejected by all those who might have helped me. My last hope was to make some desperate plea to my cousin, and I spent the last of the money I had in hiring a coach to go to see him. I was overtaken on my journey by a storm of such severity that it was necessary to seek shelter in the first inn we came across. It was here that I met Isabella Broderick, who behaved to me in the most tender fashion.'

'I would expect no more,' said Lord Angelsea.

'I had been travelling for a long time and was very tired, and after having been fed and warmed by Isabella – for so I always prefer to think of her – I believe that I fell into a slumber during which, for many months, I thought to have had a strange dream concerning Sir Roderick and his being in the room. I believe now that his presence there was, in truth, tangible.'

Sir Roderick and Isabella, together, at an inn! This caused Lord Angelsea more agitation than anything he had heard before concerning Isabella's strange history.

'How came you, madam, to believe that?' he asked.

'I did not think of it at the time, but when the storm had passed and I was able to quit the place, I found my hired coachman and groom in fervent conversation about a pair of horses that had been housed with their own. I thought then only how their prattle about how exactly the pair were marked was delaying me. But I have had leisure since to reflect on the whole occasion and am now quite convinced that the horses they described were those obtained by Sir Roderick from my cousin, and that is why, I believe, I did not dream.'

Lord Angelsea weighed all the evidence together. 'Madam,' he said with dread, 'are you completely certain that Sir Roderick and Isabella were staying in the same place together?'

'I am,' she replied.

Lord Angelsea's face fell, his heart broke and he gave a great sigh. The lady was instantly on her feet. 'Sir,' she said, 'it is obvious to me that you have a great affection touching Isabella.'

'Did! Did!' was all the lord could reply.

'Hear me, sir. I believe' – and here she placed a hand on her heart as symbol of her good intention – 'that whatever Sir Roderick intended, and we are both persons of the world enough to know what that was, Isabella had no inkling of the danger in which she had placed herself.'

'She discovered it soon enough!' cried Lord Angelsea.

'What do you mean, sir?'

'I mean this,' said the gentleman, proceeding to tell the tale he had heard from Mr Edgecliffe about the plans made by Sir Roderick for his clandestine marriage to Isabella. When he had finished this part of Isabella's sad history, Lady Amory could not help but break in with the words: 'Sir, am I to believe that on the occasion of our first meeting that one of the gentleman I allowed to run off was Sir Roderick Ducoeur?'

'It was, the other being Mr Edgecliffe.'

Lady Amory gave a great cry of regret. 'To think that I was so close to him and allowed him to escape when I might have meted out some measure of retaliation!'

'Madam, you shall have that revenge if it is ever in my power to give it to you, for know that my entire purpose now is to find the fiend and make amends for his gross misconduct to so many ladies. For the moment, though, I beg you sit down and finish your story.'

Lady Amory took her chair again. 'You have heard enough of my cousin's nature not to guess at his response when, the storm having finished and my journey being completed, I arrived at his door. At first he would not admit me, but on my insisting I was finally admitted to his room. I found a ruined man, so wasted with dissipation and drink that for much of our interview I believe he was only half aware of who I was. When I asked him if I could have a little money, he became violent towards me, telling me that I had brought about my own ruin and that he preferred that we should ever remain strangers to one another. I said that if that was what he wished on his side, he might have it, but that I, for the sake of our childhood friendship and the relationship between our fathers, would never do such a thing. This reply was greeted by language so strong and so abusive to me that I shall never repeat it. There was nothing for me to do but quit the house, my cousin declining even to shake hands. I dismissed the coach and coachman and set out alone with my bundle, to go I did not know where.

'I have mentioned that dear, good, sweet Isabella had given me a little to eat when I had been at the inn, but since then I had taken nothing and was now very hungry. I came to a place where a labourer had fallen asleep at the side of the road, half-way through taking his repast, and because I was so very hungry I could not but snatch up his remnants of bread and cheese, which I had consumed before he, in his sleepy state, knew what I was about. The following day I tried a similar expedient in a pastry-cook's, and carried away under my gown a large meat pie. I am not proud that by these means I gained enough to eat, but it seemed to me that I had no other choice and that, since all those I knew had disowned me, the only shame if I was discovered would be on my own head.

'However, though it was possible to feed myself in such a way, it was not possible to dress myself, for to do that, unless I was to deck myself out in handkerchiefs, I needed ready money. And so I turned to the trade of highway robbery, as many cashiered gentlemen have done. I found that my small stature was greatly to my advantage in this, those I stopped expecting to be easily able to overcome me, an advantage that I was soon quick to exploit. Being able to disguise my voice by talking very low, no one ever expected me to be a woman, so that even when I was caught up with and questioned by those whose jewels and purses I had taken but ten minutes before, I was never recognized. I vowed that I would keep to such a profession until I had obtained enough money to set myself up comfortably, having nothing to lose by way of life or reputation. My aim was soon achieved, and I am now again a respectable member of society, though' – she hung her head – 'I know I have behaved in a way that I can never atone for in this life or the next.'

'Madam,' said Lord Angelsea, 'I cannot answer for you in the next life, but I am sure that if there is any mercy in this it will be shown you, for, from the circumstances you have outlined to me, you were forced into this course through no fault of your own, and we all know who is chiefly to blame.'

'Sir Roderick Ducoeur.'

It now became necessary for Lord Angelsea to acquaint Lady Amory with the details of his sister's abduction and Mr Whistler's death. The lady's response was to pity the poor, unfortunate Mr Whistler and then to say she could only be thankful that her cousin had died before he could be used as Sir Roderick's messenger.

At this juncture, seeing that they had been involved in conversation for above four hours, Lord Angelsea suggested that they should take some food and resume their conversation the following day.

'Sir,' replied Lady Amory, 'if it does not tire you too much, I would rather sit on and hear every particular you have concerning Sir Roderick. Then we may break up our talk, for neither of us knows what plans such a devious mind is capable of forming in the space of a single evening.'

Lord Angelsea, seeing that the lady was very sensible in suggesting this, agreed that he would complete the story in every particular before they separated. He now told Lady Louisa what had happened to Isabella in Hawbury and how she had fled in an attempt to put him and the Bunces out of danger.

'Where is she now?' asked Louisa.

'Madam, that I do not know, though I think of her every day and dream of her every night.'

At length the two parted, each having promised that they would communicate to the other any information they had regarding the whereabouts of the gentleman or any other details pertaining to him.

At the door Lord Angelsea gave a low bow and said to Lady Amory: 'Madam, you have said things to me in this room which on reflection you might wish unsaid for fear that I should communicate them to some third party. Let me assure you that I shall never do such a thing, on pain of death.'

'I know it, sir,' replied the lady, and set off for her home.

When she had gone, Lord Angelsea spent a long time in contemplation, going over in his mind every detail he knew concerning Sir Roderick and his relationship with Isabella.

Meanwhile, the gentleman on whom his thoughts dwelt was at this time reflecting on Lord Angelsea and the means by which he had escaped from the bordello. To have had the man so much in his power and then to lose the advantage over him was a severe blow to his pride. He had returned like a dog with its tail between its legs to Ducoeur Castle, and was forced to confess to Lady Sophia what had occurred.

She, recognizing that her brother still stood in the way of great danger from Lord Angelsea, begged that she should be allowed to help him devise some new plan by which means he might escape with his life intact.

ᗦᑖ FOURTEEN ᗥᑖ

In which Isabella is recognized by
an old playmate

When Isabella had escaped from Sir Roderick's grasp she had run straight towards the body of the market and hoped to hide herself in the body of the crowd, thinking that if Sir Roderick confronted her there, the whole matter would be made very public and that she might be able to induce someone to send for the magistrate, in front of whom she could then lay all her accusations concerning the gentleman.

In her flight she was so intent on seeing that she was not pursued that she did not observe where she was going. Suddenly, she collided with one of the trestle tables on which a large pile of cabbages had been set up for display. The whole edifice collapsed, causing cabbages to scatter everywhere and making further flight on Isabella's part impossible. The farmer's wife who ran the stall was very much taken by surprise and was quite ready to remonstrate with Isabella for her carelessness when something in the girl's countenance stopped her, and, instead of cursing her for her clumsiness, she enquired if she were in some danger.

'I am, madam, and I am truly sorry for the inconvenience I have caused you.' As Isabella made this speech, the many anxious glances she took over her shoulder and round about her caused the farmer's wife, whose name was Mrs Bountiful, to believe that the young lady spoke the truth.

'Are you being looked for?' asked Mrs Bountiful.

'I am, madam, and by a man who would do me harm.'

225

Mrs Bountiful, who did not like to see any creature in trouble and who preferred the hatching of her chickens to the dispatching of them, at once decided that she would help Isabella.

'Here,' she said, taking her woollen cloak from around her shoulders, 'cover yourself with this.' Isabella did so, drawing the folds tightly around her face. When Sir Roderick passed her, in his attempt to seek her out, she was being as roundly chastised by Mrs Bountiful for her carelessness in upsetting the table as the good farmer's wife could manage.

When Isabella thought that all danger from Sir Roderick had passed, she stood up to go, thanking Mrs Bountiful profusely for the loan of her cape.

'Not so fast!' cried the farmer's wife. 'Where do you mean to go now?'

'I do not know. I am a stranger here.'

'In that case you might go around a corner and come again face to face with the gentleman.'

'Then, madam,' said Isabella, 'I pray you will let me sit on a little, until he has given up all hope of finding me.'

'You can sit there,' said Mrs Bountiful, 'until you can think of some place to go or you will come home with me. I should not like any of my children to go a-running around the countryside. Where are your family?'

'I have none,' replied Isabella. 'I am an orphan.'

Mrs Bountiful's large heart was filled with pity for Isabella. 'My poor lamb' and other such epithets were poured on her with such abundance that Isabella began to feel that she was almost Mrs Bountiful's own child. When it began to grow dark, and the last of the cabbages had been sold, the good lady turned to Isabella and once again asked where she intended to spend the night.

'If it please you, madam, I should like to return home with you.'

'Very well,' said Mrs Bountiful, who had already decided that this should be the case. She led Isabella to the cart in which she had driven to market that morning, and they set off from the town. Mrs Bountiful, who knew, from the experience of five children of her own and another five she had had to wet-nurse, that the best way to procure a secret is not to ask for it, filled the journey by telling Isabella a great many details about her family and the farm. Thus, before she even arrived, Isabella thought she had made the acquaintance of all the Bountifuls down to the smallest piglet. This easy conversation soon led Isabella into revealing a little of her history as she could remember it, and without giving out the true title of any of her friends, and, again taking for herself the name of Napier, she told the lady of the danger they had all been put under by Sir Roderick.

When she had heard what Isabella had to say, even the good-natured Mrs Bountiful was forced to declare that the gentleman was a knave and a villain, and that if by assisting Isabella she had put herself in any danger from him, she would like to have his answer when faced by the end of Mr Bountiful's blunderbuss.

At length they saw the light of the lantern that had been left out to welcome Mrs Bountiful home, and were turning into the farmyard when an elderly dog came out to greet them. As soon as Isabella had stepped down from the cart, he was at her, throwing himself on her for pats in the most adoring fashion.

'Why!' declared Mrs Bountiful. 'I would declare that he almost knows you!'

Isabella asked the name of the dog and discovered it to be Ben. She bent down to stroke it, her caresses returned in the form of some eager lickings to her face. And when they entered the house and Isabella had been introduced to the family and been invited to sit down, the dog sat so close that all its paws were on the hem of her dress.

The farmhouse was small and neat. Three of the Bountiful children now being married and with establishments of their own, it accommodated only Mr and Mrs Bountiful and their youngest son and daughter. Tom Bountiful was nineteen and his sister Mary, who was universally known as Polly, two years younger. They were most charming to Isabella, and the evening she spent in their company passed very quickly, it being after half-past ten when Mrs Bountiful declared they must all go to bed or answer to the cows in the morning. Mr Bountiful, who was as jolly as his wife, neither of them being able to bear a bad temper, swore that while he trusted his neighbours completely he would lock his door that night for the safety of Isabella and carry his blunderbuss to bed with him, so that if there was any disturbance during the night it would be to hand.

Isabella retired to sleep with Polly Bountiful. Most of the dairying on the farm fell to Polly, and in consequence she did not have much opportunity of going far from home. She was therefore most anxious to hear from Isabella about all the places she had been to, and what she knew of the fashions, and was it true that hoops were completely left off now?

She was such a cheerful companion that Isabella could not but answer her questions, and by the time sleep overtook them Polly Bountiful declared she had never had such a friend as Miss Napier.

Isabella had determined that she would leave the farm the following day, as soon as breakfast was done. The weather decided otherwise by being very wet, and Mrs Bountiful very anxious about Isabella's health, so any thought of flight became impossible. Anxious not to be a burden on her hosts, Isabella cast about to find some way of making herself useful. She soon discovered that, what with their sheep, cows, pigs and hens, and the necessary food that must be provided for them, most of the Bountifuls' time was spent outside the house, and that in consequence there was very little time to make and mend. So Isabella chose to spend the morning, Ben at her feet, turning a sheet side to centre, making a join that Mrs Bountiful declared was the neatest she had ever seen, and done with such speed. Isabella begged her that she should let her have any other such small tasks, and Mrs Bountiful, who had spent most of the day coming and going on her pattens between the house and yard, finally assented to bring her all the mending in the house.

When the weather began to be dry, night was falling, and the

Bountifuls again insisted that Isabella sat down at their table.

After dinner Polly begged that Isabella should help her to cut a pattern for a gown in the latest fashion from some pretty sprigged cotton that had been sent to her as a present by an aunt who in her youth had had the same longing for little delicacies as did Miss Polly. Again, at bedtime the door was locked and the blunderbuss carried upstairs by Mr Bountiful.

The next day being Sunday, and its being a firm rule in the Bountiful household that a visit to the church should be made, this trip allowing them to attend to their spiritual affairs and at the same time to meet and talk with two of Mrs Bountiful's married children who always attended at the same service, it was insisted that Isabella should go with them and delay her departure to the following day. Accordingly, Isabella got into the cart with the Bountifuls and Ben and a great cart-horse by the name of Dobbin, which was induced by the offer of a carrot to draw them to church.

What strange feelings the journey evoked in Isabella! She could tell before it could even be seen that they were about to come upon a ford, and she knew, with almost as much certainty as Dobbin, that they must turn left at the crossroads at the entrance to the small village in which the church was situated. Isabella began to wonder if she had not been in the place at some previous time, and whether she might not be recognized when she walked into the church. Though her entrance there with the Bountifuls caused every head to turn, it was clear to Isabella when the service was over that she was known universally to be a stranger.

After leaving the church there was a long period of chat with young Mr Bountiful and his wife, and also the former Miss Susan Bountiful, now the wife of a Mr Kindlysides, who owned another farm not far off. There was a great deal of domestic information exchanged, Mrs Kindlysides having come by the best receipt in the world for a dish of lambs' tails, which would soon be in abundant supply, and the young Mrs Bountiful having brought with her some very fine potted rabbit, which her mother-in-law said she longed to be at home to taste. Polly's new gown was discussed, and the spare pieces begged for a quilt that Susan was making, the birth of her first child being not far off, and she already planning, were it a daughter, for the happy occasion of marriage.

The adieus being said on both sides, Isabella and her hosts returned home. Again, Isabella felt the familiarity of the place. She tried to think whether she had been there with Lord Angelsea and his sister when they had gone out on some expedition, but she could not remember them ever having come in this direction.

That night, after supper, the rabbit having been pronounced very fine by all except Mr Bountiful (who made his wife the compliment of saying, 'Eliza is a very good girl, but she does not understand the seasoning of things as well as you do'), Isabella again tried to broach the subject of her quitting them.

'You cannot go until my gown be done!' cried Polly. 'I shall never remember as clearly as you what the fashion is and how the sleeves must be cut.'

Tom Bountiful, who was of an age when young men are prone to be in love, declared that if any harm was made towards her he would protect Isabella with his life. Mrs Bountiful stated that Isabella was so useful with her needle that she would keep her half a year and be glad to do so. Mr Bountiful settled the matter, as the master of the house should, by saying that if Isabella went away he would 'be quite compelled to follow!', knowing the danger he believed her to be in from a certain quarter. Finally, as if to agree with all of them, Ben set up such a pitiful whining and pawing at Isabella's skirt that the party declared that the dog had understood every word that had passed between them.

'Now,' said Mrs Bountiful, 'we must give the young lady every chance to protest that she will not fall in with our entreaties.'

Isabella could not do so. The Bountifuls were so good, so kind, that she felt it would be churlish of her not to accept their offer of hospitality. How she was embraced when she said she would stay! How thrilled was Polly to keep her friend! How glad was Tom to have a goddess that he could admire every day! How happy was Mrs Bountiful to have another young person in the house, and how delighted was Mr Bountiful that all those around him were happy! There was nothing else for it: Isabella would stay.

She had arrived on the farm at exactly the time of year when help is always required, a time when lambs were to be born, crops for harvest to be sown and much of the coppicing work to be done. Under Polly's instruction she soon found that she had an aptitude for dairying, a skill that delighted Polly, for Isabella's presence when there was milk to be skimmed gave her the liberty to put on her new gown and go to market with her mother.

Isabella herself never went any distance from the farm except to church, for she thought it better not to present herself in public in case she should be discovered. As the weeks progressed and the March winds gave way to April showers, Isabella began to feel as if she had, at last, found a haven where she might be safe from the attentions of Sir Roderick. Mr Bountiful's blunderbuss remained in its place above the fire at night, the front door was left unbolted and Isabella began to feel more tranquil. Given their son's affection for her, it soon began to appear to Mr and Mrs Bountiful that she might, at some future date, come to be regarded by them as a daughter in fact as well as in spirit.

Mr Bountiful was a keen propagandist for everything that was modern in agriculture and had for a period of years been making some experiments in the breeding of cattle. He was now convinced that his latest experiment had succeeded and was determined to display his finest calf at the fair which was to be held to celebrate the coming of May. Polly entreated Isabella to go with them to the celebrations. Isabella would not hear of it, preferring to remain at home with the faithful Ben.

'In that case,' cried Polly, 'may I beg a favour from you?'

'If it is something in my favour to grant.'

'Do me the honour of lending me your locket.'

'Oh, my dear Polly,' cried Isabella, 'that is one thing I cannot do, and I had thought I had kept it always entirely hidden.' This was a precaution that Isabella had taken since the night of the ball in Hawbury, thinking that if Sir Roderick were to put out a description of her and her jewel, she would be easily discovered.

'Will you not lend it me for my sake?' insisted Polly, for she wanted to go to the fair looking as pretty as the Queen of the May.'

'I cannot, for though I dearly love you' – and Isabella kissed her friend as proof of that love – 'I have sworn to wear it always for my mother's sake, for I believe it came to me through her, and it is all I have to connect me with her.'

Polly, who saw that pressing the matter further was pointless, was obliged to set off for the fair with a ribbon tied at an angle about her neck.

The calf was duly shown, and Mr Bountiful had the satisfaction of being awarded the first prize and his skill as a stockman being universally admired. The size of the creature and the means by which it had been produced was soon the talk of every market and fair in the county, and by this means was brought to the attention of Lord Angelsea, who decided – the reports of the animal now having exaggerated its size to one so massive that it was said to be possible to walk under its belly – that he wished to make his own observation of it. Consequently, he sought out Mr Bountiful's name and determined to present himself at the farm. This he did on an occasion when all the Bountifuls had gone to visit a market that was somewhat further away than the one they usually frequented.

Isabella, hearing a knock upon the door and thinking that it was the packman, from whom she had been charged by Polly to obtain as much purple ribbon as could be had for twopence, opened the door and saw before her the face of her beloved Montagu. The surprise to them both was great.

'How came you here?' cried Lord Angelsea.

'Sir, I was taken pity on by the good farmer's wife.'

'But how came you to meet such a woman?' asked Lord Angelsea.

'My lord,' cried Isabella, 'if you will be good enough to walk in the orchard with me, I will acquaint you with everything that has befallen me, since for your sake and that of your sister and the Percivals, and the good, kind Mr and Mrs Bunce, I ran away from you all.'

'Oh, Isabella,' sighed Lord Angelsea, longing only to take her in his arms now that he had again found her.

'Sir, we must talk.'

Lord Angelsea shivered. Why did she not call him her dear Montagu?

'What have you to tell me?' he asked.

'Only everything that has passed since our last meeting.'

'You will tell it all, in every particular?'

'Yes.'

'You will hide nothing from me?' asked Lord Angelsea.

'Indeed not. To whom should I speak the truth if not to you?' said Isabella, stepping out into the soft spring day with Ben at her heels.

'Very well,' said the gentleman. 'I will have the truth.'

So, walking in the orchard, in which every bough now was covered with blossom, Isabella told Lord Angelsea of the night she had spent with the charcoal-burners and how she had escaped from Sir Roderick, thanks to the kindness of Mrs Bountiful.

'And have you truly not seen Sir Roderick since that day?'

'Sir, I have not!'

'Isabella!' cried Lord Angelsea, drawing her hand into his arm. 'I cannot tell you what terrible thoughts I have had concerning you and that dreadful gentleman.'

'By what cause, sir?'

He told her of his interview with Lady Sophia and his going to the house of Mrs Spendlove, not for the moment telling Isabella of his meeting with Louisa, Lady Amory.

'Sir, I believe that the lady told you such a story to draw you into Sir Roderick's trap. I am only thankful, for your sake and' – Isabella dropped her voice – 'the sake of all those who love you, that it did not succeed.'

'Isabella,' said Lord Angelsea, taking her hands and holding them very fast, 'I must now tell you something more about yourself. Lady Sophia, a woman I now believe to be in league with her brother in order to prevent the law dealing with him as it should, was the woman who raised you from when you were a small child.'

'Oh, cruel, cruel!' cried Isabella.

'Wait. There is more.' Isabella began to grip Lord Angelsea's hands so tightly that he became quite alarmed for her. 'What is the matter?'

Isabella could say nothing. She shook and trembled so much that she would have fallen had Lord Angelsea not thrown both his arms around her to keep her upright. 'Tell me.'

Isabella's agitation did not cease.

'Sir,' she said, 'I do not know what commotion has occurred in my mind as a result of what I have just heard. But it has restored my memory. I know now that I am indeed Isabella Broderick and that I was raised at Ducoeur Castle by Lady Sophia Ducoeur, until, being older, I came to the attention of her brother, Sir Roderick. The lady, attempting to put me out of the reach of his passion, formed a plan for marrying me off to a certain Mr Jackson, a man who was both toadying and odious, while Sir Roderick was engaged in some business in the West Indies. Sir Roderick, returning and discovering this, came to me and told me I had been jilted by Mr Jackson, a fact in which I rejoiced until I recognized that Sir Roderick meant to marry me himself. It was in fleeing this marriage, which he had contrived in the most clandestine fashion with the help of a certain Mr Edgecliffe, that I encountered your horses. The rest of my sad history you know.'

'It will be sad no longer. Be my wife as you have already promised to be!' said Lord Angelsea.

'I cannot, sir.'

'For what reason?'

'I would not put you in danger from Sir Roderick and Lady Sophia.'

'Isabella!'

'No, sir, I beseech you. Think of what harm might come to you and your title for being married to Isabella Broderick, who was formerly under the care of such two villains.'

'I would call out any man who implied that it has touched your good nature and reputation.'

'I had rather you had not found me,' cried Isabella.

'I thank God for it!' he said, endeavouring to pick up her hand and hold it to his lips, Isabella all the while saying, 'This cannot be, sir. You must see it is impossible. Now, go, sir, I beg you.'

'I shall not,' said the young lord.

'Sir, I beg you to consider,' she entreated, 'the harm that has already befallen you and your family because of me!'

'I cannot!'

'You must.'

And so the interview continued, with Lord Angelsea saying he could never love another and Isabella urging him to leave before the Bountifuls returned. At length Lord Angelsea saw that Isabella would not be swayed.

'Then, madam,' he said, 'I beg you to permit me one thing.'

'What is that?' Isabella asked.

'Allow me to keep in correspondence with you so that I may have the liberty from time to time of enquiring after your health and well-being.'

'You will write to me as Miss Napier?'

'I shall!'

'Then, sir, I agree, but I beg you to go now before your presence puts the good Bountifuls in danger.'

'Will you not allow me to accommodate you somewhere more respectable?'

'This place *is* respectable, and I am very happy here. I do not know why, Montagu, but it has seemed since the first time I arrived here that it has been more my home than any other place I have lived, excepting Angelsea Court. And since, as I have explained to you, I cannot live there, I would prefer to remain here and perfect my skills in the art of dairying.'

Before they parted, Isabella begged to know what the news was of Lady Caroline. Lord Angelsea informed her that his sister had still not regained her power of speech.

'The poor lady! And it is all my fault!'

'Isabella, you must believe me, my sister places all the blame on Sir Roderick. And I believe she is as happy with Mrs Percival and her son as she would be with the best-connected people in the country. Indeed, Mr Percival has such an understanding of her looks and gestures that it seems that she can almost communicate with him without speech.'

'I pray you, remember me to her, and say I should have liked to have had the honour of meeting Mr Percival and his mother.'

'I shall.'

And so the interview was terminated. Lord Angelsea returned to Angelsea Court without any recollection of his objective of seeing Mr Bountiful's prize cow. Isabella watched him from an upstairs window until he was out of sight and then gave way to tears, truly believing that she would never again see her Montagu.

When the Bountifuls returned home, Polly was full of a certain young man they had met on the way, who had saluted them and been very civil and who she was sure was a gentleman of great authority. From this description Isabella guessed that the person they had met was Lord Angelsea, who had greeted them with all the respect that was their due.

It soon became important for Isabella to be able to make some explanation as to why, being supposedly friendless, she was suddenly receiving correspondence. Not liking to lie to such good, honest people as the Bountifuls, she told them she had requested, from an old friend, information that might let her know if Sir Roderick was still a danger to her.

Lord Angelsea's letter confined itself to Isabella's health and was so polite and contained so little avowal of affection that it might have been read by anyone without its ever being supposed that Lord Angelsea had begged the lady to be his wife.

The second letter was the same, but the third letter gave Isabella great anxiety by containing the information that Mr Bunce had been thrown from his horse, having gone late at night to perform a baptism on a child not thought likely to live, and had suffered the most awkward fracture of his leg, the break being so serious that there was some question of his ever being able to walk again without the aid of a crutch.

Isabella at once replied, begging that Lord Angelsea would keep her informed as to Mr Bunce's recovery. Being urgent to know more about her friends as soon as possible, with Polly, who was her usual postmistress, being away from home by the virtue of her sister Susan's confinement, an event that had carried off all the Bountifuls for the purpose of admiring the new arrival, Isabella determined that she would venture out of her secrecy and present the letter herself at the post-house. Accordingly, she set off for the town in which she had first become acquainted with Mrs Bountiful by upsetting her cabbages.

She had just handed her letter in when she heard herself being addressed from behind by a female voice. 'Why, is it not Isabella Broderick?'

Isabella turned, wondering by whom she had had the misfortune to be recognized. Behind her stood Abigail, who, having been dismissed from her place by Lady Sophia, had, by appealing to Sir Roderick, been given sufficient references to find work as a lady's maid in another household. This household was now in the process of removing itself, bag and baggage, to Brighton for the sea-bathing, a prospect that Abigail, who had never seen the sea or had the opportunity of trying if it really was salt, was greatly delighted by.

Isabella gave her a small nod and hurried on, but not before she heard her say to one of her fellow servants: 'I think that by that chance meeting I may do myself some good.'

These words rang in Isabella's head all the way back to the farm. She could suppose only that Abigail had meant one thing by them: that for the sake of some financial gain, the maid was prepared to report that she had seen Isabella. Isabella was sure that the only person to whom she, Isabella, was to be reported was Sir Roderick. Rapidly, she tried to calculate how long it would take such information to reach them, and for Sir Roderick to come after her. She felt certain that it would not be long, and wondered by what new means of flight she could this time escape him.

She then recalled the evening that they had gone to the play, and how Rosalind had escaped from her uncle by disguising herself as a boy. This now became Isabella's plan and, Master Bountiful's clothes that very morning having been washed and hung out to dry, it was easy to procure such an outfit. In five minutes Isabella had arrayed herself in jacket, shirt and breeches. In order to check on her appearance she looked into the glass, and saw that her hair could not help proclaiming her femininity. There was nothing for it. She must cut off her hair at once.

Running to the outhouse, she took down a pair of the clippers that had been newly sharpened for the shearing and, twisting her hair into a knot, cut it short just above her shoulders. Not even pausing to replace the shears or gather up her cut locks, she ran back into the house, meaning to cover as much face as she could by means of one of Mr Bountiful's hats, which hung on a peg beside the door. This being done, she had the foresight to gather up as much food as she could from the Bountiful's larder and, once again, as a fugitive set out into the world, this time disguised as a boy.

The distress of the Bountifuls, on returning from seeing the young paragon and finding Isabella missing, was pitiful to behold. Mr Bountiful lamented that he had ever sharpened the shears, Mrs Bountiful that she had hung out the clean clothes, Master Bountiful that he had not been on hand to swear to defend her, and Polly that she had suggested the expedition to her sister's in the first place. Indeed, Polly wept so bitterly that night that she might almost have been drowned in her own bed-room, and Mrs Bountiful spent the evening in constantly stroking the heavy knot of Isabella's hair.

It had been Mrs Bountiful's habit to cut a lock of hair from all the children she had suckled, both her own and those to whom she was wet-nurse. All these curls had been wrapped in small pieces of paper, labelled with the names of the child and put into the box that contained the family Bible. Picking up the Bible, placing the little packets on the table, she began to exam-ine the contents of these packets. First she looked at those of her own five children and then those she had nursed.

The last packet was labelled with the name of 'Lissy', and Mrs Bountiful could not resist drawing its contents out to com-pare them with Isabella's locks. To her amazement the colour of the hair was alike in every respect.

At first Mrs Bountiful thought that the light was playing tricks on her, but, on calling first for Mr Bountiful to come down and then her two children, they all agreed that there could be no mistake. The child that Mrs Bountiful had nursed and the young lady that she had rescued with her cloak in the market-place appeared to be one and the same.

'I do believe,' she cried to the family gathered around her, 'that, though we did not recognize her as the child I nursed here for three years, Ben did. For when Isabella was a child they were always the greatest of playmates: he would let Isabella tumble him and pull his tail, which was a liberty he did not permit to anyone else. And see the way he sits by the door, as if hoping for her return at any moment.'

'And Isabella always declared,' added Polly, 'that when she first came to us she found everything strangely familiar, and I swear now that she truly is my sister, for were we not suckled at the same breast, and did I not weep bitterly when my Lissy was taken away from us?'

'You did,' said her father. 'And you would go round the farm looking for her and calling "Lissy" for many days afterwards.'

'And did not I,' cried young Mr Bountiful, 'once pull her from the stream where she had tumbled in?'

'Indeed, Tom,' replied his father, 'and she might have drowned but for your quick thinking.'

What pleasure it gave young Tom Bountiful to think that at the age of five he had been the rescuer of Isabella.

'What do you know of her and her people, Mother?' asked Polly.

'It is a sad story,' said Mrs Bountiful, 'and not one that I should like to tell when we are already so unhappy.'

But Polly and Tom both assured her that it would greatly cheer them to hear of Isabella and her relations.

'Very well,' said Mrs Bountiful, settling herself in her chair. 'She was brought here in a manner that both your father and I found remarkable at the time.'

'How was that?' asked Polly, for whom the story could not be told fast enough.

'Why, she was brought by her father, who laid down in every particular how she must be treated, what foods she must have and what she must not, and who was to be informed should she ever be in any danger.'

'Did she have no mother?' put in the eager Polly, her eyes again filling with tears at the possibility.

'The lady was never spoken of, except for some remarks of the child looking so very like her that the father could hardly bear look at her, for she so reminded him of his dear wife.'

Polly again interrupted: 'And was that the reason he gave for bringing her here?'

'It was. And it was my belief at the time – and still is, the father being somewhat old to have such a small child – that he had made a late marriage to a young lady, with whom he had been truly happy, but who had expired on the birth of the child.'

Polly's sentimental eyes welled again with tears, for she never liked anything better than a love-story in which the couple had been parted by death, thus allowing their love to shine on for ever undiminished by misunderstanding or changes in their domestic circumstances.

'The gentleman parted from her with a tenderness I have seen only in your father and, today, in Mr Kindlysides. He talked to her in such a way that except for his calling her by the baby name of Lissy one might have supposed her to be a grown woman rather than an infant who was not even of an age to sit up, and he fastened around her neck a locket that he begged her to wear always for her mother's sake.'

'Madam!' cried Polly, at last being able to make a useful interruption. 'Was it something in the manner of an oval edged with little pearls and rubies?'

'That is the very description of it.'

'Then there can be no doubt of it, the Lissy that was my childhood playmate is the Isabella that has disguised herself and run away.'

'How can you be so sure?' enquired Mr Bountiful.

'For she had such a locket, though she took very good care to keep it hidden. I saw it sometimes at night when we were making our preparations for bed, and once I tried to obtain the borrowing of it, a loan which was denied, for she said she had vowed to wear it always for her mother's sake.'

'Preserve us!' cried Mrs Bountiful. 'If I had seen it, I would have recognized it and the child immediately!'

Here Mr Bountiful added a note of caution: 'My dear, I am not at all sure that the gentleman's name was Napier.'

'Indeed it was not!' cried his wife. 'It was Ducoeur.'

'Then how did she come to change it?' asked Tom.

'I do not know, but she never hid from us the fact that she was pursued by some person and believed her life to be in great danger from that quarter. I can presume only that the name was some attempt to prevent discovery.'

'And he must have found her out,' cried Tom, 'or why would she flee in the disguise of a boy?'

This matter, and the nature of Isabella's disappearance, was discussed between them many times over the course of the next few days, but they always decided that nothing could be done to find her, beyond enquiring at the neighbours if any young gentleman had applied to them for board and lodging, a fact they all denied. Nothing they could do would comfort poor Ben, and it began to seem that he was going to pine and die for the loss of one who had been his earliest mistress.

❧ FIFTEEN ❧

In which Lady Sophia Ducoeur decides to revenge herself upon her brother

It was not long before Abigail's report of seeing Isabella in Weyton reached Ducoeur Castle, where it was received by Sophia, who had taken on the duty of forwarding Sir Roderick's correspondence. She now learnt, from the maid's ill-spelt and badly written note to her brother, in what area of the country Isabella had secreted herself.

Lady Sophia's first instinct on this discovery was at once to inform Sir Roderick, but on reflection she decided that it would be better to plan her own campaign against Isabella. Accordingly, she sent a servant she very much relied on by the name of Joseph, to Weyton with the instruction that he was to make enquiries there and in the surrounding neighbourhood as to whether any strange young lady had come among them. Should anyone ask him why such enquiries were being made, he was to reply that he was searching out Isabella on behalf of her mother, whom she had sorely disappointed by going away.

Jacob was very thorough in his enquires and soon discovered through the gossip in the neighbourhood that a young lady by the name of Miss Napier was believed to have been lodging with Mr and Mrs Bountiful, but that recently she had disappeared without anyone being able to get the least satisfaction from the family as to why she, the young lady, had vanished almost as suddenly as she had appeared.

When the servant returned to Ducoeur Castle with this scant information, he was received by Lady Sophia, who flew into a temper and boxed his ears, insisting that by a more diligent use of questioning he might have obtained a more satisfactory report of Isabella and her movements.

'I see I shall be put to the necessity of going there myself,' she cried, raining blows on the poor man's head. The servant trying to protest that he had done all he could, she struck him in the face and declared that he was an idler and a fool.

The anger that Lady Sophia had turned on one who had been her favourite led Joseph to think that she was quite peculiarly anxious to find Isabella, and he decided to inform Sir Roderick of this as soon as the opportunity arose, hoping by that means to obtain from the brother some recompense for the injury he had suffered at the hands of the sister.

Happily, this occurred the following day, when Sir Roderick, who had again being spending his time at Mr Couchman's house, found it necessary to ride over to Ducoeur Castle to instruct an architect about some repairs to the roof. It was soon discovered that no firm plans for restoration could be made until the roof leads had been inspected, and Joseph, learning this from the architect's boy, took the liberty of following Sir Roderick there, thinking by this means to have an interview with his master that could not be interrupted by his mistress.

The servant first showed Sir Roderick the bruises that Lady Sophia had made on his arm and then the cut above his eye which had been caused by her striking him.

'I do not believe you!' said Sir Roderick when Joseph ventured to explain that that the wounds had been made by Lady Sophia, but being in truth very anxious to know what had taken place between his sister and her servant. 'What cause would my sister have to use you with such violence?'

'She lost her temper, sir.'

'And how was that loss of temper brought about?'

'I was sent to enquire after Miss Broderick.'

'By whom?'

'By her ladyship.'

'And how was my sister's anger caused: by your finding of Miss Broderick or your not finding of her?'

'I did not find the lady's person, sir, only some details of her having been in a certain neighbourhood.' The servant was gratified by Sir Roderick's being eager for more information about Isabella.

'What was the name of the neighbourhood?'

'Weyton. I have discovered she lodged there with some people by the name of Bountiful.'

'And this was not enough for my sister?'

'No, sir. She was insistent that she must have the whereabouts of the young lady. However, sir, perhaps someone like yourself, and with your connections, could discover more.'

This was the plan that had already formed in Sir Roderick's mind, and he had decided to pay a visit to the Bountifuls before the servant had descended the stairs from the roof.

Meanwhile, his sister was making a similar plan, intending to pay a visit to the Bountifuls in the guise of Isabella's mother. She thought that with a wedding-ring on her finger and an expression of an earnest desire to do good to Isabella, she would be able to obtain better information than was given to the servant.

Lady Sophia was convinced that safety could come to her brother only through the death of Isabella, which would also cancel his obsession about her and might, in time, hoped Lady Sophia, lead to his agreeing to spend a quiet life in the country with her.

To this end she had consulted Jane, who had the knowledge of a vast number of country receipts and sometimes hinted that her mother had been interested in witchcraft and accomplished in the making up of poisons, thereby becoming famous for the killing of rats and mice. After her interview with Jane, Lady Sophia armed herself with a small vial, ridged, so that its contents were indicated to be fatal even to someone feeling the vessel in the dark. Remembering how grateful Isabella had once been to her for the gift of a few drops of attar of roses, Lady Sophia decanted the poison into a phial for scent, for Jane had assured her that by being dabbed on a handkerchief and held to the nostrils the contents' effect would be almost instantaneous.

Mrs Bountiful was most amazed when, in the middle of trying to seek out a broody hen that had made its nest in the orchard, she was called in by Polly, who told her that a grand lady had arrived and was sitting in the parlour, declaring that she was Isabella's mother and that she must speak to Mrs Bountiful immediately.

'This is very curious,' said Mrs Bountiful.

'She is a very grand lady,' said Polly, 'and I have always liked to believe that Isabella was of noble birth. For was not her locket very fine?'

'Indeed,' agreed Mrs Bountiful, meaning by this means to test if Lady Sophia were really some relation of the girl she herself had almost loved as a daughter.

Wiping her hands on her apron and instructing Polly to look for the hen, Mrs Bountiful went into the parlour, where sat Lady Sophia.

At first glance there was nothing in the sight of Lady Sophia to indicate to Mrs Bountiful that she had any tie or close relationship to Isabella. The charitable farmer's wife put this down to the fact that the lady's features had been so entirely deformed by the smallpox that it was impossible to tell what her face had previously been.

'Madam,' she said when the introductions had been made, 'will you take some tea?'

'No, I am here on a matter of some urgency.'

'What is that?' asked Mrs Bountiful, though she knew perfectly well from Polly why Lady Sophia had come to their humble home.

'I wish to discuss a certain young lady who I have on good authority has been staying with you.'

'There *was* a young lady here . . . '

'Was her name Isabella?'

'There are many Isabellas in the world. If I had been blessed with another daughter . . . '

꽃꽃

Lady Sophia stopped Mrs Bountiful by holding up her hand. 'If I am correct, her name was Isabella Broderick, and in proof of this I should like to describe a locket that she always wore, a locket that I, with my own hands, placed around her neck.' Lady Sophia dabbed at her eyes. 'It was of a somewhat unusual design, being composed of pearls and rubies.'

'Indeed, she did wear such a locket.'

'Then my daughter is found!' cried Lady Sophia, her voice full of pleasure at finding her prey.

Mrs Bountiful was convinced that the lady was indeed Isabella's mother. Accordingly, believing, as in the case of her own children, that no daughter would ever seek to hide a secret from her mother, she told Lady Sophia every detail of Isabella's escape from Sir Roderick and her collision with the market stall.

'Did she ever mention her pursuer by name?' demanded Lady Sophia.

'No, madam, she did not, and indeed I believe her dislike of him was so great that she could not bring herself to mention it.'

Lady Sophia smiled to herself at this information, and, seeing that the lady looked pleased, Mrs Bountiful could not help breaking in with the words: 'There is one thing on which I am very curious.'

'And what is that?'

'How came she to believe she was an orphan?' This was a question that Lady Sophia had anticipated, and she rattled off a very pretty story of how her relations, not liking her husband, had convinced her that her child was dead and that she should leave him.

'I had just discovered that she was still believed to be alive when it was reported to me by . . . a servant that she had seen a lady in the town wearing the very jewel I have just described. Not liking to trust a servant's word, I made further enquiries and was told that you were the good woman who had taken my child in. I have therefore come at once to enquire after her, to see her, to speak with her!'

'Madam,' said Mrs Bountiful, 'I must tell you at once that she is not here.'

Lady Sophia, who knew this to be the case, nevertheless managed to express great surprise at this pronouncement. 'Do not tell me he has carried her off?'

'No, madam. When we found she had gone, we looked for the mark of a horse or a cart, for by what other means could she be abducted. No marks were to be found. But we believe, from other evidence, that she went of her own accord, disguising herself as a boy in my son's clothes and cutting off her hair.'

'But how could she support herself?'

'She took from the larder a few piece of bacon and cheese. I had that very morning carried most of its other contents over to my daughter, Susan, who had just been delivered of a fine boy.'

'Do you have any reason to believe she may return?'

Mrs Bountiful looked down at her hands in her lap, very afraid of what her guest might think of the thoughts that she had had concerning an alliance between Isabella and Tom Bountiful.

'I repeat my question!' said Lady Sophia, who was not accustomed to not receiving an immediate answer.

'She knows we will always gladly receive her, whatever her difficulties.'

Lady Sophia rose from the wooden chair in which she had been sitting, believing she could discover nothing further by remaining in the house. 'Will you do something for me?' she asked Mrs Bountiful.

'If it is my power, madam.'

'Should she return, I would ask you to give her these in remembrance of me.' And Lady Sophia took out a silk hand-kerchief trimmed with silver filigree and a scent phial which she put into Mrs Bountiful's hands, making the good farmer's wife swear that should Isabella return they would be given to her immediately, something Mrs Bountiful said that she would do a hundred times over.

Lady Sophia made her farewells and departed, leaving an address care of the Misses Timms, fully expecting that if she was ever in receipt of information there, it would be that of the death of Isabella.

As soon as Lady Sophia had gone, Polly, who had found the hen and its clutch of thirteen eggs, came running in to see what the lady had had to say to her mother. Mrs Bountiful gave her all the particulars and showed her the presents that had been left as keepsakes for Isabella. How Polly admired the handkerchief! She stroked the silver lace and held the silk up to her face; she turned the scent bottle over in her hand, admiring the scenes of love it presented on its back and front. She would have pulled out the stopper and smelt the scent had her mother not expressly forbidden her.

'They are to be kept for Isabella,' said Polly's mother, putting the handkerchief and phial in one of the drawers of the great oak dresser. 'And I only pray she may return and have them.'

The letter whose posting had been so fateful to Isabella had not yet reached Lord Angelsea. He had been called away from Angelsea Court by a sudden message from his elder sister, Penelope, Countess of Mullingar, to say that she was come from Ireland to spend the summer with a friend in Cheshire and that she requested his presence immediately. Thinking that this could only mean some fresh difficulty between the estranged husband and wife, he set off at once to render his sister any help that he could offer.

On his arrival he found the countess in a most distressed state and, venturing to enquire what had occurred to cause the lady such great emotion, discovered that it had been occasioned by the death of a friend, who had died in the most terrible circumstances. The name of the friend was Mrs Cox. The countess sat down to unburden herself to her brother.

She had been called to England by Mrs Cox, who had written to inform her that Isabella had chosen to run away from her care. No name had been mentioned for the gentleman with whom she had fled, and the Countess of Mullingar was in an agony that Isabella had gone away with Lord Angelsea.

'How I wish she had!' he cried. 'So much might have been

prevented. But finish your story, and I will tell you mine.'

'Though the letter was written long after the event and Mrs Cox had changed her place of abode, and having had nothing from your pen for a long time, I decided to set out at once. Having given instructions as to the education and care of the children, I went to Dublin to take the ferry, but I was unlucky with the weather and a storm more appropriate for February than for May blew up, obliging me to wait some days before the crossing could be attempted. I went at once to Angelsea Court, but without even presenting myself there I discovered you had gone away. Imagine, then, what my thoughts were concerning you and Miss Napier.'

Again Lord Angelsea sought to interrupt.

'Montagu, I will hear everything you have to say when I have done, for what I have to say must be said if I am to obtain any relief.

'After quitting Angelsea Court, I went straight to see Mrs Cox, hoping that she might be able to supply me with further details. I found her in Chester, where it became very obvious to me that she expected to be brought to bed of a child in a very few weeks. You can imagine my disgust at this and I did not forbear to say I wondered how she dared have any further acquaintance with me. In short, I cursed and scolded her.'

Lord Angelsea, who remembered Lady Penelope as an occasional tyrant in their own nursery, almost felt sorry for Mrs Cox.

'I was about to turn my back on her and leave when the lady put her hand to her side and declared that she was in the greatest pain and believed the child to be imminent. I retorted that it was but the start of June and she had told me the child was not expected until July. She stammered to say this was so, but that she had had other children, of which, believe me, I knew nothing, and that, though it was almost two months early, the child was coming. Such were her cries that a great fuss was stirred up in the house in which she was lodging, which made it impossible for me to leave without its being known that I was a friend of the lady's, who called with every available breath for me to hold her hand and comfort her, saying to all those around her that I had remained since our schooldays her dearest friend.

'The child, a girl, was born dead after three days' agony on Mrs Cox's part, and it was obvious that the mother's death must soon follow . . . ' The Countess dropped her head, lifting it up again after a few moments' silence and saying: 'Something in the grief that Mrs Cox had gone through in her labour and death of the child affected me, and I felt that it was my duty to remain with my poor friend until she underwent her inexorable fate. During this time Mrs Cox suffered alternately from bouts of such great pain that she could do nothing but cry out followed by periods of lucidity in which she repented bitterly of the life she had passed since the death of her husband. In one of her moments of clarity she alluded to something I had long wished to hear concerning my husband.'

'What was that?' asked Lord Angelsea.

'She told me that a friend had written to inform her that Miss Tanner had left the earl and had taken up with a member of the royal circle. Montagu, that is why I have sent for you. I would ask you to go to him and ask if some sort of reconciliation can be made between us. If not for my sake, then for our children, for I should not like to die in such regret as Mrs Cox.'

This was an altogether different aspect to Lady Penelope than her brother had seen since the earl had left her.

'Will you go at once?' she asked.

'I cannot.'

'For my sake?'

'My reasons will become clear to you, but I must now explain to you the circumstances that make it impossible.'

When she had heard all that Lord Angelsea had to say concerning Lady Caroline's abduction, Isabella's flight and his own escape from death at the hands of Sir Roderick, Lady Penelope put another question to him. 'I see that you think Mr Percival a very good and sensible gentleman. Do you think it possible that he might go to my husband for me?'

༄༅

'I consider it very likely,' said Lord Angelsea, thinking that for the sake of her sister, Lady Caroline, Mr Percival would do anything for Lady Penelope.

They agreed that Mr Percival, who would once have been considered by Lady Penelope as below her contempt, would act for her in a matter so delicate as her reunion with her husband.

The matter having been settled, and Lady Penelope having written a very kind note to the earl which Mr Percival was to put into his hand only, Lord Angelsea begged that she should return to Ireland, saying he thought it better that her husband should be seen to return to her rather than she go running after the gentleman. Lord Angelsea then went with his sister to Parkgate, to see her on to the boat, and returned to Angelsea Court, where he found Isabella's anxious letter enquiring after the fate of Mr Bunce.

There was also among his correspondence a note from Mrs Bunce saying that her husband was now very much better and that it was thought that he would make a complete recovery, and she begged him to let this fact be known to his friends. Though he had only just returned from accompanying Lady Penelope, this news, and the thought of how gladly it would be received by Isabella, made Lord Angelsea quite forget the promise he had made her of never seeing her again, and he at once set out for the Bountifuls.

The day that Isabella had departed from the Bountifuls' farm had passed well enough, though she felt very sad at bidding farewell to everything that had always seemed so familiar since her arrival there. She crossed the little stone bridge over the stream and paused for a moment or two to watch the trout that played there, and which Tom had tried to teach her to catch by tickling them under their stomachs, and where, in the course of such an endeavour, she had tumbled in and been rescued by him. It had been a pleasant summer pastime when the work of the day had been over, but Isabella now thought it might be a useful art of which to be appraised, should she find herself in want of nourishment. She passed on through the small hamlet in which the church stood and found herself curtsied at by one of the pert daughters of the parson, a curtsy she was about to return when she remembered that she was now disguised as a young labourer, and that the appropriate response was to bow. She walked on for some way when the distance that she had gone and hunger together reminded her that she should sit and take some rest. This she did, sitting down under an oak tree, and remembering that she was wearing breeches and must cross her legs.

Refreshed, and the sun not setting until late in the evening, she then walked on some way further and prepared to spend the night in the open under a dense hedge. Reminding herself that more harm was likely to come to her from Sir Roderick than from the birds and beasts of the fields, she soon fell into a comfortable sleep.

She woke the next morning to find that clouds had got up and rain was beginning to fall. In this circumstance, the hedge did not offer quite the protection that Isabella had presumed it to have the previous night, and she vowed to walk on until some more substantial shelter could be obtained. Nothing presented itself until she came to a small sheepfold roofed by some rough planks. In this abode she spent the rest of day, thinking that even in the rain it had always been cheerful at Mr and Mrs Bountiful's.

The weather was fine on the next two days, and she spent them in the manner of the first. On the fifth day she ate the last of the food that she had taken from the farm. She did not know how she could gain more except by finding some means of employment, so she decided to stop at each door she came to, offering herself as a labourer. But being small, fair and light of build, no one to whom she offered her services believed her to be of any worth in the fields, and she began to sink more and more into wretchedness.

She had just been turned away from one farm when the farmer's wife came out with a bucket of swill, which she intended to give the pigs. At that moment a terrible commotion started in the house and, putting down the pail, she ran back inside the house, fearing for her infant's life. In a second Isabella had made her way back through the gate and picked up the vessel and its contents, intending to carry it away with her, thinking that the meal of which she had deprived the pigs would last her for several days.

Lord Angelsea's second approach to the Bountifuls' farm was witnessed by Tom, who at once recognized, him from his horse and his demeanour, as the gentleman who had saluted them so civilly on the road on their return from market. He went to tell Polly, who had very often talked about their being so kindly greeted by a man so much above them in station.

While Tom went with the stranger and his horse to the stable, Polly ran into the house to wash her face and hands and then, wanting to greet the young gentleman in the style that she felt his conduct deserved, and, having no time to change from her working clothes, she remembered the phial of scent and handkerchief. She ran to the drawer in which Mrs Bountiful had put them against Isabella's return and in a second was sprinkling the scent on the silk.

At this moment Ben roused himself from his sloth and set up a frightful agitation, growling and barking and jumping up. 'Down!' cried Polly, but the dog persisted. She put down her hand to push him away and was most annoyed when, instead of going, the dog snatched the handkerchief from her hand.

'Oh, horror!' cried Polly, thinking that by this, her borrowing of Isabella's keepsake should be discovered. But her panic at losing the handkerchief turned to alarm when she saw Ben's strange jerking.

When her brother and Lord Angelsea entered the room, she cried to them that she thought the dog had been taken by a fit, but, before Lord Angelsea had crossed the room, the animal was dead, a victim of the poison that Lady Sophia had intended for Isabella, the handkerchief still in its mouth.

Without waiting for any introduction, Lord Angelsea turned

to Polly and demanded to know whence the piece of silk and filigree had come. Mrs Bountiful, who had been brought in from the cheese-room by the commotion, explained that it had been given her as a charge by a lady, and immediately began to demand from Polly an explanation as to what she was doing with the handkerchief.

'Madam, I pray you,' said Lord Angelsea, 'let us have the excuses later. For my own part I believe that the dog has been killed by some poison that has been applied to this piece of cloth.'

'How could that be?' cried Mrs Bountiful, who had lived in agony for a week when she happened accidentally to prick one of her children when putting pins in their clothes.

'I do not know,' said Lord Angelsea, 'but I beg you to give me the opportunity of making a proof of it.' He commanded Tom to bring him in some old fowl that was soon to be destined for the family pot.

The cock being brought in, Lord Angelsea instructed Polly to go through exactly the same motions concerning the scent bottle and handkerchief she had made before he had entered the room. Seizing the handkerchief from her as Ben had done, he threw it over the head of the cockerel. Straight away, the bird fell into the same convulsions as the dog had done and died in the same manner.

Lord Angelsea threw the handkerchief into the fire, snatched up the phial, carried it to the open window, and poured the poison that remained on the ground. Turning to Mrs Bountiful and her children, he said: 'I fear you have been sadly deceived.'

'Polly, perhaps that will teach you to be more honest in future,' cried Mrs Bountiful, convinced that had it not been for the poor dog, Polly would now be lying dead at her feet.

'Madam,' said Lord Angelsea, 'am I right in supposing that this was left for a young lady, whom I know to have been staying here?'

Mrs Bountiful replied that it was, and insisted that it had been brought by the young lady's mother.

Thinking that he knew of only one woman connected with Isabella who was capable of planning such an audacious scheme, Lord Angelsea demanded: 'Was she marked by the pox?'

'Very badly, sir, and it had taken most of her sight.'

'And was she very fat?'

'You could not call her beautiful, sir,' replied Mrs Bountiful, who was herself ample.

'Then she is Lady Sophia Ducoeur, a woman from whom I know Isabella to be in the greatest danger, and there is more besides.'

Lord Angelsea then asked that Mr Bountiful be sent for from the fields, so that he could repeat to the whole family everything he knew concerning Isabella and her history.

When the story had been told, and all those in the room had taken a melancholy glance at the faithful Ben, who lay before the fire on a little embroidered cushion, the Bountifuls demanded to know what they could do to be of assistance in catching two such depraved creatures as Sir Roderick and Lady Sophia Ducoeur.

'I have a scheme in mind,' cried the young man. 'If you will agree to it, I mean to find some means of bringing them both here.' But before he could expand at any greater length, a ruction was heard outside which signalled the arrival of a horse and rider.

'Two strangers in one day,' cried Mrs Bountiful.

'Pray, madam,' said Lord Angelsea, 'moderate your voice, for the window is open. If this visitor imports any danger, it is better that we should have the advantage of him. I must have a mirror,' he said to Polly in a voice so definite that she had run to her room, snatched up her glass and put it into his hand.

Lord Angelsea walked to a place where, by means of the mirror, he could observe whoever was outside. He at once saw that it was Sir Roderick.

Mr Bountiful's hand reached instantly for the blunderbuss.

Lord Angelsea restrained him. 'No, sir, we do not yet know if he has come alone. Madam,' he said, turning to Mrs Bountiful, 'do you have the heart, for Isabella's sake, to confront him and say to him exactly what I shall instruct you to say?'

'I shall,' said the stout-hearted lady. 'And for Isabella's sake I shall not be nervous.'

'Very well,' said Lord Angelsea, handing her the scent bottle. 'You must forget that this ever held the noxious poison we just now discovered it to contain. You are to tell Sir Roderick that Isabella was here and that she was taken away by a lady, who as a reward for your kindness to her gave you this bottle and a handkerchief. If he asks you where you believe the young lady to be taken, you are to answer Ducoeur Castle and ask him if he has ever heard of such a place. It is my belief that you will receive no answer, but that Sir Roderick, believing that his sister has taken Isabella away, and having proof in the form of this bottle that his sister has been here, will quit you immediately to return to Ducoeur Castle, where I must go at once if I am to have any advantage.' And pausing only to make the swiftest of bows he went out by the back door.

There now came a knock upon the front door, which made all the Bountifuls tremble.

'Take heart!' whispered Mr Bountiful as his wife stepped up to open it. Polly was so nervous that she hid herself in the shadow at the side of the door.

As Lord Angelsea had predicted, Sir Roderick at once asked after Isabella, using both the name of Napier and Broderick. Mrs Bountiful played her part and said that, though such a person had been living with them, she had been taken away.

'By whom?'

Before Mrs Bountiful could reply, the nervous Polly gave such a shiver that her skirt brushed the wall. 'You lie, madam!' he said, and in a second Sir Roderick pulled Polly roughly out of the shadow. The moment he saw she was not Isabella he let Polly go, giving her such a push that she almost fell.

For this, Tom was ready to fall on Sir Roderick, but one glance from his mother stopped him.

'By whom was she taken?' asked Sir Roderick.

'A lady, sir, of a status I should say almost matching your own.'

A dread entered the heart of Sir Roderick, who was mightily afraid that his sister had found Isabella before himself. 'What more information can you give me about the lady?'

'She was most generous, sir, indeed,' and Mrs Bountiful took the scent bottle from her pocket. 'She gave me this as a token of her esteem.'

Sir Roderick took the scent bottle and, turning it over, recognized it as the gee-gaw that had caused so much trouble between his father and his sister.

Not even pausing to ask the name of the person who had given it to Mrs Bountiful, Sir Roderick Ducoeur turned on his heels and quitted the farm.

⁕⥰ SIXTEEN ⥰⁕

In which the truth of Isabella's birth is almost discovered

Knowing what he did of Sir Roderick's sudden and impulsive nature both from his own observations and Mr Edgecliffe's account of him, Lord Angelsea felt sure that he would return to Ducoeur Castle expecting to find Isabella there. He was determined to arrive before him and had kicked his horse to a gallop as soon as he was out of the stable. As he rode he congratulated himself on having the advantage of Sir Roderick, but in this he had made a misjudgement of Sir Roderick's cunning.

Arriving at the Bountifuls' farm, and finding no one in the fields where he expected to find them all at toil, Sir Roderick had taken the opportunity to look into the stable, thinking that if their horses were still tethered, they could not be at any distance from home. Having ascertained that every stall in the stable was full, and wanting to be put to no trouble by being followed in his pursuit of Isabella, he had introduced a nail between the hoof and shoe of each horse, thinking that if he were ridden after the mount used to follow him would soon be lamed. It was a trick he had often used to outride his debtors.

In consequence of this action, Lord Angelsea's horse had not gone more than a couple of miles when it slowed from a gallop to a canter and then to a hobble. Lord Angelsea was off its back instantly and, checking its four quarters, soon discovered the nail, which he at once removed with his penknife, thinking it a confounded thing to meet such an accident when all speed was necessary. Remounted, he spurred his horse again, but the velocity with which he had been travelling, and the hard nature of the road, meant that such a great injury had been done to the animal that it was impossible for Lord Angelsea to ride the beast any further, even at a walk.

This was a bitter fact for Lord Angelsea, who must now take the horse by leading-rein to the next town and there obtain a new mount. Walking his horse and keeping it as much as possible in the grass at the side of the road, he heard the sound of a horse coming up behind him. From the sound of its hooves on the road it was clear to Lord Angelsea that it was being ridden with some urgency, and he could think only that it carried Sir Roderick.

He dropped the reins of his own horse, and with one bound jumped on to the branch of an oak tree which grew nearby. From his vantage point among the leaves, he watched Sir Roderick and his horse as they rode past, Sir Roderick's livid eyes rolling almost as much as those of his horse.

The moment that his enemy had passed, Lord Angelsea jumped down from his hiding-place and hurried his horse towards Weyton. Arriving there, he at once asked for the direction of the nearest smithy, hoping that something might be done to mend his horse. The smith disappointed him, saying he could do nothing except cauterize the injury and see that the beast was given good stabling.

He was just on the point of asking where this could be obtained when a boy came into the stable, asking if Mr Edgecliffe's horse was yet ready, because the gentleman was keen to continue his journey as soon as possible.

'Where has this Mr Edgecliffe come from?' asked Lord Angelsea.

'From Hawbury, sir,' the boy replied.

'Today?'

'Yes, sir. He says his business is very urgent, and that he has kept up sixteen miles an hour when the road was good.'

From this information Lord Angelsea guessed that Mr

Edgecliffe was riding in search of him with some urgent message.

'Where is the gentleman?' asked Lord Angelsea, thinking that the sooner any interview Mr Edgecliffe wanted to have with him could take place, the better.

'He is coming now, sir.' And looking along the street, Lord Angelsea beheld Mr Edgecliffe.

As soon as the gentleman saw him, he made as much haste as he could to shake Lord Angelsea's hand.

'Sir, oh, happy chance, I am on the point of making my way to Angelsea Court, but our meeting like this accelerates my message. I have heard word from Sir Roderick, in which he reports . . .'

'Their name is Bountiful and they have a farm not far from this place.'

Mr Edgecliffe looked at Lord Angelsea all amazement that he had already received the information he had brought him express from Hawbury.

'I have just come from the Bountifuls,' explained Lord Angelsea, 'and Sir Roderick has just paid a visit there also, without knowing anything of my presence. He is now returning with all speed to Ducoeur Castle, believing that Isabella has been carried there by Lady Sophia.'

'Oh, evil woman!' cried Mr Edgecliffe.

'I must tell you now that Isabella is not with her.'

'Then she is safe!'

'Alas, no,' said Lord Angelsea.

'Then where is she?'

Her lover shook his head. 'I do not know. All I can tell you is that she has cut off her hair and, disguised as a boy, once again disappeared. But before I attempt to find her, I mean to go straight to Ducoeur Castle and confront Sir Roderick and Lady Sophia.

At this juncture the boy who had been sent to fetch Mr Edgecliffe's horse led it around the corner at the side of the smithy.

'Take my horse!' cried Mr Edgecliffe. 'I shall find another as soon as I can and follow you directly.'

Without waiting for any repetition of this offer, Lord Angelsea was on the horse and departing from Weyton.

Sir Roderick arrived at Ducoeur Castle having whipped his horse until it bled and doing it such an injury that it was not likely that it should ever be ridden again. Without even wiping his brow, his whip still in his hand, he went straight to his sister's chambers. At the door he met Jane, who told him her mistress was engaged in conversation with the Misses Timms.

'What care I for the Misses Timms? All I care for is to find Isabella Broderick!' cried Sir Roderick, pushing his way past Jane and entering the rooms he had not cared to be in for twenty years. He glanced around him. The sight repelled him then, and time and dust had rendered the rooms still more grotesque. In her youth Lady Sophia had had a passion for cupids, and they hung from every furnishing which they could augment.

He strode through the first room and into the salon. Miss Ann and Miss Betty were greatly alarmed at his walking in on them with his face purple with exertion, his boots dirty and his whip in his hand.

'Sophia,' said Sir Roderick to his sister, who on his entering the chamber had come forward to greet him. 'I wish to speak to you.'

Lady Sophia, though disturbed by her brother's appearance and guessing what it meant, tried to delay the moment by introducing her friends.

'I do not give a fig for your friends!' said Sir Roderick, sweeping the tea-things from the table with his whip and scalding Miss Ann in the process. The lady let out a scream of pain.

'Ann!' cried Miss Betty and tried to go to her sister's aid. She was prevented by Sir Roderick, who grasped her by the arm and threw her towards the door. He dealt with Miss Ann in the same fashion, Miss Ann crying to Lady Sophia: 'My lady, help us!'

'Help yourselves!' cried Sir Roderick, now using his whip upon the backs of the clergyman's daughters and driving them out of the room like a pack of dogs.

'Dick!' cried Lady Sophia, using the pet name she had once had for her brother. 'The servants will hear!'

'What will they discover that they do not know already?' asked her brother, detesting the form of intimacy she used to him. Then, drawing the bolt across the door so that their interview could not be interrupted, he approached his sister, and, holding her arm so tightly that his nails drove into her skin, he demanded: 'What have you done with Isabella?'

'What do you mean?' asked his sister.

'Where have you hidden her?'

'Believe me, Dick, I am quite ignorant . . . '

'Then, if you will not answer me that, I shall ask you a question you may find easier. Where is your scent bottle?'

Dreading the importation of this question, Lady Sophia answered as coolly as she was able. 'Here,' she answered, and pulled a glass phial out of her bodice.

'I do not wish to see that!' cried Sir Roderick, smashing the bottle to the floor, where it broke, to be a danger to everyone who touched it. 'What I demand to see is the scent bottle that caused so much grief between you and my father. The one you purchased by coming to an arrangement with Mr Jackson.'

'Sir,' cried his sister, '*that* I disposed of as soon as I was aware of the trouble it created between me and my father.'

'I do not believe you!' shouted the brother. 'Such an action is not in your nature.'

'I gave it to my dear Jane.'

'Your dear Jane!' Sir Roderick strode to the door and threw back the catch to find Jane in the very convenient posture of listening at the keyhole. Before she could stand up, Sir Roderick had seized her by an ear and hauled her into the room. 'Is this true?' he demanded.

'Yes, indeed!' said Jane, endeavouring to take a glance at Lady Sophia and hoping that by catching her mistress's eye she would be assured of some reward.

'Then I command you to present it to me!'

'I cannot, sir.'

'For what reason?'

'I have sold it, sir. Long ago,' said Jane with a curtsy.

'A present from your lady?'

'I . . . ' Jane began to grow flustered. She looked again at Lady Sophia. 'My brother . . . '

'What care I for your brother?' cried Sir Roderick. 'I wish to know where and when and to whom you sold it.'

'It was sent to London, sir.'

'It was not,' replied Sir Roderick, taking the bottle from his pocket. 'I beg both you and my sister to look at this phial and deny it is the one of which I have been talking.'

'I cannot see it well enough,' responded his sister.

'Then take it into your hands and feel its shape,' answered her brother, stepping forward and putting the bottle into her hands. 'It is a very unusual shape for scent!'

As soon as the bottle was put into her hands by Sir Roderick, Lady Sophia guessed where he had obtained it.

'Say one thing to me,' she said. 'Tell me that Isabella is dead and will never threaten us more.'

'How could she be dead?'

'Jane's mother . . . '

Sir Roderick cast his glance upon Jane, who sank back against the panelling, quite pale at the revelation of the part she had played in what she believed to be Isabella's destruction.

'I was only carrying out my lady's orders.'

'What orders were those?' demanded Sir Roderick, advancing on her.

'I thought it best from the beginning she be done away with or sent as an orphan to some out-of-the-way house.'

'What is she gibbering of?' said Sir Roderick, turning away from the servant and facing his sister.

'You have frightened her out of her wits. She does not know what she is saying.'

'Do not call me mad, madam,' cried Jane. 'I have always known your secret, and I have kept it until this moment. Sir, I must tell you now that Isabella Broderick is your child by my lady there!' So saying, Jane stretched out her hand to point at Lady Sophia.

'How dare you lie!' Lady Sophia screamed, flinging the bottle that had contained the poison at Jane's head.

The servant crumpled to the floor. 'What I say is true.' Before she could reveal any more, Lady Sophia was upon her with her hands around her neck.

'Tell him it is not true or I shall strangle you!' Lady Sophia cried.

'Do you not believe me, sir?' asked Jane, looking to Sir Roderick for some rescue. 'Was I not the person who let you into this room and saw you safe out of it again. Let go!'

Lady Sophia would not. 'How dare you remind me of what is better forgotten,' she said, tightening her hands.

'She tried to make me believe the child had expired,' said Jane, in a voice that could only croak.

'It did!' cried Lady Sophia with such a passion that Jane's breath was completely cut off and she could talk no more to tell either truth or lies.

With Jane's death, some of the passion that had been in Lady Sophia evaporated, and she regained her composure.

'Why did you not tell me the child lived?'

'Because it did not.'

'How am I to know that?'

'These hands dispatched it,' said Lady Sophia, getting up and moving towards Sir Roderick.

Sir Roderick looked at his sister in horror.

She held out her hands towards him. 'Was it not your instruction that if it were born alive it was to be disposed of, and have I not always obeyed you?'

'When you told me Isabella was not my child . . . '

'Then,' said Lady Sophia with a hideous laugh, 'I spoke the truth.' And then, with hysterical laughter, she declared. 'But her true identity is an even better joke.'

'Then tell me,' said Sir Roderick, bringing his whip down

across Lady Sophia's face to quieten her.

'Isabella Broderick is our father's daughter by his second marriage. She is half-sister to you.' Her mad laughter broke out again as if it would never end.

❧ SEVENTEEN ❧

In which Isabella's true identity is discovered

In London happier scene was taking place. Mr Percival, to whom Lady Penelope's letter to her husband had been entrusted, had succeeded in gaining an interview with the earl.

The letter having been given to him, the Earl of Mullingar retired to a small private chamber to read it, leaving Mr Percival occupied with his own thoughts. Richard Percival was lost in contemplation of the beauty and charm of Lady Caroline Angelsea when that lady's brother-in-law returned to the room. Mr Percival stood up.

'I bid you to sit down,' said the earl.

Mr Percival resumed his seat expecting the earl to sit likewise, but the gentleman paced the room, obviously considering what he meant to say.

'Sir,' he said at last, stopping in front of Mr Percival's chair, 'I am sure you are waiting for me to give some explanation for the distress that I have caused my wife.'

'Only if you wish to give it, sir.'

'I cannot. I do not know what folly overcame me, to sunder myself from Penelope for . . . '

The earl could not utter the name that was now so repellent to him. 'I must let my actions speak for me, to my wife and all her friends. Know, then, that I have already ordered my servants to make up my trunk for me and that I intend to leave at once for Ireland, by that means informing my wife that I wish to be reunited with her quicker than by any letter.'

The earl was as true as his word. Within an hour he had left the house, parting from Mr Percival on the doorstep and begging that he would take the regards of a reunited brother to Lady Caroline.

Lord Angelsea rode towards Ducoeur Castle with the same urgency as the Earl of Mullingar rode towards the Irish ferry. He was certain that Sir Roderick, having shown no mercy towards Mr Whistler, would show none towards his sister when he discovered that Isabella was not with Lady Sophia. Thinking that his one hope of discovering Isabella's true identity lay with that lady, he was determined to reach Ducoeur Castle and Lady Sophia with all possible speed.

He arrived at Ducoeur Castle to find a stream of servants flowing out of the place. He could see from their bundles that most of them had made up for their wages by picking up anything they could carry and making off. He stopped one fellow who was struggling under the weight of a large ormolu clock. 'Tell me, sir, what is happening,' he asked.

'They have both gone mad,' replied Joseph, thinking himself adequately rewarded for Lady Sophia's attack on his ears by the prize he held in his arms.

'I always knew the child would be trouble,' said another servant as she passed.

'Do not go that way!' warned the smallest of the kitchen-maids. 'They will kill you and anyone who comes between them!'

Lord Angelsea did not heed her. He kicked his horse and rode up to the front of the house. The door was open and, there being no need of knocking for there was no footman, Lord Angelsea entered the house. Far off, up the stairs and along a corridor, he could hear the shouts and screams of Lady Sophia and her brother. He was up the stairs and approaching the chamber from which the cries came as Mr Edgecliffe rode into the courtyard.

As Lord Angelsea drew nearer the doors of Lady Sophia's

chambers, the argument between her and her brother could be heard more distinctly.

'I do not care for Isabella Broderick! I care only for you!' came the harpy cries of Lady Sophia.

'You were a deceiver then; you are a deceiver now,' came the brother's reply. 'No, do not touch me!'

There came the sound of the ripping of garments. Lord Angelsea flung open the doors to see brother and sister tearing at each other like cat and dog, each rending pieces of their fine raiments from each other and scattering them about the floor where Jane lay dead.

His first instinct was to separate them, and, using all his strength, he wrestled Lady Sophia away from Sir Roderick, the lady pulling the shirt clean off her brother's back as he did so.

Deprived of her prey, she turned on the man who had sought to be her rescuer, drawing her haggard nails across his face in an effort to scratch out his eyes. As the pair turned, Sir Roderick recognized Lord Angelsea and realized that now he had a final chance to take his revenge on him. He threw himself on Lord Angelsea's back, and the three of them fell to the floor.

Together they struggled, each trying to gain superiority over the others by any means that they could employ. Teeth, hands and feet were all brought into the terrible feud.

Mr Edgecliffe appeared in the door at the very moment that it seemed that Lord Angelsea must expire at the hands of the desperate brother and sister. Seeing this, and quite thoughtless of his own danger, Mr Edgecliffe ran to the mêlée and, seizing Lord Angelsea by the arm, dragged him from the clutches of Lady Sophia and Sir Roderick.

The brother and sister, completely inflamed by the battle, fought on.

'We must stop them, sir,' the noble lord said to Mr Edgecliffe, pushing away the cloth with which his rescuer was trying to staunch the blood running from Lord Angelsea's forehead.

But Mr Edgecliffe restrained him, as the couple struggled to their feet, their hands around each other's necks in a ghastly embrace. They looked into each other's eyes and saw there the reflection of themselves, livid and panting. Lady Sophia's hands tightened around Sir Roderick's neck, but in an instant he put his hand into the waist of his breeches, pulled out a small knife and thrust it into Lady Sophia's heart. She gave a small cry and fell towards him, catching the hand that held the blade under her as she did so. The blade that had been intended to kill his own sister was pushed from her body and into the heart of his own. They fell together, Sir Roderick stone-dead and Lady Sophia gasping her last, bubbles of blood at her mouth.

Lord Angelsea fell to his knees beside her, the lady blinking her short-sighted eyes that soon would see no more.

'Madam,' he said, 'you have but a few more breaths. Use them to good advantage by telling us the provenance of Isabella Broderick.'

'She is my half-sister by my father's second marriage.' Lady Sophia took another breath, obviously in an effort to say more, but it was too late, and, stretching out her hand and putting it into the cold embrace of her brother, she expired.

Isabella knew nothing of this release from her persecutors. In the time since she had left the Bountifuls she had grown more and more wretched and dejected. Sometimes she wished she had not decided to disguise herself in male attire, thinking she might have met with an all the more sympathetic reaction if she had chosen to retain her female status, but it was too late, and she could think of no way except theft by which she might obtain the clothes she required to once again declare herself to be Isabella Broderick.

Reflecting in this manner and being very hungry and dirty, with the clothes she wore flapping around her like those of a scarecrow, she wondered if she had anything about her person which might have any value. There was but one thing – her jewel, which she had taken great care to conceal lest it might reveal her sex.

Isabella unfastened the locket from around her neck and

drew it into the palm of her hand. Turning it over, she deliberated on the parent she supposed to have given it to her. She considered how long the money she might expect for the locket could sustain her, and whether the same parent who had given it to her might regard its sale as a necessity for the continuation of his or her child. But she could come to no decision, and so, clutching the rubies and pearls in her hand, she fell asleep in the hollow of an ancient tree.

During the night she was once again visited by a dream, so real that it seemed almost a prophecy. A kind lady came to her and urged her, with all possible haste, to find a jeweller who would give her the true price of her locket. So when Isabella awoke in the morning, the fact was quite decided upon, and, without turning the matter over in her mind, she set off to return to the town that she had lately passed through, where she thought she remembered seeing a jeweller's signboard.

She was not mistaken, and soon found herself outside a shop which bore the sign 'Mr J. Jasper, Jeweller'. Without a second thought Isabella went in, setting the small shop-bell ringing, which in turn brought the proprietor of the shop from his back room. The sight of Isabella, unkempt and dirty, caused Mr Jasper much alarm. It was obvious from the appearance of the stranger that there was nothing in the shop that could be afforded, and the shopkeeper could suppose only that he was about to be robbed.

Isabella, doing her best to stride and swagger, advanced on the old man, who trembled at her approach, thinking that any moment she would draw a weapon upon him and demand the contents of his shop and his money-boxes.

'Pray, sir,' said Isabella, opening her fist and showing the locket to Mr Jasper. 'Can you tell me what price I can expect to receive for this jewel?'

Mr Jasper, much amazed, regarded the piece in Isabella's hand without noticing the smallness of the palm. 'Where did you come by such a jewel?' he cried.

'Sir, I assure you it is my own,' replied Isabella.

'How can that be,' asked Mr Jasper with disbelief, 'unless you have stolen it?'

'Why should I steal what is my own, sir?' asked Isabella, in a tone of very great surprise.

'But how came you by it?' asked Mr Jasper, who felt from her responses to him that Isabella spoke the truth.

'Do you recognize it, sir?'

'If you will permit me to look at it more closely.'

Entirely trusting the old man, Isabella handed him the locket, which she had never before entrusted to anyone. The jeweller took out a glass and looked at the jewel, saying to himself: 'It is the very same.'

'The same as what, sir?' asked Isabella, recollecting the conversation she had had with the Bunces in Hawbury about the jewel, and how if its maker might be found she might be provided with some clue to her real identity.

Mr Jasper put down the locket and, with the same scrutiny he had regarded it, looked at Isabella. At last he pronounced: 'There is perhaps some similarity in the features.'

'To whom, sir?' asked Isabella, wishing that the old man were not so slow and careful in his deliberations.

'But I was told the child was a girl,' mused the old man, again looking at Isabella.

She could not help blushing under this scrutiny.

'And I do believe you are she!' he continued.

'Who am I, sir?' she asked, quite forgetting to lower the tone of her voice.

'Do you not know?' asked Mr Jasper.

'Only tell me,' said Isabella, 'and you will have my jewel without my asking anything else for it but what you know of my origins.'

'I made this myself,' explained Mr Jasper, again taking up the locket. 'It was a commission for a young lady on the occasion of her wedding.'

'Who?' demanded Isabella, but Mr Jasper would not be hurried.

'Her name before marriage I do not remember ever having known, but on marriage it became Ducoeur. But, madam, why do you start?'

'Of all the names in the world,' said Isabella, 'that is the one I most dread. To be Sir Roderick's daughter!'

'I do not talk of that blackguard!' cried Mr Jasper with much venom. 'If I am correct, which I believe I am, you are the daughter of Sir Penrose Ducoeur, the kindest, most gentle, generous man!'

Isabella remembered the kind face in the portrait she had so often looked at in her childhood. Now she said in wonder: 'I am Sir Penrose's daughter? How can that be?'

'This jewel was made for the occasion of a second marriage, a union that, though short, contained in it more happiness than the first. For I see by your shuddering at the name of Sir Roderick that you know that story.'

'I do not!' cried Isabella. 'I know only that it is his behaviour that has reduced me to the circumstances I am now in. You pronounced him a blackguard. I know him to be even worse than that.'

'Indeed, and I was once almost caught up with him in the most nefarious escapade.'

'Did the matter concern a lady?'

'She was not a lady by nature. She was his own sister.'

'Lady Sophia Ducoeur?'

'Indeed.'

'And what was the matter?' asked Isabella with some considerable trepidation.

'Between them, and out of their corrupted natures, brother and sister formed a wager that they could not seduce each other. And though each pretended not to have any desire for the other, the truth was very different. Sir Roderick meant to buy his sister's compliance through trinkets obtained from me. What charms the lady intended to use I do not know, for as soon as he had boasted of the matter to me, I refused to have anything more to do with him. But I believe that by some means or other brother and sister found themselves in the same infernal bed.'

'Oh, horrible' cried Isabella, almost wanting to stop her ears at Mr Jasper's story. 'Did my father know of this?'

'No, I made an agreement with Sir Roderick that I would not seek him out for debt, provided that the matter never came to the ears of Sir Penrose or his new wife.'

'Then, sir, since by this means you are still out of pocket, let my locket discharge a little of the debt.'

'I will not permit such a thing,' said the old man.

'Why not? It is but a little of what I owe you for the sake of my father.'

'You will need it.'

'For what purpose?'

'So that it may identify you to the lady who gave it to you.'

'But did you not say it was given to my mother?'

'Yes.'

'But I had always supposed her to be dead.'

'I have not heard of it. And to my certain knowledge she was alive a month ago, for I had the privilege of beating out a bump from a jug for her.'

'Sir, tell me at once where I may find her.'

'Appledown Manor.'

'Is that far?'

'No,' replied Mr Jasper. 'You may walk there in half an hour.'

'Then, sir,' said Isabella, 'I will borrow the locket from you as my means of admittance there. Now, I pray you, give me directions at once to my mother's house.'

Mr Jasper having done so, Isabella desired to set off at once for Appledown Manor, but this Mr Jasper would not allow, insisting that she should first wash her hands and face and then change her breeches for one of his granddaughter's gowns. When he saw that there was nothing that could be done about her shorn locks, Mr Jasper insisted on sending out for a hat from the milliner's at his own expense. Dressed in this fashion, Isabella set out for Appledown Manor.

Such was the speed that she made that within a quarter of an hour she came in sight of a small manor-house, somewhat old-fashioned and still with its moat. Isabella ran across the bridge to the house. She arrived at the door and beat upon it. The door was opened by the housekeeper, who told her that if she had any business with the place she should apply at the back entrance and promptly shut the door before Isabella could introduce herself by her locket.

Isabella made her way to the back of the house. At this door her reception was a little more polite.

'I wish to see the mistress of the house,' said Isabella.

The man who had opened the door said that in all matters of employment it was the butler to whom Isabella should apply.

'I have not come here in search of work, sir.'

'Then it is food.'

'No, sir.'

'You need not be frightened to beg here. It is the instruction of the lady of the house that anyone who comes in need of food should be fed. If you will go into the outhouse across the yard, bread and cheese will be brought to you.'

Isabella, thinking that by this means she would obtain a longer interview with the man, assented. When the food was brought to her, she again ventured to converse with the servant. But the fellow was very discreet and would answer none of her questions about his mistress, saying only that she preferred to remain apart from society as much as possible. The man was then called into the house to perform some duty, and Isabella was left alone to ponder by what means she might gain admittance. Eating her bread and cheese, she regarded the house and contemplated which room her mother might be in and tried to imagine what such a mother might look like.

She was engaged with these thoughts when a laundry-maid, the prospect of rain having now passed, came into the outhouse to collect some sheets that had been hung up to dry under its shelter.

At the sight of Isabella she stopped short. Feeling herself observed, Isabella turned towards her. The maid dropped her basket and covered her mouth with her hand in order not to let out a cry. Then, not believing what she saw, she took a step towards Isabella, looking hard at the locket that hung around her neck.

'It cannot be!' she said, and then took another step towards Isabella, saying: 'As I live and breathe, are you not Miss Henrietta's child?'

'If she is Lady Ducoeur.'

The maid took a step back. 'Do not think me impolite. She and I were of an age together, so Miss Henrietta she always was to me, and always will be. I am the only one she kept on after . . . but that is her story, not mine. Why are you not in the house?'

'I cannot gain admittance.'

'No,' said the maid. 'My lady is always very shy of visitors. But there *is* a way in, which is not by either the front or the back door.'

'What way is that?' asked Isabella, determined to try it at once.

'Would you like me to go to her for you?' asked the maid.

'It is kind of you,' said Isabella, 'but I should like to know if she recognizes me as you have done.'

The maid, understanding this, took Isabella by the hand and drew her across the yard to a small door at the side of the house which opened on to a twisting staircase with uneven treads. In the darkness, and hand in hand, Isabella and the maid carefully trod their way up the narrow stone steps the maid being careful to feel each one before she let Isabella place her foot on it.

At last they arrived at a small landing with a door. 'I think,' said the maid 'that from here it is best you go on alone. Open this door and you will find yourself in a corridor, very light from the window at the end of it. On the left-hand side there are three rooms. In the last room it is my lady's habit to spend the morning at her music.'

Here she took Isabella and kissed her on the cheek, saying: 'If she does not recognize you, I shall want to know why!'

The maid's certainty of who she was gave Isabella courage,

and, opening the door, she stepped into the hall. As the laundry-maid had said, it was well lit, a high window having been let into the wall at the other end. Endeavouring to make no noise, Isabella made her way along it and arrived at the third door. From inside the room came the sound of a sad air on a spinet, very well played, many hours obviously having been spent in its practice. Isabella turned the handle and went in.

The player at the spinet looked up in much alarm, not used to being interrupted in such a fashion. She looked at Isabella and cried her name.

'Madam, is it possible then that you recognize me?' asked Isabella in wonder.

To which her mother replied in the positive by fainting entirely away.

Isabella ran to the door to call for assistance and was amazed on opening it to discover Lord Montagu Angelsea and a servant. For the second time in as many minutes, she heard her name called.

'Sir, I pray you,' cried Isabella, showing him the sight of her mother.

Lord Angelsea, immediately ascertaining the situation, sent the man for salts and ran himself to hold up Henrietta.

As the colour returned to her cheeks, Henrietta, Lady Ducoeur looked round for her child. Isabella took her hand and put the locket into it.

'Then it is true!' cried her mother. 'You are my own child restored!'

'Indeed, madam,' said Isabella, 'and, if you will allow me and this gentleman to assist you to the sofa, I will tell you all my adventures and how I came to find this place.'

'Before you do,' said Lord Angelsea, 'there is something I must acquaint you with.'

'What is that?' asked Isabella in some alarm.

'Sir Roderick and his sister are no more.'

'Is it true?' cried Lady Ducoeur and Isabella in the same instant.

'They were each other's mutual destruction, to which Mr Edgecliffe and I were witnesses,' answered Lord Anglesea.

'I should not be, but I am glad of it,' said Isabella's mother, her colour returning to her cheeks. 'I was always despised by them for being born but a Miss Percival. I was not ashamed of my birth, being the daughter of a gentleman who had but two children to provide for, myself and my brother.'

'Had your brother a son?' asked Lord Anglesea, scarcely believing the coincidence of the name.

'He had, by the name of Richard, after our father, but I have not heard anything of them for many years.'

'Among my father's friends was a gentleman by the name of Sir Penrose Ducoeur, with whom he shared an interest in the natural sciences. Sir Penrose was often invited to our house, for he did not find his own establishment a congenial one. He was never disloyal enough to say so, but his wife soon proved to be an embarrassment to him, and his children by her inherited their mother's character.'

At this, Isabella recalled the sordid story she had heard from Mr Jasper, and hoped that having not reached her father's ears it would never reach her mother's.

'How Isabella and my sister know it!' interjected Lord Angelsea.

'This unhappy estate existed for some years, and the lady then went abroad with a gentleman. Very soon came word that she had expired of a fever. Sir Penrose found himself a free man and asked my father if he might be allowed to solicit my affections. Despite the discrepancy in our ages, my father agreed, saying I must be allowed a free choice in the matter. Suffice to say, I had long admired the gentleman, and admiration soon turned to love. It was agreed we should be married. Sir Penrose took me to his estate at Ducoeur Castle, where I was introduced to his children, by whom I was received with total disregard. Feeling too young to counter this by becoming a second mother to children so near my own age, I begged Sir Penrose, while still loving him, to break off the marriage. Loving me, this he would not do, and it was agreed that we should take this house, which was offered me by my father, and make our home here. We had been very happy for eighteen months and rejoiced in the birth of a strong and healthy daughter,' said the fond mother, bestowing a smile on Isabella, who sat rapt in her story, 'when my husband came to me one day in a terrible agitation of spirit. He had that morning received a letter which had been sent on from Ducoeur Castle and which was addressed to him in the hand of his first wife, a wife whom he believed to have died three years since.

'It appeared that the lady had indeed been very ill with a fever, but the reports of her death had been inaccurate. Despising her husband and not wanting to see him again, she had not sought to correct them. Now, however, she again found herself alone and without a protector, and so she had written to the man who, in law, was still her husband to beg him for assistance.'

'But was her existence not enquired into at the time of your marriage?' asked Lord Angelsea.

'It was, and, indeed, by the good, kind clergyman who married us, a Mr Bunce by name.'

'Mr Bunce!' cried Isabella. 'You are the lady whose name he could not remember, and whose locket he said was so similar to mine!'

'Mr Bunce is known to you?' asked Lady Henrietta in amazement.

'Indeed, madam, and you will hear his part in my story when you have concluded yours.'

'Very well, then,' said Lady Ducoeur. 'I have not much now to conclude. It was imperative that Sir Penrose and I should part immediately, for whatever we believed in the eyes of God we were not man and wife in the eyes of the law.

'It was a parting of great grief, with no acrimony on either side. I begged that my child might remain with me, but Sir Penrose, almost weeping as he did so, convinced me that it would be better for the child if she were sent away to grow up in some secluded place in the country under the name of

Broderick which had been my mother's name.'

'And was the name of the people to whom she was sent Bountiful?' interjected Lord Angelsea.

'It was!'

'That is why everything was so familiar and why Ben recognized me' cried Isabella.

'Were they good to you?' asked her mother.

'I believe I owe them my life,' said Isabella, 'and you will be introduced to them so they can share your happiness. But I am guilty of interrupting you.'

'A few minutes and I will be finished,' said Lady Ducoeur. 'I received news that the child had died, Sir Penrose writing to me himself to tell me of the fact. I believe,' she said, turning to Isabella, 'that he thought by such means to protect me from the great grief of believing my child alive but unable to have contact with me. For what would it have done to your reputation to be known as the child of a bigamous marriage? In order to protect them, I severed all relations with my family and wrung from them a promise that they would never mention me. I did not cease to love Sir Penrose, and grieved for him greatly when I heard of his death, truly believing him to have died of a broken heart.

'Then, some three years ago, I received the most bitter news of all. I was visited by a lawyer, who insisted that he was acting for a Mr Arthur, who had some information about the first Lady Ducoeur. Wanting to protect my solitude, I asked that the whole matter should be put in writing. This was done. The letter was so shocking that my first instinct was to throw it into the fire, but then I became more prudent, and have the letters still under lock and key.'

'What were the contents of the letter?' asked Isabella.

'It was this. Mr Arthur was a Scottish gentleman who had contracted a hasty and secret marriage, very young, with a Lady Arabella Emmett. The couple had soon parted, each vowing to say nothing of the matter and, knowing the laws of Scotland to be different from those of England, hoping never to be found out. Mr Arthur, on his death-bed, could no longer keep the secret and so confessed all, telling his lawyer and confessor exactly where the record of the marriage could be found. It is this record I now have. It proves that the only true marriage Sir Penrose contracted was with me. His union with Lady Arabella was quite void and his children by her – Roderick and Sophia – therefore had no claim on his estate.'

'But why did you not publish this information?' asked Lord Angelsea.

'I had no cause to. I believed my daughter, who was the true heir, the estate having no entail on it, to be dead. And what had I to gain except to be pitied, people supposing that I had had no happiness in my life, when I had had enough to sustain me all these years. That is my story, and now I would hear Isabella's.'

This was told with so many interruptions by Lord Angelsea that Lady Ducoeur began to laugh at them and say they were like a married couple.

Her mother thinking them so suited and leaving them alone together while she went to write a note to her nephew, Mr Percival, and her sister-in-law of whom she had always been fond, it was impossible for Isabella to find any reason why she should not now fulfil the promise she had made to Lord Angelsea to be his wife.

The letter was soon added to by Isabella and Lord Angelsea, each of whom sought to outdo the other in the description of their happiness, and concluded by Lord Angelsea's description of the demise of Sir Roderick and Lady Sophia.

The letter was received with great joy by Mrs Percival and her son and with equal rapture by Lady Caroline, who, on hearing that she and those she loved were now completely out of danger, gave a loud cry of 'Thank God' and then laughed at the sound of her own voice.

Now that her power of speech was returned to her, Mr Percival begged that he might put a question to her that could be answered with a single word. He was rewarded not only with the very word that he desired but with a kiss too.

There was then merely the difficulty of recalling Mrs Bunce and her husband from Scotland, in order that Mr Bunce could perform the necessary nuptials for Isabella and her Montagu and for Mr Percival and Lady Caroline, and the sending for of the Bountifuls and Mr Edgecliffe to dance at the wedding.

An occasion after which Mr Bunce was heard to declare that he had now seen three such happy couples as he and his wife had been on their wedding day.